SWEET BREATH OF MEMORY

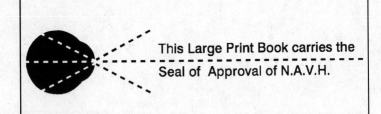

SWEET BREATH OF MEMORY

ARIELLA COHEN

WITHDRAWN

THORNDIKE PRESS

A part of Gale, Cengage Learning

GALE
CENGAGE Learning·

Farmington Hills, Mich • San Francisco • New York • Waterville, Maine
Meriden, Conn • Mason, Ohio • Chicago

GALE
CENGAGE Learning

LIBRARY OF CONGRESS CATALOGING-IN-PUBLICATION DATA

Names: Cohen, Ariella, author.
Title: Sweet breath of memory / Ariella Cohen.
Description: Waterville, Maine : Thorndike Press, a part of Gale, Cengage
    Learning, 2016. | Series: Thorndike press large print clean reads
Identifiers: LCCN 2016022453 | ISBN 9781410491978 (hardback) | ISBN 1410491978
    (hardcover)
Subjects: LCSH: War widows—Fiction. | Holocaust survivors—Fiction. | Life change
    events—Fiction. | Female friendship—Fiction. | Large type books. |
    Massachusetts—Fiction. | Psychological fiction. | Jewish fiction. | BISAC: FICTION /
    General.
Classification: LCC PS3603.O3416 S94 2016 | DDC 813/.6—dc23
LC record available at https://lccn.loc.gov/2016022453

Published in 2016 by arrangement with Kensington Books, an imprint
of Kensington Publishing Corp.

Printed in Mexico
1 2 3 4 5 6 7 20 19 18 17 16

For my mother, Kathryn,
who taught me to dream

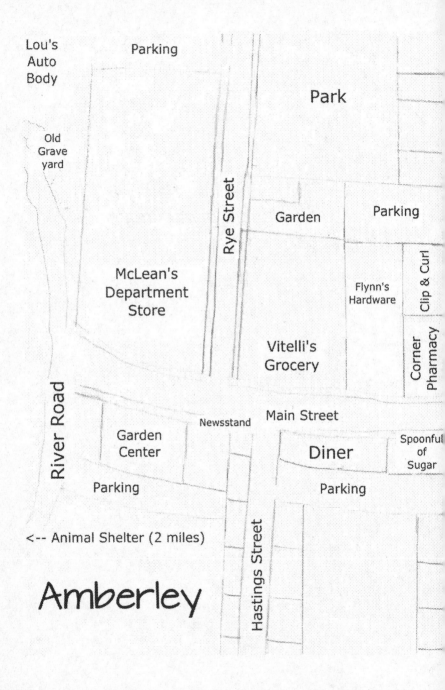

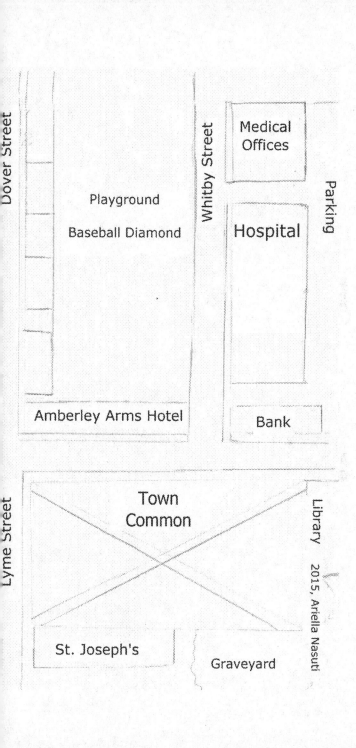

PROLOGUE

June 2008

The last months of Miriam Rosen's life, the land of her adopted home appeared to grieve. Dressed in somber shades, it seemed poised to receive her. Dust to dust.

Drought-cracked earth sent showers of lacy grit swirling down Main Street to film the windows of McLean's Department Store. Farmers paced fields of wilted seedlings, caps pushed high on foreheads that folded and relaxed like accordions with each passing cloud. Foreclosure rumors rippled through town, rising and falling with the air pressure and edging ever closer to the Amberley Cooperative Bank. Then one morning everything changed: Miriam closed her eyes and the skies opened.

Many in town believed the gentle rains that followed were her doing — a final benediction in a lifetime of shared blessings. As crops were planted and harvested, neighbors spoke of Miriam's humble manner and the quiet way she'd lived. They lamented that she'd died childless, all her family lost during that great war that had broken Europe and been the making of America. Now in the twilight of their lives, her closest friends feared that one day soon Miriam would be forgotten. They didn't know Miriam Rosen would be remembered for generations, that her story would intertwine with those of other women and seek the light like ivy on a ruin wall.

CHAPTER 1

March 2010

Rising wind ribboned its way through Boston, clearing a pathway for the rain that began to fall as Cate Saunders boarded the bus. She caught the express just before five a.m., grateful for an aisle seat until she saw the split vinyl oozing muddy-colored filling and heard the snores of an old man slumped against the window. With a mental groan, she spread her jacket on the seat and thought of the road ahead.

People said it took courage to start a new life, but Cate knew differently. Leaving Boston wasn't courageous; it was simply the only option once her home bore a black-margined foreclosure notice. That last day in the house she'd entered as a bride had seemed so unreal. Stripped bare of memories, the empty rooms had held only echoes of the woman she'd been. The life she'd lost. Packing up the last of her belongings, Cate

11

had marveled that sorrow could fold within itself so compactly. Then she'd locked the front door and stood staring at the key while a lone blue jay gave a sharp cry from the empty birdfeeder near the street. Only then had she thought to look one last time in the mailbox. There'd been a slim envelope inside that held the promise of work a hundred miles from all she knew.

Dear Ms. Saunders,
It is with great pleasure that we write to accept you into our program —

Program. More like menial work — what her grandmother would call "honest labor." Still, it was the only job offer she'd received, and it would give her the means to rescue her belongings. Cate thought back to those final moments in the storage facility's caged enclosure. A tunnel of furniture and waist-high boxes had wound its way toward a patch of bare concrete — her darkened past leading to a hard, cold future. Yet one could write the scene another way. She'd packed the boxes so carefully and taped them closed with a determined hand, as if by doing so she could keep the memories they held fresh and unspoiled by time or distance. An Easy-Bake Oven, broken beyond

repair; her first teddy bear, bald and missing a leg but still able to coax a smile; a
dog-eared copy of *Charlotte's Web* her
husband had read to her the winter she'd
caught the flu; the little trinkets they'd
bought in Boothbay Harbor that first summer in Maine. Useless junk to anyone else,
but the flotsam of their lives. To get it back
she needed a job and a home. Then she
could unpack the past.

While rain slapped the roof and the windows teared in response, the bus moved
from a shrouded world to one knit through
with gray shadows. Gradually, the sky
brightened, and colors that had drifted into
the margins hurried home — brown to yellow, navy to red. A hulking mass hugging
the road became a brick wall, and from
muddy blobs yellow forsythias emerged.
*Darkness always gives way to light just as
winter melts into spring.* Cate's husband had
believed that — had believed in hope and
resurrection. She'd tried to. After his death,
she'd sought comfort in the faith that had
sustained him, even pouring her heart out
to their parish priest who had responded
with platitudes about the Divine plan. Her
blood had boiled before she cursed herself
for a fool. It didn't matter what the priest
believed; all that mattered was that John

had faced death without her.

As a sob rose in her throat, Cate caught sight of a lone birch tree silhouetted in the pearly light. Rain beat against its unprotected bark, shredding the creamy surface into long strips that the wind sent swirling. The elements might have twisted the solitary tree into a caricature of itself. Instead, it stood defiant — its own forest. She turned in her seat, catching sight of the silvery shape out the back window before it merged into the fading landscape. When it did, a sigh escaped her and the storm loosened its hold.

The bus exited the highway onto a country road that wound its way along a river just being painted awake. "Amberley!" the driver called out, making a sharp turn and pulling to a stop. The first to disembark, Cate watched the wrought-iron streetlights lining Main Street wink out one by one as flaming sunlight crested the hills surrounding the western Massachusetts town. The sun's golden glow fell on rain-dampened streets and curbside planters filled with pale yellow narcissus. She bent to inhale their sweet breath before a slapping sound pulled her gaze skyward to where a flag played tug-of-war with the morning breeze. *Iconic small-town America: a place of undefeated dreams and forgiven sins,* she captioned the scene. And because it all looked so fresh and unspoiled, for the first time since she'd buried the remains of her husband, Cate allowed a flicker of hope to stir her heart.

All sorts of customers made their way through the etched glass doors of Vitelli's Grocery that March morning. A group of old men affectionately referred to as "the boys" arrived when the ciabatta rolls were still steaming. Gathered around the bakery counter, they sipped espresso, nibbled almond cookies, and debated the merits of this or that athlete. Then commuters trickled in to fill take-out containers from the salad bar and buy ready-made sandwiches of pepperoni and provolone; mozzarella and salami; or grilled eggplant. Farmers with wind-lined faces and muddy boots fingered unlit cigarettes and drank black coffee. Tourists gripping guidebooks that listed Vitelli's as the only authentic Italian eatery within a hundred miles made their way up and down the aisles, filling their baskets with mascarpone cheese, jarred peppers, farina flour, truffle oil, and wedges of ricotta salata. Stay-at-home moms parked their baby strollers beside the outdoor produce stalls, scrutinizing the basil, arugula, porcini

15

mushrooms, and artichokes as they chatted with their neighbors.

Vitelli's owner, Sheila Morazzo, had spent a lifetime in retail. Adept at reading body language, she could anticipate both what her customers wanted and how much they'd pay for it. It was rare for her to look up from the oak counter behind which she'd built a catering empire and find herself at a loss. But when the front door closed behind a rail-thin figure in a well-cut suit, Sheila was stumped. It wasn't the close-cropped blond hair or waif-like face that puzzled her, but a restive quality about the young woman that put Sheila in mind of an animal ready to bolt given the first whiff of danger.

When the coffee grinder roared to life and the scent of espresso filled the air, the woman who held Sheila's interest relaxed and closed her eyes in appreciation. She paused at the cheese display, her pink-stained lips pressed together before she reached out a slender hand to sample the pungent Gorgonzola. Then she tried Asiago and provolone. Sheila turned away to chat with a customer, and, when her eyes found the stranger again, she was settled at one of the bistro tables that hugged the front windows. Chewing her lower lip in concentration, the woman studied the laminated

16

menu before pulling out her wallet and glancing inside. At the look of relief on her face, Sheila felt a lump rise in her throat. *Once I was as lost as she is. But I found myself in this place. Maybe she will, too.*

Sheila's gaze swept the room, and she mentally cataloged all that needed doing. The grocery was crowded, there was a line forming before the register, and the salad bar needed tidying. But first things first. Blowing Coco Chanel bangs from her eyes, Sheila caught a glimpse of the silver that threaded her hair and suppressed a smile. She was beginning to resemble the grocery's founder, Rosa Vitelli. Rosa had been her mentor and friend, and as much as Sheila tried to mirror the woman's kindness, she feared her efforts fell short. And now dear Rosa had gone to her reward. Still, perhaps there was a way. Pulling off her apron, she made her way across the flagstone floor. "I'm Sheila Morazzo," she said to the stranger. "This is my place."

"Cate Saunders," the woman responded, her shadowed eyes skimming the room. "I didn't expect to find a gourmet grocery in a small town like Amberley. And you've got a café, too."

"My customers insisted," Sheila confided, taking the seat opposite and tapping the marble-topped table. "Seems that drinking cappuccino at the counter may be good enough for Italians, but Amberley folks prefer to sit and relax over their coffee. And dessert. We've got a full bakery — breads, pastry, cookies, and cakes," she said proudly. "Plus there's a deli and take-out counter with lunch specials every day. Today's are a spinach and sun-dried-tomato calzone with a green salad, or Sicilian meatballs with raisins and pine nuts. Over saffron rice, of course." After a beat, a look of embarrassment stole across her face. "Sorry. I'm always selling; it's an occupational hazard of the self-employed. So tell me, what brings you to Amberley?"

"Work. I'll be training as a home care aide."

Sheila exhaled loudly. "Caregiving is tough."

Cate stiffened, as though sensing in Sheila's sympathetic voice a tinge of disbelief. "I can do it!"

"Oh, I'm sure you can," Sheila said even as she tried to imagine the fragile-looking beauty bathing patients and emptying bedpans. Cate's soft hands weren't those of a manual laborer, yet she'd clearly fallen on hard times, for the job she'd taken paid barely nine dollars an hour. She couldn't live on such a salary — not without help.

"Helen Doyle hired me," Cate said, a note of contrition in her voice, as though she regretted how defensive she'd been earlier. "She mentioned Vitelli's; that's why I stopped by." Recounting her meeting at the hospital earlier that morning, Cate explained how the nurse had put her at ease.

Sheila nodded in understanding. People trusted Helen Doyle's gentle strength, born of all those years she'd spent caring for her mother before nursing became her vocation. When asked why she chose the career she did, Helen had once said that becoming a healer was a natural choice for someone whose life had been shredded by illness. Was that Cate's story? Did she hope to heal some internal wound through the work she'd chosen? "Helen and I grew up together," Sheila explained. "Her friendship got me through some tough times. I've sweet memories of her watching my back."

"Sweet memories," Cate repeated in a flat voice. "Yet even the sweetest memories can bring pain. Why is that? And why do some memories seem to steal away into the night, while others push forward at the oddest moments? But only for a moment and then they fade." She raked a hand through her cap of hair. "I'm sorry. I don't know why I said that. I don't even know you." An embarrassed flush stained her cheeks. "I didn't really sleep last night. I'm not myself."

"No need to apologize," Sheila said, casting about for a way to change the subject. "So you like to read?" She gestured toward the bag of books on the floor.

"Yes," Cate replied, the tension in her eyes lifting. "Novels mostly."

"Cookbooks are my weakness," Sheila confessed, leaning forward conspiratorially. "I've dozens of them. I love finding old ones at yard sales. I always turn to the stained pages first. Those are the most interesting."

Cate nodded. "The more dog-eared and beat up, the more a book was cherished. Those in good condition may fetch more money, but they weren't valued by their owners — not in the ways that matter." She shrugged her thin shoulders. "Then again, there's nothing like the smell of new books. Or that soft creak when you open them for the first time; it's like holding a newborn."

When Cate sighed wistfully, Sheila teased, "That's the enraptured look my husband gets when I make lasagna."

"Books are friends that never let you down."

"Unlike people, you mean?"

And just like that, the veil that had shifted momentarily fell back into place, and the sorrowful air that had begun to dissipate as they spoke wrapped itself around Cate once again. At the uncomfortable silence that followed, Sheila motioned to her assistant and ordered pastry, explaining, "It's St. Joseph's Day, so we've éclairs with custard. That's the tradition."

"No, no thank you. I'm just having coffee," Cate protested.

"On the house," Sheila said. "Call it a business expense."

"Business?" Cate asked, her face guarded.

"Yes. I'm looking to rent out an apartment upstairs, and I'm guessing you need a place to stay. It was Miriam's —" A familiar ache gripped Sheila's heart, and she rushed on. "It's nothing fancy, mind you; just a one-bedroom."

"What's the rent?"

"Rent," Sheila repeated, buying time while she turned the matter over in her mind. "To tell you the truth, I haven't given it much thought. Umm, three hundred maybe?"

Cate's sky-blue eyes lost their glint of excitement. "Oh. I can't afford three hundred a week. Thanks anyway."

"No, no, not a week. A month. The rent's three hundred a month. And it includes utilities."

Cate frowned. "That's not very much. What's wrong with the place? Are there bugs or something?"

Sheila bristled. "No! Nothing like that! The rent's low because I hoped you could help me out a bit around here."

"Help how?"

"Well, I don't live on the premises, so I need someone on site. Oh, there's a security system, but it's not the same thing."

Cate cocked her head, considering. "I'm a stranger. Why rent to me, allow me to look after your business even in a minor way? Why trust me?"

"I'm a good judge of character. As is Helen. And I think you can turn your hand to whatever's needed. That you'd be willing to." Sheila hesitated before adding, "You look as though life's dealt you a lousy hand, but you're playing it anyway. You're still in the game."

"Fair enough," Cate conceded, "and close to the mark." Then she pulled out her wallet and held it open. "Three hundred and forty-two dollars." She swallowed hard as though the words had a bitter taste. "That's all I've got. Enough for coffee as a treat now to celebrate my new job, but not enough for a deposit. I don't get paid for a week, and they won't give me an advance on my salary — I already asked. So I can't rent anything now. I've figured out that if I stay in a B&B until I get my first paycheck, I'll be okay. Maybe after that —"

"Oh no! There's no need to give me a deposit!" Sheila cried. When Cate opened her mouth, doubtless to protest that she didn't want charity, Sheila rushed on. "Normally I would ask for one. But if Helen recommends you — and I'm betting she will — it's not necessary."

Indecision warred with relief on Cate's face. Finally, she said, "Oh — okay." Then, as if to seal the deal, she sampled the éclair that had sat before her while they talked. Her eyes closed in appreciation and Sheila felt a surge of warmth, for she'd learned long ago that life's challenges are best confronted on a full stomach. "This is fantastic," Cate enthused, wiping her plate clean of all but crumbs. "As good as anything you'd find in Boston or New York." When Sheila glared at her, she amended, "Better. It's better, actually."

"Nice save. And if you think that's good, wait until you try my tiramisu."

By the time the lease was signed a few hours later, Sheila had outfitted the apartment with a basket of food, linens, towels, and some mismatched furniture. She left her new tenant to settle in and entrusted the running of the grocery to her assistant. Then she hurried across the street, a plan forming in her mind.

Cate Saunders's blue eyes took on a gray hue when she was troubled, but on that first day in Amberley, they were the color of a placid sea. By gradual degrees, her new life was taking shape, for in the course of only a few hours she'd enrolled in the hospital's home care aide program and found a place to live. Standing in the center of her apartment, she drank in the silence and wondered who else had called the four small rooms home. She made a mental note to ask her landlady. Or perhaps not, for her new home was a clean page on which she would write — what? That she didn't know was to be expected after all that had happened. That on many days she didn't care what the future held was harder to explain, especially to well-meaning strangers. When Cate had revealed that she couldn't provide an emergency contact for she hadn't any family, Sheila's brow had creased with concern. In the pregnant silence that followed, the rooms that had welcomed Cate with warmth and light seemed suddenly sepia-toned.

Then it was as though she'd heard John's voice say that the apartment was a charming place to rebuild her life. Rebuild herself.

Cate's gaze traveled over the mullioned windows, paneled walls, and pumpkin-pine floors, mentally redecorating. There was just enough space in a corner of the living room for the writing desk John had made; her grandmother's rocking chair could go near the front windows; and the hooked rug would brighten up the floor before the wood-burning fireplace.

She walked into the kitchen where vintage metal cabinets held a few groceries and a set of dishes Sheila had told her to consider her own. The small bathroom beyond boasted a stained-glass window and was dominated by a claw-footed bathtub that looked too inviting to resist. In the bedroom, a window seat looked down on a well-ordered garden sprinkled with terra-cotta pots of spring bulbs that flared with color. Gravel pathways divided raised beds where neat rows of seedlings were just beginning to poke their way through the chocolate-brown soil. Birds chirped and bees hummed as a marmalade cat made its way along a stone wall before pausing to stretch in the afternoon sun.

The scene's balance of light and shadow,

sound and stillness, was so iconic that it seemed plucked from a novel. Only on the written page could life be so idyllic, its rough edges smoothed and tapered. Or so it had always seemed to Cate. *Books are safe,* a voice in her mind whispered, the one she'd heeded before love had found her. Before John had found her.

Orphaned at a young age and raised by a grandmother plagued with health problems, Cate had been a lonely little girl who'd found escape in books. Setting her solitary childhood games against a backdrop of gothic landscapes, medieval bedchambers, and Georgian drawing rooms, she'd peopled her imagination with the heroines of romance novels and mysteries. Luckily, her grandmother had shared Cate's passion for literature. And memoir. Convinced that "Life is in the telling," she'd encouraged Cate to keep a journal. And tell stories.

The morning she turned ten, Cate had run downstairs in search of her favorite lemon cake only to find an old typewriter sitting on the kitchen table. Beneath a pink satin bow tied around its carriage, there'd been a single sheet of paper with the words FOR NOVEL WRITING typed in capital letters. Determined that the characters in her mind find their way onto the page, Cate

26

had pounded away on the Remington's black and gold keys, breathing life into strong-willed heroines who fought off rogues and found everlasting love amid the drafty castles and windswept moors of Cornwall and Scotland.

Although in time the typewriter found its way into a closet, Cate's dream of becoming a writer had survived childhood. But not John's death. Since losing him, she'd consigned her literary hopes to the midden heap. Yet words still sought her out like hungry children, leapfrogging over each other to arrange themselves into a tempting turn of phrase. Every now and then, she surrendered to their pull and dipped into the unsullied mind of the child she'd been. She did so that first afternoon in Amberley. Standing in her new home, Cate found herself thinking that old buildings speak a language all their own. They don't surrender their secrets easily, so care must be taken when translating the subtle creaks of an empty room into something that could fill a page. Surely, the give-and-take between the rising wind and the window frame was a conversation of sorts. One had only to listen with an open heart to hear the old timbers stretch and sigh.

A change in the light caught her eye, and

she looked over to see a shaft of sunlight strike a bookcase shoehorned into the corner of her bedroom. There were a few paperbacks on the top shelf. She wondered how they could have been left behind by the previous tenant; it was akin to forgetting one's children! Just the sight of those dusty, dog-eared covers made her heart beat faster in anticipation. Reaching out with eager hands for the forgotten books, she read the titles: *The Woman in White, Moll Flanders, and Tess of the D'Urbervilles.* Tragic women all, but had circumstance destroyed their lives or had it been the choices they'd made? A writer might argue both sides, but a woman who'd sent the man she loved to his death knew the answer.

CHAPTER 2

Tucked within a fold of land framed by the Connecticut River on one side and a ring of mountains on the other, Amberley is a speck on the map of Western Massachusetts. It suffers by comparison with its neighbors, dwarfed in size by the city of Springfield; in history by Old Deerfield; and in prestige by Emily Dickinson's home of Amherst. While the surrounding communities marched toward modernity, Amberley's more measured pace hadn't attracted the attention of the railroad, the philanthropy of Andrew Carnegie, or the greed of developers. As a result, no deserted mills crowd the riverbank, the downtown architecture is an appealing mix of Federal, Italianate, and Gothic Revival, and the same families have farmed the surrounding land for generations.

Sheila Morazzo grew up in Amberley, riding her bicycle along its streets and playing hopscotch on its sidewalks. She made her First Holy Communion in the old stone church on Main Street, bought her prom dress in McLean's Department Store, and had her first kiss beneath the oak tree in the town common. Memories of the Amberley Diner wove their way through her childhood for it had been a popular choice for first dates, and the place to gather after Mass, graduations, and funerals. The iconic eatery had stood on Main Street and at the heart of the town since being rolled off a railroad boxcar in 1930. Although the building now rested on a modern, cement foundation, the words BOOTH SERVICE were still splashed across its ceramic front panels in the Gothic font of a bygone era.

The diner served hearty, simple food, so the fact that it stood across the street from Vitelli's Grocery didn't trouble Sheila or affect her bottom line. Not that the same customers didn't frequent both eateries, for they did. It was simply a question of whether one wanted to be comforted or pampered. Eating in the diner brought to mind thoughts of home and childhood, while Vitelli's gourmet food made one dream of a future filled with possibility. Except for Italians, for whom Vitelli's classic favorites were a slice of home. The fact that there were so few Italians in town had troubled Sheila when she'd bought the business, but then she'd realized that, when it came to good food, there was a bit of the Old Country in every American. After all, she wasn't Italian — a fact her customers never let her forget. Dark haired, with the fair complexion and dusting of freckles so characteristically Irish, Sheila might have married a boy from Roma, but she would always be the granddaughter of Thomas Mitchell from County Cork.

We can never outrun our past, Sheila thought. *It chases us until we turn and face it, and even then it shadows us all our days.* She suspected her newest tenant was struggling with something from her past, and although Cate Saunders would eventually find her way forward, she'd get there faster with a bit of help.

Sliding into a corner booth at the diner, Sheila watched waitresses circle the room with laden plates and steaming carafes of coffee. Customers jumped up to greet newcomers, feed quarters into the jukebox in the corner, or help themselves to newspapers piled on a side table. Her eyes followed one waitress in particular who was neither the quickest of the bunch nor the most vocal. Yet something in her calm control drew the eye, making one think of a queen bee. Pretty in a no-nonsense way that wasn't off-putting, Gaby French was the Amberley Diner's owner. That she also waited tables spoke to her hands-on management style. A natural at her job, Gaby had a knack for knowing what people needed before they did. It was an admirable trait in a waitress, but annoying as hell in a friend.

The door swung open to admit a tall brunette whose shoulder-length curls were tied back with a blue-and-white bandana. The defiant look on her chiseled face put one in mind of a ship's figurehead turned in challenge to the rising wind. Well-muscled and buxom, the newcomer scanned the crowded room confidently. With a quick nod of greeting, she strode to Sheila's booth and slid her five-foot-ten-inch frame into the seat opposite her dear friend.

"You smell like gasoline," Sheila observed, wrinkling her nose.

MaryLou Rice flipped up the collar of her oil-stained overalls as if to say, "What do you expect? I work in a garage!" Of course, she did more than work there; MaryLou owned Lou's Auto Body, so named because when she'd moved to town the good folks of Amberley hadn't trusted a female mechanic. In time, MaryLou won them over with a combination of skill and grit, and built a successful business by rebuilding cars, lawnmowers, and tractors. "I was doing a tune-up when you called. Dropped everything to come here like you asked." She held her hands up for inspection. "They're clean, but I didn't change my clothes. If you'd like me to leave —"

"Oh, forget it," Sheila snapped, reaching for the menu MaryLou gripped with the strength of one who routinely shifted engines about. "Let me see that," Sheila demanded, tugging harder.

"Why? Gaby's just going to bring us what she thinks we should eat." Slapping the menu down on the table, MaryLou asked, "So who's the newbie?"

"Her name's Cate Saunders," Sheila said, still eyeing the menu for she'd heard that today's special was a meatball hero and she wanted to know how Gaby had priced it.

MaryLou's voice cut across her thoughts. "What's she like?"

"Stunning — in a peaches and cream, 'girl next door' sort of way. Looks like a strong wind would knock her down, but she's going to work at the hospital with Helen as a home care aide. That's tough work. I've rented her Miriam's apartment. Cate only brought two suitcases, so either she hasn't got much or she's not sure she's staying." Sheila lowered her voice. "The girl needs help. She looks — I don't know, broken-hearted and ashamed. Maybe it's something to do with a man. She's wearing a wedding ring, but hasn't mentioned a husband." At that, the diner's owner walked up, platters in hand.

MaryLou growled. "We haven't ordered, Gaby."

"No need." After passing a BLT to Sheila, the waitress placed a salad before Mary-Lou.

"How am I supposed to work the rest of the day on this?" MaryLou demanded, flicking a hand toward the mountain of green.

Resting a hip against the table, Gaby French fixed her closest friend with a look. "You need vegetables, Lulu. You won't eat them unless I make you. And there's broiled chicken there for protein — high-quality protein, not the fried stuff you favor. What you *don't* need are empty carbs. White bread and potatoes will just make you feel sluggish."

"Why does Sheila get bacon?" MaryLou all but whined.

"Because she eats healthy all the time, so I like to spoil her when she comes in here."

Waving to acknowledge a customer's call, Gaby moved away.

After a beat, MaryLou asked, "Did you bring them?" Nodding, Sheila passed a paper bag across the table. Pulling out a buttermilk roll, MaryLou speared a piece of chicken and began to eat. "So," she asked between bites, "if you want to know more about this Cate, why not ask Helen?"

"I tried, but she's not talking. Confidentiality of employment records and all that," Sheila grumbled. She'd phoned her old friend earlier; all Helen had said was that Cate had moved to Amberley because she wanted to make a change in her life. "Her last name's Irish," Sheila mumbled. "Saunders. So she's probably Catholic. Maybe she'd talk to Father Sullivan."

"What about a shrink?" MaryLou suggested, reaching for a piece of Sheila's bacon.

Sheila shook her head. "Vincent says the ones in town are drug-pushing morons."

"Well, what about her seeing Vincent? Maybe her problem's medical."

"No," Sheila pleaded. "Don't you dare tell my husband about Cate! He'll just say that it's none of our business and we should leave the poor girl alone."

MaryLou pushed her plate away with a

35

satisfied sigh. "Maybe it *is* none of our business." After a moment of silence, the two friends looked at each other and laughed. "It's not Vincent's fault; men just don't understand that problems won't fix themselves," MaryLou observed. "If the world was left in their hands — hang on, it is mostly in their hands." Then she sipped her coffee thoughtfully. "Seriously, though, maybe this girl's life is none of your business."

"Oh, you don't believe that; you're just saying it to get my Irish up!" Sheila groaned. "Why are you so contrary today, anyway?"

MaryLou frowned. "I'm not!" She wiped at a spot on her surprisingly clean overalls. "Okay, maybe I am." Her voice dropped. "Ran into my ex this morning."

"Were you driving?" Sheila asked sweetly.

"Very funny," MaryLou grumbled before her lips twitched. "Now that is a nice image. Harry sprawled on the street, that well-pressed suit of his splattered with blood." The twitching lips spread into a grin. "Thanks, Sheila; I needed that."

"Anytime."

A redheaded waitress approached balancing a tray on her shoulder. In one deft motion, she swung it down to hip height and slid slices of carrot cake before each woman with a murmured "Compliments of Gaby."

Sheila eyed her piece before sampling the cream-cheese frosting. "This is heaven. Very light. I wonder what Gaby cuts it with — plain yogurt, maybe?" She held the plate up and peered at the snow-white glaze.

MaryLou rolled her eyes. "Can't you just eat something without analyzing it?" She dug a fork into her own slice. "Wonderful. Just enough spice, not too much sugar, juicy raisins."

"You're doing the same thing!"

"No, I'm commenting on the taste sensations, not trying to make out the recipe."

"Semantics," Sheila whined.

"And so we come back to the starting line," MaryLou said, pulling out her compact and lipstick. "Helping this Cate is one thing; interfering another. I should know: People have been trying to set me straight all my life. That's why I hate pain-in-the-ass do-gooders."

"Point taken," Sheila acknowledged, reluctantly returning the plate to the table and abandoning her plans to re-create the cake that was rapidly disappearing under her fork's assault. "But as Gaby is fond of saying, when the women of Amberley put their heads together, great things happen."

"Sisterhood's not just in the blood,"

MaryLou finished. Fixing Sheila with a look, she probed, "You've got a special feeling about this girl, don't you?"

Sheila's lips compressed into a hard line. "Yeah, but it's not something I can put into words."

"Why not send her Gaby's way?" Mary-Lou glanced toward the busy waitress, voicing the thought in Sheila's mind. "You know she can read anybody."

"And you know what it costs her," Sheila pointed out. Her mind skipped back in time to a blustery spring day when Gaby had first confided in her childhood friend the extent of her unique ability. Although Gaby had spent a lifetime harnessing its power, Sheila knew she paid a high price for the comfort drawn from her gift of empathy, one she'd never wanted. "I don't want to call Gaby's attention to Cate until we've taken a crack at ferreting out her story ourselves. Not that Cate won't find her way to the diner in time — Amberley's a small town, after all." Sheila hesitated as a new thought struck. "Besides, Gaby's not looking too well lately." She inclined her head toward the far corner where the waitress was leaning against the wall, shoulders slumped in fatigue.

MaryLou narrowed her eyes. "Just tired, I think. Why, do you think it's more than that?" Even as the question seemed to hang in the air between them, MaryLou reached out to grip the tabletop as if tensing to spring to her feet.

Sheila moaned inwardly. *Oh, now what have I done? The last thing Gaby needs is Lulu barreling across the room and smothering her with concern.* With a sigh of relief, Sheila watched Gaby straighten at a customer's call and move toward the front counter. *She's just worn out. And no wonder. At her age she shouldn't be working so many shifts. And running the place, too. But then she's only a few years older than me, and nothing but childbirth has ever pried me from the grocery. Yet this morning I sat there with Cate when I should have been working.*

"I'll keep an eye on Gaby," MaryLou said, reaching out to cover her friend's hand with uncharacteristic gentleness. Sheila gazed down at the square-cut, fire-engine-red nails and felt a smile tug at her mouth.

"How can you keep a manicure looking so good with your hands in God knows how many engines all day long?" But then Mary-Lou Rice was a mass of contradictions. A clotheshorse of the first order, she wouldn't call it quits at the garage she'd built from nothing until the overalls she favored for work were stiff with grease. A gun enthusiast who eschewed hunting, MaryLou argued that firearms should only be used in self-defense — on a level playing field against other humans, never animals. She was also an avowed iconoclast who nevertheless took her place in the front pew of St. Joseph's whenever the diocese debated closing the small church. Catching sight of the diamond studs sparkling in her friend's ears, Sheila chuckled. "Lulu, you're one of a kind."

"I'll take that as a compliment," MaryLou shot back, twirling a curl of hair around her forefinger as she was wont to do when considering a problem. "So," she brought the conversation back on point, "do you want me to help with Cate?"

"Yes. You've got an instinct for things like this."

"For helping people, you mean?" Mary-Lou put a hand to her throat in mock gratitude.

"For finding trouble — other people's and your own. Not that you don't always land on your feet," Sheila acknowledged, thinking of all the scrapes Lulu had found her way in and out of. "Befriend Cate as I have," she advised. "But we have to move slowly; we can't overwhelm her."

"I can be subtle," MaryLou protested, only to elicit a roll of the eyes from Sheila.

40

"Besides," MaryLou continued in a rush, warming to her role, "I know what it's like to be a stranger in town. And despite the hard time I was giving you earlier, I *do* remember how people helped me and the difference it made." She paused, shifting in her seat. "Gaby told me the first day I met her that every person has what she called 'extra' — something we've been given, but don't need." MaryLou stared down at her calloused palms. "For me, it's how my hands can make an engine sing. But it took time to see that; I couldn't think beyond what else these hands have done." She took a drink of coffee as though it were a shot of whiskey. "Maybe," she proposed, "the way to help this girl, Cate, is to find out what her extra is. Any clue on that score?"

"No," Sheila whispered. "Not yet."

Before they left, MaryLou flagged down the waitress who'd brought their dessert and ordered two pieces of pie to go. When she turned away with a nod, MaryLou grabbed her arm. "No! Call out the order," she urged. "In diner speak. Please."

The waitress flashed a gap-toothed smile.

MaryLou turned in her seat to watch the back counter where the pie specials were lined up under glass domes. "Oh, here comes Gaby," she whispered to Sheila,

41

before prompting the hovering waitress, "Apple pie and lemon meringue. To go!"

"Two for a walk: Eve with a lid on, and a corrugated roof," the girl called out in a clear voice before dissolving into giggles.

Gaby paused, arms akimbo. She shook her head and shot a glance heavenward before moving to fill the order.

Sheila scolded MaryLou on Gaby's behalf. "You're like a little kid when it comes to food, ya know that? You love the silly lingo, still eat like you've the metabolism of a teenager, and are forever trying to score free pastry from me. When are you going to grow up?"

In response, MaryLou quoted Sheila's oft-repeated words back to her. " 'Life's challenges are best confronted on a full stomach.' Isn't that what old Mrs. Vitelli used to say?"

And because the memory of Rosa Vitelli saying those words to the girl she'd been was one Sheila kept in a treasure box, she smiled.

Although Cate was thrilled with her new apartment, she did foresee one problem: the divine smells wafting up from the grocery. As she unpacked, she caught a whiff of marinara and slid a tray of stuffed shells Sheila had left into the oven. Hours later, she was still nibbling on the leftovers with a whispered "I'll be as big as a house at this rate." Not that there was anyone to see or care if she gained weight. Then a familiar voice chided that even if her life was a runaway train, she could still control what she put in her mouth. "You're right, Grandma," she said aloud. "You told me once that the best exercise I could do was to push myself away from the table." So as the sun set, chasing gray and pink clouds from the sky, Cate put down her fork, covered the plate of pasta with tinfoil, and placed it in the refrigerator. That she felt empowered by such a simple act was an eye-opener, but then wasn't life shaped as much by small triumphs as grand gestures? Her beloved grandmother had thought so. As had John.

A chill hung in the air, and she slipped on a sweatshirt, recalling the first time she'd seen John on Dartmouth's campus. The sweatshirt that swam on her had been tight across his muscled chest, and his hair had been guilded by morning sunlight that pooled around him like a benediction. By chance, he'd turned away from the woman he'd been chatting with and caught Cate's eye. The earth had shifted in that split second, and the backpack she'd been carrying had slid from her grasp. Before she could retrieve it, John was beside her. He'd bent down to gather the books that had spilled out, and she'd caught a subtle scent of lemon for he took it in his tea. When he'd straighened, his gaze had held her in a green sea of interest and need. She'd decided then and there that green was her favorite color, and that losing herself in those eyes was the only way she'd find happiness. And she had, for five glorious years.

Sweet memories, she thought, calling to mind Sheila's phrase. They were like armor — initially so shiny they dazzle and in time acquiring the patina of use. But always a shield against loneliness and despair. And yet memories had been shifting in and out of focus in the two years since John had died. While some remained as crisp as a new apple, others seemed as fragile as a moth's wing — as fleeting as frost on a window-pane. She couldn't stop the past's receding with each breath she drew and dimming with each dawn. If she fought against the fog pressing in on her mind, the memories that should have filled the hole in her heart only slipped further from her grasp. Oh, she could call to mind picture postcards from the past — single images frozen in time —

but not always how it had been to *be* with John, to feel him touch her body, to sense his presence in a room. It was as if their life together were shifting to form a backdrop, one against which all she'd done since his death was thrown into relief.

To some widows that numbing was a comfort, for relegating memories of the dead to the attic of their thoughts was easier than the mental bruising of remembering. Yet for Cate, every blurred recollection and half-forgotten conversation felt as though she were losing her sweet husband all over again. Sometimes it was a struggle just to conjure his features, for although John's face floated easily into view, it took effort to recall every line of life's imprint. She did so now, painting from memory the curve of forehead over emerald eyes; the folds of skin born of laughs and smiles; the square jaw mossed with stubble that made her skin tingle when he kissed her.

Holding that image close, she leaned out the open window of her bedroom and welcomed the featherlight brush of air on her cheek. As a velvet sky took shape overhead, her city ears quickened at the strange overlay of silence beneath which insects sang and small creatures rustled through the garden below. Two white moths played aerial tag in the fading light, and she heard the *peck-peck* of a bird paying a last visit to the feeder below. When floodlights clicked on and her eyes couldn't pierce the heavy blackness surrounding their yellow pool, Cate pulled the window shut. Before turning toward the empty bed, she did what always calmed her spirit: She talked to John. Describing the town, she told him about meeting Sheila and Helen. Then she shared her plans for decorating the little apartment, and her fears that she wouldn't make a go of the new job. The familiar routine worked its magic, and she felt her body begin to relax. By the time a mantle of moonlight settled over her first night in Amberley, she had crawled between the cool sheets and fallen into a dreamless sleep.

CHAPTER 3

"Never touch the patients without gloves," Helen Doyle instructed as Cate wiped drool from the face of an old man who'd been admitted to the hospital with pneumonia. When he turned his febrile gaze on the nurse, Helen gave him a reassuring smile before telling Cate, "If you're only helping patients eat, you can take the gloves off. Except not if the other supervisors are around. Be careful about that." She paused as though her thoughts fenced this way and that. "I know caregiving isn't the type of work you're used to. Not what you would have chosen had things been different."

But they're not. And I'm hardly the first widow to find herself among the working poor. "I can do it," Cate whispered, stealing a glance at the emaciated figure before them.

The nurse followed her gaze. "The poor dear can't hear us. But don't assume everyone is hard of hearing. Or demented for that matter. And if they are, just talk to them normally, not like they're children. There's too much elderspeak around here."

Cate nodded in understanding. She'd worked the past week with a nurse who all but shouted at the more ancient-looking patients. Just that morning, they'd changed the bed linen of a woman who suffered from dementia, but wasn't hard of hearing. When Cate said as much, the nurse grumbled that the old bat was lucky anybody was willing to clean up her filth. Seething with anger, Cate would have lashed out at the callous nurse if she, too, hadn't been revolted by the diarrhea coating the patient's chalk-white skin.

Each time Cate steeled herself to accept her new life, a voice in her mind whined that an Ivy League graduate shouldn't be doing menial work. But then it was penance. Atonement. Whether God was doing the punishing or Cate herself, she wasn't sure. Nor did it matter. All that mattered was John and how she had failed him. That she hadn't been there when he died tore at her heart, but had helped to gentle her hands. Yet as resolved as she was to be compassionate and kind, the reality of caregiving was more challenging than she had expected. Many patients were grateful for her help, but the majority were either too medicated to notice her or too angry to appreciate what she did for them. That such anger might have been born of bitterness that their bodies had betrayed them didn't make the outbursts easier to take. Or so Helen assured her.

The older nurse had taken over Cate's training at midmorning. With thirty years' experience on the wards, Helen Doyle loved her job. When encouraged to move into hospital administration where the hours were easier and the pay better, she'd scoffed at the idea, insisting that she would miss the patients. And they would miss her, Cate thought, for kind words came easily to Helen and they came in droves. It was how she put people at ease.

"I'll be your supervisor from now on," Helen explained, smiling at Cate's sigh of relief. "You'll work here in the hospital. After that, we can send you out to patients' homes. You'll help them recuperate after surgery and recover from falls. That sort of thing. But before you can work outside the hospital, you have to complete seventy-five hours of training. That's how long it takes to be certified as a home care aide. Now, for the rest of today, I'm assigning you to Beatrice McLean." She led Cate to a closed door. "She's only here while she recovers from a hip replacement; after that she'll be home and you'll visit her there." The nurse shifted her weight, as though stalling. "Beatrice is quite elderly. Set in her ways, one might say. And she's given quite a lot of money to the hospital."

"And in return expects the staff to treat her like the important woman she is?" Cate supplied.

"Exactly," Helen said with a sigh. "Well put." Then she added in a lowered voice, "She'll either talk your ear off or give you the silent treatment. Either way, don't let her get to you." With an exaggerated exhale, Helen pushed open the door and introduced her old friend to Cate before shooting Beatrice a warning look.

After the door hissed shut behind Helen, Cate studied her patient. Bathed in milky sunlight that blurred her features, Beatrice McLean didn't look like a woman flirting with a second century of life. The bones of her face bore the remnants of beauty, and she seemed somehow younger than the ninety-one years noted on her medical chart. "I'm new here," Cate said, pulling off her latex gloves and tossing them in the trash. Cornflower-blue eyes studied her with interest. "I haven't done this kind of work

50

before." She finished the thought in her mind: *But how hard can it be?* Yet here she was, already at a loss. "You're recovering from a hip replacement," Cate fumbled. "But then, you know that. Just as you know that even though it's painful, you have to keep moving." She continued the one-sided chat as she eased Beatrice to a seated position and pulled a walker close to the bed. Positioning nonskid socks on her patient's swollen feet, Cate decided that she preferred the tantrums of other patients to Beatrice's silent scrutiny. "You're not going to make this easy for me, are you?" Cate mumbled after they'd made the two-step journey to a reclining chair.

Beatrice smiled then, a slow relaxing of the lines time had carved on her face. "You're lucky to be working with Helen," she observed in a forceful voice that belied her fragile appearance. "But you don't belong here." Her gaze moved over Cate's trim figure. "With your looks, you should be a cocktail waitress. You have a good bust-line for someone so thin. Men like that. You'd make a lot in tips." Then Beatrice gasped and shut her eyes against a sudden pain. Stabbing an arthritic finger toward the door, she cried, "I don't belong here either. Mark my words, I'll be home before the week is out. My family won't let me rot in this hellhole!"

When Cate moved to ring for Helen, Beatrice cried in a trembling voice, "No drugs! They're a crutch." She settled back against the seat and drew a deep breath, letting it out with a sigh. "It's passing now."

Cate reached out to touch her hand. "Medication can help."

"Pain is part of any life worth living," Beatrice said with authority. "I've lived quite a life, by the way. I've lots of stories to tell — what I've done, what I didn't have the courage to do." Cate waited, assuming the old woman's gaze was as firmly fixed on the past as Cate's grandmother's had been, and that Beatrice would prefer retracing her steps through a life that had spanned nearly a century to speaking of the present. But her patient surprised her. "You're new in town, then?"

Cate started. "Yes."

"Where are you staying?"

"Above an Italian grocery."

"Vitelli's?" Beatrice sat forward expectantly. "So what do you think of our mayor?"

Cate's eyes widened in surprise.

"Sheila Morazzo's the mayor, you know. And she's married to the best doctor in town. Quite a cutie Vincent is. Sheila's got

52

lots of energy. She's like me. Well, like I used to be back in the day. And what about you? Tell me about yourself."

Cate's answer was polite, but firm. "Ms. McLean, I really think my personal life is none of your business."

"It's Beatrice. And when you're as old as me, everything's your business." She tapped the sagging folds of skin that draped her brow. "I've the whole history of Amberley in here. Like to add your story now that you're part of the town."

"I won't be here long," Cate assured her with a tight smile.

"Don't be so sure," Beatrice cautioned. "You can make all the plans you want, but life has a way of upending things. Trust me, I know." Cate let the matter lie with a shrug before suggesting that Beatrice take her antibiotics. Narrowing her eyes at the white paper cup of pills, Beatrice barked, "Well, give them to me, then."

"I can't, actually," Cate explained, shifting her feet uncomfortably. "I can remind you to take your meds, but I can't administer them."

Beatrice snorted. "Rules! I never felt they applied to me. Wouldn't have gotten where I am if I had." She swallowed the pills with a grimace. "So, do you always play by the rules?"

She's baiting me, but I won't lose my temper. Got to get her doing something. Then inspiration struck, and Cate suggested washing Beatrice's thick, silver hair.

Her patient grumbled, "I'm too tired."

"It will make you feel better."

A gnarled hand flicked toward the bottle of shampoo in Cate's hand. "I'm not a baby. Why do they give us baby shampoo?"

Cate sighed in frustration, for Helen had warned her that older patients sometimes took a dim view of hygiene. "I'll bring something nicer next time. But for now —" She brandished the bottle.

"Oh, why bother?" Beatrice snapped. "It will just get dirty again."

"Then we'll wash it again," Cate replied evenly. "And again and again."

"Why? And why do you care? I don't! Do you know how many times I've washed my hair? Thousands! Damn sick of it. And it's so long now. Such a pain to wash. I don't want to do it. I don't want anyone else to do it!"

The outburst reminded Cate of a feral cat she'd once cared for. He'd slept in a cardboard box lined with old towels, but had refused to eat until Cate turned away. "I'm not just *anyone*," Cate said. "Helping you is my job. You wouldn't mind having your hair washed at a salon, right? This is the same thing." She shot a disparaging glance at the putty-gray walls. "Well, it's not as nice as a salon; I'll grant you that." When the older woman didn't respond, the silence between them expanded to fill the room. *Perhaps I've pushed too much. Fatigued her. Maybe she needs fluids.* Cate reached for the plastic carafe of ice water with uncertain hands. Carts rattled along the hallway outside, and she heard the distant beep of machinery. *Should I call Helen?*

"All right," Beatrice whispered, fingering the knotted mess she'd come to accept wouldn't be put to rights until she was home. "I used to have such lovely hair. Long ago. I was something to see then." The voice belonged to the ghost of a woman confident in her allure.

"You still are something to see," Cate said, relieved that the awkward moment had passed. Filling an inflatable washtub with warm water, she smiled to soften her words. "Now let's get that hair clean!"

"You're a stubborn one," Beatrice murmured as Cate worked. "Women can't get anywhere in life without being stubborn. Maybe there's hope for you yet." The undercurrent of respect to her patient's words left Cate in no doubt that beneath the gruff exterior presented to the world, a lonely woman longed for friendship. Later, as her cascade of hair dried on a towel draped over her shoulders, Beatrice described what the town had been like during her youth. The tapestry of words she wove entranced Cate, who found herself imagining the elegant, vital woman Beatrice McLean had been the day Pearl Harbor was attacked. Dressed in a formfitting navy suit and white silk blouse, she'd worn amethyst drop earrings that swayed as she'd shaken her head in disbelief at the news. That such an old woman could recall so vividly what she'd been wearing at such a moment surprised Cate until Beatrice explained. "We all remember exactly where we were and what we were doing when we heard. I was at work when the news came over the radio. I remember staring through tear-filled eyes at the fabric of my suit — blue as the waves that now covered our brave boys." Her voice broke, the pain that had seared her heart all those years ago still raw.

Before she thought better of it, Cate asked how war had affected the women of Amberley. At the sight of her patient's set face, she added quickly, "If you'd rather not talk about it —"

"No. No. I was just remembering, that's all. Remembering struggle, but also triumph. After the men were taken from us, we had to deal with rationing and shortages. Empty beds and hearts full to breaking." A note of pride crept into her voice. "I kept the store open."

"The store?" Cate asked, puzzled.

"McLean's!" Beatrice's voice rose. "Surely you've seen it!"

Cate had indeed noticed the large department store anchoring one end of Main Street, but hadn't connected the name with her patient. "McLean's Department Store. Of course. I've walked by it, but haven't stopped in yet."

"You will," Beatrice predicted, before her thoughts turned inward again. "I grew up behind the counters of McLean's, and helped out from the time I was a little girl — running errands, carrying packages. But my first real job was assisting a senior tailor at Saks Fifth Avenue. What fun it was! I loved living in New York City!" Her eyes danced for a moment. "Then, right before Pearl Harbor, I got word that my father was doing poorly. I came home to find him an embittered shell of a man and McLean's teetering on the brink of failure. Oh, I was just a slip of a thing — only twenty-two — but I had gumption. I took the money I'd saved for a trousseau and saved that store instead. It's stood on Main Street since before the Civil War; I wasn't going to stand by and see it close!" A problem solver blessed with common sense, Beatrice explained that she brought to the task the enthusiasm and optimism of youth. Her ability to anticipate the needs of her customers she ascribed to years spent observing the mercurial temperament of her father. Doing so had given her both an understanding of human nature and an innate sense of timing; she knew when to push a sale and when to step back and let customers come to her.

"I'll tell you a secret," she confided, lowering her voice. Cate leaned closer. "McLean's survived the war years because I put the women of Amberley to work. All sorts — young girls, housewives, old women everybody else had discarded. We farmed land that had fallen fallow because the men were gone. The town had put most of those fields under the plow for food, but I leased others to grow flax." She stared at the liver spots on her hands, as though seeing the calluses of long ago. "It was backbreaking work and the first harvest was spotty, but we got the hang of it. And it was all worth it because we were able to make our own linen during the war. People laughed at me, said I'd never make a go of it, but I was a spitfire in those days. I told them that flax has been grown in these parts since the seventeenth century. Well, if those farmers could do it while fighting off the Indians, I didn't see why we couldn't while fighting the Huns." When Beatrice paused to sip a glass of water, Cate marveled that a young woman born to privilege had taken to the fields and worked shoulder to shoulder with her workers. And what they'd grown had both supplied McLean's with linen and filled army contracts. Reflecting on her management style, Beatrice admitted, "I was short-tempered and demanding. Not an easy boss. But I paid top dollar, and I was the first to come in and the last to leave at night. Most important, I kept McLean's open six days a week. Had to. The women who worked for me were struggling to raise families alone. Oh, they got allotment checks if their husbands were in the service, but that only went so far.

"Those women were the soldiers in my army. They wanted to protect the salaries they'd earned with their loyalty and hard work. So, when the union fellows came sniffing around McLean's, my employees sent them packing. Troublemaking bastards left town with their tails between their legs!" She gave a snorting laugh. "I'd been prepared, you see. I knew retail would be a prime target for organizers after the war, so I got the jump on them. Offered my employees the benefits of collective bargaining without the need to pay union middlemen. Keeping the unions out made me a lot of money — money I passed on to my workers, for I never forgot I was beholden to them. The women, that is; the men I learned to live without." She paused a beat. "In business and in bed."

Cate couldn't suppress a smile.

Enjoying her role of teacher, Beatrice explained, "I kept my own counsel about the wisdom of old men waving flags while young men went to war. Knew I couldn't change anyone's thinking on that score, but I could keep the women working. So when the war ended and the men came home looking for their jobs back, I hired a few for show, but I kept the women on, too. Not many businesses did. You young people don't know that, do you? You don't understand that American women who worked during the war were expected to give up their jobs and go back to being housewives.

Well, I knew Amberley women wanted to keep working, and I gambled that my female customers would appreciate seeing women as managers, not just salesgirls. Now my male shoppers" — she made a dismissive gesture — "they just wanted to see a pretty face behind the counter. Same as today."

As the hours passed, Helen stopped by periodically to check on them. She nodded in satisfaction at the progress her protégé had made with a patient the nurses seemed to fear and respect in equal measure. Cate felt a flush of pleasure at the approving light in Helen's eyes and the whispered comment that Beatrice was rarely so talkative with newcomers.

For her part, Beatrice alternated between storyteller and ornery patient. She ate sparingly of the hospital food she complained was "nothing to Sheila's cooking" and grumbled when Cate combed the knots from her drying hair. Her thoughts often wandered along a well-worn path to the past, one signposted with success and lit with achievement in a way the present clearly wasn't. Cate understood that well enough, yet it was the quiet moments in a life — that middle ground between joy and sorrow — that always interested her most. She thought of the wheel of fortune as a

Ferris wheel; only when it was at its mid-point could one measure the hills against the valleys, and see the horizon as truly limitless.

As the day wore on, Cate guided Beatrice's sedentary body through a series of movements meant to increase her range of motion. Then she massaged cream into her patient's sagging, blue-veined arms and felt the skin move beneath her fingers like a shiver. Careful not to press too hard, she worked slowly and was rewarded when Beatrice all but purred, "Ahh, that's good. You've a gentle touch. And you've never done this kind of work before?"

"No, but my grandmother loved it when I massaged her back. She was quite a character — feisty, like you." Cate felt the pull of memory. "Grandma used to take me to a diner and let me order scrambled eggs with ketchup. She'd give me coins to feed into the little jukebox in the booth where we sat. I remember sitting on the vinyl cushion and swinging my legs back and forth in time with the music."

"You were close to her," Beatrice noted with approval.

"Grandma raised me after my parents died," Cate answered without thinking. *Now I've gone and done it — opened a door she'll*

62

barrel through.

Though Cate expected more questions and the sympathetic "poor Cate" speech she'd heard so often, Beatrice surprised her by saying, "Lucky Grandma. Being around young people keeps one young. Engaged. I see too many old folks consigned to the roadside of life. And if your grandmother liked diners, she valued home-style cooking; that shows good judgment. You know, we've a diner here in town. Right across the street from Vitelli's."

"Yes, I saw it. Is it expensive?"

"Not very," Beatrice assured her. "A friend of mine owns the place. Works there as a waitress; Gaby's not afraid to get her hands dirty. You should stop by. Gaby will see you right," Beatrice announced, before launching into a detailed description of her friend.

CHAPTER 4

Cate moved along Amberley's tree-lined streets through a chartreuse landscape of new growth. The weepy sky of that morning had given way to streaky clouds, and the air smelled of moist earth. She walked briskly, for it had been torture to spend her morning moving only as quickly as the aged and infirm. She had worked earlier with Beatrice McLean and felt a stab of guilt at the relief that had flooded through her when she'd left the old woman's room. Beatrice hadn't proven nearly as frightening as Helen had first made out, but the work was difficult in other ways, for Cate had to dodge so many questions. Whether nosy or simply curious, Beatrice routinely asked about Cate's family and education, wondered aloud why she wore a wedding ring but lived alone, and questioned whether she wouldn't be happier at another job. And the other patients Cate helped each day? A robot could do what she did, for the work required only strong hands and an iron stomach. Most of the home care aides were Russian immigrants with limited English skills and vapid stares. Although Cate knew she'd learn nothing from them, she did envy how acclimated they were to the sight and smell of the bodily fluids that gushed, spurted, and dripped from patients. She had been both disgusted and fascinated when a senior aide had turned aside from the enema bottle she'd inserted into an elderly man and proceeded to munch on a cookie.

Surrendering to the call of *her* grumbling stomach, Cate turned onto Main Street. The Amberley Diner's metal barrel roof winked as patches of sunlight made their way through the retreating clouds, and Cate quickened her step in anticipation of the hearty food she was sure to find within. She recognized the Worcester Lunch Car Company emblem on the building's blue ceramic exterior and knew the building's design had been born of the lunch wagons made popular in the late nineteenth century. Initially open only at night — when factory workers ate lunch — those horse-drawn wagons had dotted the downtown streets of Massachusetts's mill towns offering meals on wheels: coffee, pies, sandwiches, and soup.

A middle-aged woman stood in the diner's open doorway. She wore a pink and white smock with the words AMBERLEY DINER emblazoned on the pocket. "We get lots of tourists here," she said, squinting at a sudden burst of sunshine.

"Oh, but I live here," Cate answered quickly, surprised at how easily the words tumbled out. "I would have stopped by sooner, but Sheila Morazzo is my landlady; she loads me down with so much food, I haven't eaten out yet."

"That I can believe. I'm Gaby French," the waitress said, extending a work-roughened hand. Her face bore the etchings of a full life and was devoid of makeup save a coral tint on her lips. Shoulder-length, nut-brown hair was tucked behind her ears, and she pushed at it unconsciously from time to time. Her calves were muscled from long hours on her feet, and she wore comfortable flats and white ankle socks. *But you're only describing what everyone else sees,* the narrative voice that wove its way through every writer's thoughts reminded Cate. *You're supposed to look beyond that.* So, reading Gaby as she would write her, Cate imagined that a child had drooled on the shoulder that now bore the watermark left by a quick scrub; saw the thin lines of worry that fanned across Gaby's brow; and, noticed the unconscious way she fingered her watch as though time was an enemy to be kept in check.

Cate introduced herself, explaining, "Beatrice McLean told me about you."

Gaby chuckled. "Oh well, some of what she said is probably true. And you're Sheila's tenant, you say." She cocked her head. "I haven't been over to Vitelli's lately. What's she making these days? What's she been giving you?"

Beneath the gleam of competitive interest lay affection, so Cate answered freely. "Let's see. Yesterday it was spaghetti with clam sauce. The day before that, fennel-steamed swordfish with a bean salad. And there are always desserts."

"Like what?" Gaby leaned forward.

Cate's stomach rumbled at the memory of Sheila's creations. "Orange gelato, almond macaroons, ricotta cheesecake, and lemon ice. Oh, and some chocolate grappa cake; I'd never had that before."

"That one's heaven," Gaby said. "But then you haven't tried my pies. Sheila doesn't make pies."

Cate took a mental inventory of the grocery's bakery case. "No, she doesn't. I wonder why."

"Well, she'd say they're not Italian. Tarts, yes, but not pies. But that's only part of the answer," Gaby concluded in a teasing voice. "She knows she can't get a crust as good as mine. That's the real reason." They laughed then like the friends they would soon be. "Now, her panettone is another matter; it's the best you'll ever have, hands down. Moist. Lots of fruit. She keeps to tradition and only makes it during Advent. But she won't commit to a day. Just decides that morning. Word gets around town quick, though. I can't wait to —" She paused, and a look of regret took hold of her face.

"I'll let you know when she makes it," Cate said quickly. "You won't miss out; I promise."

Gaby's brief smile didn't light her eyes, and she changed the subject quickly. Turning toward the diner, she asked, "Did Beatrice tell you I grew up here? My father bought the place after WWII with a GI mortgage." She inclined her head toward the interior. "I used to do my homework at the counter. My mom was waitressing then. She'd sit me down right in front of the domed pie plates. 'Gabrielle,' she'd say, 'you only get a slice when you finish your work. And only one, mind, so choose carefully.' I used to spend as much time deciding which kind of pie I wanted as I did finishing my homework." Ticking off on her fingers, she recounted, "There was cherry, Boston cream, strawberry rhubarb, lemon meringue. Oh, and apple, of course. They were all amazing."

"No food tastes as good as when you're a kid," Cate agreed.

"You're right, of course. All those memories are painted in primary colors." Pulling open the double glass doors, Gaby said, "Come on in."

Laughter greeted them as they stepped inside the diner, for it was crowded with customers, many of whom were chatting with people in adjacent booths. The walls shone with black-and-white subway tiles, and sunlight flooded the room from the front windows on which were etched the words BREAKFAST ALL DAY. Indicating a row of high-backed wooden booths reminiscent of church pews, Gaby explained, "These are called deuce tables since they're just big enough for two people. They're original to the place, as are the marble floor tiles," she noted with pride, tapping a foot on the geometric design. "They've held up well."

At a customer's signal, she called out that she was coming before guiding Cate to a booth. When she moved off, Cate settled herself on the maroon upholstery, suddenly ravenous. A specials board that hung above the front counter read: THE ETERNAL TWINS, STEAK AND EGGS; GRIDDLE CAKES WITH FRESH FRUIT; MAC & CHEESE WITH A SIDE SALAD; MUSHROOM OMELET WITH STEAK FRIES. Debating what to order, she looked up to find a pert redhead with an infectious smile holding a tray of steaming food. "I didn't order that," Cate explained, her mouth watering in anticipation.

"Oh, there's no need to order," the waitress laughed. "Gaby always knows what people want." Setting the omelet special and a basket of whole-wheat rolls before Cate, the waitress poured out a cup of hazelnut coffee and added, "Give a yell if you need anything else." Then she circled the room in that familiar dance of serving, chatting, and clearing that made diners so predictably homey. Cate hesitated only a moment before digging into the delicious food. As she ate, she watched the redhead, who was quick on her feet and probably made a good living off her tips. One could do a lot worse than waitressing. But why did Gaby do it? Beatrice had mentioned that Gaby had a PhD from Yale. Why would someone like that spend her days in the uniform of one valued more for what her hands can do than what her mind can imagine? *Yet that's exactly what I'm doing,* Cate thought, glancing down at her cotton smock, which bore the words MY NAME IS CATE. *But then, I don't have a choice.*

Four years ago, she and John had celebrated their move to a three-bedroom house they'd hoped to fill with children. Mortgage payments had eaten up most of John's pay, so Cate had rallied to the challenge — clipping coupons, planting a vegetable garden, working part-time, and even selling a few short stories. After John's death, everything had spiraled out of control. Since Cate's wages had barely put food on the table, her savings were soon exhausted. Unable to pay the mortgage, she'd stalled, pleaded, and negotiated with the bank as long as she could. Once foreclosure proceedings began, it had been impossible to find a job: prospective employers who ran a credit check on Cate soon rejected her. The only work she'd found had been as a home care aide, and the only place she could afford to live was a small town. Not that Amberley was so bad. It seemed a cute enough place, with tree-lined streets and friendly people. Besides, in a year or two, she might be able to repair her credit enough to try for a better job. *And then I'll build a bonfire and burn this damn thing,* she resolved, running a manicured finger over the cheap cotton of her smock. It had seen its share of vomit, blood, and urine in the short time she'd worn it, and although each night she washed it clean, somehow she couldn't scrub her memory so easily. "Badges of honor," a senior nurse had quipped one day at the sight of Cate's soiled uniform. "You've helped a lot of people today. Should be proud." But Cate wasn't, or not as she should be. She was angry. With herself, with God. Sometimes even with John.

As her mind twisted this way and that, she looked down in surprise to find that she'd cleaned her plate of all but the garnish of sliced orange and parsley. She was picking up the former when Gaby drew near. "So you liked it then?"

"Oh, yes," Cate replied, dropping the orange slice. "It was just what I needed."

Gaby threw her a knowing look. "I'll send over some dessert and have your coffee topped off." She cocked her head and studied Cate. "I recommend the cheesecake special. Raspberry chocolate with a Chambord sauce on the side." When Cate closed her eyes in anticipation and sighed, Gaby laughed. "Good. That's settled. Now, I hear you're working with Helen Doyle at the hospital. As a caregiver, right?"

"How did you —"

"A friend mentioned it," the waitress explained, inclining her head toward a tall figure in blue overalls who had just come in the door. "That's a good job for a writer," Gaby continued. "Caregiving, I mean. So many old folks have lost their stories, while others feel the need to share them. You can help with that."

"What makes you think I'm a writer?" Cate asked in surprise. Before motioning to another customer that she was coming, Gaby pointed to the notebook Cate was scribbling in. That she still carried a little notebook with her even though she'd fore-sworn writing was hard to explain. Truth was, she'd gotten in the habit of having one handy so she could jot things down, for if not committed to paper those flashes of inspiration often melted away.

Looking up, Cate saw the friend Gaby had indicated studying her with blatant interest. With ruby-red lips, high cheekbones, and clouds of glossy curls, the woman was stunning. And she moved so confidently, at ease in her own skin and at peace with the world around her. "I'm MaryLou Rice," she said, walking up to the booth and pumping

Cate's hand.

"Cate Saunders," Cate replied, her heart sinking, for good smalltown manners dictated that she invite the woman to join her, and the last thing she wanted was company. With a resigned sigh, she motioned Mary-Lou to sit before turning her attention to the wedge of cheesecake Gaby had sent over. As expected, it was fabulous — creamy and rich, but not overly sweet.

"I hear you've just gotten to town," Mary-Lou said. "I remember the day I moved to Amberley. It was right after I got out of prison." She sat back, waiting for Cate's eyes to widen in surprise. In the pause that followed, MaryLou said, "You're too polite to ask. Not many people are. It was robbery. I'd like to say that the woman I used to be is gone forever, but every once in a while the selfish bitch flexes her muscles, and I'm reminded that the past is never really past." She gave a tight smile. "Still, prison wasn't all bad. It's where I learned to fix cars. A work-release program placed me with a mechanic. Joe was his name — a real old-timer who worked out of a dump of a garage. Some folks looked at Joe's place and saw only chipped paint, ripped Naugahyde stools, and linoleum floors veined with age. But it was more than that to me, because I was like that — beaten up, but with a bit of usefulness left. At least that's what Joe saw. He took an interest in me. Oh, not like the guards did; not Joe. No, he just wanted to teach me. Hadn't met a lot of men who gave more than they took. Hell, I hadn't met any! And Joe was patient, started me off with the basics: tune-ups, some simple bodywork. I loved it. Being able to fix things and make them new again is what got me through."

Although surprised that a total stranger was sharing her life story, Cate couldn't help but respond to the narrative's pull. Like all writers, she was hungry for a good story. And if she wasn't going to write it herself — "So when you got out of prison, you came here?" she prompted.

MaryLou nodded. "The first person I met when I got to Amberley was Gaby. She was working the morning shift, just like she does now. I sank onto the cracked vinyl of that booth over there," MaryLou said, pointing across the room. "I was wiped out. Not the 'didn't sleep well,' 'up too late' kind of tired, but the spirit-crushing, mind-numbing sort most people never know. My head dipped closer and closer to the tabletop until I was stretched out over the paper place mat. You remember those?" she asked with a crooked smile. "Used to have ads on them for funeral homes, termite inspectors, and sewage treatment — just the sort of thing you want to read before you eat." Cate smiled, recalling just such a place mat in the diner she'd gone to as a child. One day, her grandmother had given her a pair of scissors to cut out the ads, and she'd made a deck of playing cards. The rules of the game had been simple: Three septic tanks and a pair of termites beat even a full house of mourners.

Drawing a deep breath, MaryLou continued. "So there I was, passed out or near to it. Next thing I know, someone's sliding a cup of coffee, a plate of scrambled eggs with onions, and a pile of rye toast under my nose. When I looked up into Gaby's face, I knew I was home. She had a way about her that just made you feel safe. She said, 'Hi, I'm Gaby.' And, still feeling a bit out of sorts, I answered, 'Hi. I'm not. Gabby, that is.' Well, she just burst out laughing and slipped into the seat across from me. She sat with me while I ate, not saying anything. Finally, she asked if I was an artist. Can you imagine? Me! I told her I was just a mechanic, but she shook her head." MaryLou's eyes narrowed in thought. "Gaby said that the way I moved my hands was so deliberate, controlled, and fluid that I had to be an artist." MaryLou stared for a moment at her work-scarred palms. "When I found out the town needed a mechanic, I stayed. Made an offer on an abandoned auto body shop near the river and found rooms to rent. Gaby spread the word to her customers that Lou's Auto Body was the place to go. Just like that, I had a home."

"Gaby seems very nice," Cate offered in a neutral tone.

"It's more than being nice," MaryLou corrected. "Scrambled eggs with onions and rye toast, coffee with just a dash of cream — that's what she brought me that first morning. That's my all-time favorite breakfast. And she knew, just knew by looking at me. Knew what I liked, knew that I needed to see something familiar, something that reminded me of better times."

"You're right," Cate agreed haltingly, glancing down at the crumbs on her plate. "Gaby did the same thing with me. And I saw her do it with other people. It's like a game."

"It's not a game; it's a gift for making people feel safe by sending the fear we each carry around scurrying into a corner."

Cate pulled back at the intensity of the older woman's words. As though sensing she had gone too far, MaryLou changed the subject and spoke of other things until the moment passed. With an apology that she had intruded on Cate's meal, she made to get up.

"Hang on," Cate said, a hand shooting out to grip the sleeve of MaryLou's overalls. "Why did you tell me all of this? Not that I don't appreciate your confiding in me, but — well, it's a little odd. We don't know each other. Why — ?"

"I should think it was obvious."

"Indulge me," Cate pleaded. "It's been a long day."

MaryLou softened. "Yeah, I don't imagine working at the hospital is easy. I told you about when I came to Amberley so you would understand that I only made it because I had help. We all need help sometimes, Cate. No shame in that."

"I never said there was," Cate bristled, for since John's death there had been far too much unsolicited advice flung in her direction. "If you're implying that I need help too, you're mistaken."

MaryLou cocked her head. "So you've a temper. Good. Means you've got spirit."

"God, you're infuriating!"

"You're not alone in thinking that." Mary-Lou smirked. "Still, if you don't need help, then you can give it." When Cate blinked widely, MaryLou added, "There are lots of folks in need. What life experience do you bring to the table? Tell me about yourself."

Cate sputtered before giving way to the laughter bubbling up her throat. "So if you don't manage to get me to open up one way, why not try another?"

"Worth a shot," MaryLou said sheepishly, getting to her feet. "Think about what I said, though. I may not be the easiest person to talk to, but there are others. Sheila. Gaby. Even Beatrice when she's in the mood. Reaching out to the women of this town isn't a sign of weakness. We all help each other." With a slight nod, as though congratulating herself on a job well done, the blunt, down-to-earth mechanic made her way to the door.

CHAPTER 5

Sheila had set up a baking area near the front of the grocery years ago, reasoning that customers wanted both to see the pastries and breads being made and smell them as they baked. It had proven to be a brilliant move, and ever since, her mind had swirled with plans for further expansion. But not on the stormy day her husband left; without him at her table and in her bed, Sheila was irritable and distracted. Thankfully, tending the business gave her a way to forget her worries until a familiar song on the radio reminded her of Vincent. Then her busy hands stilled, and her thoughts scrambled.

When a clap of thunder startled her from her reverie, she noticed the government postage mark peeking out from a pile of mail on the counter. She slit the envelope open before noting the addressee. "Shit!" Her new assistant jumped. "No, you didn't screw up," Sheila growled. "Not this time, anyway." The girl relaxed, hand moving to her phone, doubtless to text a friend. "But why are you standing about? The pickle barrel is almost empty! The counter needs wiping down!"

"Right. Sorry, Mrs. Morazzo."

MaryLou ducked into the grocery to escape a sudden downpour. Dark curls were plastered to her face, and she shook them free like a dog, sending a spray of water to the floor at her feet. Sheila grimaced at the sight and snapped, "What if someone slips on that?"

MaryLou frowned. "I know you're missing Vincent, but don't yell at me." When Sheila glanced pointedly at the floor, MaryLou said, "Oh, for pity's sake, it's only water!" Then she caught sight of her friend's whitened fingers wrapped around an envelope. "What's that you're holding? Is it from him?"

"No!" Sheila made to slip the envelope into the pocket of her apron, but MaryLou's reflexes were as fast as ever, and she snatched it away with a cry of triumph before her face fell.

"Oh. It's not even yours."

In lowered tones, Sheila explained about

the letter.

"So now you're opening Cate's mail?" MaryLou scolded.

Sheila pointed to the envelope. "It was the Commonwealth of Massachusetts postmark! I thought it was another notice about some idiotic food-safety regulation, so I ripped it open without thinking."

MaryLou had walked over to a cheese display and reached for a sample. At Sheila's words, she made a great show of pulling her arm back. "Food-safety regulation," she repeated slowly. "Violating a lot of those, are you?"

Sheila punched her friend in the arm. "As if. My kitchen is spotless! The freezer temps are always within the guidelines; my grease traps are cleaned every day; I've —"

"Okay, okay! Don't get your knickers in a twist," MaryLou cried, popping a slice of mozzarella in her mouth before scrutinizing her friend. "Your business might be in good shape, but you're not. I barely felt that punch."

"Focus, Lulu," Sheila hissed, taking back the envelope and brandishing it. "Cate's getting survivor's benefits from the military. That's what this says."

"Meaning what?"

"Meaning that she's a war widow *and* she

has a second income. But then why is she living hand-to-mouth? The army pays her more than eleven hundred a month. Tax-free. Combined with her salary — well, it's not a lot of money, but it's over two thousand a month."

"Sheila, is this any of your business? You're the one always telling the busybodies of this town that unsolicited advice is the root of all evil. It's like that *Star Trek* thing your daughter's always quoting —"

"The Prime Directive," Sheila interrupted. MaryLou was right, of course, but only to a point. It was true enough that Sheila had little patience for Amberley's gossips; how could she after they'd tortured her mother because she'd been a Divorced Catholic, a title both capitalized for emphasis and whispered in the tone used when saying "cancer"? "I saw how my mother suffered because of the divorce," Sheila recollected. "Not that it was her choice. She told me at the time it was out of her hands. Well, I was seven, so I didn't understand that concept until it hit me one day during recess that Mama could no more control where my father went than I could make a baseball fly where I wanted; some things in life are out of our hands. Except the Church taught that divorce was a sin." When MaryLou snorted in disbelief, Sheila tried to set her straight. "You have to understand that Catholic Amberley was pretty evenly split then between Irish and Italian immigrants, but we were of one mind regarding the authority of the Pope. In those days, his photograph seemed to be everywhere. Rosa hung it in the window of Vitelli's; I even remember it being over the rinse sink at the Clip & Curl."

"What's all this to do with Cate, then?" MaryLou asked, always able to cut to the heart of a thing.

"Mama only got through that tough time because she had help. From friends and Father Sullivan. He made sure people understood she never wanted the divorce, that it was all my father's doing."

MaryLou raised a well-groomed eyebrow. "James Sullivan as a maverick? I can't see it," she confessed, for she'd only known the snowy-haired priest in the sunset of his life.

"Believe it," Sheila said. "He was something of a firebrand — always clashing with the bishop. But he revitalized St. Joseph's, which is Church-speak for the fact that he brought in a lot of money. So they let him be. Still, the black-veiled matrons of the St. Joseph's Rosary Society were scandalized when he gave Mama Communion. I learned

84

a valuable lesson from him: You've got to involve yourself in someone's life if you think you can help."

"But maybe Cate just has debts to pay off and that's where all the money's going. Did you think of that?"

Sheila shifted her feet as though to find solid ground. "No. I'm a nosy pain in the butt." She ran her hand back and forth along the envelope's now broken seal.

MaryLou stated the obvious. "You're obsessing over this to avoid thinking about Vincent. Worrying yourself sick won't make him come back any sooner."

"You think I don't know that?" Sheila snapped. "That I haven't been through this before? Do you know how many times he's volunteered?"

"No. But I do know that when he comes back this time, you've got to make sure he sees a way clear to leave again. Without guilt. You can't back him into a corner; men are like animals that way. I should know; I've tried to trap enough of them. They just bite and claw to be free. Now, that can be fun in its own way, but it doesn't make for a good marriage. I know that, too."

"Think you have all the answers, don't you?"

"Not all. Most, but not all. For instance, I

know you'll have to take it on the chin and own up to opening that letter."

"It was an accident! Cate will understand."

MaryLou shrugged. "She probably will; that girl thinks you can do no wrong. 'Course you've won her over with food, whereas I've used charm." Ignoring Sheila's snort of laughter, MaryLou said, "Speaking of food, I hoped you'd compensate for Vincent's being gone by working more." Her gaze slid to the bakery case and she licked her lips.

With a resigned sigh, Sheila moved behind the counter and weighed out half a pound of chocolate lace cookies. MaryLou clapped her hands together like a child on Christmas morning. "Any chance of an espresso with those?"

As slate gray clouds gave way to watery sunlight, Cate stepped into the grocery later that day to find only a handful of customers. Sheila would normally have been chatting with them about this and that. Instead, she stood mechanically filling cannoli, her face blank. Cate asked how the new assistant was working out. Sheila shrugged. Then Cate observed that the walnut pesto was selling well. Sheila mumbled agreement. Only when Cate's stomach growled did Sheila come out of herself, the nurturing side of her nature trumping all else. She passed Cate a cannoli with a brisk, "Eat something; you'll feel better."

"Thanks," Cate mumbled, savoring the crunchy shell and sweet cream within. "This is fabulous!" She licked her fingers in appreciation. "Oh, there's nothing like a cannoli! It's just what I needed."

"Tough day?" Sheila asked sympathetically, her gaze straying to the telephone for the hundredth time.

"Yes. No. I mean, it was pretty much the same as other days. Which is to say, I'm getting used to the patients. The nursing staff is another matter. So many of them refuse to see that patients are people."

Sheila nodded. "They see the sick as a collection of symptoms, or pains in the ass. Rarely as people. Well, except for Helen, of course; she's a gem."

Moving to wash her hands, Cate agreed with a weak smile. "The day wasn't a total waste; I spent the morning with Beatrice McLean."

"Are you two getting on?"

"She can be a handful, but I like that she's so feisty," Cate revealed. "She's nosy, though. Keeps asking me about myself."

Sheila waved a hand dismissively. "That's to be expected: you're new here. People are curious. Hell, I'm curious."

"You are?" Cate tensed. For a fleeting moment, she wanted to bolt from the room rather than be besieged with questions. Then an inner voice reminded her that she liked and respected her landlady. The woman was a workaholic with incredible energy and a prodigious memory for details about her customers' likes and dislikes. Furthermore, Sheila was honest, loyal, and funny — everything one could ask for in a friend. And friends could be trusted, should be trusted. "I grew up in Boston and went to Dartmouth, where I studied literature," Cate began, lowering the drawbridge around her heart one creaky link at a time.

"Is that where you met your husband?"

Cate's eyes widened before she held up her wedding ring. "Of course, you've seen this. Yes, we met in college. And married after graduation. John was wonderful. He encouraged me in everything I wanted to do, especially writing. I spent years trying to make a real go of it. John worked two jobs so I could. One of those jobs was the National Guard." Her voice took on a flat tone as images replayed in her mind like a worn newsreel that looped back on itself

88

over and over — the closed coffin, folded flag, and hard face of the officer who had stood on her doorstep and mumbled a scripted condolence. "John's unit was sent to Iraq. He died there."

"I'm so sorry."

After a moment, Cate managed, "It isn't easy for me to talk about. Even after two years."

"You don't have to. But if you want to, I'm here. Or, well, there must be resources for army widows — people who can help."

Cate explained about the army bereavement councilor who had urged her to attend a support group. He'd argued that it couldn't hurt, only it did. Although there was strength in fellowship, Cate soon found that the last thing she wanted to do was spend more time thinking about death; when she was with other widows, that was all she did. Hearing them speak of their fatherless children, or how they were struggling to reenter the work force, just made her feel worse than she already did. And always in the back of her mind a litany played: *Our husbands are dead; our husbands are dead.* She couldn't explain her reasoning to those who had traveled a path she'd only begun to stumble upon. So she avoided war widows and support groups — anything connected with the military. She said as much, hoping that would close the matter. Then she made herself go on. "After John died, it was hard to find work. When I saw an advertisement for the program here, I applied, never thinking much of it. I was trying so many things those days — anything to put food on the table. You see, my credit rating is crap. Nowadays employers run credit checks before they hire you. Luckily, the hospital didn't, or if it did, my background didn't matter. Anyway, that's how I wound up in Amberley." She shrugged her thin shoulders. "So that's my life. No big mystery." At the strained expression on Sheila's face, Cate asked, "What? What's wrong?"

In answer, Sheila pulled an envelope from her pocket. In a halting voice, she explained what had happened.

Cate accepted the envelope, but made no move to read the letter within. Instead, she shoved it in her pocket. "So you know that the army sends me money every month." Reaching for a knife to occupy her hands, she proceeded to chop pistachios with quick strokes. "I — I was furious when I got the first payment — a lump-sum hundred thousand dollars. I wanted to rip up the check and send the pieces back to — well, that was the problem. Who was to blame — the Massachusetts National Guard, the Pentagon, that jerk in the White House? I carried the check around for days, staring at all the zeros. It was enough money to pay off the mortgage, and keep the home I'd made with John. But having it made me feel dirty, like I was betraying his memory by taking a payoff. It was a stupid reaction; I know that. And I know John would have wanted me to keep the money. In the end, though, I didn't have to." At the question in Sheila's eyes, Cate said, "John's grandmother needs to be in a nursing home. Keeping her in a good one costs a lot. So you see, the hundred thousand was a blessing in some ways. And the stipend I get every month goes to pay her expenses, too. But it's not enough; I'll have to start making real money someday."

"What about government programs? Maybe they can help."

"I don't qualify. The survivor benefits I get put me above the income level for those programs. Even though I don't use the army's stipend for myself, it still counts as income." At the look of sympathy on Sheila's face, Cate hastened to add, "I'm not unique. Lots of army widows find themselves in the ranks of the working poor."

"The working poor," Sheila echoed grimly. "You shouldn't be reduced to that. Shame on our country." Her eyes flashed. "And shame on those idiots in Washington who are so clueless."

As evening beckoned, they closed up the grocery together, both women mourning absent husbands. Sheila threw herself into the familiar routine of tidying up, storing food, and setting the place to rights. After pulling down the front shades, she poured two glasses of amaretto liquor and gestured toward the bistro tables near the window. "Can you stay a few minutes?"

"Sure."

They sat quietly until Sheila said, "I want you to know you're not alone. War has touched many of us in town. Some women have lost loved ones, and some have seen the men in their lives come back from war changed in ways they could never have imagined. My own husband —" She paused, and Cate leaned forward. Although she'd never met Vincent Morazzo, she'd heard talk of him, for the Italian-born internist was highly regarded. She'd often thought to ask why she'd never seen Sheila's husband in the grocery, but then perhaps they were having marital problems. Was that what Sheila wanted to tell her?

"Vincent's been working extra hours since you got to town," Sheila said, as if reading Cate's thoughts. "That's why he hasn't been around here. And now he's taken a leave of absence from his practice to go back to —" Sheila stopped and turned her attention to the front window. Jumping up to fetch a cotton cloth, she proceeded to scrub the glass. "This is covered with fingerprints. Just covered!" Cate waited in silence, for there was nothing else to do until the emotional wave broke, and well she knew that it might be a minute or an hour before that happened. Slowly, Sheila's hand stilled. "Actually, I'm not sure exactly where Vincent is at the moment. Turkey, Jordan, Iraq." She walked to the table and sat down wearily. "He volunteers with Doctors Without Borders. He's done it since before we were married. The first time he went, he told me over the phone he was leaving. Just like that, he called to say he was off to the sub-Sahara for six months. I was furious. And hurt that he could up and leave me — leave our life — for, well, strangers. I wanted to shout at him, but there was a customer here. A bitter woman who preferred the echoed soundtrack of other lives to the silence of her own heart. She was eavesdropping, and afterward she said that Africa sounded like a dangerous place filled with disease. I heard her words as if from a distance, for I was still holding the receiver — staring at the smudges of flour on it. I'd been making bread when he called, you see." Sheila looked down at her hands. "Making bread is like making life. It's miraculous what yeast can do if you've the touch. After Vincent called, I didn't. Slapped the dough I'd been kneading so hard I killed the yeast within. That's the only batch of bread that didn't rise for me in all these years."

She tugged the cloth she still gripped this way and that. "After the first time he went away, I thought long and hard about breaking things off. But I loved him too much. I was over the moon for that man. Still am. As hurt and worried as I am when he goes, I'm proud, too. I think you understand that. And I think you understand why I've never told Vincent how I really feel. Why I've never asked him to stay. An ultimatum might just push him away. I can't — *won't* take that risk."

How damaging silence can be, Cate thought, for the cry of objection that had frozen in Sheila's throat had surely birthed resentment. That might be a slow-acting poison, but in large-enough doses, it could kill the strongest love. *So she's never told him how she really feels about his leaving, just as I never told John. Why didn't I beg him not to go to Iraq, to run away to Canada instead? Why do we hold back like that when war seeps into our lives? We convince ourselves it's right to surrender what's most precious, but is it? Is it really?* For a moment, Cate gave herself over to loss. Then a curious thing happened. Instead of drowning under a wave of sadness, she bobbed to the surface — some yards from where she wanted to be, but no longer struggling against a rising tide. Grateful for that small step forward, she reached out to give Sheila's hand a squeeze.

Sheila nodded, gathering the remnants of the story. "When Vincent came back home that first time, I thought it was all done with — that he wouldn't go again and that my doubts had fled for good. Instead, they've dogged me like ghosts that won't rest, for he can't say no when they call him. Not even after our daughter was born and he knew — knew how much we needed him here." Her voice broke, before flattening out. "He's volunteered three more times. Each has been different, but this time — this time I'm worried because I'm not sure where he is. He flew to Turkey, but beyond that, I don't know." She met Cate's gaze then, and there was a hard glint to the look. "What I do know is how often doctors and journalists — all noncombatants — die side by side with soldiers."

"Y-yes, but it's very rare," Cate said lamely. Then it hit her that although the conversation had begun with her needing comfort, it was ending with her giving it. At the realization that by sharing her own pain Sheila had thrust her into an empowering role, Cate felt a wave of gratitude. With a silent prayer that her next words were true, she said, "Your husband's probably working so hard he can't get to a phone. He'll call you soon. I'm sure of it."

Sheila nodded in agreement, although she seemed far from certain Vincent was safe. Yet even her doubt brought a curious comfort, for uncertainty rested as solidly on hope as fear. Cate had only to look in the mirror to see the damage wrought when the battle between those twins is at an end.

Chapter 6

On her next day off, Cate lingered over a breakfast of French toast and strawberries before taking a walk toward the town common. Out of habit, she glanced in the front windows of Flynn's Hardware, for Sheila's neighbor had a unique approach to merchandizing his wares. A pyramid of oil cans that bore a "4 Sale" sign sat next to a pile of khaki overalls that could be had "2 For A Jackson." She paused to peer closer. Twenty dollars for two pairs of pants wasn't a bad price, after all. Maybe — no. No! Times might be tough, but she wouldn't stoop to buying her clothes in a hardware store! Not yet, anyway.

Her wallet was rather slim due to Mary-Lou, not that Cate was having second thoughts about spending that bit of money. "You can't walk to work in the heat of summer," the mechanic had announced the day before, pulling a red ten-speed bicycle out

97

of her truck. "Won this in a poker game, and I don't need it. It's brand new. Fifty bucks and it's yours." When Cate blinked in surprise, MaryLou had lowered the price to forty. Tempted to pull away from anything that smacked of charity, Cate had surprised herself and accepted the outrageously low price, determined to repay MaryLou's gesture in kind.

Wondering how long it would take her to do that, and save up for a proper biking helmet, she peered in the window of a block-long florist and garden center, where she'd bought a few plants when she first moved to town. The owner was a middle-aged woman who had introduced herself as "a friend of Sheila's" before hurrying away to hoist bags of manure into a customer's truck. Cate had wandered down the aisles of perennials and annuals, admiring how healthy everything looked. With a pang of longing, she had recalled the small garden she'd planted around her house in Boston. Her last day there, a clump of double narcissus had begun to bloom. Leaving that small spot of cheery yellow had hurt more than she'd expected. So she'd bought a Van Gogh–yellow ceramic bowl to hold a six-pack of purple pansies. They'd flourished in their new home, and every morning Cate moved the planter from the windowsill to the kitchen table so she could admire the tiny garden as she ate breakfast.

Thoughts of food brought Vitelli's to mind. "No," she whispered to herself, "not until you've at least walked a mile." Continuing along Main Street, she passed the Amberley Cooperative Bank, where her meager savings were kept, and the library she had yet to visit. Veering onto a brick pathway that meandered its way through the common, she picked up the pace, inordinately proud that what had begun as a leisurely walk had become, if not a run, at least a jog. Outside the diner, she paused to read the menu pasted to the front door.

SPECIALS

French onion soup with red cabbage
coleslaw and potato salad
chicken potpie with a green salad
grilled cheese with sweet potato fries
apple crisp with pistachio ice cream

Imagining how Gaby would present each dish, Cate concluded that if she was to continue partaking of her new friend's cooking, she'd best keep moving. Quickening her pace, she crossed Main Street to admire the window displays of McLean's

Department Store. She thought of the stories Beatrice McLean had shared with her. As each piece of the puzzle that was her patient's life fell into place, Cate came to appreciate the unique contribution Beatrice had made to Amberley. A rich, successful businesswoman who had saved her family's business when her father couldn't, Beatrice had lived life outside the four walls that constrained women in her day: submissive daughter, dutiful wife, proud mother, and pious communicant. Yet for all her strength, at times the old woman seemed vulnerable. That came from engaging with the world and putting herself out there. From taking risks. There was a lesson to be learned there, one best pondered over caffeine.

Although Cate hadn't lived in Amberley long, when she made her way into Vitelli's, she was greeted by name by staff and customers alike. Cappuccino in hand, she headed for one of the bistro tables near the front windows, choosing the seat she'd taken her first day in town. She thought of how her life had changed since then and wondered how much it would change in the months and years to come. Would she see those changes through in Amberley or make her way back to Boston? In Amberley, she hoped, feeling warmth suffuse her at the prospect of putting down roots again. And wasn't it strange that the very thing she'd initially found difficult about moving to a place John had never been was what now made it so attractive? For the fact that the town was free of memories was a blessing. That had been difficult to get her mind around until it struck her one day while she was shopping for a colander. She'd had a lovely stainless steel one at home that had been John's before they married. He'd used it to make spaghetti and meatballs the first time he'd cooked her dinner. So why had she found herself in the housewares department of McLean's holding a white ceramic replacement? An extravagance, she'd told herself, before putting it back on the shelf. Only it hadn't been, for she'd needed the colander precisely because it evoked no memories. So she'd gone back the next day and bought it. If asked why, she'd have said that some things in her new life needed to be what she'd come to think of as neutral colored — neither stained nor tinted by the past.

Still, the past was ever with her — in scraps of memory and emotion, discarded hopes and weathered dreams. She accepted that, but there was a sweet balancing point between remembering and rebuilding. Between honoring what was and embracing what could be. But how could she move forward without knowing the truth of John's death? She'd been told he'd died in a roadside bombing, but not where or how it happened. Some of her friends had seen John's passing as a threshold to be crossed blindfolded. They'd counseled acceptance and pressured Cate to accept whatever crumbs of information the army chose to share. Try as she might, she hadn't been able to make them understand her fury at being stonewalled, for even if she couldn't change what happened, she deserved to know how it had. So she'd bombarded John's commanders with letters, e-mails, and phone calls. And learned little. Then she'd lost her home and her will to keep fighting. Or was that true? Even if she hadn't — *yet* — won her battle against the Pentagon, she might find the courage to try again.

In the meantime, she stumbled forward, measuring success some days by the hour, others by the minute. When night fell on her spirit, despair circled like a hungry animal, darting in to bite and gnaw whenever the darkness overcame her. Yet as often as the tide of grief rose, it receded. In those respites, she carved a path through the pain, and each time she managed some task alone — hooking up the generator during an ice storm, getting through the holidays without reaching for a bottle — she felt both proud and guilty. It hadn't been easy adjusting to life without the man she loved, but it hadn't been impossible. And it should have been.

As her thoughts turned this way and that, she looked up in surprise to see that Sheila had taken the seat opposite. Cate hadn't the heart for conversation, but welcomed the distraction — anything to keep from torturing herself with unanswered questions. Unquestioned answers.

Circling her shoulders, Sheila blew wispy bangs from her brow. "I'm beat." After glancing at her watch as if gauging how much of a break she could give herself, she gestured toward Cate's plate. "Almond cookies. Good choice."

Cate found a smile. "They're heaven."

Sheila shrugged. "Not tough to make."

"How do you — ?"

Sheila held up her hands, surrender style. "Trade secret. Even from you." Her gaze shifted to the door, and she inclined her head toward a slim woman in yoga pants who was just leaving. "An old friend. She's getting together a team for the bowling league. If you're interested." When Cate stiffened, Sheila rushed on, "Oh, nobody's very good, but I hear it's fun. Not that I've been myself. No time. So, do you bowl?"

"No."

"It's okay, they can teach you. No problem."

"Oh. That's nice, but —"

"You don't want to," Sheila said without judgment.

"Not really."

"Okay. Well, if not bowling, what are your hobbies?"

What are my hobbies? Cate repeated the question in her mind. *How bizarre it sounded. A common enough query to anyone else, but not in my world.* Sheila's face shuttered just a little when she didn't reply. Without allowing herself to overthink the decision, Cate tried to explain how disconnected she felt. "To tell you the truth, there was a time when I would have answered that question easily and defined myself without thinking. But since losing John, I've begun to sort of fade away. It's like I'm only an echo of who I was. Not the real Cate. Sometimes I feel as though I don't even cast a shadow or have a reflection."

"My daughter would say that means you're a vampire, so be careful," Sheila said

104

before her tone became serious. "I do understand how you feel, actually. I'm always Mary Sunshine at work. Always up. But you know how I worry about Vincent. Worry that without him, *I'll* lose my reflection. But we shouldn't feel invisible. Fear's the enemy, after all; Roosevelt was right about that." She got up and drew her shoulders back in characteristic fashion. "So if I was to ask you what your interests are, to describe yourself, what would you say? Quick, without thinking."

"I'd say I'm a frustrated writer. An out-of-shape runner. A reluctant caregiver. A widow."

"So nothing positive then?"

Cate felt a jolt at the simple truth of those words. In the days to follow, Sheila's question became a haunting refrain. Although Cate had celebrated and cherished her life with John, since his death life had been something that happened to her — something to get through. She floundered and thrashed about, made headway in spurts and starts, but usually managed only to keep her head above water. To cope and survive. Even that much took effort, and along the way she'd lost herself. It had happened so gradually, this shift to something less than three-dimensional. Her grandmother would have called her a remnant woman torn apart by grief. Bits and pieces of her old self remained, but not enough to form a full person. And she couldn't return to who she'd been — to John's Cate. She would never be that woman again. But she could become — who? Who did she want to be? That question became a well-gnawed bone, but it also birthed what she began to think of as "Project Cate" — a construction project for rebuilding herself. Resolved not to let a day go by without putting in some work on it, she began by pulling out a notebook and writing in capital letters across the top of a clean page: THINGS I LIKE. At first, the list that followed sounded like a dessert menu. Gradually, the seams of such narrow thinking strained outward, and she wrote: WATERCOLORING. BIKING. GARDENING. Her heart skipped with excitement. WRITING. AMBERLEY.

As Project Cate developed, so grew Cate's friendship with Sheila. Both women were eager to lay a foundation devoid of cracks, so things had progressed slowly. That changed the day customers surged through the grocery's front door and Cate grabbed an apron to pitch in. She chopped nuts, washed up, and swept the floor. When Sheila insisted that Cate take groceries as payment, she bristled until Sheila explained that she didn't sell day-old bread or pastries. "What you and I don't eat goes to the food bank, and they can't take it all. So I wind up feeding the birds, who eat quite well as it is." Cate relented.

The next time Sheila tried to give her food, Cate pointed out that the rent she was paying was far below market. Brushing aside her concerns, Sheila said the peace of mind she derived from knowing Cate was on site couldn't be valued. As if the matter were settled, Sheila held out a bag of vegetables. "Here. You'll be helping me out taking this stuff; it will just go bad otherwise."

Cate peered into the bag and blanched. "These artichokes are perfect!"

"They're going soft."

"And the lettuce?"

"Wilted, or as good as."

Sheila prudently waited a day before trying again. This time, the bag contained a dish of eggplant Parmesan and a heel of garlic bread. Cate did her best to check such generosity, but it was no use. If she refused to accept something, Sheila just left twice as much food in her refrigerator. When she confronted her landlady about this, Sheila smiled and pointed out that the lease gave her right of entry to the apartment.

Resigned to the inevitable, Cate resolved two things. First, she needed to exercise more. Second, she would pay her landlady back in kind. Sometimes, Sheila looked up from the morning baking to see Cate scrubbing the sidewalk produce bins, others to note that the trash had been hauled to the curb for pickup. Cate also weeded the vegetable and herb beds, for although a novice gardener, she could distinguish weeds from edible plants. Most of the time.

In the weeks to follow, both women threw themselves into this competitive tug-of-war in which the rule of the game was simple: Give more than you take. "Not a bad blueprint for friendship," Helen observed when she caught wind of it. And that was something both Sheila and Cate could agree on.

CHAPTER 7

Dawn had tinted the sky a soft pink, but by midmorning it was overcast and brooding. Gaby watched the sun struggle to pierce the blanket of clouds above much as her spirit fought against the demands of her aching body. How she longed to crawl into bed and surrender to the oblivion of sleep. But she couldn't, even though it was Sunday — her only day off. Cate had called and asked her to brunch, and the hopeful undercurrent to the younger woman's voice had been enough to push all thoughts of rest from Gaby's mind. Mostly.

Pulling on a pair of jeans, she frowned in dismay for they swam on her hips. She'd lost weight, enough that people would begin to notice. But perhaps they'd think it was intentional. *You can never be too thin or too rich* — wasn't that the popular phrase? Well, one out of two wasn't bad. She chuckled at the thought of what it had taken for her to achieve the willowy shape of a supermodel. Then she fed a handful of kibble to her two kittens and headed into town.

Cate welcomed her guests with a broad smile before ushering them into the living room, where soft music played. Jam jars of wild daisies dotted the room, and there was a hint of vanilla from a score of scented candles. She'd managed to save up enough money to have some of her things sent from Boston, and she was proud of how good they looked in her new home. When Sheila's gaze moved approvingly from the mahogany end table to the writing desk John had made, Cate felt a satisfied thrill. Exhaling the breath she'd been holding, she gestured toward the couch. "Won't you sit — ?"

"Oh, we're not sitting in here," MaryLou said dismissively with a curt shake of her signature curls. "We'll help in the kitchen."

"But —" Cate began, a frown gathering the skin on her brow.

"Lulu's right," Sheila threw over her shoulder, moving through the rooms she knew so well. "We want to help, not be waited on."

"Best go with the flow, Cate," Gaby advised, following her friends.

With a resigned air, Cate switched off the radio, blew out the candles, and hurried to catch up with her guests. Soon she was positioned in what John had termed a kitchen's "command post": that magical triangle formed by sink, fridge, and stove. The coffee was percolating, and she was bent over a waffle iron from which cinnamon-scented steam rose in wisps. "My husband's waffle decorations were legendary," she explained. "Banana slice smiles, blue-berry noses, kiwi eyes, and orange-segment ears." Gesturing toward the fruit bowl on the table, she added, "I'll do my best to re-create the effect, but I'm nowhere near as talented as he was."

"I'll help," Sheila volunteered, reaching for a knife to slice the fruit. MaryLou set the table with Cate's mismatched set of dishes while Gaby poured coffee.

"No, no! Sit, please! Relax!" Cate cried.

"Don't know about them, but I can't sit still," Sheila explained. "You should understand why." Cate did; they all did. They also knew that although Sheila had learned Vincent was safe in Turkey, she still didn't know where he would be sent next or when he would be home. Such uncertainty would paralyze some women, but with Sheila it had the opposite effect: She had more energy than usual.

"So your husband did the cooking?" MaryLou asked Cate, sorting through a drawer for cutlery. "Sounds like the perfect man."

"He was. Or as close as," Cate said before rubbing a hand over her brow. "I had such a vivid dream about him last night," she added in a whisper.

MaryLou cocked a hip. "A vivid dream," she repeated in a throaty voice. "Does that mean what I think it does?"

"Lulu!" Gaby scolded. "Get your mind out of the gutter!"

Cate smiled. "No. It's all right." She addressed herself to MaryLou. "Yes, actually. Although sometimes I don't exactly remember John's touch, or I don't think I do, my dream self seems to have no problem in that regard. I'm jealous of her. Dream Cate, I mean."

"Ah." MaryLou nodded sagely. "I can relate. Dream MaryLou has a hell of a time. Every night."

"Awake MaryLou doesn't seem to do too badly," Sheila quipped. "Five marriages and counting."

"But only three husbands," MaryLou corrected, before sliding her gaze to Cate's astonished face. "I married two of them twice." A smile lit her eyes. "Gaby introduced me to my last husband. Ryley. Southern boy. Very charming." She turned her burgundy fingernails to the light for a quick check. "I love Southern men. They take their time saying things, but then they're thorough in everything, and that's good news for women. Yeah, Ryley was worth marrying twice, despite the pain he caused me." And therein lay a surprising truth: MaryLou was a romantic. Her failed relationships weren't testament to poor judgment so much as a firm belief in nothing ventured, nothing gained. "Without love," she explained to Cate, "the world isn't worth much. But it doesn't just fall in your lap; you've got to go looking for it, sometimes in the oddest places. And if what you find is fool's gold, try again. You'll have better odds the next time."

In the pause that followed, Sheila dropped her bombshell. "I've been thinking about putting off the surgery." She stepped back to consider the cascade of luscious color that only moments before had been a bowl of fruit. "I just can't deal with being sliced myself, what with everything else now."

"Sliced? Surgery?" MaryLou asked sharply. "What surgery?"

"On my hand."

"Wrist," Cate corrected, flipping a blueberry waffle.

"Right. Wrist," Sheila agreed. "They need to cut something or other."

"It's carpal tunnel surgery," Cate reminded her in a low voice. "You know that."

"Whatever," Sheila muttered. "Damn nuisance is what it is."

"They need to cut something or other." MaryLou repeated Sheila's words in a mocking tone. "This from a doctor's wife!"

"Exactly. His wife. *I'm* not the doctor," Sheila reminded them. When the three women stared at her, she threw them a bone of sorts. "I've got a mental block about medical stuff, okay? Especially when it comes to my own health. And I don't want to have surgery while Vincent's away."

Gaby reached out to give Sheila a hug. "But if you're in a lot of pain —"

"If it gets worse I'll reconsider. Okay?" Sheila shifted her gaze from one friend to the next. "Okay?" Each nodded in turn, and she let out a breath before sniffing the air. "Are those waffles done? I think they're done."

"Backseat driver," MaryLou grumbled. "You're telling Cate how to cook just like you told me on Christmas Eve!"

Gaby filled in the conversational gap. "You

see, Cate, MaryLou cooked us dinner last Christmas Eve. It was — interesting," she concluded diplomatically.

"That's one way of putting it," Sheila recalled with a snort.

MaryLou took offense, or pretended to. "I don't know what you're complaining about. We ate by ten, nobody was rushed to the hospital with food poisoning, and the dishes were done before New Year's."

An hour later, MaryLou pushed her empty plate aside with a satisfied sigh. "Fabulous. You two had better watch out," she cautioned Gaby and Sheila, "or Cate will open her own restaurant and give you both a run for your money." Then MaryLou dug in her pocket for the lipstick she was never without.

"Funny, Lulu," Sheila said.

"Lulu," Cate repeated. "That's an unusual nickname."

"My daughter, Sara," Sheila explained. "Oh, you haven't met her yet because she's away at school. Anyway, when she was little she couldn't pronounce MaryLou."

Sorting through her memories, Gaby added, "Then we all took to calling her that because it fit. MaryLou's a bit of an exotic bird, one with bright plumage and a distinctive call. A Lulu."

"So I'm showy and shrill," MaryLou joked before considering. "You know, I can live with that."

Gaby's voice took on a serious note. "Don't laugh this off. Your name is special because you are. You're someone who shimmers with life."

"Amen," Cate added quietly.

MaryLou swallowed hard and shifted in her seat.

"Uncomfortable with compliments?" Sheila teased.

"From men, no, but from you lot — yeah, I guess so."

"Why's that?" Cate asked.

"Because when we're being nice to her, she can't taunt us or be as annoying as she wants," Sheila observed.

"Sure I can," MaryLou decided briskly, snapping her compact closed. "I've been thinking about Vincent." When Sheila frowned, MaryLou shrugged her shoulders in a way that made her hefty bosom rise and fall suggestively. "Her husband's quite a cutie, you know," she spoke confidentially in Cate's direction. "You wouldn't think that one so muscled could be smart." A sigh escaped MaryLou. "That's rarely the case, at least in my experience — and I've had

116

plenty. No, it's a cruel fact of nature that delicious food is unhealthy and gorgeous men are either gay or stupid. But then Vincent Morazzo is the example that disproves the rule."

Gaby read Cate's expression for what it was: surprise that MaryLou would be so insensitive as to bring up Vincent's name. But then, Cate didn't fully understand the friendships forged by the women around her, or the architecture of Sheila's mind. So Gaby hastened to assure her hostess in a lowered tone, "Cate, this bantering they do is nothing more than the give-and-take between close friends."

"Didn't he do a neurology internship once upon a time?" MaryLou continued, seemingly oblivious to how Sheila tapped her forefinger on the kitchen table in a staccato beat. "Neurology," MaryLou repeated in a throaty voice. "The study of all those nerve endings. Sources of so much pleasure. And pain, of course. But then I'm not into that sort of thing. Although —"

"You're skating on thin ice, MaryLou!" The words exploded from Sheila.

"Take it easy!" MaryLou held her hands up in mock surrender. "You husband's safe from me. I don't poach."

Cate jumped into the conversation. "You

may not poach men, but food — that's another matter."

MaryLou blinked widely. Then blinked again. "Our girl made a joke." She reached out to give Cate's hand an avuncular pat. "It wasn't very funny, but nice try."

"I thought it was funny." Sheila smirked, sitting back against her seat. "Funnier than you were."

"I wasn't trying to be funny; just wanted to needle you."

"You two are incorrigible," Gaby chided. "Poor Cate went to all this trouble —"

MaryLou waved a manicured hand in the air. "She's a friend; she understands." Mary-Lou chatted on to Sheila, not noticing the impact of those simple words.

Cate needs this — the easy teasing of sisters, or those as close as sisters, Gaby thought. *I don't think she has many friends. But why? There's a story there she hasn't shared yet.* As Cate cleared the table and put things away, Gaby's keen eyes noted the nearly empty shelves. *Not much food here, and she reused her tea bag. Twice. Yet she comes into the diner nearly every day for lunch. My prices aren't steep, but still — must be she craves the company. And my cooking, of course.* Gaby smiled inwardly.

When the three women took their leave,

MaryLou commented that she had shown great taste befriending yet another good cook. Sheila complimented Cate on both the meal and how she'd turned the barren apartment into a home. Gaby insisted that Cate stop by the diner for lunch the next day as the meal was on her. "It's only fair, for I've got to repay the favor of those lovely waffles!"

After closing the door behind her guests, Cate tidied up the kitchen and opened a bottle of wine she'd been saving. She relit the candles, switched on some music, and curled up on the couch. As afternoon gave way to evening and candlelight danced across the ceiling, she told John about her day. She found herself thinking the words she usually spoke aloud and wondered when that had happened. She couldn't recall, for the change had been so gradual. She tried to get her mind around whether it was a sign she was healing — oh, how she hated that word! Like *closure* it suggested that her life with John was something she hoped one day to consign to a box in the attic of her thoughts. But that wasn't what she wanted! She gave herself over to the moment before noticing something wedged between the far bookcase and the woodwork. Why hadn't she seen it before? Her tears ebbed as she walked across the room and bent down. Wiggling some rolled-up papers free, she spread them flat on the floor. A spider ran out, and she pulled back instinctively. The yellowed pages recurled slowly, as if to shield the words within, and a hushed silence seemed to fill the room. She hesitated before reaching out a curious hand.

From the moment I stepped off the bus, Amberley felt like home. The streets were tree-lined, children played in grass-filled backyards and lines of wash flapped in a gentle breeze. I wandered through downtown, passing planters overflowing with purple flowers I've learned are called petunias. It seemed like a movie set. No bullet holes marred the buildings, no shouts filled the streets, no fear hung in the air. *Amberley is a town untouched by war,* I thought, only it wasn't so. I didn't know then how many wars have touched this quiet place, for its scars are well hidden.

I turned toward a massive hotel that dominated one corner of Main Street before studying the address I'd been given and walking farther on to a brick and stone building. The green awning outside read,

"Vitelli's Grocery" and beneath that, "imported foods — baked goods." Bins filled with fruit and vegetables crowded the front sidewalk, and the smell of spices and fresh baked bread filled the air. I pushed open the etched glass door, and a bell jingled overhead. An apron-clad woman stood behind a gleaming wooden counter staring at a wheel of wax-covered cheese. She looked up with a smile, her gaze moving to the suitcases I carried. I introduced myself, and she nodded, wiping flour-coated hands on her apron and saying, "I am Rosa Vitelli." Her gray-streaked hair was pulled into a severe-looking bun at the nape of her neck, but her brown eyes were warm and welcoming. "Come, see your rooms."

Picking up my bags, I followed Rosa up two flights of stairs to a small corner apartment that looked down on the back garden. Clean and neat, it was papered in a violet print and well furnished. Most important, it boasted a door that locked and windows open to the air of freedom. Rosa told me my English was good, and I blushed with pride. "I studied for years before I came. But I have a heavy accent."

Rosa waved a hand dismissively. "As I do." She watched me unpack, murmuring

121

that I was too thin but that she'd soon fix that. I smiled, for it was impossible not to respond to so maternal a figure. Rosa surprised me by saying in that lovely Italian accent of hers that she saw steel beneath the thinness of my body and compassion in a face that hadn't been hardened by sorrow. She said she knew something of sorrow and assured me that the haunted look in my eyes would soon fade. Rosa told me she, too, had fled the ravages of war and left the land she knew. I came to see how her hunger for work matched my own, and how profoundly her friendship would define my new life.

Cate turned the pages over, but there was nothing further. From context and the handwriting, she concluded that the writer was a woman. Since the text bore no salutation or signature, it seemed to be a journal entry of some kind. Although undated, given the state of the papers, they must have fallen behind the bookcase long ago. She skimmed the text again, the emotional undercurrent drawing her in as before. Then her gaze traveled over the paneled walls to a spot behind the fireplace mantle. A small patch of old wallpaper was visible. With an indrawn breath, she ran a finger over the violet print. So this *had* been the writer's apartment, one with a "door that locked and windows open to the air of freedom." But why had someone fleeing the memory of war come to Amberley? It wasn't to be with family, for the writer had rented rooms from Rosa Vitelli — a stranger. Surely Sheila would know who the writer had been. Cate considered seeking her out immediately before deciding against it. Sheila had been so preoccupied with Vincent and, truth be told, Cate feld an inexplicable desire to keep her discovery to herself. At least for a while. With a glance at the overflowing laundry basket, she dropped the yellowed pages into a desk drawer and pushed it closed with a swift movement. The faded words were once again plunged into darkness, but the plea tucked beneath the inky scrawl half a century before had already slipped free and was making its way toward Cate's heart.

CHAPTER 8

The next morning was sun-splashed. As Cate crossed Main Street, she called out a greeting to Zelda Malory. Cate had seen Zelda many times before she'd stopped to chat with the woman whose newsstand was a downtown fixture. And despite her love of dogs, Cate hadn't petted the Irish setter who routinely ran up to her in the common until one day his russet fur had caught the light in such a way she'd laughed despite herself.

Why had she been so closed off and determined to pull back from life in ways both small and large? John, of course. Zelda reminded her of his grandmother, the dog of the puppy he'd had in college. She didn't know why calling those memories to the forefront of her mind was painful, but it was. And yet memories were armor. That armor didn't shield her from sadness, for that was as constant as the rising sun. But it did keep the chill wind of despair from snaking its way toward her heart. So why did she sometimes resist remembering? Perhaps because it was human nature to live in a world of opposites where darkness was the absence of light, fullness the lack of hunger. Recalling a joyful moment with John often pointed up his loss so sharply that a curtain wall rose around her heart. When that happened, a fearful voice whispered that perhaps it was better not to remember at all. Why risk the pain of a burning sun when the half-light beckoned? For love, of course; one only risks for love. The days when she answered fear with those words, she moved forward. On those she didn't, she lost ground.

She couldn't guess that April morning that meeting her next patient would set her on a path where she'd risk so much. No, that day she felt only surprise when she glanced from the address Helen had texted her to St. Joseph's, a Gothic Revival church that anchored one corner of the common. Looking up at its castellated tower, stained glass windows, and stone façade, she wondered if James Sullivan was the caretaker of the church. Or perhaps he was a groundskeeper, for she'd glimpsed a walled garden to the rear.

Running up the granite steps, she pulled open the heavy oak door and entered the cool interior. As the door hissed shut behind her, Cate's eyes adjusted to the dimness even as her right hand reached out for the holy water font. Old habits. Her gaze lit on a statue of the Virgin flanked by banks of red and white candles. How many times had she prayed at just such a spot, reciting a penance of Hail Marys? She could almost feel the sensation of cold marble on bony knees and the dread that would flood through her when she entered the confessional. An oppressive silence would close around her as she waited for the wooden screen to slide open, and her heart would pound when the priest's shadowed profile came into view. Enjoined not to look directly at the confessor, she'd stare instead at the maroon leather armrest and intone the refrain: *Bless me, Father, for I have sinned.* Then her mind would go blank. A monotonously well-behaved child, she often confessed to sins she hadn't committed, for one had to have *something* to say.

The church was quiet save for the low murmur of whispered prayers and the creak of wood as the few parishioners who dotted the pews shifted their weight. Cate's throat constricted at the achingly familiar smells of incense, burning wax, and a subtle mustiness. Then the nostalgic feeling gave way to memories of her third-grade teacher: "We'll be late for the novena, girls. Line up now, two by two!" Invariably, as the class marched past her, Sister Francis would catch sight of Cate and cry, "Catherine Mary Elizabeth, straighten your uniform! And pull up your socks!" Cate's shoulders stiffened at the memory of those gray knee socks bunched around her ankles. The elastic inevitably wore out before new ones could be bought. Rubber bands did the trick — when Cate remembered them. When she didn't, Sister's sharp tongue ensured that the class knew it. Funny that the humiliation hadn't paled in all the intervening years, but then she wouldn't have thought of Sister Francis if she hadn't come into the church. That realization fed an irrational resentment of James Sullivan who seemed to be nowhere in sight despite their appointment.

There was a rustle of movement in the last pew before a figure disappeared through an archway that probably led to the rectory. On impulse, Cate followed and found herself in a small kitchen. An elderly priest stood before her, holding a cane in one hand. He swayed slightly, and she rushed forward to help. "Are you all right?"

"Yes," he said in a voice that sounded as thin and crackly as old parchment. "I just wanted a glass of water. Got a bit dizzy, though." When he introduced himself, Cate stiffened. James Sullivan's faded blue eyes narrowed. "Don't like priests much, do you?"

Something in his manner made her opt for brutal honesty. "No. Not really."

Easing himself to a chair, Father Sullivan gestured toward her uniform. "Now, I could judge you by the packaging, but that would be unfair. It doesn't define you any more than mine does me."

Cate shifted her weight, acutely aware that she was on the defensive and at a disadvantage. "It's not really the same thing."

"Oh?"

"We have rather different jobs. I clean up people's messes, get them back on their feet, and help them make it to the next day," she said briskly.

"Sounds familiar," he countered, cocking his head of unruly white hair as if asking a question.

"Except you work for God."

"We all work for God. I've just been lucky enough to make my living at it."

She let the matter lie with a shrug. After

checking her patient's vital signs, Cate made him a bit of lunch and tidied the kitchen. While he ate, she opened a window that looked out on an herb garden, all the while trying to order the questions swirling in her mind. What excuse could she give Helen for not working with the priest? She could say she was uncomfortable caring for men, but she'd already proven otherwise. When an Alzheimer's patient had thrown his breakfast tray at a nurse and threatened to slit the woman's throat, she'd screamed, but Cate had approached the patient calmly. Noting that although the *Boston Globe* on the bed was turned upside down and spotted with coffee, it was opened to the sports page, she had asked, "Who do you think will pitch tonight?" Her face impassive, she'd waited for his answer as though discussing baseball with a red-faced stranger clutching a knife in his vein-corded hands was the most natural thing in the world.

"Wha-what?" the old man had stuttered before she'd looked into eyes bloodshot with fatigue and clouded with confusion. Then she'd had her first inkling that her new career might prove to be more than a means to an end, more than a way to pass the time between the life she'd lost and the one she had yet to find.

"I think it'll be Beckett," she'd said, straightening the man's rumpled blankets as though by putting the bed to rights she could reorder his thoughts. "Beckett has the arm to take them to the World Series, don't you think?" Only when he'd nodded mutely had she eased the knife from his trembling hands. Helen had rushed in then, eyes wide with concern. Taking in the scene, she had thrown her student an approving look that made Cate flush with pride. Although afterward her knees had turned to jelly, Cate's composure in the face of Old Man Simmons's tirade became the talk of the ward. It earned her the respect of the more battle-scarred nurses and something approaching friendship from Simmons who refused to have anyone else bring him his breakfast.

After seeing how she'd handled that situation, Helen would never believe Cate couldn't work with the mild-mannered priest. And it wasn't as though Cate could say that, as an ex-Catholic, she had an aversion to clergy, for the agency's rules prohibited even the appearance of discrimination. Then she recalled that Father Sullivan's health insurance only covered home care for two weeks. That wasn't very long; she'd just adopt a professional manner and think of him as a patient, not a priest. Not John's priest. As an image of the unctuous prelate who had prodded her husband to do his duty and go to Iraq took shape in her mind, she felt her hands tighten into fists. But James Sullivan had nothing to do with that, and he'd been pleasant since the moment they'd met. Surely she could find a way to get past his dog — *Roman* collar. She had only to find some sort of common ground, a way for them to connect. Then her mind took a turn. She hadn't seen Sheila yet that day, so she hadn't found out anything about who might have written what she'd come to call "the journal entry." Thinking that the priest must know just about everyone in town, she asked him who used to live above the grocery.

If surprised by the question, Father Sullivan didn't show it. "Miriam, of course."

"Miriam?"

"Miriam Rosen, a Polish immigrant."

Cate's heart began to thud inexplicably. "Did you know her? Can you tell me about her?"

Taking a moment to consider his response, he sipped the tea Cate had brewed and reached into the cookie tin she'd placed before him. Studying a piece of shortbread, he spoke simply and quietly about the resettlement program that had brought Miriam Rosen to America. "Miriam was a war refugee. Amberley sponsored a hundred or so World War II refugees." He paused then to ask what she knew of Amberley's history.

"Nothing really."

"Then you'll not appreciate that the town was founded by those fleeing the intolerance of Puritan Boston. Fitting, then, for us to welcome Europe's homeless." He stoked the gray stubble at his chin, and his voice dropped to a whisper. "I was proud of how people banded together then. Very proud. Although the resettlement program was underwritten by a grant from McLean's, it seemed that everyone helped in one way or the other."

"McLean's?" Cate was surprised. "The store paid?"

The priest nodded. "For all the refugees' travel costs. But, as I said, the program was a town effort in the purest sense. Local farmers set up a community food pantry; schoolchildren went door to door, collecting a mountain of used clothing, dishes, and linens. The town's GP, Doc Wesley, opened a free clinic for the refugees. Local businesses provided housing; as you know, Miriam lived above Rosa Vitelli's store." The priest took a sip of tea before continuing.

"While the town prepared itself to receive the refugees, I navigated my way through all the immigration paperwork. It was a Herculean task, but I was younger in those days, and so sure of myself. It never occurred to me that we wouldn't succeed, and I thought it would all take a few months at most." He shook his head ruefully. "There were strict immigration quotas, even after the war. So I argued that the refugees were fleeing Communism, and it worked. It wasn't until 1955 that the first refugees arrived. Miriam came even later." At Cate's look of surprise, he shrugged. "Not unusual at that time. You're far too young to remember, but people spent years in displaced-persons camps and then traveling across Europe waiting for just such an opportunity." He reached up an unconscious hand to finger the crucifix at his neck. "Most of those who came were Jews like Miriam, but I'm proud to say that there were a fair number of Christians who, even in the midst of hell, stayed true to their faith. At great personal risk, some fought with the resistance, while others helped Jews escape capture."

Cate exhaled loudly, unaware she'd been holding her breath. "And was that Miriam's story? Had she escaped capture?"

Father Sullivan paused, as though tempted

to tell less than the truth. "No. Miriam Rosen didn't escape; she survived. Miriam was a Holocaust survivor."

"Oh, my God." Cate felt the knot in her stomach tighten.

"She lost all her family in the war." The priest paused, as if weighing a memory to balance the ugly truth that lay before them. His gaze found the pile of books Cate had pushed aside when she'd set the table, and he gave a slow smile. "Miriam had a fine mind. She was fluent in French. Yiddish and Hebrew as well, of course. I studied some Hebrew at the seminary, and she was quite patient with my bumbling attempts to recall it. She'd been raised in a religious home, but much of what she knew of the Jewish Bible was studied in secret."

"In secret?" Cate repeated, thinking that Miriam's father hadn't approved of his daughter's education. Then she learned how wrong she was.

"During the war," Father Sullivan said, "Miriam spent years in a Polish ghetto."

"Ghetto?"

The priest let loose a sigh. "Before killing their victims, the Germans enslaved them. Miriam was in one such ghetto — the second largest in Poland. Her three brothers were with her — well, initially. None of them survived." He crossed himself quickly. "As you can imagine, life in the ghetto was brutal. There were random killings and mass deportations, and a small number of collaborators terrorized and beat their own. Everything was rationed. Miriam worked all the hours God sent to buy food and enough fuel to avoid freezing to death. But she was one of many women who also struggled to feed their minds by studying Jewish law. Can you imagine that? They broke curfew to travel the streets and meet in secret. Doing so was a double rebellion: against a tradition that entrusted such learning to men, and against the enemy that threatened all. In time, the rabbis gave their approval, for if Jewish men were taken from the earth the responsibility to safeguard the past and carry it forward would fall to mothers and daughters, wives and widows — women like Miriam."

When her patient's eyes watered, whether from fatigue or the effort of recalling painful memories, Cate suggested that he take a rest. After settling him in his study with a glass of water at his elbow and the phone nearby, she made her way back through the church.

Her mind swirled with questions. She had imagined the journal writer to be a woman like herself — someone who had come to Amberley seeking work. But Miriam Rosen's life couldn't be compared with hers. With anyone's. Who knew what horrors the woman had seen and yet — and yet there was a thread of hope that wove its way through her writing. How was that possible? Wouldn't one who had seen the raw brutality of war be bone-weary of life? Perhaps Miriam had been and that's why she'd so valued her apartment's "door that locked and windows open to the air of freedom."

Cate hoped the Polish woman had found both in Amberley — safety and freedom. Even if Miriam could never forget the war, perhaps she'd found a way to efface the horror of being abandoned by her own government and probably betrayed by those she took to be friends. Although Cate believed that no evil before or since equaled the Holocaust, she couldn't help comparing Miriam's fate with John's. But that was ridiculous — Miriam had been a civilian and John a soldier! Yet the American government had betrayed soldiers like John by providing shoddy body armor, and hiring contractors to replace military personnel. Faulty intelligence was the norm, and Iraqis routinely turned on their allies. But that couldn't be compared to a society turning its Jewish citizens over to the enemy. Could it?

Cate fingered her wedding ring, her mind echoing with phrases she'd heard John's commanders fling about as though they explained chaos. "The fog of war"; "collateral damage." But Miriam hadn't been collateral damage — an unintended victim caught in the cross fire; she'd been targeted for death because of her religion. And John? He'd died in a roadside bombing that might have killed coalition forces as easily as an Iraqi child or a running dog.

She wondered if wearing a uniform and dying with a gun in one's hand made a difference, before deciding that it did. John had had a fighting chance; Miriam hadn't. Yet in the end, the gun, the body armor, and the training had meant nothing because Miriam survived, and he didn't.

After Cate left him, James Sullivan's thoughts turned again to Miriam Rosen. It was she who'd reminded him, when self-doubt reached for his heart, that he was a man who had found God in war. Strange to think of his chaplain duties that way, but he supposed she was right. It was certainly how he'd come to appreciate the way war shapes women's lives, as it had hers. He'd been

137

able to do little for the Korean wives, mothers, and daughters who'd crossed his path. A meal here and there, a bit of money pressed into the palm of a girl so she wouldn't turn to prostitution, or at least not that day. But it had all been a pitiful effort that made little difference — like spitting in the wind, his mother would say. Then he'd learned of the continuing plight of Europe's homeless and begun to plan what he would do to help when his tour of duty ended. It was during the numbing cold of his first Korean winter that the idea of refugee resettlement took shape in his mind. When at last he returned to Amberley in 1953, his heart scarred and his nights sleepless, he'd pushed hard for the program that eventually came to pass. Not that it had taken much to persuade Beatrice McLean and the rest of the town; they'd all been on board from the get-go. His eyes traveled to the wall opposite, and he wondered at the flare of recognition he'd seen in young Cate's eyes when she'd noticed the framed photograph there. Had her pupils narrowed in something approaching pain at the sight of all the army uniforms, or had he only imagined it? She had opened her mouth to say something before thinking better of it, and in that pause he was certain there'd been a story. Or a secret.

CHAPTER 9

"Why are you scowling?" Beatrice asked, rubbing her temples.

"You're still having those headaches aren't you? Why didn't you tell me?" Cate demanded, holding out an ice pack. "Lay this on your forehead."

"If it will make you leave me alone, I'll stand on my head."

"Now that I'd like to see." Arms akimbo, Cate scrutinized her favorite patient. "You have to take your migraine medication. If, as my grandmother would say, you want to make old bones."

"I don't take drugs," Beatrice shot back petulantly.

"Not *drugs,* medication."

"Semantics. Drugs are a crutch; once I start taking them, I'll be hooked."

And lose what little control she has over her body, Cate added to herself. "Having migraines predisposes you to a stroke. That's serious business."

Beatrice fixed her with a look. "Then I need blood thinners. Like aspirin."

"Yes, Helen says aspirin can help."

"And alcohol. That thins the blood, doesn't it? I'll just drink more."

"Beatrice!"

"I'm kidding you, dear. I'll take an aspirin every day. I promise. Okay?"

"Well, it's a start," Cate mumbled, checking her patient's vital signs and making notes on her laptop.

Half an hour later, it was clear Beatrice was feeling better. "I'm going stir-crazy!" Flipping a thick braid of silver hair from her shoulder, she swung her legs over the side of the bed.

Easing Beatrice back under the satin comforter, Cate softened her voice. "You can't go out yet. You're still recovering, and the doctors want you to rest."

Beatrice's eyes flared in characteristic fashion. "Doctors? What the hell do they know? I've outlived most of the doctors in this town!"

"It's only a few more days," Cate repeated as if speaking to a child — a stiff-necked, petulant child.

"Might as well be a year for someone my age!" Beatrice snapped, folding her arms across her chest and breathing heavily. "I hate being cooped up in this hellhole!"

Cate glanced around, thinking that only the melodramatic Beatrice could call the richly paneled room a hellhole. Damask curtains framed French doors leading to a small balcony that overlooked lovely gardens. The inlaid floors gleamed, and the four-poster bed was covered in Irish linen sheets. "Why don't you read a book?" Cate suggested. "You can go anywhere with a good book."

Beatrice wrinkled her nose in dismissal. "That sounds like a commercial for the Library of Congress."

"But it's true. When I was a kid, I read all the time. Books took me around the world, back in time, and into the future." Sorting through a corner bookcase, she said in surprise, "You've only got business stuff here — no fiction."

"So much for my travel plans," Beatrice snorted.

"No matter," Cate assured her, pulling a wing chair closer to the bed and extracting a notebook from her bag. "I'll take you to the diner."

"Now you're talking!" Beatrice cried eagerly, throwing back the comforter.

Cate laughed. "With words, Beatrice, only

with words." At the suspicious look dawning on her patient's face, she explained, "I'm going to read you a description of someone at the diner. You know everybody in town, so it shouldn't be too hard to guess who it is. Okay?"

When Cate glanced down at her notebook and flipped through the pages, Beatrice shrugged and mumbled that it might help pass the time. Nodding when she found what she was looking for, Cate read aloud: *"She can see cracks in people, the kind no one else would notice. Like the hairline breaks you find in fine china. Ignore them and they widen too much to repair. That's how it is with people, too. We all have something that needs fixing — a disconnect between mind and spirit. When she looks at her customers, she doesn't just know what they want to eat, she knows what they want to feel and how they want to love. Some days, she treats a broken heart or fractured spirit; others, a splintered dream."*

"It's Gaby, of course!" Beatrice cried, clapping her hands together and smiling broadly. "Yes, you've captured her. Well done!"

An absurd surge of joy filled Cate at the compliment, and she felt her cheeks flame. "Thanks. Gaby and I only met a short while ago, but I feel as though I've known her so much longer."

"Who else do you have?" Beatrice asked, leaning forward to peer at the pages filled with neat handwriting.

Cate flashed a mischievous smile. "Here's one. *The burden of her years is obvious in the stoop of her shoulders and the swollen joints of her hands. But what nature took with one hand, it bestowed with the other, for she's blessed with an unclouded mind: Her memories are sharp, and her reasoning sound. A matriarch figure, her name is often coupled with old-fashioned words like* grit, moxie, *and* pluck. *When I picture avenging angels, her face comes to mind, for she's passionately devoted to those she loves. Stories about her past are Amberley legend. A witness to the great changes of the Twentieth Century, she saw the Depression force neighbors from land their granddaddies farmed. During World War II, she planted a Victory garden in the town common, sold war bonds in front of the courthouse, and kept her own counsel regarding the wisdom of old men waving flags while young men went to war.*"

Beatrice blinked back tears and cleared her throat noisily. "It's me, isn't it?"

"Yes."

It was some time before Beatrice found

her voice again. "So you're a writer! I should have suspected that; I've seen you scribbling in those little notebooks. Then why —" Although she left unsaid that emptying bedpans for a living was far from a literary life, her meaning was clear enough.

Cate shook her head violently. "I'm not a writer. Not anymore. This is just —"

"Not anymore?" Beatrice repeated. "One doesn't stop being an artist, dear. You either are or you aren't. No choice there. And you're good, by Jove; a lifetime in business taught me to recognize talent when I see it!"

No rejoinder sprang to Cate's lips, for what could she say? That she knew full well the power of words, especially those waiting to be written. Beatrice knew, too, for the unspoken words in her heart had poured out the day they'd met. Had the need to share her story with a virtual stranger been born of loneliness, or something more? What if Cate hadn't been willing to listen? And her other patients — who was listening to them? Were they waiting to tell stories as Beatrice had been? Cate thought then of Miriam's journal entry. On impulse, she asked Beatrice what she knew of the Polish woman.

"Miriam? You want to know about Miriam Rosen?" Beatrice's expression brightened as if her thoughts had passed through a shadow. "She was a petite little thing. Like you. With strawberry-blond hair and a heart-shaped face. Wide-set blue eyes. Blond and blue-eyed." Beatrice shook her head. "I didn't expect that. She worked at McLean's, you know. Designed our in-house label. I told you how we grew flax for linen during the war. Well, what we made then wasn't a designer line — nothing to what Miriam did for us." Beatrice pointed to a nearby bookshelf. "There's a sketchbook of hers there. On the end. The spiral one. Take a look at it and you'll see how talented she was."

Cate found the notebook and thumbed through it slowly. Some of the designs were streamlined and practical, others whimsical and extravagant. There were drawings of tailored blouses, flaring skirts, practical trousers, and form-fitting dresses. Cate fingered the swatches of fabric taped beneath each piece — plush black velvet, mauve silk that rippled like water, and starched linen as stiff as an ocean breeze. Further on in the book, she found designs for trenchcoats, riding clothes, spring suits, cocktail dresses, nightwear, bathing suits, and wedding gowns. Each outfit was paired with some coordinating item: a purse, shoes, stockings, a belt or a hat. She bent closer to read the description scrawled beneath the last sketch. *Black satin cloak over hand-beaded evening dress, embroidered purse, patent-leather heels, sheer black stockings, diamond stud earrings.* "These are lovely," she muttered. "All so different, yet you can see her hand in each of them."

"She was one of a kind. And a hard worker," Beatrice recalled. "Still, at first I was reluctant to hire her."

"Why?" Cate asked, setting the sketchbook aside.

Beatrice fingered the lapel of her robe, folding and refolding it as though organizing something in her mind. "Miriam only survived the war by sewing in a Polish ghetto. Lodz, it was called." She paused as though that explained everything. "Don't you see? Most of what passed for problems in my life were setbacks and challenges that could be surmounted with time, effort, and money. And given how I'd spent the war years — working hard, but in comfort and safety — how in God's name could I relate to what she had suffered? How could she relate to me? Plus, it was 1960 — fifteen years after the war. I didn't know at first what Miriam had been doing all that time except that she'd spent time in Paris. Now why in the world would a talented designer leave there to come here? I couldn't imagine. Not that McLean's wasn't something to see in those days. No registers for we kept our cash trays beneath the counters. The floors were the same black-and-white marble as today, but the mahogany display cases gleamed in a way I don't think they do now. And there were glittering chandeliers — not these newfangled lights. We had doormen at every entrance, and a uniformed operator in the elevator," Beatrice recalled proudly.

"You said you didn't know at first what she'd been doing all those years in Europe. Did she ever tell you?"

Beatrice nodded. "She was in a DP camp after being liberated. Sick as a dog for a while. TB, I think. Then she was searching for her family. She looked all over. Germany. Poland. She even went to the Soviet Union a few times because so many Jews had escaped there. All that time in Eastern Europe worked to her benefit; Jim Sullivan got Miriam a visa by arguing that she was fleeing communism!" She paused as if sorting through memories. "You know, I assumed Miriam had been a seamstress before the war, but that wasn't the case. It wasn't until she was made to sew that she learned."

As if reading Cate's face, Beatrice said, "I thought the same thing you are: Why in the world would she want to keep doing what the Germans forced her to do? But Miriam explained it to me. I'll never forget what she said: 'Every time I stitch something beautiful, the knot around my heart unravels just a bit.' Miriam wanted to use the skills that kept her alive to create what she called 'moving art,' fabulous clothes that celebrate life. I asked her how, after all she must have seen, she could believe in the power of beauty. I just blurted it out without thinking."

"What did she say?"

"She said, 'How can I believe in anything else?' We chatted for a while until it was clear her hands were itching to start sketching. Well, that's how we got the first collection. Like those to follow, it was elegant and functional. And it was a sellout, as were all of them really." Beatrice drew a deep breath and let it out with a sigh. "McLean's did well over the years. I'm proud of that. Love wasn't my portion in life; I never married or had children. But that store's been my baby. And Miriam Rosen helped make it a success." Beatrice's expression grew wistful. "I miss her."

"When did she die?"

Beatrice wrinkled her brow. "Oh, about two years ago."

Cate sat forward. "So recently? I thought somehow — I assumed, well, she must have been quite elderly."

"She was about my age," Beatrice pointed out before adding, "but I've no plans to check out just yet, so don't concern yourself on that score."

"I'm glad to hear it," Cate replied in a teasing voice, before repeating in a more somber tone, "very glad."

"You found one? Where? When?" Sheila's voice rose sharply. Before Cate could respond, Sheila turned aside to issue a slew of orders to her assistant. Then, with a glance around the crowded grocery, she ushered Cate into the back of the store. When the door to the kitchen closed behind them, she pointed toward the marble counter that ran the length of the room and proceeded to uncork a bottle of Chianti.

"You never drink at work; well, not that I've seen," Cate observed, a question behind the words.

Sheila paused before pouring two glasses of wine. "I have a feeling we'll need it. Well, I will." By way of proof, she took a deep drink. "Vincent e-mailed that he's leaving

Turkey any day. He's not sure where he'll be sent next. It's the uncertainty and the waiting that are so hard; I'm not a patient person." She took another drink before her mind shifted gears. "Why didn't you tell me before about the journal entry?"

"I didn't get the chance," Cate explained. "You've been swamped with work."

"That's true," Sheila conceded. "It's been nuts around here. Still, you should have said you needed to talk about something important!" At Cate's confused expression, Sheila rushed on. "Oh, how would you know it's important? But tell me, where did you find it?"

"Behind the living room bookcase," Cate explained, pulling the journal entry from her pocket.

Sheila took the pages, uncurling them reverently. "Yes. That's her hand." She traced a finger over the faded writing, recalling the furtive look in Miriam's eyes as she'd ripped apart the journal she'd spent decades compiling. It was the worst cruelty that, after war ravaged her life, the many years she'd survived had wrought untold damage to Miriam's mind. Still, paranoia and fear might have led her to destroy the journal, but at least some of her words had survived. That was something. "Behind the bookcase, you say?" Sheila asked before wondering aloud, "Why would she hide it there? Or maybe she didn't. This was yellowed by the sun. Maybe it fell behind the bookcase long ago. I wonder —"

"There aren't any others." Cate finished the thought. "I gave the apartment a proper going-over, but I didn't find any more. So, did you know Miriam well?"

"Yes. We were friends," Sheila said, although the word felt inadequate somehow. "Miriam was a very special person."

Cate's gaze rested on the journal entry. "Her English was excellent. I was struck by that when I first read it and I had no idea then who she was. Where she was from."

Sheila smiled, recalling how Miriam had struggled with grammar and spelling. "She studied English before she came over here. She was always studying, actually. She used to carry a little notebook in her pocketbook. When she heard a word she didn't know, she'd jot it down so she could look it up later. I found piles of those notebooks after she died. She'd moved into a nursing home months before, but I hadn't cleaned out her apartment. Doing so seemed like, well, like an admission that she was never coming back here. Stupid, I guess. She was so sick by then; of course she wasn't coming back."

"It's not stupid," Cate said softly. "It's sweet."

Sheila shrugged off the compliment and sipped her wine, pausing from time to time to pull strips of raffia from the wine bottle as she described the final months of Miriam's life. Her dear friend had taken to layering her clothing, as though to add dimension to her vanishing form. The frayed raincoat she favored had seen a decade of hard use, been mended, patched, and mended again. Like the woman within, one day it simply gave way, as though its seams rebelled against the pressure of conformity. "To see her give no thought to her appearance left me in no doubt her mind was affected. She wasn't herself; it's as simple as that. The entry you found came from a journal Miriam kept as a sort of therapy. But at the end of her life she became paranoid. Frightened. She — she thought the journal would be taken. Confiscated."

"Confiscated?" Cate asked, confused.

"Her thinking was muddled. She thought she was back in — she thought the journal would be turned over to the Germans. So she destroyed it."

Cate felt a shudder run down her spine. "Oh, the poor woman! To lose her grip on reality after everything she'd been through!"

As shadows gathered in the corners of the room, the import of Sheila's words hit home. "How many other entries were there?"

"Lots. As I said, Miriam destroyed them at the end." Her gaze found the faded papers. "Or so I thought."

Gaby picked up the phone on the second ring. She listened quietly, surprise nudging aside the bone-weariness that always claimed her by day's end. "Have you read it?"

"I have," Sheila reported. "It was written when Miriam first moved here. Cate found it quite by accident."

"Or not," Gaby offered.

"Meaning?"

Gaby hesitated, unsure how to put into words what she suspected was true. "Perhaps Miriam's words resurfaced because they can help Cate. I don't think she has many friends."

Sheila considered. "You may be right. Aside from her husband's grandmother, she doesn't talk about anyone in Boston. But then she plays life close to the vest. And she doesn't get much mail. But she's making friends here. That brunch at her house was a way of reaching out."

"True," Gaby conceded, "but then, healing from the loss she's suffered will take more than friends. More than a job and a new home."

Sheila frowned at the arc the conversation was taking. Blunt by nature, she was the first to admit she lacked subtlety, except when creating pastries. Only in the kitchen had she a delicate touch. "You're going to have to spell this out for me, Gaby."

"Maybe Cate and Miriam have something in common that connects them despite the passage of time. Despite even death."

"That sounds rather creepy."

"Yeah, it does. Sorry," Gaby backpedaled, hearing a warning behind her friend's words like the distant growl of thunder. Yet as much as they'd all reached out to Cate in one way or another — Beatrice, Sheila, Father Sullivan, and even MaryLou — something more was needed. Gaby felt it in that way only she could.

After hanging up the phone, Sheila sank down on a stool before the marble island in the grocery's kitchen. Her mind flitted this way and that before settling on a cold spring morning decades before. It had been Easter time; Sheila remembered because she had been wearing her new navy pea coat. She'd headed into town early, cutting across the common and shuffling through a pile of late-winter leaves that a cool breeze had sent cartwheeling across the path before her. That's when she'd seen Gaby sitting on a park bench, her young eyes liquid pools of fear and anguish. Sheila had offered to walk her home, but Gaby's pale lips had tightened stubbornly. Glancing toward a couple sitting across the lawn, Gaby had revealed that she knew what they were feeling, for when she looked at people, she saw colors. Red meant someone was angry, while purple meant sadness. Other times, she saw shadows of things that would happen to them, or already had. But the insights came to her in a mixed-up way, like photographs all bunched together. Only when she placed them in sequence did the impressions make sense. Sheila had thought then of a book she'd seen with pictures of Fred Astaire and Ginger Rogers, for when the pages were flipped at just the right speed it looked as though they were dancing. When Sheila had commented that knowing things nobody else did must be fun, Gaby had said that it wasn't.

In the decades since, Sheila had come to both understand the burden of her friend's eerie intuitiveness and trust her instincts about people. If Gaby thought Cate had found the journal entry for a reason, she probably had. Perhaps it was as Gaby believed: Cate and Miriam shared a special bond. Only time would tell. Pushing the matter aside for the moment, Sheila focused on her own problems. Vincent. The looming surgery. Vincent. Picking up the wine bottle, she put it back down with a sigh. A veil of liquor might soften the sharp edge of worry, but when it lifted, the world would be unchanged. Except that she'd have a bitch of a headache.

Chapter 10

"Don't you know anything about pastry?"

Cate responded by blinking the remnants of sleep from her eyes and peering out the grocery's back door at a clouded moon. "It's still dark."

"Of course it's dark! It's three in the morning!" Sheila grimaced at a sudden stab of pain. Pulling a tray of butter cookies from the oven with one hand, she reached for a bottle of liquor with the other.

"You'll never heal from the carpal tunnel surgery if you keep this up," Cate chided, elbowing Sheila aside and pulling on an apron. "It's only been a few days! You shouldn't be working yet, even with one hand." When her patient's mouth thinned to a stubborn line, Cate eased the tension by gesturing toward the liquor and joking that one shouldn't start drinking until after three p.m.

Reluctantly surrendering the kitchen,

Sheila mumbled that although she'd intended to use the rum to ice a tray of napoleons, perhaps a drink would ease her pain — both physical and emotional. For although grateful to Cate and relieved she wouldn't be managing the baking alone, it wasn't easy for Sheila to watch someone else do the work she took such pride in. Her eyes strayed to the veined marble counter, as she mentally checked off the things Cate was neglecting. *She has to spread the flour more evenly! And cut the pastry at an angle! Oh, get a fresh cloth to cover the biscotti dough before it hardens!* Even as her brow furrowed, Sheila imagined MaryLou calling her a controlling pain in the butt. But she had a right to fret over a business it had taken her decades to build. The grocery was her baby, one born of love and hard work much as the child of her body had been. And as painful as it would be to watch another woman care for her daughter, seeing even a friend in her kitchen made Sheila's heart ache. But it was nothing to the misery of being without Vincent.

When he'd finally called, she'd been grateful for the poor quality of the overseas line, for her voice had broken when he'd told her he was in Iraq. She shuddered at the thought of his driving around that wartorn land in a mobile hospital van. Who knew what danger lurked around the corner or what enemy waited in the next village? She'd forced a calm note into her voice even as her imagination took flight. Then she'd found herself assuring him, "Of course I won't postpone the surgery. In fact, I'm scheduling it today. It will all be over by the time you get home."

Thankfully, the procedure had gone smoothly. When the hospital assigned Cate to help in Sheila's recovery, the young woman had surprised her landlady by volunteering to work the grocery's early morning shift as well, fairly certain Sheila wouldn't heed the doctors' orders unless closely supervised. Cate had been right of course: Sheila was learning to compensate for the bandage that covered her right wrist, but otherwise didn't intend to change her behavior a whit. But like dead leaves fleeing a gathering storm, even her most determined thoughts couldn't outrun the pain that ravaged her. Not since childbirth had Sheila's body so rebelled against her control. That had been decades ago, and time had taken its toll on her stamina and her spirit. So although it set her teeth on edge, she'd accepted Cate's offer of help. But she hadn't expected that Cate couldn't tell a pignoli cookie from a spumenti. "How is it possible that someone who grew up in a city and purports to be educated is so woefully ignorant of Italian food?" she demanded, only to have Cate shrug good-naturedly as she scurried around the kitchen, spilling as much flour as she folded into the mixing bowls lined up before her.

Perched on a stool from which she could watch and critique, Sheila filled her lungs with the nutty base tones of toasted almond flour, the sharp tang of molasses, and the lingering sweetness of melted chocolate. Her gastric juices responded to the familiar aromas as predictably as her heart did to the sight of her husband even after nearly three decades of marriage. Thoughts of the nights she'd spent in Vincent's arms brought a flush to her face, and a contented glow suffused her for a moment. It dissipated rapidly when she imagined what he might be facing at that very moment. Then she caught sight of Cate wielding a rolling pin as though it was a weapon. "Don't attack the dough," Sheila cried in a voice cracking with emotion. "Handle it as you would a lover — with confident hands, but carefully! And the vanilla icing on those pastries has to be as featherlight as new snow — so delicate a strong wind will carry it away.

Remember that baking is about illusion, promise, and the fragility of beauty."

Somehow, they muddled through. As dawn streaked the sky, Cate brewed them both espressos and gestured toward the worn oak table. "Let's take a break. We've twenty minutes before those cheesecakes are done, and I want to ask you something."

Although she welcomed the opportunity for some girl talk, Sheila's eyes strayed of their own accord to the sink full of dishes. With effort, she took a seat facing away from the wall clock so she wouldn't be tempted to track the minutes until opening. Stretching out her legs, she crossed her ankles and waited. She expected that Cate might want to talk of John. Or Miriam. "Rosa?" Sheila sat forward. "You want to know about Rosa Vitelli?"

Cate nodded, arching her aching back. "She was such a big part of the town, and I've come to understand how much place matters. How we heal in a community. Especially women. And she was a friend to Miriam."

"That's true." Sheila took a sip of espresso and nibbled a biscotti. After the first bite, she sniffed the biscuit and squinted at its texture. With a nod of approval, she mumbled, "Not bad," before taking another bite.

"So you want to know about Rosa. Well, where do I start? She lived in Amberley a long time and knew everybody in town. Or at least that's how it seemed to me." Sheila glanced around the room, seeing it as it had been all those years before. "Some of my earliest memories are of Vitelli's. It was such a magical place then. It smelled of Rosa's baking and just-ground coffee. Heaven. The store was smaller than now, but neat as a pin, with cans of olive oil and bags of spices lined up just so. There were refrigerated cases filled with fancy meats, strings of sausage, and wedges of cheese." Her face softened with memory. "You know, my father left us when I was little, so Mama was always struggling to make ends meet. Rosa knew that. She used to send my mother little care packages of food — a bit of cheese or tomatoes from her garden, a loaf of focaccia, or her famous almond cookies. Once we cut the string from a bakery box to find a chocolate cake topped with creamy zabaglione!" Sheila laughed. "And those shopping bags! Burlap they were, with the word *Vitelli's* printed in green letters. I asked Rosa once why she didn't just use paper like everybody else. She said that because burlap was stronger, custom-ers didn't hesitate to buy big cans of olive

163

oil or an extra pound of cheese. And once they got home they could use the bags for other things. Everybody did, of course. Kids put schoolbooks in them; men used them to carry lunch; housewives to hold wet laundry or store potatoes in root cellars. Seemed like everywhere you turned in town, you saw those burlap bags. And the Vitelli name." Sheila tapped her brow. "Rosa was one smart businesswoman. And such a baker! Father Sullivan used to say that her bread was the closest thing to manna one could find on this earth. Of course, some in town didn't shop at Vitelli's. I couldn't understand why until I overheard someone say that during the war Rosa had lived in Rome. I gave this all considerable thought at the time before concluding that Rosa must have been keeping the Holy Father company!" Sheila gave a sharp laugh before her tone sobered. "I was defensive of Rosa because I saw how hard she worked. It wasn't easy for a woman to run a business then, but she did it. I wanted to follow in her footsteps, so I started planning. And making lists. Oh, I was always a list-maker, just like now," Sheila explained. "Some lists I put to paper; some only lived in my mind. I made lists out of habit and necessity, in anticipation and expectation. I used them to chronicle the past and plan the future. There were chores to do and sins that couldn't be undone. All those years ago when my mother struggled to raise two children alone, I made a list of the things beyond my control that God seemed to have forgotten were in His. I even had a list of dreams: I wanted to own Vitelli's, marry an honorable man, and have a family."

"And you did all three."

"Yes. Yes, I did. I remember a neighbor telling me once that lists are rubbish because life is chaos. You should just try to get through it. Well, I decided then and there that my life would be more than something to get through." She paused before adding, "And it's been as good as it has because of Rosa." Then, seeing Cate reach for one of the few cookies she hadn't tried yet, Sheila teased, "You eat as much as MaryLou and that's saying something!"

"I'm sampling," Cate protested. "It's quality control." Brushing crumbs from her fingers, she asked, "So Rosa sold the business to you?"

"Eventually," Sheila said proudly, explaining how gradually the idea of being the boss had taken root in her mind. She'd kept her wrinkled dream tucked away in a pocket of her thoughts until the day she brandished a savings passbook in the air and announced to her family that she was going to buy Vitelli's. "I got an accounting scholarship to the community college. I worked all day at the grocery, learning the business. Then I was in class every night. It was grueling. And weekends? Those were spent studying and sleeping. Until I met Vincent, but that's a story for another day."

As the sky lightened, the two women entered a new phase of their friendship. For Sheila, speaking of Rosa served to frame the day to follow with light because she'd loved the woman so dearly. For Cate, those glimpses of Rosa Vitelli provided another piece of the Amberley puzzle. And Miriam's life.

Passing by the diner one evening, Cate paused, recalling that she had nothing but a wedge of cheese and some stale crackers at home. When the door opened, she caught the scent of onion rings and melted cheese. Her stomach growled in response, and she made her way inside. Grateful to find a seat at the front counter, she caught Gaby's eye and mimed the act of pouring coffee. The waitress walked over slowly, her face pinched and drawn. "Are you all right?" Cate asked anxiously.

"Sure, just a little tired." The blithe response was accompanied by a rub of the temples before Gaby announced, "I've a special treat for you today." When she ducked into the kitchen, Cate allowed her mind to imagine all sorts of cheesy, gooey comfort food. A moment later, Gaby returned, carrying a bowl of soup and a basket of rye toast.

Cate blinked. "Oh. Soup."

"Try it," Gaby urged.

Tasting the rich broth, Cate moaned in appreciation of its delicate flavoring. "This is delicious! Thyme and garlic. And there are carrots, potatoes, onions, and celery. But what else do you put in it?"

"Don't ask her," MaryLou advised, slipping onto the stool next to Cate's. "There isn't a recipe. Gaby just throws stuff in. That's why she calls it — don't remember what. My memory's French today."

"She means her memory's on strike," Gaby supplied, sliding her friend a cup of coffee. "And the soup, well, MaryLou's right on that score. I don't have a recipe because it's made of what's left over from my cooking the day before. I take all the 'must goes' and dump them in an iron pot of my grandmother's. She used it every day — for stews, porridge, even soda bread.

167

She'd cook that bread over an open fire. I'll never forget how it smelled. Anyway, the reason you like the soup is because of all the memories in that pot. You see, it's the pure taste of home that makes the soup so good."

"What the hell does that mean?" Mary-Lou asked derisively.

Gaby rolled her eyes at MaryLou and addressed herself to Cate. "For you, I think this town is like my grandmother's iron pot. It will bring out the best in you. If you let it."

Cate sat silently, absorbing what Gaby said, while MaryLou snorted. "Amberley's like an old pot. Or the soup that's in it. That's what you're saying? All that education and that's the best you can come up with?"

Gaby frowned. "You don't exactly have a perceptive turn of mind, do you, Lulu? I was using the analogy to make a point — oh, forget it!" Setting the impulse to enlighten her old friend aside, she addressed herself to Cate. "I've tried for years to expand MaryLou's horizons, but the finer things in life are wasted on her. Wasted!" She ticked off on a work-reddened hand the top three of what she said was a long list: "Good wine; classical music; *and* literary speech."

"You're right," MaryLou agreed, reaching for her coffee. "Give me a beer-loving, banjo-playing plain speaker over a sherry-sipping, opera-singing poet any day."

After a beat, the three women dissolved into laughter. Slapping a hand on the counter, MaryLou asked, "What about you, Cate? What's your idea of the ideal man? Tell us more about your husband."

Cate paused for a moment to gather her thoughts. "From the start, John's voice was the soundtrack of my thoughts. When something funny happened, it was his laugh I imagined; when I gave less than my best, it was his calm tone that prodded me to work harder." A shy smile lit her face. "He drank Irish whiskey, but loved red wine. He liked all kinds of music really; he was forever humming something while he worked. And I'd say he was a plain speaker who never said a mean thing. Not that I heard. Oh, he'd lose his temper like anyone else, but be intentionally mean to someone? No. I never saw that."

MaryLou grew quiet. When she spoke again, her tone was sober. "That's about the best thing you can say about somebody." The words were simply spoken, with no trace of the levity and sarcasm that were her stock-in-trade.

"Amen," Gaby agreed, before moving off to help another customer.

MaryLou took her leave soon after, but not before relieving Cate of a piece of rye toast. "For the road," she explained with a grin.

Cate was finishing her second cup of tea when Gaby joined her and changed the course of her life with a simple question. "So will you be entering the writing contest?"

"What contest?"

"The local VFW is sponsoring it. Someone in town left them a bequest — don't remember who. Anyway, they're using it to fund a twenty-five-thousand-dollar first prize. You should enter." She said the words casually before turning away to call an order to the cook in the kitchen.

Cate's heart began to thud. Twenty-five thousand! Such a sum would support John's grandmother for almost a year. With a catch in her voice, Cate asked, "The contest — do you know anything else about it?"

Gaby frowned in concentration, her eyes skimming the room. "Only that the library's helping to organize things." Then she waved broadly toward the door, raised her voice, and called out, "Marion! Come here a minute, will you?" Gaby turned away to help a customer, and Cate watched the elderly, prim-looking librarian approach.

Marion Puttner had steel-gray hair and a temperament to match. Pushing a pair of tortoiseshell glasses up her long nose, she squinted at Cate and said sharply, "I don't know you. Why don't I know you? Why don't you have a library card?"

"Well, I — I haven't had a chance to get one yet," Cate stuttered.

Marion sniffed her disapproval, her thin lips growing thinner when pressed together. "Everyone else here has one." Her gaze swept the room as though taking attendance. " 'Course some use the library more than others. You can learn a lot about people by what they read. Or don't read."

"Yes, I suppose that's true," Cate agreed lamely.

"Well, if it's a card you're after, you'll have to come in for it; I don't carry them around with me."

When Marion turned away, Cate grabbed her sleeve. "Wait! Please! The writing contest — can you tell me a bit about it?"

Marion turned back. The years had etched frown lines on her face, and they deepened as she considered Cate. Giving a quick nod, she said, "You're Cate, aren't you? I heard about you. You're something of a writer."

Cate stiffened. "Who told — ? Oh, never mind, I've lived in Amberley long enough to know there are no secrets."

"Well, there are a few," the librarian said cryptically, pursing her lips as if to say more. Then she apparently thought better of it.

The conversation made Cate nervous. When in any way off her game, she had the habit of flipping the hair from her shoulders. But that was in the past, for the veil of long curls John had said was the color of summer wheat was long gone. When she had bid good-bye to the little writing house he had built for her in the backyard, she'd cut her hair in a gesture of — what? Anger? Sorrow? In her mind's eye, Cate could still see the hair swirling toward the slate floor John had laid. She'd stared at the glossy pile before picking up a broom to sweep it briskly out the door, for what a moment earlier had seemed to arrange itself in *s* and *o* shapes that hinted at a message suddenly looked like the dead thing it was. She allowed the memory to flutter away under the pressure of Marion Puttner's scrutiny.

"If you're *not* a writer, then why are you interested in the contest?" the librarian pressed. "And why do you have a little notebook there?" She pointed toward the spiral pad at Cate's elbow. "Unless you're making a shopping list, of course."

"No. No, it's not a shopping list! Look, I write down little things," Cate admitted. "But it's not for any specific purpose. I mean, I just don't want to forget a phrase that comes to mind or a snatch of conversation that might —"

"Find its way into a story one day?" Marion suggested with a knowing smile. "Thought so. I was just giving you a hard time, dear," she added, patting Cate's arm as though bestowing a blessing. "I've too many amateurs entering this thing as it is. Now, you've obviously got the writing bug. Might be you've got talent, too. Time will tell." Pulling a bright orange leaflet from her handbag, she handed it to Cate. "Here are the submission guidelines. Take a look at them; if you have any questions, stop by the library." With a farewell nod, Marion moved away and Cate exhaled the breath she'd been holding. After shooting a glance toward Gaby who was slicing into a pie at the opposite end of the counter, Cate read the leaflet.

The Amberley chapter of the Veterans of Foreign Wars is sponsoring a
FIRST NOVEL CONTEST

Winning entry **must** be from an
unpublished novelist <u>and</u> address the
civilian legacy of war
Contest open to Amberley residents only
No entry fee
100,000 word maximum
Contest closes on November 11th —
Veterans Day
Short-listed entries will be announced on
New Year's Eve
$25,000 first prize AND a publishing
contract with a major New York publisher
Good Luck!

Cate reread the leaflet, and her heart sank.
The thought of entering, let alone winning,
a contest sponsored by the VFW given how
angry she was with the military — well, it
was either laughable or the sweetest revenge.
And she had only six months until the
deadline; could a novel be written so
quickly? Had she the talent to do it? Certainly, Beatrice had been pleased by what
Cate had written, and she had sold a few
short stories. But those were nothing compared to the challenge of constructing a
book-length narrative that held a reader's
interest page after page. She always likened
good writing to butchery: cutting to the
bone Hemingway-style before rebuilding

with the simplest of tools. Only then could truth dance off the page like the chorus line at Radio City Music Hall — every syllable enticing the eye forward, and no divas stopping the flow. That had worked with short fiction, but she'd never tackled a novel.

She considered the topic and wondered how in the world to approach "the civilian legacy of war." Widows were part of that legacy, of course, but not the only part. She thought of Sheila and her husband, and how Beatrice's life had been changed by WWII. Of Miriam Rosen. Her experiences couldn't be compared to anyone else's in Amberley, yet there was common ground. Perhaps only a bit, but enough to build on.

With a jolt, Cate realized that perhaps she had found a way into the novel. But were the ideas taking shape in her mind brilliant or rubbish? John would know; John always knew. He had predicted that one day she would find the courage to try a book; but then, he'd believed she could do anything. And she'd felt that way, too, when he'd been by her side. Every evening after work he would ask what she'd written, for he knew that the ideas she scribbled down only gelled in her mind when spoken aloud. He would pull on his reading glasses and pore over the latest draft of whatever she was working on, giving her feedback and encouragement. Her body suffused with heat at the recollection of how often those collaborative sessions had ended in passionate sex. Hours later, she would slip from his arms and attack her laptop with restless energy, her fingers barely keeping up with the narrative in her thoughts. And now John was gone, leaving an aching void in her mind and her heart. Without him by her side — encouraging, critiquing, and prodding — she couldn't undertake such a project. Could she?

CHAPTER 11

The next afternoon, Cate went for a walk
through the common. Father Sullivan sat
alone on a bench; when he smiled in greeting, she moved to join him. They'd seen
each other many times since their first meeting weeks before, but Cate hadn't yet found
a way to apologize for her behavior that day.
Taking the seat next to him, she did so by
way of greeting. "I need to explain — for
you to understand why I was so rude when
we met. You see, it was my husband's priest
who encouraged him to go to Iraq. Well,
among others. But I just can't forgive Father
Morton for that. John trusted him so much,
you see. And afterward, after John died, I
went to see Father Morton. Even though I
was angry with him and had closed my
mind to the Church in many ways, still I
went. To give him a chance to say he was
sorry, I think." She shrugged. "Well, he
didn't, of course. I don't think it even oc-

curred to him that he was in any way responsible. That made me furious. So when I first saw you in the rectory, I saw red." She smiled tightly. "Or rather black-and-white. I couldn't see past your Roman collar. Not at first."

"And now?"

The tone was neutral, but she knew the answer he was looking for — one she couldn't give. Not yet. "Let's just say I don't see you as the enemy. Maybe not a friend yet, but not the enemy. That's the best I can do."

"It's enough, Cate. And there's no need to apologize. This Father Morton shouldn't have pressured your husband in any way. And he should have helped you deal with your loss; he should have been a comfort. Clearly, he wasn't. I'm deeply sorry for that. If there's ever anything I can do to help you, please let me know." He spread his hands in a gesture of submission. Or entreaty. They sat companionably, watching birds dart in and out of the trees overhead. Finally, the priest said, "So you've decided to enter the writing contest."

Months before, she would have been surprised that he'd heard her news so quickly, but now she was accustomed to small-town life. "You're certainly up on what's going on."

"Oh, I hear things," James Sullivan said breezily. Then, in a more serious tone, "Given the topic, it should either prove to be a cleansing experience or very difficult, I imagine."

Cate sighed eloquently. "You've hit the nail on the head. Still, I think I have an angle — so to speak." He waited expectantly as she gathered her words. "Women make war possible by keeping everything on the home front going, mostly by keeping our mouths shut. But we bury our stories, just as we do our hopes and needs, when family beckons. I think it's high time women shared those stories."

"In what way?"

"My grandmother used to say that life is in the telling. If mothers, daughters, sisters, and friends shared their memories of war, maybe men would begin to understand the price we pay for their decisions. Not that women don't serve as well as men — they do. But it's still mostly men who do the fighting and women who do everything else." Her tone was hard, unbending. "That we're silent casualties of war is partly our fault. No, it's entirely our fault. Whether anyone pays attention to what we say is one thing, but if we don't even try —"

When her voice trailed off, Father Sullivan nodded slowly. "You're right that the history of war has generally been written by men. And it's still mostly about battles won, prisoners taken, soldiers killed. Not about what happens to women behind the lines. I saw that firsthand during my time in Korea. Those women's stories were certainly lost — or as good as."

"Maybe I can take a stab at changing that. At redefining the civilian legacy of war." Her voice was tentative, but edged with hope. "The stories of sisters-in-arms are an integral part of the tapestry of war. *The Tapestry of War,*" she repeated with a nod. "That's a good title. Makes you think of a backdrop of intertwined threads of narrative. And it's only against that backdrop that the horror of war is best thrown into relief. Now all I have to do is find and piece together enough stories. Join them one to the other."

The priest crossed his ankles and glanced up at a crab apple tree beneath which they sat. The fragrant blossoms that had suffused it in early spring had been replaced with glossy fruit and masses of small leaves. He spoke in his best Sunday Mass voice. "And will doing so help you find out what you want to know?"

"Me?" Cate asked in confusion. "The

book isn't for me!"

He raised his hands in a gesture of surrender. "My mistake. I view writing as a chance for the artist to explore unresolved issues in his or her own life."

"Fiction writing is storytelling," Cate corrected, her heart beginning to hammer in reaction to his words. "It's make-believe — a product of the writer's imagination. That's all. Of course, this will be based on true stories. Maybe of people right here in Amberley." Her gaze traveled around the green space. "But how do I gather the stories? How do I tell them?" She fell silent, lost in thought.

Father Sullivan bent down to retrieve a crab apple from where it had fallen on the slate path beside them. "There's so much fruit in the Bible," he mused, "so many parables around which to build a homily. Which story I choose each Sunday depends on what theme I wish to emphasize, what lesson I want to teach. But what most lay people don't understand is that the homily is instructive for the priest as well as the parishioners."

"Your point being," Cate finished the thought, "that the stories I choose to tell are the ones I need to hear."

"Perhaps. How would you characterize the

way you want to construct this book? How would you describe it to a stranger?" His salt-and-pepper eyebrows joined to form a line of inquiry.

Cate frowned, for pitching a book idea was far from easy. "I hope it will tell stories of loyalty, friendship, and hope. And explain how women coexist with grief — for that's really the word. It can be contained in the main, but not more than that, for it's always there in the background. Even as we go about our lives and keep doing the things that need to be done, the loss is always there. I guess I hope it will emphasize how women's lives may be shaped by war, but don't need to be defined by it. I'm thinking of women I've met who have had their lives ripped apart by war, and yet they're still standing. They're not victims."

"You describe an amazing group of people," the priest observed quietly. "Just the sort of friends someone recovering from loss would seek out."

She cocked her head. "Point taken. The question is: Can I tell these stories? Will people respond to what I write?"

"You know," Father Sullivan said, "before I learned to read, I would spread the newspaper out on the floor of our kitchen. I so desperately wanted the letters to speak to

182

me and share their secrets. Oh, I could pick out some of them — fat *O*'s, tall *T*'s and graceful *L*'s — but when they crowded together, I was locked out. I remember crying, shaking my head from side to side such that the letters wavered and blurred. I think of that sometimes when the line of my bifocals sets the words of my book dancing." Pitching his voice low, he explained, "You see, before I learned to read, I was frustrated and ignorant. I knew books and newspapers were filled with wonderful things; I just didn't have the tools to discover them. Once I did, I understood that words have power. Trust in that power, Cate, and in the talent God gave you."

A blast of warm air yanked Cate to a new level of consciousness as she stepped outside the diner. She had sat writing in the artificial cool for hours, and it was invigorating to feel the breath of summer. As the sun set in fiery splendor, her feet took her across the common to the town library. On the rim of her thoughts a scolding voice reminded her that she had assiduously avoided the place since coming to town. Strange behavior for one who loved books, but sometimes the sight of a "New Fiction" display just reminded her that she might never be published herself, and that the characters she birthed would live out their lives in the confines of her crowded mind.

Pausing outside the two-story brick building, she saw that a small garden had been planted around the dedication stone. Words were chiseled on the stone, and she bent down to read what the library's founder had said:

LIBRARIES ARE THE GUARDIANS OF MANKIND'S MEMORIES. THEIR COLLECTIONS ARE THE SCRAPBOOKS OF CIVILIZATION, FOR THEY PRESERVE THE WRINKLED DREAMS AND WHISPERED LONGINGS OF THOSE WHO'VE COME BEFORE. THAT NEED TO CHRONICLE LIES AT THE HEART OF WHAT IT MEANS TO BE HUMAN.

Then Cate saw the name beneath the quotation: Beatrice McLean. So she'd paid for the library! But was that really surprising? From their first meeting, the older woman had stressed how important it was to remember and be remembered. And now she'd agreed to have her story included in the book. As had Sheila.

Cate felt a familiar excitement, for although the stories she would tell weren't born of her imagination, it was she who would decide which bits cast shadows and which remained a backdrop. That thought brought a slow smile, one that deepened when she was assailed by a subtle lavender scent that brought to mind her grandmother. *I should write about how smells trigger dormant memories and bridge the past. And about how we so often allow those bridges to rot through. Or burn them outright.* For the first time in years, she found herself planning a series of writing projects. What should she tackle first: a story about her grandmother or one about her life with John? Oh, there were so many stories to tell!

Her thoughts ran ahead of her as she walked home through the common. A frog chorus bellowed from a small pond, a rising wind teased the grass, and fireflies decorated the trees. All around her, the summer darkness pulsed with life that seemed magical. Full of mystery and promise.

When she got to the grocery, Cate ran up the side steps to unlock her door. Eager to get back to her writing, she stepped across the threshold and stopped. Something crackled underfoot and she glanced down to see a few sheets of wrinkled notebook paper on the floor. Bending down to pick them up, Cate drew a sharp breath. The handwriting was Miriam's! She wondered if

Sheila had — but no, that didn't make sense. If Sheila suddenly discovered another journal entry, she wouldn't just slip it through the mail slot. Then who had left it? And why? Switching on an overhead light, Cate sank onto a chair and read.

My father, Judah Berkson, was a religious scholar and a diamond cutter. The former fed his soul and the latter his family. The same curious nature that drove him to uncover layers of meaning in a Talmudic tract guided his hand in revealing a diamond's hidden brilliance. He was at peace in both worlds, for he took pleasure in the camaraderie of the yeshiva and the solitary nature of his art. Whether shaping an uncut stone or an uncut mind, Papa's goal was the same: *tikkun ha-olam* — repair of the world. Jewish tradition held that although the world was broken, man had the power to repair it and move the clock forward to the Messianic Age. There were many ways to do this. For his part, my father perfected the world through prayer, good deeds and hard work.

Cate turned to the next page.

Papa passed from this world to the next

in 1935. He was buried beside my mother in the cemetery that had served our community for a century. My heart ached that he didn't see me marry or my brother Samuel become a man. Dear Samuel. Long before the gates of the Ghetto closed behind us, long before the column of steel-gray uniforms marched down Pabianicka Street, it was he who foresaw what was coming. Samuel was blond like me, and he spoke peasant Polish with his friends. He'd even been to a Catholic Mass. Samuel had friends in the Zionist movement and after Papa's death he argued that we should all emigrate to Palestine. We refused. I couldn't bring myself to leave our parents' graves. And my brothers Joseph and Benny were blind to the darkness that was Germany. In the end, our stubbornness doomed Samuel for he would not emigrate alone.

On September 1, 1939, German troops crossed the border. By the end of the month, Poland surrendered her liberty. Soon after, she would surrender her Jews. Months before we were forced to wear the Stars of David, soldiers could tell Jew from Gentile by the mark of Abraham. Men and boys were stripped in the street. Beaten.

Shot. I pleaded with my brothers not to go outside. Why face death for a loaf of bread?

It fell to the women and girls of Lodz to brave the occupation in a way men couldn't. Children were the fastest runners and the bravest, for to them it was all a game of hide-and-seek. Hide from the soldiers. Seek the safest route through town. They carried messages and we used them as spotters, for when they shouted an alarm the Germans mistook the cries for play.

Each time I slipped from the house into a waking nightmare, my heart hammered in my chest. Moving through streets I knew so well, I was sick with fear. Jews were forbidden to walk on the sidewalk, yet I did so boldly, my blond hair uncovered. One day bled into the next, and we women played our part as the wheel turned for a new year, and the trees surrendered their golden leaves.

One morning as I stood in line to buy what rationed food there was, a truck pulled up to the curb next to me. It was filled with children, and I saw Rabbi Weiss among them. Even as his name formed on my lips, the woman behind me hissed a warning. I hesitated, and in that moment the soldier guarding them shouted and the truck moved on. I told myself I could do nothing to save them, that the meager vegetables I would buy might mean the difference between life and death for my brothers.

I folded guilt away when hunger and worry stretched that day to breaking. Only in sleep did the rabbi find me. I saw his tired eyes light with recognition before glinting with tears. With a strangled cry, I jerked awake.

Forgive me.

"Wow. Just — wow." Sheila carefully refolded the journal entries and handed them back to Cate. "I've never read these before. And of course I didn't leave them in your apartment. But then who did?"

"Not Gaby," Cate said, glancing across the diner to where their mutual friend stood amid a circle of smiling children. "I already asked her. And not Helen either. I asked her, too, since she was Miriam's nurse at the end." Cate lowered her gaze to the paper place mat before her. Ripping it into little strips, she said, "I've been doing some research. On the Lodz ghetto."

"Oh?" Sheila leaned forward. "Tell me. I'm ashamed to say I know little aside from

189

what Miriam told me."

"I knew nothing," Cate confessed, keeping her eyes downcast. "I'd heard of the Warsaw ghetto of course, but I didn't realize there were others. Didn't want to know, I suppose. The Holocaust is just impossible to get your mind around, so I took the coward's way out and avoided reading about it. Thinking about it." She swallowed hard and reached for the cold coffee before her, for the words had a bitter taste. "Lodz was a big city. Over two hundred thousand Jews lived there before the Germans invaded. A few months after they did, they walled off a section of Lodz — the poorest, dirtiest section. That became the ghetto. There were no sewers, unlike Warsaw, so you couldn't smuggle food or weapons in. The ghetto was overcrowded and life was primitive. Out of thirty thousand apartments, only fifty had bathrooms. If Miriam and her brothers were lucky, they had cold water."

"But — but what about bathing? And if there were no bathrooms, how did they — ?"

"Feces was piled in the street or in courtyards and then collected. And bathing? There were wells in the common area, and I guess people heated what water they could on whatever stoves they had."

"And that's where Miriam learned to be a seamstress," Sheila mumbled. "In a place of filth."

"And yet she was lucky to have work. Lucky that Lodz was the most profitable ghetto. Its factories didn't just make uniforms, either. Some designed high-end fashion for German department stores. Imagine sewing delicate lingerie amid the brutality of random shootings and rape. It's that juxtaposition, that — that perversity that's always made the Holocaust so hard for me to read about."

"What do you mean?"

"Well, having victims send happy postcards back to relatives before they were murdered, asking people to remember which peg they hung their clothes on before herding them to their death. Even having people strip before you kill them. Human history is full of slaughter, but there's something about the way Nazi Germany went about it that's uniquely sick. And Lodz was a test ground for so much of that. Did you know that having Jews wear armbands, and later the Star of David, was the law in Lodz *two years* before it was in Germany?"

"I didn't know that," Sheila admitted. "I should have. I should have read more. I will now."

The conversation petered out as both women wrestled with dark thoughts, imagining a life so very different from their own. Noise circled around them: diner sounds — life sounds. When MaryLou stepped in the front door and spotted them, Cate felt her stomach clench. She hadn't the heart for the mechanic's biting sarcasm. But perhaps that was just the point, Cate thought, sitting up straighter. MaryLou was so vibrant and full of energy. Perhaps that was just what she and Sheila needed.

Slipping into the seat next to Sheila, MaryLou winced as peals of laughter filled the air. The children at the front counter were now clapping their hands in delight as Gaby lit the candles on an enormous chocolate cake. "Oh, great," MaryLou whined. "A birthday party. Give me the whirl of a motor over the scream of a kid any day."

"I like children," Cate said, making an effort to nudge melancholy aside. "They're so full of hope, so unfiltered."

"I'm unfiltered," MaryLou pointed out.

"Yes, but in a different way."

MaryLou snorted. "Diplomatically put. What Gaby would call a well-crafted response. Typical of a writer." Adept at reading emotion, MaryLou shifted her gaze from Cate to Sheila. "What's up with you two?" While Sheila explained, MaryLou reached over to take a French fry from Cate's plate. "So someone just dropped it through the mail slot?"

"Apparently," Cate said before a thought struck. "Lulu, you didn't —"

MaryLou held up her hands. "No way." At the pause that followed, the easygoing expression slipped from her face. "Hey, I don't lie. Well, just to men. And then only between the sheets."

"Sorry." Cate shrugged. "I just — well, there aren't a lot of people who know I found the first entry. You, Sheila, Gaby, Helen." Her eyes sought the waitress who was singing Happy Birthday along with the children. "Of course, there's no reason to believe I'll get more of them. Except —"

"Except I know there were lots," Sheila put in. "I told you that. So it stands to reason that whoever had those" — she pointed to the pages Cate now gripped tightly — "has the others. Clearly, Miriam entrusted them to someone. But who?"

"A mystery," MaryLou announced, rubbing her hands together. "My money's on the priest, by the way."

"Father Sullivan?" Cate asked in surprise. "He doesn't know about the journal. At least I don't think he does. When we talked

193

about Miriam, he didn't mention it."

"He wouldn't, would he?" MaryLou shot back, pulling Cate's plate closer and sorting beneath the remains of her salad to find a few fries. "Keeping secrets is his business. And don't kid yourself: He knows everything that happens in this town. As does Beatrice. For all she's pushing a hundred, she's another one to watch."

"Beatrice?" Sheila repeated with more than a touch of exasperation. "She's just out of the hospital and using a cane. How do you think she managed the steps to Cate's apartment?"

"I wouldn't put anything past her. That one's as tough as they come," MaryLou observed, before turning back to Cate. "So will you use Miriam's story in your book?"

"I don't know. It doesn't seem right somehow. It's not as though I can ask her permission or anything."

"And she has no family you could speak with," Sheila pointed out. "Except us." She glanced across the room toward Gaby. "Her friends. I can tell you that she always intended that her journal be shared. But as to what she was feeling at the end of her life, well, I'm not sure about that. On the one hand, she wouldn't have ripped it up if she wanted it safeguarded; on the other, perhaps she thought that doing so was her only option. And if she did give the other entries to one person, someone who's now giving them to you, that might mean he or she is doing what Miriam would have wanted. Hard to say."

"I really do wish I could figure out who's leaving them," Cate murmured.

"Like you said, it has to be someone who knows you found the first one," MaryLou pointed out. "Someone in that group you mentioned. I mean, it's not as though Miriam's sending them herself."

CHAPTER 12

Gaby stepped outside for a breath of air and to marvel at the simple beauty of a sunrise. First orange and then lemon yellow streaked the mauve sky; within minutes a golden glow was inching its way across the parking lot. She leaned against one of the stone planters that bracketed the diner's back entrance. The herbs within had been given a good soaking the night before, and the stone's gray hue had darkened to midnight blue. *But just as it drank of my watering can, soon it will drink of the sun and surrender its life-giving blood. Then the rich color will fade to the gray of ashes. That's the way of things.*

When a wave of nausea swept over her, she stumbled back inside the diner, cursing, for she knew she would soon be crippled by searing pain. She made it to the storeroom, gulping air as her vision blurred. When the room swayed, she grabbed wildly, losing her balance. Strong hands caught her before she hit the stone floor.

"I've got you," a reassuring voice said. "Thank God I saw that back door open and came in." Anxious eyes bent over her — eyes she knew so well. When her mouth filled with bile, Gaby turned her head and emptied her stomach. Muttering a string of oaths, MaryLou heaved her friend up with the strength of one who spent her days welding and wrestling all manner of metal into shape. Then, with equal tenderness, she eased Gaby to a chair. "What the hell's the matter?" MaryLou demanded, the initial stab of fear she had felt tempered by a new thought. "You're not pregnant, are you?"

Gaby gripped the burning muscles of her abdomen and grimaced. "I'm almost sixty, just how —" She made an explosive sound as a fresh stab of pain brought tears to her eyes. When MaryLou reached for her phone, Gaby flung out an arm to stop her. "No. Duh-don't."

"You need an ambulance!" MaryLou hissed.

"I know what this is. It will pass." Soon the nausea began to subside, and the pounding in her head lessened. "It's better now," Gaby whispered. "I — I've got to get to work. It's almost time to open."

MaryLou stood with arms akimbo.

"You're not going anywhere."

Gaby groaned. "You're a bully, Lulu, do you know that? I'm not something you can bend to your will like a — a carburetor!"

"After all these years have you learned nothing from me? Cars don't have carburetors anymore, Gaby!" MaryLou thrust her hands into the pockets of the faded overalls she favored for work, and her eyes narrowed. "You're wearing makeup!"

"Wha— what?" Gaby stuttered, mentally scolding herself for the time lost that morning experimenting with bottles and tubes filled with colored goo. That MaryLou would see through her efforts — literally — was to be expected, for the mechanic could apply war paint to her face as expertly as she could detail a car.

MaryLou stepped closer, tipped Gaby's face up, and read the skin she knew so well. "Makeup! Foundation and blush. You never wear makeup except for lipstick! I've been trying for years to get you to — wait. Why now? And at this time of day? What are you trying to cover up? What the hell's going on?"

In response, Gaby coughed violently. MaryLou spotted a bottle of ginger ale on a nearby shelf. She grabbed it, twisted off the cap, and held it out. "Drink," she commanded in a voice that brooked no refusal.

Pushing sweat-drenched hair from her face, Gaby accepted the bottle gratefully. "Thanks." She took a cautious sip and bought time by allowing her eyes to slide around the storeroom. The window opposite let in a slice of sunlight that fell across the floor at her feet, highlighting a two-foot-wide area markedly cleaner than the rest. *That's where I dragged the box of pickles yesterday. Had to drag it for the damn thing was too heavy to lift. They shouldn't overpack those things!* But of course the box hadn't been heavier than usual; it was she who had changed. Too weak to haul the trash out in the evening, she now allowed it to pile up until the morning staff could help; too easily winded to climb the hill on Federal Street, she made excuses for driving her car to the post office — she was running late; there were so many packages to pick up; it might rain. She'd told so many lies and hidden so much from her friends, that as painful as the truth was to admit, she felt a flood of relief at the prospect. Then she met MaryLou's tear-filled eyes.

"Well?"

Gaby's resolve faltered, but only for a moment. Drawing a breath, she found the strength to tell the woman she'd trusted with all her secrets save one that she was dying. "It's brain cancer." Seeing her friend's face crumble, Gaby rushed on. "Don't say it. Don't say there's a treatment, because there isn't. I've been to the best doctors and read everything there is. Prayed to God and pleaded with Him. I tried drugs, herbs, meditation, and visualization. But the fact is that I'm done for, or as good as. I've got a few months tops."

A gasp exploded from MaryLou, and she doubled over as though she'd been punched in the gut. Her head jerked up and her eyes lit. "I knew there was something wrong with you! For weeks, you've looked like crap. I told Sheila!" MaryLou paced the room in quick strides. "No. This can't be happening! There has to be something we can do. Some doctor somewhere. An experimental treatment. Something —"

"Lulu," Gaby pleaded. "Don't make me spend what time I have left chasing shadows. The simple fact is that my body is all used up. I've accepted that." She lifted her shoulders in a gesture of resignation. "But before you go thinking I'm not falling to pieces, you should know that I went through a really tough time a few months back — drinking and feeling sorry for myself."

"When —"

"You were taking that class in Boston. It worked out well because I couldn't have hidden this from you of all people."

"But you did." The hurt was raw.

"Because I'd much rather talk to you about your love life or a new cheesecake I've put on the menu than the fact that my brain's being eaten cell by cell." That was true as far as it went, but not the whole truth. *Truth is I'm a coward. And I'm scared to death.* She smiled grimly at the choice of words.

"I'm so — so angry with you!" MaryLou cried, her voice breaking as she grabbed Gaby and hugged her roughly.

"God, you're strong."

Pulling away, MaryLou wiped a hand across her wet face. "And don't you forget it. I'll kick your ass if you lie to me again, cancer or not!"

"Okay." Gaby held up her hands. "But you'll help me get through this?"

"Oh, so now you need me."

The sculpted chin jutting up in challenge called to mind a long-ago bar brawl. A biting comment from someone who'd known something of Gaby's past had brought MaryLou barreling across the sawdust-coated floor to confront the woman. *Funny to think of that now, but then memories have* been cropping up at the strangest times. *It's as though they want one more chance at center stage before fading away with everything else. With me.* "There's so much left to do," Gaby mumbled. "Cate is still so lost."

"With all you're facing, you're worried about *her*?" MaryLou asked with such gut-wrenching emotion Gaby felt her throat constrict. "You barely know her!"

"She needs help," Gaby repeated. "And as much as a part of me wants to enjoy the last of life's sunshine in peace, I can't ignore how much needs to be done. I'm not going to go sit on a beach when Cate is so broken. I can see that in a way others can't; you know I can. Just as you know it's taken me a long time to accept that this — insight happens to me for a reason."

MaryLou nodded, for she knew the burden Gaby carried because of her gift of empathy. That burden was made heavier by working in a diner where customers thought nothing of telling their problems to a waitress just as they would a bartender. There'd been a time when feeling the sorrow and pain of others had so overwhelmed Gaby that she'd avoided crowded places because the weight of people's crushed dreams was so great. "You told me once that you did your PhD because you wanted to escape to academia, where dead words might engage your mind, but they couldn't touch your heart."

Gaby gave a brittle smile. "It was cowardly to run away from who I am; I know that now. Just as you know why I left Yale. The same reason I have to try and help Cate. Maybe she's the last person I'll ever help."

Reading the fear behind the words, Mary-Lou warned, "Don't even think you've got something to atone for! You've more than —"

"It's not enough, will never be enough," Gaby revealed. "I have to try — I have to believe it's still possible to leave this world having given more than I took."

"What happened was an accident!" Mary-Lou exploded. "How many times do you have to hear that?"

Gaby looked into her friend's eyes — eyes she'd so often seen crinkle with laughter, sparkle with mischief, and glint with anger. Now they were wet with tears, and there was a trembling in the corners as though MaryLou was fighting for control. *I can't burden her with my guilt. Done too much of that already.* "You're right," Gaby said with forced brightness. "But you know me, Lulu; I have to keep moving forward. I've got to do what I can for as long as I can."

And then MaryLou asked the question Gaby knew she would. "Why haven't you told Sheila?"

"I can't. She's so worried about Vincent. I can't add to her troubles. Besides —"

"I know that look!" MaryLou pointed an accusing finger. "You know something. Something about Sheila! What? What is it?"

"Nothing bad, just — just a challenge down the line. Something she's not prepared for."

"What the hell does that mean? Oh, never mind. You won't tell me! But I'm watching you, Gaby French. Any sign that all of this is taking too much of a toll and —"

"Okay, okay," Gaby agreed, for she felt the breath of winter in her bones and was grateful she wouldn't face the cold alone. And then, instead of plunging into her day and burying herself in work, she sat quietly with her friend. They cried together and comforted each other as the familiar sounds of the diner drifted in the door and a blazing sun climbed the sky.

Helen glanced around the hospital storage room with a frown before returning her gaze to Cate's stricken face. With an inward sigh, she mentally sorted through the patients she'd assigned to Cate that day. Beatrice in the early morning — no problem there as far as Helen knew. Surprising, really, that the two had hit it off. More than that, Cate had gained the old woman's trust. Helen wrinkled her brow in thought before recalling that Cate had also visited James Sullivan. The priest and she hadn't gotten on at first, but that was all in the past. Pulling off her glasses, Helen proceeded to polish them with the hem of her smock. Lourdes Garcia! Of course. "It's Lourdes, isn't it?" she asked. The jerk of Cate's head was confirmation enough.

As a brilliant sunset lit the sky and crimson spread along the horizon like a blanket to receive it, Cate gave voice to the horror of caring for the delirious Cuban woman. "She told me things — things she should have told her priest, not a stranger. Horrible things about her life in Cuba. What the guerillas did to her. What she did to survive. Who she betrayed." A shiver ran through Cate's body. "I didn't want to know, but she said she had to tell someone before she died. And she did. Die, that is. I — I was there."

Helen sighed. *So she's seen her first death. And heard the confession that preceded it.* When Cate turned stricken eyes on her,

Helen thought, *I first saw that tortured look in the mirror years ago. Before the promise of youth bled away. Before I came to accept my role as confessor.* Pulling her thoughts back to Cate, she wondered, *How do I comfort her? How do I explain that she must be a friend to her patients, but only to a point. She needs to be compassionate and kind, but keep an emotional distance. She must care, but not too much.* Helen turned to gaze out the window at the vibrant colors of a summer day. *Soon darkness will mellow it all to dull blues and grays. Too many nurses only see shades of near-death. Can't let that happen to her.* "Lourdes trusted you with her secrets. Other patients will, too," Helen said. "You'll find a way to handle it. It won't be my way or anyone else's, but you will. And you won't be doing it alone. But," she concluded briskly, guessing Cate wouldn't take kindly to pulled punches, "you have to accept that this is part of the job. You'll see patients at their most vulnerable, hear them say things they don't even tell their families. Perhaps some stories shouldn't be told, but they weigh on the soul unless given voice."

"Weigh on the soul," Cate repeated softly, her shoulders straightening as though some invisible string were pulling her upright. "Yes. You're right. No one should die without someone to listen. Without loved ones to hear them."

Is she talking about Lourdes or her husband? And then it was as though Helen's old friend stood beside her — supportive and encouraging. "This talk of Lourdes reminds me of something Miriam shared while I was nursing her."

"Miriam?" Cate wiped at her face.

"Her father was a diamond cutter. He died before the war."

"I — I knew that, actually."

Helen nodded. "Well, after Poland was invaded, Miriam and her three brothers divided up his diamonds, each hiding a portion and vowing to keep the location secret even from each other. That way, if any of them were questioned, only one hiding place would be compromised. Imagine family members fearing betrayal at the hands of each other? Hiding diamonds rather than pooling them? But Miriam said that it was the right thing to do, for under the stress of torture even the strongest can break. Later, in the Lodz ghetto, they were able to dole the diamonds out in trade for food and fuel. But only for a time, for the world tipped on its axis so far that one day a diamond didn't buy a loaf of bread." The pale oval of Cate's face was very still. "After the war, Miriam met two sisters who had survived in a similar fashion: They'd sold or traded family jewels one by one. In the years following, one sister became very materialistic, convinced that as possessions had saved her once, they would again. The other sister joined a kibbutz, equally convinced that no amount of jewels had stopped the horror, and that only by working to build a homeland could Jews hope to survive."

Cate exhaled the breath she was holding. "I understand those sisters. But I don't understand Lourdes. I can't condone what she did. You can't tell me you do?" Cate challenged.

Helen lifted her shoulders slightly. "I don't know the details and I don't judge her. How can I? The choices people make when confronted with the unthinkable can't always be understood — at least not by those of us living in comfort."

"There's right and wrong, Helen!"

"Yes, that's true. There's also a lot of gray that young people running so fast don't see. But as your hair grays, so does your sight: a black-and-white world is a very stark and lonely place." The gentle rebuke behind the words seemed to echo in the now silent room. Helen glanced at her watch. "It's time I was heading home. You, too. Come on, let's call it a day." Cate nodded mutely, clutching her bag to her chest and turning toward the door. As they made their way out, Helen promised, "Tomorrow things will look different." *I hope that's true and Cate finds her way. I hope those sisters found a measure of peace just as dear Miriam did.*

When she got home, Cate brewed a pot of tea and thought of Lourdes's final moments. Cate had felt so helpless watching the woman slip away. There'd been a nurse there and other aides, but it was toward Cate that Lourdes's gaze had turned at the end. The intensity of that desperate look had stripped Cate to the core.

Turning away from her thoughts, Cate glanced over at the phone, tempted to ignore the blinking light. For some reason, the sight of it sent a chill down her spine. Perhaps the message was from the nursing home. Had something happened to John's grandmother? Her hand hovered over the Play button. If anything was wrong, she could hardly help from one hundred miles away. Then, again, she had to know. Punching the button, she heard the familiar voice of her husband's commander. As his words settled over her, Cate felt the walls of her bedroom recede; in fact, all of Amberley seemed to fade from her sight until only shadows of her new life remained.

She replayed the message, thinking how easy it would be to do as the army urged: accept the futility of a struggle she had lost before. Perhaps John would want her to move on; so many people had told her that, and she'd allowed herself to believe it — once. She'd even left the city they'd called home, determined to start afresh. But the shame born of her failure to discover exactly what had happened to her husband had shadowed her; it still did. And now the army wanted her to sign some sort of release agreement, one it argued would help her put the ugly business of John's death behind her. As if that were possible.

She heard movement in the garden below and pulled the curtain aside to see Sheila cuddling the marmalade cat that slept in the greenhouse. Although her visage was hidden, Cate read sadness in the hunched shoulders and guessed thoughts of Vincent were the reason. Sensing she was being watched, Sheila looked up and gave a brief nod of her tear-stained face. It was the type of greeting given a friend, someone so much a part of one's life that grief need not be hidden. Or explained. For some reason — inexplicable then and for decades to follow

— that simple gesture of acceptance was the push Cate needed.

CHAPTER 13

The plaque hanging outside Father Sullivan's study gave Cate pause. "Life is fragile. Handle with prayer," she read aloud. It was a maxim John would appreciate; her grandmother, too. She rubbed a hand over her gritty eyes. Her sleep had been fitful and plagued with dreams. Perhaps it wasn't the right day to do this, perhaps — Before her nerve deserted her, she raised a hand, fisted it for control, and knocked twice on the paneled door.

"Come in," a familiar voice called out.

She found the priest teeter-tottering on a stepladder set before floor-to-ceiling bookcases crammed with books, papers, boxes, and file folders. "What are you doing?" she cried, rushing forward. "You'll fall!" Reaching out, she pulled her hands back for the only body parts she could grab were leg or buttocks. "Get down!" She all but stamped her feet.

"All right, all right," he said in a grudging tone. "As soon as I —" His words were cut off by a sharp oath that bore witness to James Sullivan's working-class roots. He shifted his weight awkwardly, and one foot slipped off the top step to dangle in midair.

Scrambling up the ladder, she grabbed him around the waist and guided him safely to the floor before giving vent to her fears. "Are you crazy? You've only just recovered from knee surgery! You shouldn't be climbing ladders!"

Father Sullivan dismissed the notion with a wave of the worn leather volume he held in a death grip. "Found it." Face alight, he opened to the first page and muttered, "Aquinas. Knew I had it, just didn't remember where." His gaze sought the shelf above before flicking to Cate's flushed face. "I wonder what else — ?"

She held back a smile. "Deftly done. All right, I'll take a look for you. Provided you sit down." When he grumbled a protest, she added in what she'd come to think of as her home care aide voice, "You may not be my patient any longer, but if you want my help —"

"Okay. Okay."

Only after Father Sullivan was settled in an armchair did Cate mount the stepladder.

Soon a pile of books covered the green blotter paper of his desk. After half an hour, she waved aside a puff of dust, opened the room's only window, and held up her hands. "Enough. You can't read more than that now."

The priest sent one more longing glance toward the bookcase's uppermost shelf before acquiescing. Surveying his treasures with hungry eyes, Father Sullivan ran a reverent hand over the leather spine of the nearest volume before recalling how often Miriam and he had debated theology. "She had a keen mind, you know. She was always reading."

"You told me how she studied Jewish law," Cate reminded him.

Father Sullivan nodded. "One of her brothers was religious. Soon after the invasion, Lodz's synagogues were burned. He was one of those who hid the community's holy books. Imagine worrying about protecting a library when you're facing persecution. Death." He shook his head sadly. "Of course no one knew those books would face a unique martyrdom, for in all the lands Germany controlled not a single set of Talmud survived. But then what one army took, another gave back. Did you know that after the war the U.S. Army arranged for a special printing of the Talmud? America was the first government in history to do that."

"Wow. And the Talmud — that's an important holy book?"

"Books," Father Sullivan corrected. "Imagine a set of encyclopedia — millions of words long — that analyzes the Bible and Jewish law." He nodded thoughtfully. "The army understood — Truman understood — that it isn't enough to feed and clothe the civilians who survive war. A rebuilding army has to do more."

His meaning was clear, and Cate found herself lamenting how little modern armies did to safeguard holy books. How many stories had she read about copies of the Koran being desecrated by Western soldiers ignorant of its meaning and dismissive of its value? When her thoughts circled back to Miriam, she told the priest about the journal entries, asking, "Did you — was it you who left the second one?"

"No. And before you ask, I've no idea who did. But I'll give it some thought." Reaching in his pocket for a handkerchief, he used it to wipe his glasses before asking in a tone halfway between invitation and command, "Tea?"

"What?"

"Would you like some tea? As Rosa Vitelli

used to say, 'Life's challenges are best confronted on a full stomach.' And Mrs. Andrews made apple tarts today." His eyes lit in anticipation, for the middle-aged woman who did his cooking was celebrated for her baking.

"All right. But I'll phone her. You need to rest," Cate said, motioning him to stay seated while she dialed the rectory kitchen. A moment later, a high-pitched voice answered the call, promising tea and tarts within the quarter hour. The words Cate had strung together as she walked to the rectory deserted her, so they sat quietly until Mrs. Andrews bustled in to serve the tea and tsk-tsk at the fact that her charge had skipped his afternoon nap.

After she'd gone, Father Sullivan studied Cate. "How is the book coming along?"

"Some days I think I'm doing great. That what I write is brilliant. Others I feel like a sham. Know I'm a failure." She stiffened, expecting either stock assurances or sympathy.

Instead the priest surprised her by changing the subject. "And caregiving — how are you getting on with that?"

"Oh. Well, it's not the most exciting work." At his raised eyebrow, she hastened to add, "Not that what I'm doing isn't meaningful, of course. It's just —"

"Boring?"

She considered lying, but something in his steady gaze made her swallow the pat answer that leapt to her lips. "Not boring so much as monotonous. With some patients." An image of Old Man Simmons sharpened into focus as her mind's eye replayed that morning's routine. She had changed his diaper, showered, dressed, and fed him. By the time he finished breakfast, it was time to check his diaper again. So much of what she did was about getting food and medication into one end of her patients and getting it safely out the other. As Helen often told her, "Digestion should be a one-way street with no roadblocks. It's your job to keep the lanes moving." When Cate explained to the priest what her day had entailed, the underlying frustration was obvious, for at times she did feel it was work a robot could do.

Father Sullivan regarded her sympathetically. "It's because you only see a slice of your patients' lives. That's not very different from my work; one can't view a parishioner simply in terms of what is learned in the confessional. That doesn't tell the whole story. There is as much unsaid in a person's life as said, as much below the surface as what we see."

Surprised at how easily they had found their way to common ground, or at least onto a path they could walk together, she regarded him with new respect. "You're right, of course." In the silence that followed, she found the courage to speak of John. Father Sullivan listened quietly until she stammered out the question uppermost in her mind, the one that had drawn her to the rectory that day. "I — I want to know exactly what happened to my husband. I know he was killed in a roadside bombing, but —" She pulled a file from her bag and grasped it with whitened fingers before shaking it for emphasis. "What does 'injuries sustained in enemy action' mean? What precisely happened to him?" She saw the sympathy in Father Sullivan's faded eyes; before he could offer comfort, she rushed on. "These are John's e-mails." When she opened the file to a pile of papers, her mind registered the fold marks born of repeated reading, being carried next to her heart, and tucked beneath her pillow. "One — one is from that last morning. In it, he says he's going on patrol 'a few clicks outside the wire.' That means he was only a couple kilometers off base. But I can't find out more than that! I tried to contact a priest he mentioned," she said, sorting through the e-mails before choosing one. "Father Murphy. He was the chaplain on base, or one of them. And John always went to Mass, so they'd have known each other. I want to talk to Father Murphy, but I haven't been able to find out where he is. I called all over, but nobody will help me. I thought — I thought maybe you could —"

Father Sullivan anticipated her. "I'll certainly try. May I see the e-mail that mentions him?" She surrendered it reverently, and the priest read carefully before handing it back. "What about the other men in John's unit? Have you spoken with them?"

She shook her head violently. "No one will talk to me." The words caught in her throat. "Maybe they were told not to. I don't know."

Something flickered behind James Sullivan's eyes — a light that had once flared before time's assault dimmed it to little more than a banked ember. "So you're getting stonewalled on all sides," he murmured, turning the crucifix that hung from his neck first this way, then that. "It may take some doing to find Father Murphy now that the army's leaving Iraq. Many of those troops are now in Kuwait. He could have been reassigned there or sent back home. Tell me, where exactly was your husband stationed?"

"Camp Fallujah, in the Al Anbar province," Cate said. When the priest made some notes on a slip of paper, she reached out to lay a hand over his, both of them surprised by the impulse. "Thank you."

"Don't thank me yet. I haven't done anything."

She heard the caution behind his words and understood he didn't want her to expect too much. She wouldn't, or so she told herself. Yet when she stepped out of the rectory an hour later, her heart felt lighter. As her grandmother would have said, "A burden shared is a burden eased."

Cate sought out MaryLou during what she assumed was the garage's lunch hour, a pleading cast to her features when she asked if the mechanic had a few minutes. Since customers paced the waiting room of Lou's Auto Body, MaryLou opened her mouth to ask, "Are you kidding?" Instead, she read the urgency behind the words for what it was and ushered Cate into her office even as her assistant raised an eyebrow in inquiry. Shooing him back to work, MaryLou shut the door and reached for a bottle of water. Twisting off the cap, she downed half the contents before frowning at Cate. "What are you looking for?"

"Some papers," Cate murmured, rummaging through her handbag.

"Why do you carry such a huge pocketbook?" MaryLou demanded. "All you need is a lipstick, some money, and gum."

"What?"

"Oh, give me that!" MaryLou snatched the bag from Cate and upended it on her desk. "There," she said with a satisfied sigh. "Now, let me look at this thing." Scanning the bag's interior, she grumbled, "There should be a light. Damn impossible to find anything otherwise. I can jerry-rig something that's battery operated. If you want." When Cate didn't reply, MaryLou looked up. "What are those?"

Cate handed over the papers she clutched. "E-mails. Can you tell me what they mean? John sent these to himself. I — I accessed them after he died."

MaryLou scanned the e-mails before reaching out an unconscious hand to switch on an oscillating floor fan. "They look like maintenance schedules. Don't know exactly what for, but I'll figure it out. How long ago did John die?"

"Two years." The question MaryLou didn't ask vibrated in the air between them. "I did show them to someone at the time. Someone in his unit." Cate shrugged her thin shoulders. "He said they were just routine stuff that John had probably meant to delete but forgot to. After that, I didn't really think about it. But something's happened. Something's changed."

"What?" MaryLou asked, never one to let a matter lie. Cate explained about the message she'd received and the document she was being urged to sign. The release of liability the army had sent her was so broad in scope Cate felt sure it violated her constitutional rights. When she showed the release to MaryLou, the mechanic fumed, "This is bullshit! It says you can't bring a claim against the contractors who handled base security and maintenance, or suppliers who provided protective gear — oh, just about anyone who might have been at fault. I can't believe — hang on!" She shook the paper for emphasis. "Why do they need this?"

"They don't want me to make trouble. Bring a lawsuit."

MaryLou handed the paper back. "You can't anyway. At least I think you can't. Those guys — contractors — they're immune from lawsuits. Like the government is. A good friend told me that; someone who should know." She cocked her head. "But then why would the army need you to sign

222

anything? Why would they need you to waive a right you don't even have?"

Cate shrugged. "I don't know. But I'm not signing. Even if what you say is true and these guys are above the law, I'm not signing." Her voice shook when she added, "It would feel like a betrayal of John."

MaryLou nodded approval as part of her mind tucked away what she'd learned. There was only one reason the army would need such a release: It knew that the legal mumbo jumbo used to protect contractors in war zones wasn't a shield after all. That bore thinking about. In the meantime, she needed to support and protect her new friend. "Sorry I flew off the handle. I just hate seeing people bullied. Seeing women bullied." Then the sharp eyes that never failed her noted that although Cate reminded her of those glass figurines they sold at McLean's, perhaps Sheila was right about there being steel beneath the fragile shell. "Give me some time to think about all of this," MaryLou said, sweeping a hand toward the e-mails that now lay scattered on her desk. "I need to touch base with a friend of mine — an ex-marine. I'll call you when I know something." She pulled open the office door, eyes scanning the waiting customers. "I've got to get back to work."

"O-oh," Cate stuttered, making no move to leave.

With an effort she rarely took, MaryLou gentled her voice. "I can't do more now, but I will. I promise."

James Sullivan's heart was heavy. The day had started well enough. By chance, he'd tracked the chaplain who had been John Saunders's confessor during his time in Iraq to a New Jersey parish. They'd spoken briefly that morning, the conversation strained as the younger prelate recalled the disciplinary action taken against two members of John's unit. Father Murphy's description of events had been sketchy because the army's investigation had not been made public. Not that it mattered to Seamus Murphy, for he knew what he did from other sources. He couldn't share those sources, for the seal of the confessional couldn't be broken even to help another priest. Still, James Sullivan had noted the anxious tone and read the worried pauses of their conversation for what they were. He'd pieced together a basic understanding of what had happened on that far-away army base, and the enormity of it was staggering. Yet as much as he thought he knew what had transpired that awful day John

Saunders was killed, it was another thing entirely to give voice to his suspicions. He couldn't tell Cate anything with certainty. But how could he keep silent when learning the truth might give her a measure of peace, or at least some kind of closure? Turning the matter over in his mind, he sought comfort in the faith that never failed him. Closing his eyes to the distractions of this world, he emptied his mind, methodically sweeping it clean of doubt and fear as he had been taught. Then he allowed prayer to soothe his spirit, and in so doing glimpsed an outline of what had to be done.

CHAPTER 14

A week passed before Cate spied MaryLou in Vitelli's one evening talking in low tones with Sheila. She called out a greeting, and, although Sheila acknowledged it with a wave, MaryLou did not. Was the mechanic avoiding her? Why? Was it because Mary-Lou had been as unsuccessful as Father Sullivan? He'd called earlier to say that although he'd tracked down Father Murphy, the Irishman had been unable to tell him anything concrete. Hearing the regret in the priest's voice made Cate wonder if the time had come to live on whatever scraps the army threw her way and push the questions she wanted to pepper MaryLou with to the back of her heart. She took a mental step toward complacency, then another before hurrying across the room. "Did you find out anything about those e-mails?"

MaryLou fixed her with a remorseful look. Usually blunt to the point of rudeness, she avoided answering even as her eyes swept the grocery as though seeking an escape. "This really isn't the place, Cate. Perhaps —"

"Lulu," Sheila cut in, pulling off the apron she wore and folding it with purpose. "Take her in back. I'll grab some cookies." Giving her old friend a subtle shove, she hissed, "Stop putting this off! You have to tell her!"

Tell me? Tell me what? The room blurred for an instant before MaryLou grabbed Cate's arm and guided her back to the kitchen. Cate sank onto a chair at the worn oak table while MaryLou took the seat opposite.

Sheila joined them and pressed a glass into Cate's hands. "It's grappa. Drink."

Like an obedient child, Cate lifted the clear liquid to her lips and took a sip. She coughed when the alcohol hit her throat, but then nodded in thanks, for it had helped to penetrate the fog surrounding her thoughts. She stared at MaryLou. "Wha-what did you find out?"

Refusing the glass Sheila held out, MaryLou opted for an almond cookie, which she proceeded to crumble between her fingers. "About those e-mails," she began in a flat voice. "I wasn't sure what they were until I had a friend take a look at them. Eddie

227

Fallon. An ex-marine. He served in Iraq and Afghanistan. Eddie's a contractor now. More money in that work." Sheila elbowed MaryLou sharply. "Sorry. Not relevant. Anyway, Eddie says what your husband sent were maintenance schedules. For armored vehicles called MRAPs. MRAP stands for Mine Resistant Ambush — something or other."

When Cate opened her mouth to speak, no sound came out. Sheila elbowed Mary-Lou again. "Tell her the rest, Lulu."

MaryLou pulled back in her seat as though to distance herself from the dirty task ahead. "Look, Cate, I'm the last person who would defend the military, or any authority figure for that matter. I've seen too many people in power abuse their position for that. And what I found out may have no bearing on John's death. On any death. Maintenance screw-ups like this probably happen all the time. And I know from experience," she added in a rush, as though relieved to find herself on familiar ground, "that the maintenance schedules manufacturers call for on most things are excessive. Certainly that's true for new cars."

"What the hell are you talking about?" Cate demanded, eyes wild. Between the words MaryLou spoke, a yawning darkness began to take shape. It couldn't be; it couldn't be —

"Eddie's familiar with the MRAP. He knows how things should be done and how they shouldn't. Those e-mails," MaryLou finished with a sigh, "they show that the MRAPs in John's unit weren't being maintained properly." At Cate's indrawn breath, MaryLou shot a glance at Sheila as though debating whether to ask the obvious question. "Do you know if John was in one of those when he died? If not, maybe what I found doesn't matter."

MaryLou's words were swallowed by the roar in Cate's ears. She didn't know if he'd been in a vehicle when he died — didn't know because the army wouldn't tell her. Because they lied. Lies. The Pentagon lied to Congress about how the war was going, lied to soldiers who depended on proper body armor and allies who wouldn't betray them. Lies, lies, lies. She pushed away from the table, the bottle of grappa gripped in her hands. "It wasn't terrorists! The army killed John as surely as if they'd set that roadside bomb! They killed him with one lie after the other! Maybe he was in one of those things. Maybe it broke down, or was driving too slowly because it hadn't been taken care of. Maybe —"

Cate raised the bottle above her head, held it there for a moment, before flinging it to the floor with an anguished cry. She wanted to break something — break everything — as she'd been broken. Glass crunched underfoot as she paced in aimless circles. "I've had those e-mails for two years! Why didn't I *really* look at them? Why?" She was dimly aware of hands guiding her to a chair and pulling off her sodden, glass-encrusted shoes. In the distance, she heard muffled tones of a conversation. But none of it penetrated her grief. A red haze seemed to veil her sight, distorting the room she had come to know so well. *I didn't want to know the truth. I didn't have the courage to face it until I came to Amberley. I wish I'd never come here! Thank God I did.*

When a soft voice whispered that it was all right to cry, she did. Wave after wave of heartrending sobs racked her body. She cried until her eyes were too gritty to keep open. Then she gasped, for when she closed them the tortured images followed her into the dark: John's coffin, a folded flag, the empty bed she had to conquer every night. The realization hit her that as much as the army was to blame, as much as John's priest had encouraged him to go to war, it was *she* who had put John in danger. "Because of me, he joined the National Guard! Because of me!" she wailed over and over. Cate felt the pressure of a hand on her arm. Then she was being guided upstairs and undressed like a child. She opened her mouth to protest, but sleep beckoned, and she welcomed it like the coward she was.

Crawling into bed, she escaped into a dreamscape where John waited. She rushed forward eagerly, but the earth beneath them shifted and fell away. She called to him, but a whistling canyon of swirling blackness swallowed her words. Reaching out to pull him to safety, she gasped out his name and tightened her grip. But, no, it was only a pillow she clutched in her trembling arms. And the cheek she thought bore the imprint of his kiss was, instead, wet with tears.

Curling her body around the pillow, she buried her face in it and welcomed pain into her heart. It expanded within her, filling the space to breaking so quickly her breath caught. She mourned the children John hadn't fathered and the old man he would never become. She wept for all he'd learned and thought, believed and valued. For the mind he'd nurtured through a lifetime of questioning. That his lifeblood had fed the sands of a land not his home, that his body

231

might have been mutilated after death, might have been —

She threw the pillow aside, eyes wild, for the images running through her tortured brain were the stuff of madness. She'd read that crowds gathered around the bodies of slain Americans, spontaneously kicking, cutting, and burning in a frenzy of hate. Oh God! Was that what had happened? Was that why the army was stonewalling her? No! Not to John! Not to John! Her breath came in ragged bursts as her eyes narrowed with a feral instinct to sweep the shadowed room. Was that something moving in the corner? Did a figure crouch there? *When it's too dark to see, look for outlines* — John had taught her that. She peered into the feathered blackness, searching for any hint of thinner air encircling a solid mass. Her right hand reached for the light switch, knocking into something sharp. "Shit!" Books flew and a glass vase crashed to the floor. Then a dull pool of yellow light took shape over the carpet. She bent down to pick up the lamp, her movements jerky as she set it on the nightstand. Her gaze swept the room methodically. *A grid pattern. That's how you search. In a grid pattern.* But there was no one. *I'm alone. Alone. I'm alone.* The words ricocheted through her broken mind.

■ ■ ■ ■

The morning was humid. A murky haze clung to the edge of MaryLou's property, smudging the world beyond. She sat outside on the balcony of the small apartment she'd built above Lou's Auto Body, a fresh batch of catalogs from her favorite suppliers on her lap and a pot of coffee percolating on the stove. The Red Sox were playing at home that afternoon, and MaryLou imagined herself with her feet up, listening to the game. Then she looked at the parking lot below and caught sight of the wreck that had been towed in the previous evening. So much for quiet time; her day would be spent under the business end of a Corvette.

Hours later, when she heard a familiar voice address the other mechanic, MaryLou slid out from under the car. "Father!" Jumping quickly to her feet, she knocked over a can of engine oil. "Shit!" Bending down with a rag, she mopped at the spill. Then she looked up, an embarrassed blush staining her face. "Sorry. Poor choice of words."

"Quite apropos, I thought," James Sullivan observed, leaning against the workbench opposite and pulling a bottle of Scotch whisky from a bag he carried.

MaryLou abandoned her task, wiped her dirty hands on her overalls, and reached out before thinking better of it. "Hang on. Let me wash this gunk off first." She moved to a sink in the corner and proceeded to scrub her hands vigorously. Drying them on a paper towel, she returned to the priest and gave a low whistle. "Isle of Skye. Nice." She cocked an eyebrow. "Is this a bribe? Or did you do something you need to apologize for?"

Father Sullivan bristled. "Neither. Can't I bring a gift to a friend without an ulterior motive?"

MaryLou snorted out a laugh. "Sure. But you wouldn't part with this stuff unless you had a damn good reason." When he explained in detail what he wanted her to do, MaryLou reluctantly pushed the whisky out of reach. "Look, I'd like to help, but I don't want to go behind Cate's back. She's still pissed at me."

"That's unfortunate, for I know she considers you a friend," Father Sullivan said. "I've already spoken with her and explained that Father Murphy alluded to some irregularities concerning John's death. Cate is trying her best to bring pressure officially and find out what happened, but I thought perhaps your marine friend could help."

"Eddie Fallon? Sure. He's the best at what he does, and what he does is understand the military. And I get the impression Eddie worked for the government in other areas, but he won't cop to that even when he's drunk. And when he's drunk, he takes to cursing in Arabic, Russian, and a bunch of other languages I don't recognize, so I'd say he's served his country across time zones, if you take my meaning. Yeah, Eddie will probably help. For a price. But then he owes me big now: I overhauled his heap of a Mustang last week. Again. He drives that thing into the ground. Damn shame, 'cause they don't make cars like that anymore." After a beat, she added, "And they don't make men like Eddie anymore either."

Eddie Fallon rubbed a hand over his chin, regretting that he hadn't taken the time to shave that morning. Or the day before for that matter. Sitting back in his chair, he considered the priest. The Jesuits of his youth had been skilled in interrogation and intimidation — familiar territory for any soldier, whether one fought for Christ or country. So when confronted with men of the cloth, Eddie felt the grudging admiration of one professional for another. Yet Father Sullivan didn't seem to fit the priestly mold, what with his welcoming smile and warm handshake. Now the woman was easier to read. When she turned sky-blue eyes on him, blond curls tickled her cheeks, and he felt an urge to reach out and smooth the worry from her face. Normally, vulnerable women didn't attract him. Or hadn't until now. There was no time to linger over that thought, for Cate Saunders was studying his inscrutable face with an intensity that was unnerving. Her gaze was direct and questioning, but camouflage in all its forms came naturally to Eddie, and his inner thoughts were his alone. But not hers: Her needs and fears were plain to see.

They sat in the rectory kitchen at a worn oak table set beneath a ticking clock. The cups of tea Father Sullivan had poured grew cold as Eddie questioned his spur-of-the-moment decision to hop in the car and drive to Amberley. He'd phoned MaryLou en route, and she'd agreed to pass on his request for a meeting with the two people now fixing him with expectant looks. "Since MaryLou phoned me," Eddie began, addressing himself to the priest, "I started asking around, trying to find out what happened." He shifted his gaze to Cate. "I don't have the whole story, but something about it doesn't add up. That's why I came. To tell you in person."

The priest arched an eyebrow. "How can you know something so quickly?"

"Yeah, well," Eddie shrugged. "I called in a favor. Didn't take long to piece the story together. Or part of it."

"And?" Father Sullivan prompted.

Eddie hesitated before deciding he could no more dress up the truth than turn a Ford into a Ferrari. With the unemotional, detached bluntness that was his trademark, he explained how John Saunders had died. "He was in an MRAP with two corporals named —" Eddie pulled a pad from his pocket and flipped it open. "Lance Bruno and Roy Kapunski."

Cate sat forward to grab his arm. "He was in one of those? Did it break down? Did it?" Her voice was breathless.

"I don't know. Maybe they had trouble with it, maybe not. What I do know is that the vehicle stopped just inside a village they apparently knew well." Eddie closed the pad and tapped it absentmindedly on the edge of the table. "What happened next was — unusual."

"Unusual?" Cate repeated, confused.

Finding himself on solid ground, for military procedure was something he knew well, Eddie explained, "If they encountered a problem, the protocol would be to radio in. If they'd broken down, for instance, they'd be sent an emergency response team. But your husband didn't do that. Didn't allow the others to, either. Now, the radio was in working order, so that wasn't the problem. For some reason, instead of radioing in, he ordered Bruno and Kapunski to stay in the vehicle, but got out himself. He walked across the road. Over a bomb. I don't know whether that triggered it or it was triggered remotely. There was an investigation afterward, but I don't have a copy of the report. And I may not get my hands on it," he added quickly, forestalling Cate's next question. "So, the next step is to talk to Bruno and Kapunski. Both survived by the way; they weren't injured. But they were disciplined afterward for not following protocol."

Cate was silent, her eyes saucers, so it fell to Father Sullivan to ask, "Have you any idea how to find these two men? Do you think they'll talk to Cate?"

Eddie shrugged. "I don't know. And finding them might take some time." He fixed his gaze on Cate's pale face. "You'll have to be patient."

"Yes, yes," Cate said so weakly that Eddie wasn't sure she understood what he'd said.

Then any doubt was cast aside when she asked in a low voice, "Why would he do that? Why would he leave the safety of an armored vehicle to strike out on his own? Why?" Her voice rose sharply.

In the porous silence that followed, Eddie exhaled deeply.

"Tell me!" Cate pleaded. "Tell me what you think happened. You must have some idea, some —"

"I just don't know," Eddie said more sharply than he intended. "Look, people make mistakes in combat. Things happen and they get careless."

"What the hell does that mean? What are you trying to say?"

The priest reached out to cover Cate's trembling hands with his own. "Eddie doesn't know more now, Cate. But he will. We will." Then he added as if in prayer, "God willing."

After her meeting at the rectory, Cate made her way back home in a daze. What Eddie Fallon suggested couldn't be true: It made no sense. She'd known John, not as a soldier perhaps, but as a man — a deliberate, responsible man who wore safety goggles when using power tools, never drank to excess, and generally drove the speed limit.

He wasn't careless. He wasn't! The prickle of unease she'd felt when MaryLou's friend folded his tall frame into the chair opposite hers had quickly flowered into genuine dislike. That made dismissing what he'd said easier, for Fallon was so — what? Tattooed. As coiled as a spring under pressure. And there'd been a wild, untamed glint in his dark eyes that unbalanced her.

Not that John hadn't had a wild side, one that grew bolder the longer they were married. That it only surfaced during lovemaking made it their secret, one that gave her a silent thrill whenever friends complained about their predictable husbands and dull sex lives. John had been different, for he'd reveled in her body. He'd loved life — loved their life together. He wouldn't have taken chances and jeopardized their future for anything. She couldn't — wouldn't — believe otherwise. Steeling her will against doubt, by the time she'd opened the door of her apartment she'd pushed what Eddie Fallon had said to a quiet corner of her thoughts.

She hadn't expected to find another journal entry waiting for her, but there it was. Instead of picking it up, she circled the faded writing slowly. It had been such a draining, awful day. Perhaps she should wait, perhaps — "Oh, get a grip, Cate," she scolded, bending down to snatch up the paper. "I'll read it in the garden. I need to be outside. And if I am," she promised herself, "I'll stop talking to myself."

Settling herself on a low bench beside a patch of basil, she began to read.

In the Ghetto, it was routine to randomly execute people, or grab them off the street to fill slave labor quotas in other towns. One morning, the worst happened: While I was at work, my brothers were taken. I never found out what happened to them, and from that day I kept moving around the Ghetto, staying with one friend after the other. Somehow, I survived for two more years. The war wasn't going well for Germany, and the Jews of Lodz were needed to make weapons and sew uniforms, so at least I had work.

When it was clear the war was lost, they decided to liquidate the Ghetto and send us to Auschwitz. I was one of eight hundred left behind to sort through what the Germans had stolen from their victims. There were warehouses full of clothing, furniture, and musical instruments. A church packed with mattresses. Storerooms of buttons and ribbons, dishes and books. Those small mementos that define a life.

We were housed together in Rembrandtstrasse. The atmosphere in the Ghetto was eerie — deserted streets; buildings that had been gutted for their wood half collapsing all around us. We were all waiting for the quiet to be broken. There were more and more air raids. I read what newspapers I could and knew the Russians were close. That the Allies were winning.

On a bitter day in January of 1945 we were taken out to the Marysin cemetery and ordered to dig our own graves. The weather was raw and the ground all but frozen. It was backbreaking work after five years of near starvation. A cool mist rose from the ground and mixed with the puffs of breath that escaped our mouths as we struggled, shoulder to shoulder. I knew that the moment we stopped digging, we'd be shot. Still, some hurried, eager to embrace what we'd fought to hold off for so long. Others found their eyes straying beyond the brick walls to where birds, untouched by the madness of war, circled in an ashen sky. I kept my eyes focused on the chill earth at my feet, the earth that would soon claim me.

Then softly, so softly, a chant began. Kaddish. The prayer for the dead. We would say it for ourselves as there would be no one left alive to say it for us. When the digging stopped, my face was wet with tears. I gripped hands with the women next to me and prepared to face my father. Would he be proud of the life I had lived without him? Would the choices I had made merit my seeing him again?

An officer approached us and smiled. He drew out the moment for an eternity before ordering us back to Rembrandtstrasse. All was silent as we prisoners looked at each other. Instead of joy, there was confusion. We had prepared for death. For release. Then he shouted and we broke into a run, or what could be managed on stiff legs and frozen feet.

The next day, Soviet troops liberated Lodz and we were free.

Letting the paper fall to her lap, Cate began to tremble, for in her mind's eye she saw the German's vulpine grin. Being ordered to dig your own grave was a horror beyond imagining. And yet — and yet Miriam survived it. Without her family, without anyone to help, she'd survived war. But John hadn't.

Chapter 15

"There's someone I want you to meet. Come with me," Helen said briskly.

They stood in the bathroom of a patient's room, Cate bent over the sink as she dumped dirty water from a plastic tub. She frowned, blowing at the bangs that clung to her sweaty brow. "I haven't finished Mrs. Peterson's bath."

"Do you want to?"

"Not particularly," Cate admitted freely, for the old woman she was working with was notoriously ill-tempered regarding matters of personal hygiene. Combine that with the fact that she weighed twice what she should, and the unfortunate aide assigned to bathe her needed to be well-muscled *and* thick-skinned. Most days, Cate qualified on the first count, but on that particular day she admitted she wasn't up to being insulted. "Fine. I'll let the other aide finish up." Rubbing her sore biceps, she grumbled,

"I can't decide if lifting Mrs. Peterson hurts my arms, my back, or my spirit more."

Although Helen wanted to enfold the younger woman in a hug, she schooled her features into a neutral mask. Cate hadn't mentioned what she'd learned of John's death, and Helen wasn't letting on that Sheila had filled her in. Of course, Sheila had only done so after Helen had revealed that Cate's work performance had deteriorated to the point that she might be fired. The change from model employee had begun with showing up late and missing meetings. That was bad enough, but when Cate snapped at a patient, Helen had to move quickly to persuade the hospital administrators that although lately distracted and irritable, Cate Saunders was still an asset. Without going into detail about the body blow the young widow had recently taken, she'd explained that her protégé was dealing with a personal matter that would soon resolve itself. And it had to, for as accommodating and easy-going as Helen Doyle was in most things, when it came to caring for the sick, her golden rule was that personal problems be left at home. When that rule was violated, Helen's reaction was always the same: She read the offending aide the riot act. It wouldn't be fair to do less with Cate. Then, again, these were unique circumstances, and Cate's work thus far had been exemplary. It was while debating how best to set the younger woman straight in a way that would also speed her emotional healing that Helen hit upon a compromise: Zelda.

"So who are we going to see?" Cate asked, her red-rimmed eyes hidden behind sunglasses as she and Helen made their way into town. Instead of the buoyed walk that was Cate's trademark, Helen noted that she shuffled along, one foot periodically scuffing the other as though picking a fight.

"A patient who's a special case. Someone who needs your help," Helen replied laconically.

Cate opened her mouth to respond before apparently thinking better of it. Fixing her gaze on her uncooperative feet, she focused on putting one foot in front of the other — all she seemed able to manage at the moment.

They made their way the few blocks to Main Street. Then Helen picked up the pace. "It's just here."

Cate looked up at the Amberley Newz sign as the newsstand's owner stepped into view. Zelda Malory's face was a canvas upon which the hot Southern sun of childhood and the cold Northern winters of adulthood had recorded her life. The jokes she'd heard, the worries she had known, and the sorrow she'd felt had all left their mark. Time had sharpened some features into prominence while others had softened such that she appeared of indeterminate age. That sweltering day, as a blanket of humidity seemed to hold the world in check, she was dressed in patched shorts and a frayed cotton shirt. One toe peeked out of a pair of worn tennis shoes, and her socks were mismatched. The shabbiness she wore unconsciously did not extend to her spirit; far from tattered, it seemed instead to light her careworn features from within.

"Turn on your hearing aids," Helen shouted by way of greeting.

Nodding her cap of white hair, the older woman fingered the bits of plastic in her ears. "Switch 'em off so I don't hear the traffic," she explained, the trace of an Alabama accent still slowing her speech even after forty years living among Yankees. She smiled and Helen responded by giving her a brief hug. When they pulled apart, the nurse ran a hand down Zelda's thin arm, lingering at the wrist long enough to check her pulse. Helen's gaze fell on legs dotted with black-and-blue marks, for depth perception was a problem for Zelda. When she stumbled, she'd curse under her breath before rummaging through her memories to discover where she'd left the thick, horn-rimmed glasses that brought the world into focus. Helen had recently affixed them to a silver chain Zelda could wear around her neck. It helped keep them within reach — when Zelda remembered to put the chain on.

"This is Cate," Helen said.

Cate stepped forward and pulled off her sunglasses for she'd noticed Zelda squinting at her. "We've met." Cate smiled for the first time that day — not a broad grin, but one heartfelt.

"I remember. You told me my name wasn't easy to forget. Said I shared it with some writer gal."

"Zelda Fitzgerald," Cate reminded her. "A Southerner, like yourself." Her gaze flicked to the sign overhead. "So is that why you used a z, why it's Amberley Newz?"

Zelda shook her head ruefully. "Nah. That was my nephew's doing. Nice boy. Well meaning, but not the sharpest tool in the shed. Still" — she jerked a thumb toward the sign — "folks remember the z. Remember me. So maybe he ain't so dumb after all."

Helen watched the exchange with pleasure. She hadn't known the women were acquainted, but now that she did her inner voice proposed a change to the plan she'd formulated earlier, and she reordered her thoughts accordingly. Her intention that morning was first and foremost to get Cate out of the hospital, reasoning that a change of scenery would lighten her mood. And it had, Helen realized with satisfaction. The second goal of their outing was to allow Amberley to work its magic, for Helen knew from experience that one suffers loss alone but heals best in a community. Zelda was proof of that. Eyeing the former psychiatric patient, Helen noted how the broken woman she'd treated all those years ago had been eclipsed by the business owner before her. *We can remake ourselves. With a bit of help. Zelda certainly did. Cate can, too.*

When a customer fingering a copy of *Elle* asked a question, Zelda turned away, and Cate stepped back to consider the newsstand that occupied a corner of Main Street between the diner and a block-long garden center. She gave a low whistle of appreciation, saying to Helen, "This place is amazing. It's only about, what, eight feet long by

249

three feet wide? Yet it's like a mini convenience store." Racks of newspapers, glossy magazines, crossword puzzle books, and comics shared space with candy, chips, packages of cookies, bottled water, maps, umbrellas, lip gloss, pens, batteries, and panty hose. "You don't see newsstands like this anymore. People either read the paper online, or buy a copy from one of those automated machines."

Helen nodded. "Amberley doesn't have those downtown. That's one of the perks of having Sheila as mayor; she got an ordinance passed banning them."

"Because of Zelda?" Cate guessed, her voice rising in surprise.

"Yes. She needs to work. To be out and about. And the town needs this newsstand. It's a bit of the past we don't want to let go of."

When the customer walked away, Zelda turned back to her visitors and pointed up at the red and white awning overhead, the edges of which flapped in the warm breeze. "That's new this year. Used to have hard plastic, but the canvas is so much nicer." She shifted her weight before pulling a folding chair close and settling her thin frame on its pink nylon straps. "Damn rheumatism. Hurts something awful today."

"So we'll have rain later?" Helen asked. Zelda nodded, for her joints were known to predict the weather with great accuracy. "Aside from the swelling, how are you feeling?" Helen asked in a matter-of-fact tone, slipping a stethoscope from her handbag with fluid ease. Bending down behind her patient, she slid it over the thin fabric of Zelda's blouse.

Although neither woman acknowledged the impromptu exam, Zelda drew a series of deep breaths as she spoke. "I'm holding up, Helen. Heat should break when it storms."

"I hope so," Helen said. Then her gaze moved across the street. "I've got to run some errands, Zelda. Can I pick up your meds for you? Wouldn't want you to miss any sales doing it yourself."

"Well —" Zelda made a show of considering, but Cate had seen her eyes light at Helen's offer. "If it's no trouble."

"None at all. We'll be back in two shakes of a lamb's tail." Gesturing for Cate to follow her, Helen picked up her bag and held a finger to her lips to silence any questions until they were safely out of earshot.

Once Helen and Cate stood together at the prescription pickup desk of the Corner Pharmacy, Cate asked, "So what's the story?

251

Why doesn't she come in for her checkups?"

Helen pursed her lips. "Technically, Zelda's not a patient."

"Technically?"

Helen shrugged, sifting her words. "She's a special case. Had a bit of bother a few years ago. Trouble with the law. She wound up in a psych ward, but she's pulled her life together since. Meds help. It's important that she take them. I check that she does, but I'm not the only one." She gave Cate a measuring look. "Sheila does her part. And Gaby. Lots of folks. You could help, too."

"Me?" Cate held a hand to her chest. "How can I help?"

"Keep an eye on her when you're in town. Remind her to turn her hearing aids on, to wear her glasses. Check that she's taking her meds."

"How will I know — ?"

"She'll behave strangely. If you see anything like that, call me. Or tell Sheila."

Cate rubbed a hand over her brow. "I don't get it. Why isn't she someplace where people can take care of her?"

Helen's eyes were hard. "She is. She's in a community. If you're suggesting an institution, Zelda wouldn't consider it. And it's not going to happen without her consent. Not so long as there's breath in my body.

252

The woman's been through enough. Besides, there's no need; she gets the help she needs here. Everybody takes a turn." When Helen pulled an envelope from her purse to pay for Zelda's medication, she forestalled Cate's next question by saying, "She hasn't got insurance. Doesn't qualify for government benefits and can't afford to buy the meds herself. So we take up a collection. Folks put in what they can every month. Speaking of which, give me a dollar." Helen held out her hand. Cate opened her wallet wordlessly before handing over a five-dollar bill. Helen gave her change. "Only need a dollar from you. I take from each according to his or her ability to pay, and I decided your contribution should be a dollar a month. From now on."

"*You* decided," Cate repeated, two bright spots of color rising on her pale cheeks. "I'll freely contribute, but I won't be told to. Or coerced. Not even by you."

Helen gave a quick nod. "Point taken. And I didn't mean to offend. I'm not by nature pushy, unless it's on behalf of patients."

They exited the pharmacy and made their way back across the street. Zelda accepted the medication without comment, slipping it into her pocket and holding out two bottles of lemonade. "On the house. It'll be a scorcher today." She gestured toward the sun — a pale globe that had moved behind a bank of clouds. "But we'll have a spot of rain before long. Mark my words."

Helen and Cate took their leave, and, as they made their way back to the hospital, Cate asked, "Why did you really bring me here today? It's because I've been screwing up, isn't it?" When Helen didn't respond immediately, Cate exhaled a sigh. "I haven't been able to focus on work lately, haven't — well, I haven't cared." She eyed Helen and, seeing no surprise at her words, guessed the truth. "You know, don't you? About how John died — what MaryLou's friend found out?"

Helen nodded before gesturing toward the common. "Let's sit for a minute under that oak tree." She shook the bottle of lemonade that had begun to sweat in her hand. "Maybe we can catch a bit of breeze." When they'd settled themselves on a bench and taken a long sip of their drinks, Helen threw her head back. "It's pleasant here. This is a nice tree. A good place to sit a spell." When a rumble of thunder sounded far away, she nodded slowly. "As usual, Zelda's right about the weather changing. 'Course a storm can clear the air. And cool things down." She turned on the bench to face

Cate. "I wanted you to meet Zelda because she was so broken once, so destroyed by what fate threw at her. She's rebuilding her life — slowly, and with a lot of help. Well, the reason for wanting you to see that is obvious. But I also wanted you to become part of her rebuilding, to see that whether or not you get up every morning and move forward matters to other people. Zelda needs your help, so you have to be strong. You're part of a community here."

"I think you're exaggerating," Cate disagreed. "If I left Amberley tomorrow —"

"You'd be missed. By your patients and your friends. If you give up and throw in the towel, it impacts others. We all send out ripples — of kindness, need, and love. We don't always appreciate who they impact or how far they travel; that's part of the mystery of life. We can't see the whole picture, but it's there regardless."

"That sounds like something my grandmother would have said. Or Father Sullivan." Cate thought then of the last journal entry she'd received. Actually, she'd been thinking of it all day on some level. Now it bubbled to the surface of her thoughts and, on impulse, she spoke of it to Helen.

Helen nodded. "I know about the ghetto's final days. I've heard the gist of that story from Miriam's own lips." Reaching out, she gave Cate's hands a squeeze. "It must have been tough for you to read it."

"It was." Cate wiped at her wet cheeks, unaware she'd begun to cry. "Who's leaving me these journal entries? You were with Miriam at the end; have you any idea who she gave them to?"

"No." Then a thought slid into Helen's mind. "You know, as much as it's tempting to see what's happening only in terms of how it affects you, that might miss the target."

"I don't understand."

"Perhaps whoever Miriam entrusted her words to is suffering under the weight of that responsibility. Perhaps he or she is looking for someone to take over safeguarding the journal entries. To do what's best with them."

Cate's voice rose. "You mean this is a compliment?"

"Maybe in a way. But that doesn't make reading about the ghetto any easier."

They sat for a time as pewter clouds gathered overhead and a rising wind brushed the trees. Finally, the nurse said, "Ripples. We all send them out. As do other people in our direction. And those ripples aren't always good, as Miriam's story illustrates. But it's interesting, isn't it, that you received that particular entry after meeting with MaryLou's friend?"

"What do you mean?"

"I'm thinking of what you learned about those armored vehicles in Iraq." When Cate stiffened, Helen gentled her voice. "If there's a lesson to be learned from what happened to Miriam, it's that good can come from what we think is evil. I see that makes you uncomfortable. It does me, too. As I'm sure it did Miriam. But in her case, it did. Don't you see, Cate? If not for that German officer's sadism in making Miriam and the others wait for death, they would have died that last day. But they didn't; they were liberated. Because of a horrible, twisted man, those eight hundred Jews survived."

"But what — ?"

"It might be the same with your husband. You can't know — may never know — but it might be. If his vehicle *did* break down, maybe the other soldiers with him were saved as a result. Don't you see? If they'd driven over that bomb, they might all have died."

Cate tried to wrap her mind around the possibility that the army's sloppy maintenance had saved lives. "No, that can't be! It can't!" Then her voice caught. "Can it?"

"I don't know," Helen said softly. "And you may never know. It may be that you will always live with uncertainty. Or with the knowledge that even if the army's actions led to John's death, it might have been —" She paused, unable to finish the sentence that stretched between them.

"Worse. It might have been worse," Cate whispered, the words arrowing their way to her heart just as the storm broke.

CHAPTER 16

Ruins from the town's original settlement were located on River Road, and the hilltop graveyard there dominated the surrounding landscape. It was a lonely, neglected place of sunken earth and leaning stone. The site was enclosed by a wrought-iron fence into which a gate was set atop a thick slab of New England granite. Shaped by use into a crude smile bearded with a thin layer of moss, the worn gray stone doubtless had a story to tell as poignant as the headstones within.

The gate squeaked when Gaby pushed it open, moving only two feet before catching on a clump of grass. "What a mess," she muttered, eyes sweeping the overgrown patch of earth. "The town can certainly do a better job of keeping this place up." To Gaby, there was nothing sadder than a graveyard reclaimed by weeds and abandoned by the living. *We are all tenants of nature,* she thought, *living on sufferance. So we build our homes with walls to shelter thought; windows to draw in the light; and, a stout door to keep out the darkness. But graveyards — what thought do the living give to them?*

One of the few in Amberley to visit the dead, Gaby did so in that quiet hour when the stars dissolved and dawn leaked over the horizon. Nature's boldest colors torched the sky before the sun crested and her breath caught in her throat, for surely such a display presaged a glorious day. Or was that yet another example of the human need to hope, to believe that miracles lay right around the corner? Often they did; she knew that, just as she knew that no miracle would keep her from returning to the earth when her time came. And it was coming.

With a sigh, she walked between the graves as pine needles crunched underfoot and the wind whispered in the trees. She read the names of the dead aloud, as though by reciting them she was bringing comfort to those long gone and all but forgotten. "Eunice McCaffery, beloved wife, died in childbirth; Phillip Thomas Riverton, cherished son, lost at sea; Margaret Ellen Wells, loving sister, stricken by scarlet fever." She imagined a stone pulled from the earth that would soon bear her name. And when nature polished it clean, who would remember her? Her eyes teared in regret for the children she never bore and the husband she might have loved. Then MaryLou's face swam into view, and Sheila's laugh floated through her thoughts. Family in all but name, their friendship had gotten her through the toughest times of her life. And it would see her to death's door; of that she was certain. She felt a pang of regret for adding to Sheila's worries, but MaryLou had been right. After Gaby told Sheila about the cancer, she'd responded predictably by making a list of the food she would cook, "To put some meat back on your bones. Then you can fight — *we* can really fight this thing. Together."

Gaby turned at the sound of footsteps to find Cate behind her. The younger woman's eyes were red-rimmed from lack of sleep. And tears. Gaby treaded lightly, for although she knew the gist of what MaryLou had discovered about the maintenance schedules, Gaby didn't know exactly how that knowledge had impacted Cate. When a cardinal fluttered in the canopy of trees overhead, Cate's shadowed eyes followed the swatch of red as it took flight. So intent was she on the bird's departure that she stumbled and would have fallen had Gaby not rushed forward to steady her. "Careful there."

"Thanks," Cate said, staring at the serpentine, gnarled roots of a huge conifer. "What a strange tree."

When she lifted her gaze, Gaby glimpsed the past through those cobalt-blue eyes, like images reflected in a mirror. She saw young Cate standing over twin graves beside an elderly woman who enfolded the girl's sobbing body in a sea of black cotton. Cate's spirit had been bruised, not broken, for with love she'd bridged the loss of her parents. And now? Would the support of friends be enough to lighten the burden of living without her husband? Inhaling deeply, Gaby filled her lungs with the tree's heady fragrance and therein found inspiration. "It's a yew," she said, gazing up at the evergreen. "Quite an old one by the looks of it."

"Yew," Cate repeated. "There are yews around the churchyard where my parents are buried."

I know, Gaby thought. "Yew trees can spring from what appear to be dead trunks, so they're associated with immortality and resurrection. That's why you find yew groves near churches and monasteries. And yews emit an alkaloid that acts as a hallucinogen.

I've often wondered how many monks experienced otherworldly visions brought on by just such a drug effect."

The change of subject had shifted Cate's focus, but only slightly. "I — I've never heard that. I didn't know — about yew trees, I mean." Then her thoughts turned inward again. "There was one near my parents' grave, but I don't remember feeling anything strange. And I went there often. I only felt —"

Guilty had been the word cut off when Cate drew a breath to steady her conscience; Gaby was sure of it. She knew well enough the strength of that emotion, but wouldn't add to the younger woman's burden by explaining how. Settling herself on a stone bench, she asked, "Do you want to talk about your family?" To her surprise, Cate nodded slightly before coming to sit beside her.

"I'm an only child," she began. "My parents died in a car accident when I was little. I was in the car and should have died, too. But at the last minute, right before the crash" — she shivered at the memory — "I bent down to pick up my doll." Her voice dropped. "If my father hadn't swerved. If I hadn't dropped the doll. If John hadn't crossed that road —" She paused to shake

263

her head. "I can't accept that life and death are determined by such random acts." She seemed about to say more, but instead released a sigh.

"Why did you come here this morning?" Gaby asked quietly. "Were you just out for an early walk?"

"No, no," Cate said, getting to her feet. She glanced around the graveyard. "I was looking for a grave. For Miriam's grave. I want to see where she's buried. Need to, I think. I learned something about her, about what happened during the war, and I wanted to see for myself that she's at peace. That sounds strange, I suppose." She shifted her feet as though she'd wandered onto uneven ground. "Anyway, I was working extra hours the past few days, trying to make up for — well, for messing up with some patients. I couldn't come until today." Her gaze moved again around the small graveyard.

"Miriam's not buried here," Gaby pointed out. "She's in the Jewish cemetery in Amherst."

"Oh." Cate looked disappointed. "Where's that? How do I —"

"I can take you," Gaby said easily. "Come on." She gestured toward the beat-up blue Ford she drove. "I've time now."

Half an hour later, they stood at Miriam Rosen's gravesite. The headstone was a simply carved piece of granite over a mound of earth covered with Irish moss. "There's moss like this on John's grave," Cate murmured, bending down to run a finger over Miriam's name and date of death. "I go there every month. I used to plant flowers, but now that I'm so far away, I can't really care for them. Moss is easier." She recited a Hail Mary before wondering aloud if it was a fitting prayer.

"I don't think Miriam would mind," Gaby said.

"I hope you're right."

"Besides, she and Mary had something in common. Both lived as oppressed minorities under occupation."

Cate gave a tight smile. "I don't think Father Sullivan would see it that way."

"Probably not," Gaby agreed, "but then he's not a writer like you. Writers are always looking for ways to daisy-chain one story to the other."

"That's true," Cate replied, spreading some wildflowers she'd gathered on the grave. Then she stood up and walked over to where Gaby stood. "Thanks for driving me here. I really wanted to pay my respects. I've been reading about the war, about —

about the killing. I never studied the Holocaust before. I think I didn't want to know too much. It's so overwhelming. Paralyzing even. I can't get my head around it."

Gaby's voice was sympathetic. "Nobody can get their head around it. Well, nobody sane. But I think reading up is a good thing given your interest in Miriam." Turning from the grave, she took a half step toward the car, her suggestion that they head back subtle. "So you've been using the library?" she asked.

"No, actually. Well, not the one in town," Cate explained, falling into step beside her. "Father Sullivan's allowed me to use the library at the rectory. He's got quite a collection there." Then she asked the question Gaby knew had been circling her thoughts.

"Pictures? Of Miriam?" Gaby paused. "I think Sheila's got an album, actually. She put it together for Miriam's eighty-fifth birthday." Noting the eager light in Cate's eyes, Gaby urged, "Ask her about it."

"I will. Thanks."

When Sheila learned of Cate's desire to see some photos of Miriam, she retrieved a large album from the attic of her home and brought it into the grocery. Covered in green velvet and bits of colored stone, it contained dozens of pictures held in place with tiny triangles of paper. There were black-and-white shots, colored Polaroids on glossy paper, and digital images. Over coffee and a plate of cookies, they sat at a corner table while Sheila walked Cate through five decades of Miriam Rosen's life. There were photos of her posing beside her McLean's designs; laughing with a heavy-set woman Sheila identified as Rosa Vitelli; holding a cocker spaniel puppy she'd found during a snowstorm; having coffee in the diner; playing cards with Beatrice; posing on the back of MaryLou's motorcycle; bent over the pastry counter at Vitelli's as she taught Sheila to make challah bread; and, reading a book in the atrium of her nursing home.

When Sheila got up to help a customer, Cate gazed at the woman in the photographs — first trim, with blond curls and arched brows over shining eyes; then heavier with short hair of tarnished gold and a contented smile born of security and comfort; and, finally, thin again with a face lined by experience. *I've heard stories about you and read your journal, seen the impact you had on your friends.* She said the words in her mind, somehow sure Miriam heard them. *I wait for your journal entries, disappointed when I don't get them and filled with something like dread when I do. I know you understand that, just as I know you understand how broken I feel. How guilty and angry. Every day I manage a step forward, I think I take half a step back. Then some days I don't seem to move at all. But I keep trying. I have to. When I see John again, he'll ask me what I did with the time I had left — the time he didn't have. You must have felt the same, must have imagined your family asking what you'd made of your life.* Pulling the latest journal entries from her pocket, Cate spread them flat on the table. *After reading these, I wanted to see your face and imagine the girl you were.* She shifted her gaze to the now-familiar handwriting.

From the day I turned seventeen, my hand was sought. My three brothers didn't consider the young men who pursued me worthy and Papa agreed. For his most precious jewel, he wanted nothing less than a kindhearted Talmudic scholar from a good family. Over glasses of sweet tea, the men who watched over me despaired of ever finding the right husband. Then they met Isaac Rosen.

Isaac was the eldest son of a well-respected scholar. Polish by birth, he was raised in England where his father taught mathematics. After the family returned to Poland, Isaac enrolled in university.

"He's learned," Pious Joseph commented favorably one evening after Isaac came to supper. "He lives in the modern world, but he's well versed in tradition."

"He's kind," my brother Benjamin put in, according the man I would love the highest compliment.

"Yes, yes," Samuel, the realist, interrupted, "but what's important is that he's a Zionist!"

"All you say is true," Papa agreed, stroking his gray beard thoughtfully. "But the most important thing is that our Miriam loves him. Did you see her eyes shining tonight? We have found a man who is worthy of her and who makes her heart sing. Isaac is a scholar who will not permit his sons to forget the past. A Zionist who sees that Palestine is our future. That is all good, but you can't support a family with prayers and dreams. Fortunately, he wants to study medicine and the world will always need doctors."

The first time Isaac came to our house, I peeked through the kitchen doorway while he spoke with my brothers. I remember wondering whether his jet-black beard was soft to the touch or scratchy like Papa's.

And his hands — what would they feel like? Beneath the suit he wore, Isaac was well muscled. Samuel had told me that. He and Isaac had worked side by side building a classroom in the basement of the synagogue. Afterward, Samuel joked that you would never know by the way Isaac Rosen swung a hammer and hoisted lumber that he was a scholar and not a carpenter.

Cate set the first journal entry aside and bent her head to the next.

Before we moved into the ghetto, I asked my brothers what we should pack. Everyday things like dishes and linens, or things that couldn't be replaced like Papa's favorite books? Samuel wanted to take practical items that would keep us alive, while Joseph filled a sack with religious texts. As important as it was to feed body and soul, Benjamin knew that memories of better times would keep our spirits up during the darkness to come. So he packed things of symbolic value — a photograph of our parents, Papa's favorite pipe, a watercolor our mother had painted.

Since the Ghetto apartment we'd been assigned would be brutally cold, Samuel

said we should bring our warmest clothing, wearing as much of it on the day of
the move as possible. We practiced layering shirts, sweaters and coats until it was
difficult to move without falling over. "Help
me," Benjamin cried, lying on the floor of
the parlor and flapping about like a fish in
an effort to coax a smile from me.

As he flailed about, scarf trailing across
his grinning mouth and booted feet
squeaking on the wooden floor, I couldn't
help but laugh. "Get up, you fool. We've
work to do."

Rolling over on his side, Benjamin pulled
a serious face and looked me up and
down. I wore three dresses, slacks, two
sweaters and an overcoat. "Miriam, I've
been meaning to tell you this for some
time, but I didn't want to hurt your feelings." He exhaled loudly. "You've grown
fat." I threw a pillow at him. "Really, really
fat." Another pillow. "Waddle like a duck
fat."

I plopped down on the floor and pum-
meled him with pillows. Tears of laughter
ran down my face for the first time in
months and I wiped them away with a
grateful hand. "Oh, Benny, you always
make me feel better. What would I do
without you?"

I did not know that within days he would be lost to me forever.

Cate sat for some time, her mind shuffling through the journal entries she'd read that day and before. Sorting through the album, she cast the different images of Miriam into the starring roles of each story in an effort to reconstruct — at least in part — the life of a woman she'd only come to know in death. When the day faded and the grocery began to empty, she shut the album with a sigh. As the now familiar face slipped back into the shadows, Cate felt an aching sense of loss but also a profound sense of gratitude for the gift of Miriam's words.

CHAPTER 17

Sheila poured espressos for herself, Cate, and Gaby. They sat in the kitchen of the grocery the following Sunday afternoon, chatting over the remains of Sheila's signature grilled eggplant lasagna. The talk was easy and light as Cate discussed the book's progress. The atmosphere changed abruptly when Sheila said, "Cate, I want to tell you about Rosa's life in Italy." She shot a glance at Gaby, who nodded imperceptibly. "Gaby thinks it will help you to know about Anthony."

Cate sat forward for there was a strange undercurrent to the conversation. *Anthony? Who was Anthony?*

"Where to start?" Sheila wondered aloud. "I told you how I came to work with Rosa. I was sixteen when she hired me — green as grass — but she soon took me in hand. Taught me everything she knew. So one day, when a very special letter came from Italy

— a letter that incapacitated Rosa — I was able to run the grocery. That letter changed Rosa's life. Changed so much." Sheila's gaze moved about the room she knew so well, and her voice fell to a whisper. "Sometimes, when I think of those days, it's as though the present shimmers and falls away. There are no stainless-steel appliances in here, just the eggshell-white ceramic that was the postwar norm. I don't hear the hum of traffic from Main Street, but the voice of Mario Lanza, for Rosa favored him above all singers. She played his albums when business was slow, not that it often was." A faraway light lit her eyes.

"You don't have to tell me, Sheila," Cate said softly. "Not if it upsets you."

"No. I want to. Or Gaby thinks I should." Sheila licked her lips as if to swallow the last of her reservations. "So. The letter. I was working hard that day, and as busy as my hands were, my mind was skipping into the future. As usual, I was making a mental list of the things I'd change about Vitelli's when it was mine. I wanted to add a few woven wicker chairs and tables in the corner by the front windows so customers could have coffee while they waited for their orders to be filled. That turned into the café. I planned to replace the creaky wooden floors with something easy to clean, like tile. Well, I used flagstone instead. I even dreamed of splurging on a beaten copper ceiling. Took a few years to afford that. Anyway, back to the letter. It came on a July morning so hot waves of heat rose from the sidewalk. I had just finished misting the outside vegetables when the mailman walked up holding a thick envelope. It was addressed to Rosa and postmarked Rome. I left the letter behind the register and began restocking shelves while Rosa sliced cheese for the McLeans' housekeeper. When I looked up a bit later, the store was empty, and Rosa was slumped over the front counter, pale as the creamy stationery in her hands. She seemed to be in a daze, and I thought that she was having a stroke. I helped her into the kitchen before running upstairs to Miriam's apartment.

"Why I didn't just call an ambulance, I can't say. Instead, I pounded on Miriam's door even though I barely knew her for she kept to herself. When she answered, I babbled out what had happened, and we hurried downstairs together. Miriam said that Rosa was just upset and that she'd stay with her while I kept the grocery open. She shooed me out of the kitchen and shut the door before I could stammer out how inexperienced I was. I remember turning around in the silent store, my eyes skipping over the aisles. I'd helped Rosa for years and knew every inch of the place. Still, by closing time I was exhausted. After I locked up, Miriam sat me in the kitchen with a steaming mug of tea. She said Rosa was upstairs resting. Then she told me that the letter had upset Rosa because it was about her son. I was stunned, for in all the years I'd known Rosa she'd never mentioned her family. I thought she was a widow with no children; everybody in town did. Well, that wasn't true. Rosa had a son named Anthony. A priest. During WWII, he helped those fleeing the Fascists. He was arrested, and Rosa thought he'd been killed. After the war, she came to America because this is where Anthony wanted one day to live. She felt that by doing so, she was fulfilling his dream."

"But he wasn't killed?" Cate guessed.

"No. He was imprisoned, but Anthony survived the war. Rosa didn't know until the letter came twenty-eight years later. I couldn't get my mind around that, but Miriam explained that after Anthony was arrested, Rosa's friends would have nothing to do with her. They feared that associating with her put them in danger, so they shunned her. When she left Italy, she told no one — there was no one to tell, no one who would care. Then, six months later, Anthony came home to find Rosa gone without a trace. He looked for her, but didn't think she would have left Italy."

"Then how —" Cate asked.

"Father Sullivan," Gaby answered. "One day, a few months before the letter came, I was in the grocery shopping. I saw Rosa staring at the calendar, tears running down her face. It was Anthony's birthday, you see. Well, Rosa told me about him, and I told Father Sullivan."

"She told *you*," Cate said to Gaby before she shifted her gaze to Sheila, "and not —"

"Not me," Sheila finished, the hurt no longer raw, but still coloring her words. "I wondered the same thing until Miriam reminded me that Gaby has a special gift of empathy, one I've benefited from more than once." Sheila reached out to lay a hand over Gaby's. "Anyway, Gaby told Father Sullivan because he had contacts within the Church. In time, he was able to locate Anthony in Rome, living not a stone's throw from Rosa's former home.

"Rosa was devastated to get the news that her son was alive. I didn't understand that at first, but Miriam opened my eyes. She explained how Rosa was convinced that a mother — a good mother — should have known her son was all right. Felt it somehow. Miriam knew better, so that afternoon while I minded the grocery she told Rosa about her own son. And that evening she told me." Sheila's voice trailed off before she found it again. "Miriam rarely spoke of her life in Europe, but that day she did. She wanted me to learn from her story and Rosa's, convinced that one day I'd be a mother. Oh, I was too young then to imagine having a family of my own. I wasn't beautiful like my sister, and boys don't like freckle-faced girls. One boy in my class used to tease that I was a girl even the tide wouldn't take out. I told Miriam that, and her voice was barely a whisper when she said that, by my age, she'd seen such horrors. That put me in my place, for what problems did I really have?"

As shadows began to gather in the corners of the kitchen, Cate learned that Miriam had married Isaac Rosen shortly after losing her father. "The couple moved to Krakow, where Isaac enrolled in medical school," Sheila explained. "They were blessed with one perfect child: a son they named after Miriam's father, Judah. When little Judah was just a toddler, Miriam went to Lodz for a visit. It was 1938, and with war imminent, she was desperate to see her brothers while travel was still possible. When she returned to Krakow, Isaac met her at the front gate of their small house. He was pale and nervous, so Miriam knew something was wrong. They sat in the garden on a small bench, and Isaac said that they'd had a visitor. Miriam looked around, but there was no one else there, and the house was quiet. Isaac told her that the visitor had first come years before and asked him to safeguard a precious jewel. While Miriam was away, the visitor returned to claim it. With tears in his eyes, Isaac said that he had surrendered the jewel. Miriam told him that he'd been right to do so, for it had never truly belonged to them. And that is how Miriam's husband told her that their son was dead. That God had taken their precious boy home." Sheila wiped tears from her eyes. "Telling that story, even so many years later, brings back the heartache I felt at the anguish in Miriam's eyes. But I understood why she wanted me to know what had happened to her. You see, both she and Rosa lost their sons during the war, each in her own way. As it turned out, Anthony survived, but Rosa lost decades with him, lost the young man he'd been.

Miriam wanted Rosa to see that not knowing what had happened to their sons didn't make them bad mothers, for how could they have known? How could Rosa have suspected her son was alive any more than Miriam could have known that hers had died?"

Cate's breath caught and she made a choking sound.

"What? What is it?" Sheila asked anxiously. "Cate! Are you all right? Cate!"

But Cate couldn't answer, for guilt had pulled her thoughts back to that horrible night in Atlantic City. Blaring music. Shots of tequila. It wasn't until the next day that she'd turned on her phone and learned the truth. Although mortally wounded, John had clung to life — calling for her, waiting to hear her voice. Even passed-out drunk, she should have felt his pain. His need. But she hadn't. As the love of her life lay dying, she'd known no more than Miriam or Rosa had.

Cate awoke to a pounding in her head that made her wince. She sat up gingerly, blinking unfocused eyes. *Still in my clothes. Why am I still in my clothes?* And then the fog that obscured her memories of the night before began to dissipate. More pounding. In answer, she raised a hand to her temples.

"Cate?" The voice was insistent. "Cate, are you there?"

Not my head pounding. The door. The door is pounding. And calling me.

She stumbled into the hallway, adjusting her clothes and pushing spiky hair from her eyes. Fumbling with the dead bolt, she jerked the front door open to find Gaby standing in a shaft of morning sunlight. Cate stepped back in surprise. "What — ?" Her voice sounded strange in her ears, and she swallowed hard before trying again. "What are you doing here?"

Gaby held up a container of coffee and a bakery bag. "Almond crescents and a latte."

"I don't feel well. Please just go away!" Cate pleaded, moving to shut the door.

Gaby softened her voice. "I don't want to intrude, but perhaps I can help." She held out the coffee like a peace offering.

Cate hesitated a beat before accepting it and making her wobbly way to the couch. Sitting down with an undignified plop, she drank the coffee in silence. Then she reached for the bag of cookies.

Gaby's normally disciplined hair was uncombed, and weariness stained the skin beneath her eyes. She took the seat next to Cate and heaved a sigh before apologizing. "I didn't sleep well for worrying. I'm so sorry about yesterday. I was convinced having Sheila tell you about Miriam's child and Rosa's son was the right thing to do. I thought knowing how those fine women faced the same guilt you carry would help, that the wound you've kept hidden would only begin to heal if exposed to the light. I was wrong." She reached out to lay a hand over Cate's, and in that movement was reflected every person Gaby had helped, every life she'd tried to mend.

Cate realized with a start something her muddled brain hadn't the day before. "You knew. About where I was when John's commander called to tell me he was dying." She rubbed at her temples as if to push aside the headache that pounded there. "How did you know?"

Gaby took a long time responding, and when she did her words were carefully chosen. "I'm not sure exactly how I knew. I've come to believe there's a sort of errant space in my mind — a gathering place for thoughts not my own. Excess emotions that swirl around people, stray flashes of pain or loss they can't contain seem to wind up there. With some people, I can untangle their emotions, sometimes see the things they keep hidden. Things they want to forget. It — it reminds me of something

Miriam told me once. About the world's being broken."

"Broken?"

"Yes. She said that long ago pieces of the Divine were scattered and lost. Only when they are gathered together again will the world be repaired."

"*Tikkun ha-olam.* That's the phrase in one of Miriam's journal entries," Cate supplied.

"Yes. That's right. Well, Miriam believed one affected *tikkun ha-olam* through prayer and good deeds. But I've come to understand the broken world in terms of all the damaged people in it. We're all broken in some way. Sometimes, I can see — I can know what people need, or think they need. Not just food, although that's a good door in and a quick way to bring comfort. Of course, there are people I can't read at all, even if they want me to. I don't know why that is. Or why this happens to me. I suppose it's a blessing. And a curse. Mostly a curse because I can't really control it. If I try to focus on someone, things may come, but they might have anyway. And I can't stop it from happening; I've tried to, with meditation and alcohol. But I can't run away from my destiny. I can close my eyes, but what I'm supposed to see is still there."

Cate felt a pang of sympathy, for it was a

burden she wouldn't welcome. "My grand-mother was Irish. She would have said you have 'the sight.' "

Gaby nodded, as though relieved to be understood. "My grandmother used that phrase, too. Some say it's an ability passed down from mother to daughter, although I don't think my mother had it. Or not that I remember. And since I don't have children —"

"It ends with you," Cate finished the thought. After a pause, she asked softly, "When did you first know about my being in Atlantic City?"

"I sensed it only recently." Then Gaby circled the conversation back to John. "If you want to talk about him, I'm here." She sat back in her chair as if to give Cate space. "And what you tell me won't go any fur-ther."

Cate studied the half-eaten cookie in her hand. When pressed, its hard outer shell gave way to the soft almond paste within. Much like her landlady. "You know, I don't mind if you tell Sheila what we talk about," she said, surprised that it was true. "Or Lulu for that matter. Like you, they're — they're friends. The only ones I've got now."

CHAPTER 18

Feeling her way through the emotional landscape of another's pain was always tricky, so Gaby took her time. She scrambled Cate eggs for breakfast. For lunch, she made grilled cheese, moving about the apartment's small kitchen noiselessly as Cate's story poured from her. The words tumbled out in such jagged pieces that Gaby fought hard to set them in a mosaic. In the end, she did. "It wasn't your fault," she said in a gentle voice. "You went to Atlantic City to comfort a friend — your best friend. She needed you."

"For a bachelorette party?" Cate cried. "It was all so meaningless!"

"It wasn't," Gaby countered. "She was nervous before the wedding, and you kept her company. That's far from meaningless."

But Cate wouldn't allow herself to be so easily comforted. "I was drunk when the army called me. Couldn't have heard my phone ringing even if I'd had it on. Couldn't hear anything but the pounding in my head." Tears fell unchecked as she revisited those fateful hours. "If I'd answered the damn phone I might have spoken with John and said — something. I might have comforted him. Told him I loved him."

Gaby watched her with trepidation, for pain enveloped her new friend like a gray mist. Not visible to most people, it was easy enough for Gaby to see. Still, as they spoke arrows of light began to pierce the darkness. Would they be enough to keep Cate from surrendering to despair? Gaby wasn't sure. "Stop torturing yourself! You put your fears for John aside when your friend needed you. It was the right thing to try and comfort her. You couldn't know what would happen any more than Miriam could have known when she left her son that she'd never see him again."

"You would have known." Cate sniffed.

Her words were like a slap, for when those Gaby had loved most were seconds from a death wrought by her own hands, she'd known nothing. But she didn't say that or indulge her guilt, for doing so wouldn't help the woman across from her. She could see that Cate had turned a corner in the time they'd spoken, one around which she might glimpse a way forward. If she had help. "This isn't about me," Gaby said simply. "It's about you and the friend you were with."

"Jenny," Cate whispered, wiping at her face. "We grew up together. She lived next door. And she was my roommate in college."

"Then she knew John."

"Yeah. We all used to hang out together."

"And after his death, did she help you to — ?"

"I haven't spoken to her since he died."

"I don't understand."

Cate met Gaby's gaze with bloodshot eyes. "I haven't spoken to any of them since then. Not Jenny. None of the friends who were there. I can't. Don't you see?"

Gaby did. She saw that from the moment Cate lost her husband, she had begun punishing herself by turning away from her friends. But without them to comfort her, how had she carved a path through the void created by John's death? It was surely as Sheila believed: There was a core of strength to the younger woman. "Tell me about John," Gaby urged.

Cate seemed about to refuse, but then the dam that had broken earlier continued to flow. "He took a job with the National

Guard because we needed the money. And the only reason we did was because I wasn't working full-time." She stabbed a finger at her chest. "I wasn't contributing the way I should have been!" She was breathing quickly, eyes flashing before her temper sputtered to a slow burn. When her voice flattened out, Gaby read a weary resignation in the tone. "I'm sorry. Sorry to dump this on you. I thought — I thought I was doing better. That I wasn't as angry as before. At myself, I mean. But every time I think I've taken a step forward, I get pulled back into grief. Into guilt. Because no matter what new life I try to build, or how much time passes, the facts don't change: If I'd been working, John wouldn't have had to take a second job."

"You *were* working; you were writing."

Cate gave a hollow laugh shot through with regret. "Writing. Pounding away on that damn computer every day. What a waste of time! The few short stories I sold never amounted to anything!"

"But surely your husband was proud of your gift, of how hard you worked." Then Gaby saw, as clearly as if she had been in the room with them, a tall man holding Cate close. He was speaking of the future he was sure awaited them. *"Someday, we'll live in an old Victorian by the sea. There'll be a swing on the front porch and a houseful of children. We'll collect driftwood and build sandcastles. And we'll be happy."* As the image faded, Gaby felt the loss of John's presence like a physical blow, for she had tapped into Cate's pain. Gaby understood then just how much John had encouraged his wife to believe in the dream that pushes every writer. He had assured Cate that her stories would survive her own death, that the characters she birthed would one day live in the minds of readers. With his death, that dream — now as fragile as gossamer — had been relegated to a quiet corner of Cate's thoughts. Gaby knew then with a calming certainty that writing was how Cate would recover her life. Recover herself.

"All those sleepless nights." Cate's tone was bitter. "All those times when I could have been with him and instead I was staring at a computer screen. Do you know how terrifying it is to sit in front of a blank screen? It's almost as horrible as staring at one filled with words and not knowing if they're brilliant or crap! You would think you'd know when you wrote something good, that you'd see with utter clarity you'd succeeded, but you don't. The more you write, the more unsure you become. But

John" — her voice broke — "John never let me give up. When my mind strayed into self-doubt, he pulled me back. Knowing I'll never hear his voice again, see myself reflected in his eyes, I feel only partly alive."

"It sounds like you had a wonderful marriage," Gaby murmured, a hint of longing in her voice. "And although I didn't know him, I'd wager your husband is still proud of you."

Cate was unbending. "Proud of me? I lost our beautiful home! And I empty bedpans for a living!"

The derision in her voice tempted Gaby to snap that caring for the sick was the most honorable work one could do. Instead, she read the outburst for what it was: born of pain, guilt, and loss. "I can only imagine how much you miss John."

Something in Gaby's quiet strength calmed Cate. She picked up a mug of tea that had long since gone cold and took a sip. "He was a carpenter, you know. Well, more than a carpenter: He was a cabinet-maker."

"So an artist, like you."

"Yes. He could build anything." She stopped, her face flushed with shame. "When I think of all the times he tried to tell me about a piece he was working on.

I'd listen and encourage him, but if I was working on a story, I was too distracted to really understand. I thought at the time I was being supportive, but I know now I wasn't. Not really. What I'd give —" She didn't finish the thought; she didn't have to.

Gaby reached out to give Cate's arm an avuncular pat. "He sounds like an incredible man."

"He was."

When Cate's breath caught, Gaby read doubt in the silence that followed. "You'll see him again. You know that."

"Do I?" Cate asked in a weary voice. "After my parents died, I was so certain they were waiting for me. I even convinced myself I could feel them watching over me."

Gaby hesitated, finding irony in the fact that it fell to her to reassure Cate that John's death wasn't the end of their love. Yet perhaps that was why she had been spared all those years before and lived as long as she had. "When my parents passed," Gaby said, "I prayed for them as I'd been taught. Mostly I prayed that I would live a good life, one that would earn me the right to see my loved ones again. You see" — she took Cate's cold hands in hers — "I wanted to be worthy of their love." Gaby shrugged slightly as if to suggest that she might not have succeeded.

"You are worthy! You'll see them," Cate said quickly before adding, as Gaby hoped she would, "just as I'll see John." Reaching for a tissue, Cate found a weak smile. "I haven't cried this much in a long time."

Gaby accepted Cate's change of subject with the instinct of one who had spent decades helping others find their way. "Oh, don't give it a second thought. We all cry now and again. You know what you need?" she asked, pushing to her feet. "Some fresh air. 'A change of scene and society,' as Jane Austen would say. I have a delivery I need taken out to a friend. It would really help if you could do it for me."

"Oh, well," Cate fumbled, "I'm not really up to —"

"She's a veterinarian," Gaby continued. "Her name's Leah Mitchell; she's Sheila's sister."

"I didn't know —"

Gaby anticipated her. "Leah works long hours. She doesn't get into town much. And she doesn't eat right half the time. Her clinic's out on River Road. Just follow Main Street to the end, and you can't miss the turnoff. My car's parked out front; the keys are in the glove compartment." When Cate drew breath to protest, Gaby rushed on,

"Before you go, why don't you take a few minutes to pull yourself together? I'll just clean up these dishes." Without waiting for a response, Gaby turned toward the sink, troubled that she might have pushed too much. Only when she heard Cate make her way to the bathroom did she reach for the phone.

Cate drove out of town past fields of swaying cornstalks before spotting a sign for the Amberley Veterinary Clinic. She turned onto an unpaved track and came to a stop beside a barn with peeling paint and a patched roof. Parking in a gravel lot, she saw a striking redhead clad in denim overalls stride out of the barn. She was leading a black horse toward a fenced paddock. "Good afternoon!" Cate called out.

The woman waved in answer before passing the horse off to a teenage girl who ran up to take the reins. "Can I help you? I'm the vet here. Leah Mitchell," the redhead said to Cate, pushing horn-rimmed glasses up her nose. Blessed with near perfect skin, the doctor had arresting green eyes and the athletic build of a dancer. When Cate introduced herself, Leah said, "Oh, you're living above the grocery!"

"And you're Sheila's sister."

293

"That I am. Sorry we haven't met before this." When the horse whinnied, she turned to watch it paw the ground. "She's a Morgan. A bit quick at the trot, but skilled at cutting."

Cate laughed. "I have no idea what any of that means, but it sounds impressive." After she confessed that the closest she had been to a horse was watching the mounted police parade through Boston, Leah led her over to pet the mare. Cate laughed when the horse nuzzled the bag under her arm.

"She thinks you've got a carrot in there. Better yet, an apple."

"I don't know. It's for you from Gaby," Cate said, peeking inside the bag. Sure enough, there was a Granny Smith apple inside. "Now what are the chances?" she murmured before catching Leah's eye. "This is all a setup, isn't it?"

As skilled as Dr. Mitchell was at earning the trust of her animals and coaxing smiles from the children who brought their pets in for treatment, she was a lousy liar. "Gaby did let me know you'd be stopping by. And she mentioned the book you're writing. She probably thought you'd be interested in the animals here." She swept an arm to indicate the property. "I run a shelter of sorts."

"Of sorts?"

"Western Massachusetts doesn't have a proper animal shelter. Well, not a no-kill one." She grimaced, but didn't explain further. "Since I'm the only vet in town, I get a lot of drop-offs — stray dogs, feral kittens, wounded horses." Her eyes traveled over the property. "Somehow, we find room for them all until they can be placed in forever homes. I also rehabilitate animals sent back from war zones. Iraq and Afghanistan. Other places, too. Once the physical problems are taken care of, they have to learn how to behave in family settings." She pointed to a large German shepherd across the yard. The dog was cowering in fear from a young man who was kneeling beside him. "Animals can learn to trust humans again. With help. You could write about that in your book — about how these animals are victims of war just as the soldiers who cared for them." She glanced at her watch before adding, "Why not stay and lend a hand if you've the time? It's the merciful hour, after all."

Cate's heart skipped a beat, for the phrase was one she hadn't heard in a long time. She recalled her grandmother's saying that God's mercy was greatest at three o'clock — the hour Christ died. "The merciful hour," she repeated softly, tempted to point out that as she felt as abandoned and needy as the animals, she was in no position to help. Then she met the veterinarian's pleading eyes and relented.

Over the next few hours, Cate learned to tack a horse and muck out stables. She was feeling rather proud of herself until she tried to clip the claws of an uncooperative Siamese who squirmed in protest at the indignity of the process. The cat only relaxed when Leah approached, for in the doctor's presence her patients purred, drooled, cooed, neighed, and generally flashed the equivalent of a smile. Picking up the cat, Leah turned it toward the wall where the sun cast shifting patterns of light. Momentarily diverted, the animal forgot its anxiety, and Cate quickly finished her work. "You've got such a way with animals," she observed.

Leah shrugged. "I've always felt more comfortable around them than people."

Cate laughed. "I can relate." Then she grew serious. "You know, I work with so many elderly who view the time remaining them as a burden, whereas these animals seem to see a future filled with possibility. As if all of life is a game. A chance to play."

"That's true," Leah conceded. "Now if only the government didn't make it so tough to bring healthy animals here!" At

Cate's raised eyebrow, she explained. "I'm trying to get two dogs flown out of Kuwait. The soldiers who cared for them are coming home and want to bring their comrades — for that's what those pups have been." Leah pushed a mass of red curls from her face impatiently. "It's so frustrating! We know how much having animals can help soldiers readjust to civilian life. I've seen it time and again."

"I'm sure you have, and that you're right. How did you get involved in all of this, anyway?"

"A veteran in town. He wanted to help a friend and reached out since I was the only vet he knew. I hadn't a clue what to do, but one thing led to another. Because I've the room here, I started taking in and retraining some of the returning dogs. And housing animals for families sent to overseas posts who couldn't afford to take their pets. The military will pay to move a family, but not its animals." She shook her head ruefully. "Damn government agencies. I'd rather shovel manure than deal with them!"

"But you do it."

"Yes. For the animals I do it."

Cate made her way to Leah's many times. One evening, as dusk claimed the sky in a sweep of shocking pink and mauve, she found herself bent over a sink scrubbing puppy vomit from her hands. An unexpected grin split her face at the realization that she had spent her day off up to her elbows in the same bodily fluids that were her bread and butter at the hospital. Before she left, she sought out the veterinarian. "Thanks, Leah. Volunteering here is exactly what I needed."

The older woman nodded in understanding, for she knew about John. "You have to learn to trust again. In life. In yourself. I've seen even the most broken animals recover. It takes courage. But I think you know that, Cate. Just as you know it takes time to make a new life — that's true no matter what your species. So don't rush your fences. But do think about including these animals in your book." Her passion was infectious, and Cate said as much. "Without passion — for the people and work we love — life would be pretty colorless, wouldn't it?" Leah asked. "We all need something to strive for. A dream to stretch our eyes."

"I let so many dreams die with my husband," Cate said. "With him by my side, the future was brightly lit. Without him, my focus for so long was just on surviving from one day to the next."

"And now? What do you want? What do you dream about?"

"I'm still working that out."

That night, Cate began to compile a list she entitled WHAT I WANT. First, she wrote: FINANCIAL SECURITY. Well, she was working toward that. She'd even managed to save a few hundred dollars. FRIENDS she added next, thinking of the three women who'd come to brunch, and of Beatrice, Leah, and Helen. Then she wrote: TO GET BACK IN SHAPE. She ran a hand over her belly for it wasn't as flat as it had been. *I'm such a coward. Why can't I admit to the one thing I want above everything else? Well, John back of course. But I can never have that. No, the thing I can have, the thing I deny myself every day.* FORGIVENESS. But then she'd taken a giant step down that path the day she'd come to Amberley. And every day after that had been another step forward as she found her footing — more or less. Working with animals had helped, for amid the neighing, barking, and purring, a calming peace had entered her thoughts on stocking feet. In time, it would nudge her spirit forward, smoothing the hard edges of her mind. She felt as though she were crossing a threshold, one from which she could look back on the good life she and John had shared. *I made him happy. Made him laugh. And I didn't hold him back — with tears or pleas— when he heeded that siren song that lures men to war. I wish I had. I'm proud I didn't. How screwed up is that?* That she would never find an answer to that question, or consign the argument raging in her conscience to the back of her mind, was part of the new normal. Admitting that pointed up a barren corner of her life she was now ready to fill.

Picking up her phone, she punched in Boston's 617 area code, her heart thudding. Would the call be welcomed or refused? Did she have the courage to find out? Swallowing her fears, she dialed the number. Her oldest and dearest friend, Jenny, picked up on the third ring. When Jenny heard the familiar voice, she cried, "Caty? Caty? Oh, thank God you called!"

CHAPTER 19

A few days later, Cate received a letter from Jenny. She stared at the envelope for a long time, for the handwriting was so achingly familiar it made her breath catch. Steeling herself to accept whatever came, she slipped a fingernail under the flap and gently ripped the blue stationary. A single sheet of notepaper was inside. As she pulled it out, a snapshot fell in her lap. The photographer had caught the infant gurgling a smile and kicking her pudgy legs in the air. Dressed all in pink, the baby girl wore a T-shirt embroidered with her name: Catherine. Cate swallowed a sudden lump in her throat and read the letter through a film of tears. Jenny wrote of how happy she was that Cate had phoned. She sent regards from her husband and a few mutual friends. Then she dropped the bombshell she hadn't wanted to on the telephone: Her firstborn had been named after her childhood friend.

I should have known, should have been at the christening. I should have — but it's not too late to be part of little Catherine's life. To make her part of mine.

As one day melted into the next, Cate acclimated to life in Amberley. Her work on the novel was progressing slowly since she could only work on it in the evenings, but ideas for how to present the underlying themes continued to take shape in her mind. As for caregiving, she still found the work demeaning, frustrating, and emotionally draining. But as trite as it sounded, at the end of the day she often felt she'd made a difference. Providing her patients with simple comforts — clean hair, laundered sheets, or hot food — was satisfying in a way she couldn't put into words, even to herself. And the payoff was so immediate, not like writing where one might invest years in a project only to discover that the time had been wasted. And not like office work, where the difference between a shoddy job and one well done was measured in profit margins. The work of a home care aide might be humbling, but it was also fulfilling, for Cate helped lessen the pain and discomfort her patients felt. She did for them what she hadn't been able to do for

John, and that beat making money or running after a publishing dream. Most days.

What got her through the rough patches weren't the times when she'd been no more than a pair of hands and a strong back. No, it was finding ways to tend her patients' spirits as well as their bodies. That might not be her job, but she considered it an essential part of their healing. Wondering what drove her to do more than many other aides, Cate questioned if she was so eager to help ease the mental strain of her patients' battles because she hadn't faced the end of John's life with him. Or was it simpler than that; was she doing for her patients what she hoped would one day be done for her? Helen believed it was the latter. She'd pointed out that since Cate loved songbirds, it had naturally occurred to her to place a baby monitor beside a pile of sunflower seeds outside the window of a bedridden patient known for bird-watching. A stroke had robbed the old man of his speech, but his eyes had lit when she'd switched on the receiver and he'd heard the coo of a mourning dove.

That same look of surprised gratitude had illuminated the face of an end-stage cancer patient when Cate had suggested to the woman's six-year-old daughter that she make a memory garden. The wide-eyed girl had listened intently as Cate had explained that it would bring her mother as much comfort as the pill bottles that lined her bedside table. "Memree gar in?" the girl had repeated with a baby lisp. "What 'dat?"

"A memory garden," Cate had explained, "is for flowers you remember your mommy loving. Now you'll have to think hard: Does she like pink flowers or white? Purple or yellow? We'll have to collect just the right ones and plant them outside her window. It will be hard work, and you'll have to water the flowers. Can you do that?" The girl had nodded solemnly before skipping outside to plan where the garden would be planted.

"Thank you," had come a relieved whisper from the bed. "She needs to be in the sunshine. And have something to do. A garden," the woman had mused. "I'd like my ashes buried in a garden. But then you've thought of that, haven't you?" Cate had, but still the tears came.

News of the memory garden spread rapidly, and more than one person stopped Cate on the street to tell her what a good idea it was. Wives who'd buried husbands, children who'd lost grandparents, even those mourning pets took to the idea, adapting it to their needs and making it their own. Marveling at the ripples sent out by such a simple concept, Cate stood on the sidewalk outside Vitelli's one June evening as the sun set into velvet softness. She was waiting for her boss.

Helen Doyle had just turned eight when her father's bomber was shot down over Vietnam. After he was reported MIA, Helen's mother, Charlotte, had miscarried twin boys and fallen into a severe depression. For years she'd drifted in a twilight state between consciousness and sleep, reality and dreams. That Charlotte preferred the company of the dead to the pain of living without them had been clear to her daughter. Growing up in the shadow of ghosts, Helen would often cry for attention. Emboldened by the yawning silence, she'd scream. It made no difference; emotion bounced off Charlotte like rain on a windowpane, streaking the surface of her grief for only a moment. Helen's best friend, Sheila, had supported her when the enormity of Charlotte's indifference cut too deep. But Sheila wasn't alone.

As Charlotte retreated from life, neighbors, friends, and hired help had looked after Helen. From the women of Amberley, Helen had learned how to do laundry, cook simple meals, and handle the social workers who visited monthly, notebooks in hand. With the help of live-in caregivers, she'd ensured her mother ate, bathed, and took her medication. The responsibilities thrust upon such young shoulders had weighed heavily, yet Helen never considered institutionalizing her mother, for despite Helen's frustration, anger, and resentment, in a corner of her mind lived the hope that one day Charlotte could come back to the living. Although assaulted daily and starved, year after year, into submission, somehow that hope had survived.

The story of how Charlotte eventually fought her way to the light was one Helen didn't share easily. Yet when she learned about the book Cate was writing, she'd begun to open up. Little by little, she'd shared her story, promising that evening to tell the rest of the tale.

Cate looked up at the sound of her name. Hurrying down the sidewalk, Helen apologized for being late. "A patient needed help, and I just couldn't get away." Then she nodded approvingly at Cate. "I heard about the memory garden idea. It's brilliant."

"Oh. Thanks."

Helen inclined her head toward Vitelli's. "Let's chat over coffee. And if one of Sheila's pastries finds its way onto my plate, I won't complain."

Cate smiled before sharing, "She was just filling some cannolis. And she made her legendary seven-layer chocolate cake this afternoon. I've heard she doesn't do that often. I could let you know when she does. If you're interested."

Helen gave a quick laugh. "You almost sounded like MaryLou there. Enticing words, but with a hint of something naughty beneath. As if you'll let me in on a secret, provided I do — what?"

"Nothing!" Cate protested. "Really. I was just making conversation."

"Yes, but you were doing it Amberley style," Helen observed sagely. "And you didn't even know it."

Over cannoli and hazelnut coffee, Cate studied her boss with the eyes of a writer. Helen's auburn hair was streaked with gray and pulled back with a headband. Her unpainted nails were cut short, and her lined face had a glow Cate's grandmother would have attributed to "clean living and straight shooting." And the way Helen ate —

"What?" Helen wiped a napkin across her lips. "What are you looking at?"

"Oh. Just —" Taken aback, Cate gestured toward Helen's plate. "You cut your cannoli. Into neat little pieces. Most people don't."

"Made a study of this, have you?" the nurse asked between bites.

"Not as such. But I can't help noticing things. Writers do that." Cate leaned forward. "MaryLou, for instance, can down a cannoli in four bites. She takes off the two ends first, then attacks the middle. No neat cuts for her. Sheila always seems to be analyzing her food, so she's a slow eater. Gaby rarely sits still and is usually jumping up halfway through."

"And you?"

Cate glanced down at her empty plate. "As you can see, nothing interrupts my eating a cannoli. I plough right through uninterrupted, saving the second end for last. That way, I finish with those bits of pistachio." She paused to lick her fingers. "And you can dispense with napkins when eating pastries. That's a rule of mine."

"You've given this far too much thought."

"I give everything far too much thought. Another rule. Or fault." Cate pushed her plate away. Her tone sobered as she pulled a paper from her handbag. "This is a journal entry of Miriam Rosen's. About your mother. It was only after you agreed to speak with me that I received it." At Helen's raised eyebrow, Cate added, "Yeah. I know. It's weird, huh?"

"I knew you'd been getting these, but not that Miriam had written about Mama," Helen said, leaning forward. "What does it say?"

"Perhaps you should read for yourself," Cate suggested, holding out the journal entry. Helen accepted it with a nod and bent her head to the paper.

"Unclouded memory is both a blessing and a burden, for to remember what was, and know that it can never be again, is the sweetest pain." My dear friend Charlotte used to say that, but then she spoke with the authority of a woman who'd sent two babies to the wilderness of Limbo after losing her husband to the jungles of Vietnam. Those precious boys breathed their last before being baptized. A river of Charlotte's tears didn't persuade Father Sullivan to bury their tiny bodies in the graveyard behind St. Joseph's for canon law forbade it.

Charlotte gave birth to stillborn twins after learning of Robert's disappearance. Rather than accept the death of her husband and sons, she retreated into the past, folding within herself like a flower faded

309

from its summer glory. She didn't speak or acknowledge the world around her, for to do so was to admit Robert and the boys were gone. So she lived in her memories, for they were dressed in comforting shades, smelled of familiar things. But there was a price to pay, for when Charlotte listened to the past, she didn't hear her daughter's voice. And she lost her own. I wanted to help her find her way back to the living. In time, I did.

Helen refolded the journal entry and passed it back to Cate. "Miriam did help; that's true."

"Can you — would you tell me how?"

"So you can include the story in this book you're writing?"

"If you agree, yes."

Helen considered. Then her gaze found the journal entry again. "I think watching Mama struggle to accept death reminded Miriam of her own loss. I was too young to understand at the time, but when Miriam's thoughts circled back to Poland it was as though she feared shadows of the past could escape the prison of her mind. That they'd stain the present. Maybe sometimes they did. Still, she tried to find ways her pain could help others. Just as I have through my nursing and you can through your writing. Maybe your book will encourage women to tell their stories. Convince them those stories are worth listening to. How can I refuse to help with that?"

By the time they'd worked their way through double espressos, Helen and Cate had reached a new understanding. Both caregivers by profession, each woman recognized that the other's character had been molded by terrible loss. Cate had been orphaned young, and Helen had grown to maturity with only a shadow of her mother. Her father had been a career soldier for years before his death, and her memories of his months home on leave were sketchy at best. It was as Helen was articulating just how much the two of them had in common that the front door of the grocery swung open to admit a tall man dressed in scuffed jeans and a torn T-shirt. His tanned face was shadowed with stubble, and his eyes had a wild, unfocused look. The corded muscles of his forearms were those of a manual laborer, yet he moved with a grace and deliberation that belied his working-class appearance. Beneath the haggard face, the features were as finely drawn as an aristocrat's.

"Who is that?" Cate whispered, for the

newcomer held Helen's interest as well as her own.

"Vincent. I heard he just got home. God, he looks awful."

Cate returned her gaze to the town's most popular doctor with surprise. He'd moved to stand before a display of olive oil and was running a hand back and forth through his unruly black hair as he gazed at the bottles and cans that lined three shelves. "Jesus. Why the hell is all this here?" He asked the question of no one in particular, and Cate looked around with relief to see that the grocery was empty of other customers.

"Vincent," Sheila said in a level voice, hurrying to his side. "Why don't you come in the back? I'll make some coffee."

Her husband turned angry eyes in her direction and repeated his question. "Why the hell is all this here?" His gaze flicked to the olive oil and then back to her anxious face. "So much of the world goes hungry, and you stock shelf after shelf of stuff to make Americans even fatter than they already are?" Before she could respond, he swept out a hand to knock the middle shelf's contents to the floor. Bottles smashed and metal cans bounced down the narrow aisle. "What a waste! What a fucking waste!"

"Vincent." Sheila's voice was pleading, fearful. "You're not yourself. Please come with me!" She grabbed his arm, but he shrugged her off and lurched toward the door.

"Leave me alone! You don't understand! You can't understand!" Before yanking the door open, he spared a backward glance, and Cate thought she saw regret claim his face for a moment. When the door shut behind him, she and Helen were on their feet.

"You!" Helen called to the cashier who stood staring at her boss as though thunderstruck. "Bring a mop over here and get this cleaned up. Move it!" The girl hopped to, conditioned after months of working with Sheila to respond to a strong woman's voice. Helen shot Cate a questioning look, and they both nodded in unison before guiding Sheila toward the kitchen. They seated her at the marble work area where she proceeded to wring her hands.

"I don't know what to do; I don't know what to do," Sheila cried, wiping tears from her cheeks. "He's not himself. I don't know what to do." Cate retrieved a bottle of liquor from the cupboard where she knew Sheila kept a supply, and Helen found some chocolate. Prodded by her friends, Sheila ac-

cepted a glass of grappa and downed the
contents. She coughed as the fiery liquid
burned her throat. Then she started on the
proffered truffles, all the while debating
aloud whether she should go after Vincent
or give him space. Half an hour later, she
pulled out a tissue and blew her nose.
"Thanks. That hit the spot." Getting to her
feet, she wiped crumbs from the black leg-
gings she habitually wore and drew a calming breath. "I have to find him. Have to —"

"Already done," Helen announced, pushing her phone back in her pocket. "Mary-
Lou texted that she saw him wandering
along River Road, and gave him a ride back
on that horrible motorcycle of hers. He's at
the diner, well, in Gaby's office. Lying down
on her couch."

Sheila's shoulders relaxed with a sigh.
"Yeah. He's run off his feet. He hasn't been
sleeping. It's the dreams, you see. Nightmares more like. He doesn't want to close
his eyes. Of course, he won't take sleeping
pills. Or even a cordial to relax." She threw
a sad smile in Cate's direction. "My husband doesn't imbibe. Can you imagine? An
Italian who won't even drink wine. Shocking."

When Helen suggested that Sheila head
home, she bristled. "Home? It's two hours

until closing." Squaring her shoulders, she stalked from the room, head thrown back.

"What a stubborn woman," Helen muttered. "She needs to —"

"She needs to work," Cate supplied. "That's what keeps Sheila going."

Helen started, for she knew that well enough. And so, apparently, did Cate. "You *are* becoming a woman of Amberley," Helen observed, nodding with approval. "Look, we didn't finish talking about Mama. Let's get together on Sunday. We're both off that day."

"Great."

Walking back through the grocery, they stood watching Sheila. In classic fashion, she was feverishly running to and fro, serving customers and filling orders. She was in her element and would accept no more help that night, so they made their way out into the balmy air. The minds of both women had circled back to Vincent's behavior, and after a moment they spoke of it.

"He may have changed, but at least he's home," Helen said.

"And the anger won't be permanent," Cate pointed out, turning toward the side entrance that led up to her apartment. After a step, she turned back. "You know, in time, he'll find his way back to the man he was.

315

The man Sheila loves. Or most of the way back. But you're right; at least he's come home. At least he's alive." With those words, each remembered her own loss and the wounds that would never fully heal.

CHAPTER 20

As she crossed Main Street toward the diner the next day, Cate looked up to see Mary-Lou bearing down on her. Their meetings had been awkward and brief since that fateful conversation about John.

"So," MaryLou said by way of greeting, "are you still pissed at me?"

They stood inches apart, but separated by so much pain. After a moment, something shifted in the air, and Cate felt the last vestiges of her anger begin to ebb away. Or had that happened long before and she'd only just allowed herself to admit it? Truth was, in finding out about John, MaryLou had done nothing more than what Cate had asked. So why shoot the messenger? And how could she reject the hand of friendship, even a rough-textured one like MaryLou's?

"I'm not mad at you. At myself, yes, but not you. I asked for your help and you gave it. How can I resent that? And although you're as relentless as a pit bull, beneath the prickly exterior is a caring person."

MaryLou shivered. "Don't let that get around." Then she nodded as though a page had been turned. "I've got to eat something. Come on." She motioned Cate inside the diner and settled into a booth. "It's been a hell of a day," MaryLou said before looking up at the specials board. A hand flew to the back of her neck, and she grimaced.

"Are you in pain?" Cate asked, leaning forward. "Do you need — ?"

"A drink." MaryLou cut her off. "I need a drink. Not that this joint has a liquor license."

"And we never will," Gaby supplied, gliding up to the booth with the fluid ease that Cate concluded all great waitresses possess. Gaby looked across the room toward one of her employees, who nodded before hoisting a tray of food on her shoulder.

MaryLou followed Gaby's gaze. "Hang on. We haven't ordered yet."

"I know what you want," Gaby replied, not shifting her gaze from the other waitress who was weaving her way across the room.

"Just how the hell do you know what I want?" MaryLou snapped.

"Even if you're feeling bad, that's no excuse for taking your foul mood out on

Gaby," Cate cut in. When the mechanic glared, Cate added, "Or me."

"First of all," MaryLou barked, tapping a blood-red fingernail on the tabletop, "kudos for jumping in and defending Gaby. Second of all, butt out. She doesn't need your help, and you don't know what you're talking about." Shifting her eyes back to her friend, she repeated, "We haven't ordered yet."

"Fine," Gaby exhaled, raising her shoulders and releasing them in a flourish. She turned to Cate. "What would you like?"

"Whatever you recommend."

"Oh, she's hopeless," MaryLou cried. "Spineless and hopeless. Ask me!"

"MaryLou, dear, what would you like?" Gaby asked with exaggerated politeness.

MaryLou squinted at the specials board before deciding. "Muddy. And a First Lady." She sat back smugly, arms crossed in front of her.

Gaby didn't miss a beat. She beckoned the waitress closer and reached for a cream-colored plate heaped with steaming food. "Feta cheese and spinach quiche, new potatoes with dill sauce, and corn chutney," she announced, passing Cate her lunch. "You'll get a pot of tea with that, of course. Now let's see what we've got for the grease monkey." She fixed MaryLou with a penetrating look and paused for dramatic effect before slipping a mug and a platter onto the table. "Black coffee and the barbecued ribs special," Gaby said. "Just like you ordered." Seeing Cate's eyes widen, Gaby explained. "Black coffee is 'muddy' and ribs, well, we take our Bible seriously here. We call those a First Lady."

After Gaby walked off with a smug swing of her hips, Cate wondered aloud, "How did she know?"

"She always knows," MaryLou replied matter-of-factly, already digging into her meal. "Damn annoying."

"So if she always knows, why do you — ?"

"Go through the charade?" MaryLou finished the thought. "Tradition. Because it's fun." She held up a rib to make her point, "And there's always a chance I'll catch her up. One can hope."

"Live in hope, die in despair," Cate supplied with a shrug. "My grandmother used to say that when she was in a melancholy mood."

MaryLou licked her fingers and chuckled. "I think I would have liked her."

Cate grinned. "I think you would have liked her, too."

"Liked who?"

They looked up to see Sheila standing

beside them, her normally calm expression tense. Cate scooted over to make room for her to sit. "We were talking about my grandmother," Cate explained. "She had a dark side I think MaryLou would have appreciated."

"Oh," Sheila muttered before her eyes lit on a stylishly dressed woman across the room. "Is that Shelly Lamont? I should talk to her about a catering order." She placed her palms on the tabletop and swung her legs out of the booth in one fluid movement.

MaryLou rolled her eyes. "Can't you sit for a minute without thinking about work?" Dipping a rib into barbeque sauce, she asked, "You're still worried about Vincent, aren't you? I realize he's different since coming home, but at least he's safe now."

Cate glanced up sharply. That morning, she'd asked Sheila about her husband, and the brief answer had convinced Cate not to raise the painful subject again.

"He's home, but he's not," Sheila said in a flat voice. "I mean, his body's here, but not his mind. At least not all the time. He's depressed. And short-tempered. With me most of all."

"His body's here, but not his mind," MaryLou repeated, eyes twinkling. "That body would be enough for me. Enough for most women."

Sheila's cheeks flushed and her eyes narrowed. Then her jaw relaxed a bit, and she blew out a sigh. "That's not funny."

MaryLou pushed her empty plate away. "I wasn't trying to be funny, just to nettle you. And it worked. All Vincent needs is time. That and some home cooking. And sex. Lots of sex." Patting at the lipstick that looked flawless despite the gusto with which she ate, she added in a serious tone, "Speaking of which, you know I would never go after him, don't you?"

Sheila lifted her chin in challenge. "As if he'd look at you."

"Oh, he'd look, honey. He'd look."

Cate slapped the table. "Enough, you two. Can I please eat in peace?" she asked, indicating her full plate.

"You haven't even touched your food!" MaryLou scolded, reaching out a hand that Sheila promptly slapped away.

"Leave her be! You've had your lunch!"

And so the meal passed with MaryLou trying to sneak food from Cate's plate and Sheila beginning to relax into the familiar teasing routine of her friendship with the larger-than-life mechanic. Steering the conversation toward Cate's writing, MaryLou said, "I hadn't thought of it until now, but if this book takes off, it could help the town." She paused. "You *are* using Amberley as the setting, right?"

Cate explained that, although fictionalized, the stories she would tell were based on the lives of Amberley's residents. "So the town's something of a character in the book."

MaryLou nodded. "That's what I thought. Just think of how many people will flock here after reading about it."

"I already get more than enough tourists," Sheila protested.

"Send the overflow my way," MaryLou said, stretching her arms over her head and arching her back like a cat. "I'll convince them to get an oil change from the famous MaryLou. Hang on," she asked, her voice edged with doubt. "I *will* be in the book, right?"

"No. Why would you want to be?"

MaryLou shrugged. "Why not? It's like taking part in an oral history project, or being on a reality show. I've got nothing to hide. Yeah" — she nodded vigorously and addressed herself to Sheila — "send the tourists my way. I can always use the business."

Gaby joined them and picked up the narrative. "Me too. Then we'll send them on to

Father Sullivan. St. Joseph's isn't getting the traffic it used to, so the bishop's threatening to close it."

"Really?" Cate asked, taken aback. A wave of concern washed over her, and something shifted inside. It was a subtle change — a rebalancing of spirit. Increasingly convinced that the peace of mind she'd found in the past few months was due in no small part to the town's working its magic, she took to heart anything that threatened the Amberley she'd come to know. Or threatened her new friends. Her gaze moved over the faces of the three women who were so different in temperament and inclination, they could fight like alley cats one minute and chat contentedly the next. She'd seen them close ranks, cross swords, and finish each other's sentences. That they had welcomed her so easily into their lives still surprised her. And sometimes brought tears to her eyes.

When her phone rang, Sheila took the call with a nod of farewell and headed toward the door. Gaby waved to a customer that she was coming, before observing, "Sheila's much calmer than when she came in."

"Yeah. We did good," MaryLou agreed.

"There are two types of good," Cate said, thinking again of her grandmother. "No good and good for nothing."

"I've been both in my time," MaryLou confessed. "Still, we earned dessert. We can go to Vitelli's for it, or —" She had just begun to study the specials board when movement across the room drew her attention. Her face fell. "Shit."

"What?" Cate asked, turning around to scan the crowd. "What's wrong?"

"I saw somebody outside I have to talk to." MaryLou's voice was toneless. Pulling a few bills from her pocket, she tossed them on the table without looking and pushed to her feet. "See ya, kid."

"Right. Okay. Bye," Cate said before her eyes lit on Benjamin Franklin's face.

MaryLou felt the vein on her forehead begin to throb even before she pushed open the door and strode outside. Grateful for the blazing sun, she slipped on the sunglasses she'd hooked to the front of her shirt. It was childish to believe that because her eyes were hidden, her unease would be, too. Why *did* the sight of him make her so hopping mad? It had been two years since the divorce — two years! What was the statute of limitations on anger, anyway? *But it's not anger,* a voice whispered in the shadowed recesses of her mind. *He still gets to you; even after everything the bastard's done, he still gets to you.* "What do you want, Harry?" she demanded, hands on hips and chin thrust out in defiance.

"Now don't take a swing at me again!"

MaryLou felt her teeth clench at the sound of that gravelly voice she'd once thought so sexy. "That only happened once. And I was drunk at the time."

"Still —" He rubbed the stubble on his chin as though he could still feel her knuckles connect.

"You're such a drama queen!" She turned away and threw over her shoulder, "I've got to get back to work."

He grabbed her arm roughly just as the front door of the diner opened. "Wait! We have to talk about the alimony!"

"Get your hands off her!" Raising her handbag over her head, Cate brought it down in one deft motion. Shaking with fury, she sputtered. "I — I won't let you bully her!"

Letting go of MaryLou, the man Cate had assaulted spun on her and cried, "Who the hell are you?" He shifted pain-filled eyes from MaryLou's surprised face to Cate's livid one. "You're as crazy as she is!" Cradling one arm in the other, he beat a hasty retreat.

The tension MaryLou had felt earlier was

released with a whopping belly laugh. "Nice move!"

Cate stared at the leather bag clenched in her whitened fingers. "I — I forgot I've got a flashlight in here. Do you think I really hurt him? Oh my God!"

"Oh no." MaryLou waved a hand in eloquent dismissal. "I'm sure you didn't. Unfortunately. So earlier you defended Gaby from me and now me from Harry. Why did you, by the way? I'm not usually cast as the damsel in distress."

Cate looked uncomfortable. "When I saw him grab you, I just did — just did —"

"What came naturally," MaryLou supplied.

"Yes." Cate exhaled. "I hate bullies."

"Yeah. Me too. Actually my ex is a lot of things, but that's not one of them."

"Your ex?"

"One of them. And the love of my life." MaryLou's voice was edged with regret. "Or at least I thought so when I stole for him. Prison was an eye-opener, though." She jerked her head toward the retreating figure. "Harry only came to visit me once when I was inside. Wanted to make sure I wouldn't rat him out. I didn't. I also didn't divorce him. Not for years. But I wised up eventually. Then I married him again a few years ago." She shrugged. "I'm a moron when it comes to men." MaryLou glanced down at the wad of cash in Cate's hand. "Honey, put that in your pocket. Amberley's a safe-enough place, but still —"

"Oh, it's yours, actually." Cate held out the money.

"You lost me, kid."

"You left two hundred dollars inside. I'm sure you're a good tipper, but that's a bit much."

"I thought I left two tens. Now that's funny." MaryLou slipped the cash back into her pocket. "Thanks. I'll need this if I decide to pay alimony this month." She pulled a face. "Excuse me, *spousal support.* Blood money, more like."

"If you decide to — *you* pay?" Cate asked in a stunned voice.

"Life ain't fair."

"*You* pay?" Cate repeated, her eyes widening.

"Oh, don't worry," MaryLou hastened to assure her. "Harry still deserved what you did."

Cate shifted her weight from one leg to the other as if undecided. "Maybe I shouldn't ask this question, but after what I just did I think I deserve to know. Why do *you* pay?"

MaryLou wrinkled her nose. "Might have something to do with my calling the judge a spineless jackass. Plus I make good money, and Harry hasn't got two nickels to rub together. But I don't pay it without a fight," she said proudly. "Every month Sheila has to make me write the check, and I don't do it until the day it's due. I fight until the last minute. Like it says in that poem Gaby read me once, the one that Welsh fellow wrote."

"Dylan Thomas," Cate offered. "But he was writing about death."

MaryLou shrugged. "Death. Blood money. Same thing." She glanced at her watch. "I've got to run." She took a step away before turning back and pulling a twenty-dollar bill from her pocket. "I still owe you for lunch." She handed Cate the money, saying, "Thanks again for breaking Harry's shoulder."

Cate's face took on an ashen hue. "You said I didn't hurt him! You said —"

"I'm kidding! Besides, Harry's got great insurance. I should know; I pay for it."

CHAPTER 21

Cate and Helen sat together in Cate's apartment as the muted sounds of a Sunday morning drifted in the open windows. Strips of lemon-yellow sunshine painted the walls of the rooms Miriam had first made a home. Over a pot of tea, Helen spoke of her loss. And of her mother. Cate was tempted to ask questions, to push the narrative one way or the other. Instead, she waited until Helen found the right door to the past. "Thinking that my father was alive kept Mama living in a twilight state. Even when the army admitted it would never find him, there was no sense of closure, for there was no body to bury. So she retreated from life. Retreated into memories of him. They insulated her spirit. I didn't deal with grief that way. Instead of my mother's stillness, I craved movement. Action. I became a dancer." She glanced down at her pear-shaped body. "You wouldn't know it by looking at me now, but I was actually quite good. The training was grueling, but I welcomed the release. When I danced, my mind was free of worry. And guilt." Helen paused to sip her tea, as if gathering strength to say what came next. "Every day Mama stayed locked in the past, I felt I'd failed her. Like if I was just good enough or smart enough, I could find a way to reach her."

How we blame ourselves for the choices of others, Cate thought. *Yet how much can we influence even those we love most dearly? Could I have made John stay when he was convinced duty called him to war? Should I have tried harder or was I afraid I'd fail, that he preferred the camaraderie of soldiering over the life we'd built together?* Giving herself a mental shake, she asked, "So how long were you Charlotte's principal caregiver?"

"About a decade. Oh, there were live-in aides, but Mama didn't trust them. She wanted me to do everything. I resented that. A lot. Not that I admitted it then. But I did when Mama found her voice again. Found it with Miriam's help. That took years, and the truth is, when someone refuses to deal — with loss, illness, whatever — somebody else has to. I loved my mother, but I was angry about how much fell to me. It was a normal reaction, especially for a kid. And we had many years after she recovered to repair our relationship. Many years before she died. But how Mama found her way back to me is a story for another day." Helen's hazel eyes clouded then, and lines dragged at the corners of her mouth. "I think that's enough for now, don't you?" she asked, before rising to her feet and stretching. "I've been sitting too long. I'm not used to that. I think I'll head home."

"Oh, I'm sorry," Cate said, jumping to her feet. "Let me walk with you," she suggested. "I need to stretch my legs, too." Helen nodded her thanks, and the two women made their way through Amberley's streets together. They spoke easily of small things, avoiding, by unspoken agreement, talk of the hospital and the topic that had brought them together that day.

After Helen waved farewell from the eggplant-colored porch of the Victorian she called home and stepped inside, Cate stood for a moment in the gathering gloom. She imagined Helen as a child, playing hide-and-seek among the birch trees and rolling on the grass. The burden thrust upon her had been heavy, yet she hadn't given up on her mother. And her faith had been rewarded because eventually Charlotte had found the courage to leave the past in the past.

Thinking of how Charlotte had clung to memories of her husband, Cate felt something akin to envy. Her memories of John were often spotty and increasingly fluid. Being unable to keep every bit of their life together in the forefront of her thoughts seemed like failure. Truth was, her mind resembled an overstuffed filing cabinet that no longer closed properly. Some bits were easy to find, while others were mislabeled. Thankfully, enough had been properly filed for her memories to be armor, yet as much as armor protects and shields, it also separates. It certainly had for Charlotte.

A week after Vincent's outburst in the grocery, Gaby tucked a dishtowel around a steaming pie plate. With a glance out the window at an ashen sky that had been gilded by morning sunlight only an hour earlier, she pulled off her apron and headed across Main Street. Charcoal clouds let loose the first drops of rain as she pulled open the door of Vitelli's. The air within was redolent with the aroma of coffee, yeast, and almonds. As the door jingled shut, Gaby inhaled deeply and waved at the woman standing behind the worn oak counter. Her vibrant, high-energy friend was consumed with worry, and it showed. Sheila's bobbed hair was pulled back into a spiky ponytail, her slim figure was tending toward gauntness, and her normally sparkling eyes were heavy-lidded with fatigue. *The civilian legacy of war,* Gaby thought, calling to mind the topic of Cate's book. And it was a silent legacy because Sheila wouldn't share her heartache with the love of her life. Convinced that Vincent mustn't see her pain or know the toll his passion for healing took on his family, she buried her hurt and played the supportive wife. And that was yet another cost of war, Gaby concluded, for women not only suffered in silence, they tried to do it with a smile.

"Gaby!" Sheila cried, noticing the pie. "You don't have to bake for me! With all you're facing now!"

Gaby's chin jutted up. "Since when can't I bake for a friend?"

"You can, of course." Gesturing toward the still steaming pie, Sheila sniffed. "What kind did you make?"

"Wild leek and new potato, seasoned with Provençal herbs and just a hint of goat cheese. Maybe Vincent will like it." Placing the pie on the counter, she affected a casual air. "So how is he, anyway?"

Sheila tensed, but only for a moment. "Back at work, but not eating much. Still, I doubt he can resist your cooking as he has mine." She found a smile. "Nobody can resist your onion pies."

Gaby smiled for she was known in town for her prize-winning, showstopping, take-the-ribbon-at-the-county-fair onions. Vitelli's featured big baskets of her onions in its sidewalk stall, and locals filled their root cellars with mesh bags of goldens and topped Fourth of July burgers with thick slices of her sweet reds. When the diner served "Gaby French's French Onion Soup," it sold out within the hour. The onion patch where she worked her magic was a sunlit bit of open ground bordered by marigolds and patrolled by rabbits and chipmunks. Her onions grew to maturity amid Queen Anne's lace, creeping thyme, and goldenrod. When asked her secret, Gaby would say, "I feed the earth and then give my onions to it. Nature does the rest. They drink the rain, stretch out their roots, and slowly relax into the warm dirt. All it takes to grow an onion is faith. I bury them alive, pushing them into the ground when they're just little bitty things. It takes faith not to panic when you're thrust into darkness. If you do, doubt rots you from within.

The onions that have faith survive and flourish; those that don't have backbone turn to mush."

And it's the same with people, Gaby mused. *Once doubt gets inside us, it eats away. I know that well enough. And look at what the uncertainty of Vincent's future is doing to Sheila.* After locking the front door, Gaby moved around the counter to give her friend a hug. That simple contact opened the floodgates as Gaby had known it would.

"I know that fighting the bloody trinity of war, famine, and disease is part of being a healer," Sheila sniffed. "And Vincent's a healer, first and foremost. But he's also my husband." Her voice waivered. "I want him home, Gaby. Really home. Mentally and emotionally here. One hundred percent. But I also feel guilty, as though by insisting he act normally I'm asking him to deny what he saw over there. Deny who he is."

"You're just trying to help him readjust. You're just worried. He'll understand that in time."

"Will he? Trouble is, I can't leave well enough alone. I can't stop trying to repair all the broken moments between us." Easing a foot out of the flats she wore, Sheila flexed her toes and exhaled the tension she had been holding in her shoulders. "I've been cooking around the clock, as though if I just put enough food on the table, he'll decide to eat. And I've been chattering to him nonstop because the silence is deafening. But it's all rubbish because I can't say what I really want to."

"Which is?"

"Snap out of it!" Sheila slapped the counter. Then her shoulders sagged. "No, not really. And yes, actually. I understand that he's still trying to process what he experienced; he wouldn't be the man I love if he could do that easily." A note of fear crept into her voice. "I just don't know if he wants to be here. Sometimes, he looks at me like I'm invisible and the life we've built is shallow and meaningless. Sometimes, I think — I think he's sorry he came home."

Gaby suppressed the soothing words that sprang to her lips, for, as eager as she was to offer comfort, she guessed that Sheila wouldn't welcome platitudes and unsolicited advice. So instead of muddying the waters with empty words, Gaby let her friend have a good cry. In time, tears streaked her own cheeks, for grief was a language she spoke all too well.

Vincent Morazzo sprinted along River Road. Sweat blurred his vision, and his breathing was labored. He gripped an unopened water bottle in his right hand, his fisted left hand punching the air as he ran. Five miles into the run, the demands of a middle-aged body slowed his pace. By the time the old graveyard came into sight, he was bent over and gasping. Disgusted with himself, he propped a foot on the stone wall that protected the dead and stared at the water bottle. He didn't deserve to drink. Or rest. Shielding his eyes against the sun, he studied a sky free of helicopters and drones. He lowered his gaze to sweep the paved road, the only danger in sight a small pothole that might claim a hubcap but never a life.

Pushing off the wall, he squared his shoulders and began to run again before wincing, for his calf muscles had tightened in those brief moments of rest. With an oath, he heeded the physician within and stopped to stretch. And drink.

Why was he pushing himself so hard? His wife would say he was running away from their life together, but that wasn't true. Or not the whole truth. He wasn't trying to distance himself from her, but from himself. Volunteering had always left him emotionally spent, physically exhausted, and spiritually battered. But self-loathing was new territory. He couldn't explore its boundaries with friends who seemed to think his work entitled him to a halo. Father Sullivan might understand, but unburdening himself to the elderly priest seemed like weakness. No, there was only one person he could talk to. Should talk to.

Turning around, Vincent headed back into town at a moderate jog, drinking as he ran. Tempted to head straight for the grocery, instead he headed home to shower and shave. It was while pulling on clean clothes that he realized how long it had been since he took any care with his appearance. Grabbing a razor from the medicine cabinet, he set to work uncovering the man Sheila had fallen in love with all those years before.

When Vincent stepped into the grocery later that morning, Sheila's breath caught. For a fraction of a second her hands stilled before she continued cutting provolone for a customer. From the tail of her eye, she watched her husband walk up and down the aisles, cringing inwardly in fear of what he might smash. Or say. But his gait was slow and steady, and she allowed herself a moment's relaxation, all the while continuing to fill orders, smile, and make change. Shoving a stray bit of hair behind her ear, she looked up to find him at the pastry counter. Instead of the worn jeans and grubby shirts he'd taken to wearing lately, he was dressed in black dress pants and a white cotton shirt. As lean as the day she'd met him, he walked the length of the counter, moving with the economy of an athlete. Sheila's heart beat double-time, and that part of her mind able to think clearly marveled that after decades of marriage the sight of his slate-blue eyes locking on hers still turned her knees to jelly. He wore the wire-rimmed, Trotsky glasses she found so sexy, and she saw with surprise that his face held a hint of suntan. "Can I help you?" she asked in a neutral voice.

His eyes swept over her, flicked to the pastries, and then returned to her face. "Everything looks so good, it's hard to decide."

Cheeks flaming, Sheila felt like a schoolgirl. She was dimly aware that her customers had stopped to stare, but didn't give a fig. "Perhaps you'd like a pound of cookies? That would give you a bit of variety."

Vincent leaned his arms on the counter and cocked his head, lowering his gaze to her lips. "Variety's all fine and good," he said in a velvet-smooth voice, "but once you find something you really like, there's just no going back. Don't you think?"

She held her breath, not daring to hope until his grin disarmed her and she rushed around the counter to fling herself into his arms. He picked her up with a flourish and spun her around, all the time muttering that he was a damn fool for pushing her away. She clung to him, tears stinging her eyes. When he swept her into the kitchen, all control fell away, and she wept.

"Forgive me," he pleaded, trailing kisses down her face and neck. "Please."

She clung harder. "Forgive *me.*"

He pulled back and took her face in his, a question in his eyes.

"I shouldn't be so selfish. I should be ready to share you with the people who need you. I'll be a better wife; I promise."

He put a finger to her lips. "No. Don't change. Please don't change. You're my rock. You and Sara — you and Sara mean everything to me. When I pull away from you, it's because I'm punishing myself."

Sheila drew a deep breath to protest, but he silenced her with a look. "You don't know what it's like, how it feels to leave desperate people behind and hop on a plane. They can't escape the ugliness, but I can. I can come back to this." His gaze swept the spotless kitchen. "I can come back to you. To freedom."

"You're right; I don't know what it's like. So you have to tell me," she pleaded. "Somehow, you have to find a way. Please." She linked hands with him. "Please be my friend, not just my lover. Trust me with your doubts and fears, not just your body and heart."

"Be my friend," he repeated softly. "You sent me that book of poetry once, remember? When I was finishing my internship in New York."

Sheila blinked widely. "You — you remember that?"

"I remember everything." His voice was low, with a trace of the rumble that only surfaced when they were making love. Stepping back, he half closed his eyes and recited the poem Sheila had bookmarked all those years before.

"Be my friend
And I will show you
Where the wild violets grow.
I will help you count the stars
And if we're lucky
We may catch a summer wave
And keep it 'til the fall.
I don't ask much at all:
A gentle touch

A kind word.
Just accept me as I am,
Rather weak
Sometimes foolish.
And in return I promise you
No small lies
Or large deceits.
A smile when you are lonely,
A hand when you are lost,
Faith in dark times
And the secret of where the wild violets
    grow."

Unable to speak, Sheila simply opened her arms. When Vincent stepped into her embrace, she took a silent vow to never let him go. He might leave her side when his conscience bade him, but her heart would hold him close.

In the weeks that followed, they spoke about their feelings in a way they hadn't since those early days of their marriage. Gradually, they found a path back to the simple pleasures born of shared confidences and intermingled laughter. It was slow going, but each day brought its own reward. As did each night.

CHAPTER 22

At nine o'clock on a crystal-clear evening, Cate pulled open the front door of the diner and stared at what could only be described as a carnival atmosphere. Tables had been cleared from the middle of the room and balloons hung from the ceiling. There were disco-era lights blinking in time with music that blared from speakers spread around the room. People milled about laughing, eating, and talking. "Excuse me," a voice said from behind her. "Either go in or step aside, will you? My stomach's growling something awful."

"Oh, pardon me," Cate said, moving inside just ahead of a bleached blonde who waved at someone across the room before plunging into the crowd. Cate looked around, her gaze settling on Father Sullivan. She made her way over to him just as the music died away.

MaryLou climbed up on a chair and shot

the cuffs of her cotton shirt with a flourish even as her eyes scanned the diner. "She plans this birthday party for me and then takes off. Typical! Now where is she? Sheila! Get out here!"

The swinging door to the kitchen opened, and her friend stepped into the room, face flushed and eyes flashing. "What is it? I'm busy back here!"

Like actors in a well-rehearsed play, Mary-Lou thanked Sheila, and Sheila grumbled that she'd prefer being left alone to cook in peace to being thanked. Then they both turned in Gaby's direction, and Cate got her first glimpse of Gaby who appeared wan even in the poor light. "Thanks, Gaby, for letting Sheila mess up your kitchen," Mary-Lou said. "You're a saint." In response to what the uninitiated would take to be a heated exchange and Cate knew to be playful bantering, Sheila turned on her heel and returned to the comfortable world of bubbling sauces, boiling water, and sizzling oil.

Cate turned to Father Sullivan. "Gaby looks tired."

"She does," he agreed. "I'll call in after Mass tomorrow morning and have a chat with her." Sweeping a hand to encompass the room, he asked, "So are you getting to know the town's cast of characters?"

"Bit by bit. I know some of the people here." Her eyes picked out a tired-looking Beatrice sitting with an elderly couple. "Who are they?" Cate asked, pointing.

"Beatrice's sister Pearl and Pearl's husband, Jeremy," Father Sullivan said. "Nice fellow. Owns the Amberley Arms hotel down the street."

Cate nodded, the puzzle that was Amberley gaining another piece in her mind. Her gaze lit on the blaring jukebox. Zelda stood beside it, tapping her foot contentedly; she'd clearly chosen to wear her hearing aids that evening. Sheila's husband came in the door then, his shoulders tensing at the sight of the crowd. Cate hadn't seen him since that time in the grocery when he'd vented his anger and pain on the dream his wife had made a reality. Although she didn't know the details, Sheila had intimated that Vincent was doing better. It seemed to be true for the haunted, vacant look was gone from his face. Cate glanced over at the priest. "There are lots of people here. Are they all close friends of MaryLou's?"

Father Sullivan answered in an amused tone. "Well, they are and they aren't, if you take my meaning. I think only Sheila and Gaby know her really well, but as she's been in Amberley so long, others think they do, too. That's how it is in a small town, you know. Although given her caustic nature, you'd expect MaryLou to quickly disabuse folks of the notion that they know her at all. She doesn't, in fact. She's a bit like Fort Knox in that respect: formidable on the outside, but with the same heart of gold."

Cate laughed at how apropos the description was as she watched the woman of the hour with a mixture of awe and admiration. Like a politician working the crowd, Mary-Lou touched a shoulder here and locked eyes with an acquaintance there. She bellowed songs, shouted out greetings, and enfolded all in bear hugs. Then someone proposed a toast in a booming voice, and Cate looked around to find Peter Flynn, the owner of the hardware store that stood next to Vitelli's. Wearing his signature worn jeans and open-necked denim shirt, he held a brimming glass of beer aloft. Flynn's lined face bore witness to his age, but his silver hair was thick, and he had the lean, muscular build of a man who still worked with his hands. She'd seen him at the grocery where his taste ran to black coffee, red meat, and white bread, and he was one of the few in town Sheila couldn't charm into sampling more exotic fare. "To MaryLou!" he cried. "I'd marry her in a second if she'd have me!" Laughter greeted these words, and the object of his desire threw him a smacking kiss. "Happy sixtieth! May your neighbors respect you, trouble neglect you, the angels protect you, and heaven accept you!" Raising her own glass of wine, Cate joined the "Amen" chorus.

"Coming through! Make way!" Sheila called out, balancing a tray above her head and weaving a path from the kitchen. Catching sight of Cate, she rolled her eyes and elbowed two giggling teenagers out of the way. "This is nuts!" she cried. "There are too many people here!" Then she smirked. "But it's a compliment, I suppose." Her head shot up in characteristic fashion. "They came for my cooking, of course." At a shout from the kitchen, she called out, "I'm coming! I'm coming!" Handing the tray to Cate, she pointed toward the front counter. "Lay this out, will you? And then mingle. Have some fun."

Cate was just arranging the last of the antipasto Sheila had given her when Helen made her way across the room. As the jukebox bellowed, Cate inclined her head toward the door, and Helen followed, plate in hand. They settled themselves on a bench just outside the diner, plates of food balanced on their laps and drinks at their feet.

Moonlight etched a maple tree onto the smooth surface of Main Street, and crickets hummed a steady beat. A soft breeze lifted the air and brought the scent of honeysuckle their way. Cate looked around the small patch of Amberley she knew so well and sighed contentedly. Then she turned her attention to the steaming manicotti and selection of salads heaped on her plate. The two women ate in silence for a time before Helen brought up the subject of her mother.

"I want to finish telling you about Mama. You know by now that she found her way back to me. To life. And you know that Miriam was a part of that." Helen set her empty plate aside and reached for the iced coffee at her feet. She took a sip and waited, as though considering how to proceed. "Miriam helped Mama most just by listening to her silence. She understood Mama's fears. How comfortable she was with a stagnant life. Like shutting the door on a messy room you don't know how to set to rights, Mama's mind had pushed to a dark corner the hopeless task of healing. Of course, I didn't think it was hopeless. Miriam didn't either. She told me once that Mama was living in a sort of ghetto, with walls I couldn't breach until she let me. Miriam talked to me a lot about Mama. I remember one time in particular because we were sitting in the kitchen of Vitelli's watching Rosa ice a lemon cake." She smiled. "For me, memories linked with food are always the sharpest. Anyway, Miriam told me that even though Mama knew my brothers were dead, part of her couldn't accept that they were gone. That part still tracked the lives they should have lived and saw them as the men they might have become. She said Mama probably counted their birthdays and tried to imagine the sound of their laughter. Turns out that was true; Mama told me afterward. And in that make-believe world, my brothers ran, played ball, opened Christmas presents, got married, and had children of their own. I came to see how Mama's mind created the lives they'd lost because the alternative was beyond imagining. Of course, to do that, to live in that unreal place, she had to pull away from the living. From me." Helen swallowed hard. "Miriam understood Mama so well because she lost her only child. Just as Mama lost my brothers."

"I know about Miriam's son. How he died before the war," Cate said softly.

"As did her husband. He contracted the same virus that killed the child. Did you know that?"

"I didn't. Oh, how horrible. That explains

a lot, actually. Explains why she was back living with her brothers when the Germans invaded."

"Miriam moved back home, well, back to Lodz after her life fell apart. Doing that — heading for what was comfortable, what she knew — was sort of what Mama did. Except that Mama retreated into memory, back to a time before her loss."

As Helen spoke, Cate wondered why, when grief had shredded her own life, she hadn't reached out to friends for comfort. Instead, she'd exiled herself, refusing even Jenny's calls. *I didn't have Miriam's wisdom. Or strength. And now? Now, at last, I'm letting Jenny into my life again.*

"Miriam never remarried, you know," Helen continued. "Never knew the joy of motherhood again. But she did learn to live in the present despite the horrors of the past. And she felt that, in time, Mama would fold away thoughts of the boys, storing them carefully but out of sight. She said that grieving people do that. If they're strong enough."

Cate sat forward. "How? How do we — how do they do that?"

Helen cocked her head in thought. "Miriam told me that the mind is like a series of rooms. Oh, how did she put it?" Helen stared off into space for a moment. "She said something like this. There's a parlor we live in every day and sweep clean. Then there's a back room we only visit when we need to; that's where we keep memories of family we've lost and dreams that are dead. And there's a locked room where we put selfish thoughts we don't want anyone to see. Not even God. Now the last room is one we wish we could forget exists, for it holds echoes of all the horrors we've seen." Helen paused, as if replaying the words in her mind. Nodding that she'd gotten them right, she added, "Miriam said that everyone's mind is like that. A sane person learns to keep the rooms separate. During the war, she did that by focusing on surviving. Afterward, she tried to find a reason every day to get up and keep that front parlor of her mind tidy. Sometimes, it was just the hope of a sunny sky; others, looking forward to a good cup of coffee, the scent of a flower, or the sound of children playing outside her window.

"The key," Helen finished, "is to find something to cling to. A bit of beauty or a scrap of hope. I found that in dance. And later with my children, and my husband before he died. We just needed to figure out where Mama would find comfort once she'd given up hope of my father's ever coming home. And she finally did give up hope once Clinton normalized relations with Vietnam. Even if there were POWs and MIAs still alive — and there was talk of slave-labor camps that had operated for decades — nobody in Washington wanted to deal with the political fallout of actually finding them. Mama understood that even in the state she was in. If she hadn't connected with the living again, she'd still be lost to us."

A loud shout from inside the diner drew their attention, and Cate could have cursed with frustration before wishing fervently that her readers would be as caught up as she was. "The last part of this story will have to wait," Helen said, getting to her feet. "Lulu's cutting the cake, and this party's about to get even noisier."

Peter Flynn looked around the hardware store that was his life's work and heaved a sigh. Doubtless the mental cobwebs that caught on every thought were due in no small part to the hangover that had yet to release its grip despite two pots of black coffee. Rubbing a work-scarred hand across his brow, he cursed the limitations of a seventy-year-old body. Not that it had failed him the night before when he'd matched

MaryLou shot for shot until the wee hours. They'd traded innuendo, the ribald talk spiced with descriptions of what she'd do with her ruby-red nails given the chance. That's when he'd gotten as tongue-tied as a teenager and headed home to bed. Alone. He'd invited her along as he often did, the knot in his stomach born of equal parts hope and fear. She'd given an enigmatic smile and a shake of those dark curls before saying she was too tired to do the invitation justice. His chest had puffed up then, and he'd marveled that rejection could feel so good.

A sliver of sunlight glinted off the power tools that hung on the far wall. The glare made his eyes ache. Why the hell had he opened up the store this morning, anyway? Only a handful of customers had come in, most of them more interested in the rumor drifting about town that MaryLou Rice had finally succumbed to old Peter Flynn's considerable charms. He made to shake his head at the improbability of that before thinking better of it; best not to move unless necessary. Still, it was ridiculous to imagine such a luscious woman taking up with the likes of him. Not that they didn't spend time together talking shop, a pastime she never tired of. And hearing MaryLou describe the thrill of a well-greased engine's roaring to life could make any man salivate.

A movement caught his eye, and Peter fixed his gaze on the sidewalk outside. That young woman who lived above Sheila's place was pacing back and forth, as though debating whether to come in. When she strode purposefully toward the door, he straightened up in anticipation before she took a step backward to lift her head to the sign as though unsure where she was. What the devil was the matter with her? Either come in or not, but get on with it! Then he softened, remembering that she'd lost her husband. Her warrior husband. That was a pity, for she was a pretty enough thing, if a little athletic for his taste. And such short hair wasn't appealing — nothing to grab on to, no silky veil to tease a man. Now what in the world had put those thoughts in his head? He wasn't in the habit of appraising his customers like fillies to be bought or bred! Concluding that his uncontrollable hormones were all MaryLou's fault, he reminded himself that women were trouble. Hadn't his philandering ex-wife taught him that if nothing else?

Squaring his shoulders, Peter walked to the door and pulled it open. "Can I help you?" he asked, taking pity on the indecisive widow. He tried to remember her name, but it hid under one of the boulders strewn about his memory that so often tripped him up.

"Oh. Yes. Thank you," Cate answered, picking up a box at her feet and following him inside. "I'm Cate Saunders," she announced.

"Peter Flynn. Nice to meet you." He took her small hand in his and couldn't help comparing it with MaryLou's generous one. Then he looked into her eyes and saw such anxiety that it sobered him, or seemed to. "Is there something wrong?"

Cate exhaled loudly. "No. It's just the smell."

Peter took a step back. He'd showered that morning, hadn't he? Perhaps not, for things had been a bit fuzzy when he'd awoken with a tongue dry as sand and eyes that slit open only under protest. "Sorry." He moved an arm as unobtrusively as possible and took a cautious sniff.

Cate laughed. "No, not you. This place. The sawdust. The wood smells. The man smells."

Had she said "man smells"? Prepared to like her for she was a friend to Sheila and a woman alone, he was now more inclined than ever. "You were at the birthday party last night," he said, suddenly remembering.

"Yes, that's right."

"It was a good turnout," he remarked.

"MaryLou has a lot of friends."

"She does. Hard not to like the woman," he observed before adding, "not that she can't be infuriating at times."

"Like when she steals food from your plate," Cate supplied.

"Or flies through town on that motorcycle of hers at two in the morning," Peter countered.

They laughed in unison before Cate wagged a finger in his direction. "I saw what you did for her last night." When Peter raised a shaggy eyebrow, she recalled how after MaryLou had ruminated aloud on the downside of turning sixty, he'd announced in a booming voice that his throat was parched and his stomach empty. That had prompted Gaby to fill glasses and Sheila plates. "You turned Lulu's mind to living," Cate observed. "And flirting, which are one and the same."

Suddenly interested in the floor at his feet, Peter mumbled, "Just can't stand seeing her sad. A woman like that —" He swallowed hard, his throat muscles working. Then he lifted his eyes to Cate's, and his voice took on a clipped, professional tone. "Why were you unsure about coming in?" He waved a hand toward the street.

Cate looked around the store, empty save for an elderly couple examining a battery-powered lawn mower. "I was building up my courage to ask for your help," she said weakly, then stopped, as though unsure how to frame the words that now hung in the air. Lifting the cover off the box she held, she proceeded to spread the contents out on the counter. Peter whistled low at the sight of the chisels, block planes, files, and carving knives. They were top-of-the-line carpentry tools and had clearly been well cared for.

"I want you to have them. Sheila told me how you're always tinkering — fixing and building things. Fine, beautiful things."

Peter followed Cate's gaze toward the scarred workbench that ran along the side wall. It was well-known he could be found there whenever the store was empty, his perch a swivel stool he'd picked up for a song when the Esso gas station closed down years before. He'd whistle quietly while his nimble fingers patched, rewired, and mended things broken by hard use or long life. At one time or another, all the neighborhood children had huddled around that workbench — including young Sheila.

Although she'd had no interest in things mechanical, he recalled how mesmerized she'd been watching him strip and stain a table that had seen better days, or coax a cough of life from an old motor. Years later, she'd told him his hands were those of an artist, one whose medium was oil and rusted metal much as hers was pastry flour and almond paste. Clearly, she'd told Cate the same thing.

Although a great teller of tales with a mug of coffee in his hand or a cigar in his mouth, when confronted with a compliment Peter usually communicated with grunts, sighs, and mutterings. In response to Cate's offer, he shook his trademark thatch of unkempt hair, cleared his throat, and shifted his booted feet. "These are fine tools. And, sure, I could put them to use, I suppose. But why are you giving them away?"

It was a question Cate had obviously anticipated. "They belonged to my husband. He was a carpenter — a cabinetmaker, actually." She reached out to trace a finger across a wood-handled instrument with a hooked end. "This is called a scorp. I remember that." The black-edged tone to her words softened. "John loved these tools. He was always sharpening them, tending them like children. They — they should be used by someone who appreciates them, someone who can create the things he did. I couldn't part with them until now." She turned shining eyes on Peter as though glimpsing a bright future for her husband's treasures. "Sheila says you're very talented. That's important, of course. But the real reason I'm here is because of the kindness I saw in you last night. My John was so loving." She extended a hand toward the tools again only to draw it back. "He'd want someone like you to have them."

Peter was speechless, the urge to comfort like a fist around his heart. How could he accept such a gesture from someone he didn't even know? Then he saw the plea in her eyes, one mixed with relief as though these reminders of her dead husband were both treasures and an albatross. "I'd be pleased to hold on to them for you, but only that." He wrapped them carefully. "On one condition."

Cate blinked in surprise. "What?"

"That you let me teach you how to use them. Or at least begin to."

"Wha-what?"

The spur-of-the-moment proposal began to take shape in Peter's mind. "You've probably absorbed quite a bit just watching your husband, probably know more about the craft than you realize. You're a writer, right? I think I heard that somewhere." Cate nodded mutely. "So you've the artistic touch. And you've got small hands." He gestured toward hers with approval. "They'll serve you well. Not in construction or straight carpentry, but for detail work. For cabinet-making." He reached out to run a hand down her bicep, before nodding with approval. "You've got good muscle strength; you'll need that for power tools. To cut the wood."

The turn of conversation took her so by surprise, Cate couldn't respond with more than a stutter. "B-but —"

He waved away the objections he knew would follow. "All it takes to learn is the right tool for the right job, a good teacher, and commitment. You've got the first two. And the third? Well, you just have to decide to try. Whether you've got talent or not is another matter, of course. No knowing that until you give it a go. When you're ready to do that, come on by. In the meantime" — he made a show of stowing the tools under the counter — "these will be safe and sound. Waiting."

CHAPTER 23

Cate looked back at the hardware store, now two blocks away and bathed in morning sunshine. Her mind took a mental tour of the space that was half again as large as the grocery. Well lit, it had tin ceilings and wide-beamed oak flooring roughened by years of sawdust underfoot. No wonder Amberley loved that store. It was the type of family-owned business fast disappearing from downtown America, and the place had everything. If you wanted a snowblower or a space heater, try Flynn's. Plumbing supplies, auto parts, or lumber — Flynn's had it all. And if someone couldn't afford to buy a tool, Peter would lend it for the price of a black coffee and a bit of conversation. Such open-handedness was good business, but how the man made a living selling ten-dollar pants and ten-cent screws, Cate couldn't imagine.

Yet Peter Flynn did a brisk business not

only because of his prices but because he was admired for his Yankee ingenuity; it was an established fact that he'd rather fix something old than sell something new. He could jerry-rig a twenty-year-old washing machine that was on its last legs, design solar-powered lighting for the manger scene that took pride of place in the common every December, and keep the county's wheelchair-accessible van running on what was jokingly referred to as "a wish and a prayer." He'd been a fixture in town for so long that his name had become parlance for repairing rather than replacing. "Why buy a new stove when you can Flynn the old one?" Sheila once asked a customer in the certain knowledge she'd be understood.

Needless to say, MaryLou idolized the man, for his storage room was crammed with inventory. By the murky light cast by aging florescent bulbs, amid all manner of tools, piping, filters, and spare parts, he always found just what she was looking for. "If he were twenty years younger, I'd marry that man," she'd confided to Cate once. If drunk, it was said MaryLou cut the term to a decade. "What a couple those two would make," Cate found herself thinking aloud before a grin split her face.

Relieved that John's tools had found a

home, Cate turned her mind to those bits of his clothing she'd held on to. Some things she would keep — to wear or just grasp to her when her hands ached for him — but some she now felt she could part with. Like his tools, they should be used. Thinking of the tools, she wondered if Peter was right and one day she'd balance them in her palm as she'd seen John do. Not as expertly, or with as much confidence as he had, but with the same reverence. It was something she'd never imagined herself doing. And yet once the book was behind her, and she could see a clear path ahead, perhaps she'd take Peter Flynn up on his offer. The idea became commitment when she decided her first project would be a keepsake box to hold the letters John had sent her over the years. He'd passed her funny notes between their college classes, written poems of love once they started dating, and penned heart-wrenching missives in Iraq. His writing deserved a special resting place, one she might find a way to carve with his fine tools. And a lot of help.

She wondered if any of her husband's talent had rubbed off on her. John would often stare at a block of wood as though willing it to reveal its secrets. Once it did, he'd reach for a tool and begin the work he'd always maintained was more archeology than creation. And hadn't she found the same thing with her writing? Weren't the words her characters spoke so often whispered to her heart more than written in her mind? When her spirit was open, stories were easy to discover — as though they lay waiting for her like buried treasures. But how had John unlocked the secrets of his craft? Why hadn't she asked him more questions when she'd had the chance? Why hadn't she — No! She wouldn't take that path for it led nowhere, only circled back on itself again and again.

When Cate saw Vincent later that day, he strode past her on the sidewalk before turning back. "You're Cate."

"Yes." She extended her hand.

"We haven't met properly. It was too crowded at MaryLou's party, and the first time I saw you — at the grocery — I wasn't quite myself." He managed a tight smile. "I was a bit out of my depth, or perhaps in too deep." He shrugged.

"There's no need to explain," Cate said, wanting to ease him out of what sounded like an apology. "I won't say I know how you were feeling — I hate when people say that to me. But I do know how pain can warp thinking and distort your vision."

"Warp and distort," he repeated. "Yes, that's true." Then he fixed Cate with an appraising eye. "You've been a help to my wife these past months; I'm indebted to you."

"Oh, well," Cate stumbled over her words, "she took me in, so to speak. Without her help, I'd be homeless." He withdrew slightly and Cate winced inwardly. "That's a stupid thing to say to someone just returned from helping refugees. Please forgive me."

"Don't apologize. It was an apt word. In normal circumstances, I wouldn't have reacted as I did. No one would." They'd been walking along as they spoke and now stood across from the common. "Have you got a moment?" he asked, gesturing toward a bench.

"Sure."

They sat quietly for a time while crows swooped down from the canopy of trees overhead to peck at a bit of bread someone had left on the slate path. A woman pushing a baby stroller threw Vincent a wave, and he raised a hand in return before thanking Cate.

"For what?"

"Not asking about Iraq."

"Why would I? I barely know you. And — well, I imagine it's not something you want to talk about, or at least not casually."

"No. No, I don't. Even with Sheila, it's tough." He eyed Cate sharply. "You must know that." She nodded. Then he changed the subject, or seemed to. "I hear you've been given some of Miriam's journal entries."

"Yes."

"She was someone who really lived in the moment. Few of us manage that. And she knew what it was to be a refugee in her own land," he added as if speaking to himself. "To be driven from her home because of the vicissitudes of war." His voice rose in volume, and he sat up straighter. "Do you know that when she learned her family's house would be turned over to German-Poles — to collaborators — she scrubbed it from top to bottom?"

"You're kidding!"

"Seems strange, I know. She was obsessed with leaving everything as spotless as when her father had been alive. And she hoped one day to return. I've seen that same hope in the eyes of refugees. To watch it fade and see the moment when resignation replaces resolve, well, it can't be put into words. Miriam understood that. Eventually, she let go of the past, or as much as was possible. But then she was luckier than the refugees I work with." His eyes swept the path before them where children skipped, dogs barked, and flowers bloomed. "Miriam found work, peace of mind, and good friends here. With those building blocks, anyone can make a new life." Whether his last comment was directed at Miriam Rosen's memory, the Iraqi refugees he'd come to know, or Cate herself she couldn't say.

As evening approached, she told Vincent about the manuscript that was slowly taking shape, describing how she hoped it would highlight the civilian debris left in the wake of war. Discussing her work, she circled around the thing that had sprung to the forefront of her thoughts the moment she'd seen him. He waited with the instinct of one who had spent decades earning the trust of his patients. While stars awakened in an enameled sky, Cate spoke of John, surprised at how easily the words came. Many people in Amberley had asked about her past, always with the best of intentions. Polite but distant, she usually dodged their questions and doled out the sketchy details of her life like hoarded breadcrumbs. Like MaryLou, some people tried to draw her out with glimpses of their own suffering. Yet no loss was like another, or so Cate used to think. But Vincent Morazzo had seen war firsthand, and something about his quiet manner had her pulling a photograph from her wallet. She saw Vincent's eyes take in the worn state of it — edges thinned by anxious hands and curled by perspiration.

How many times had she stared at John and the child as though by doing so she could inject herself into the scene? John hadn't ever mentioned the boy with the football, but she'd found over a dozen photos of him among those John had taken in Iraq. "Probably just another kid shadowing the soldiers when they go on patrol," she had been told by the bereavement counselor she'd met with in Boston. He had given her a look equal parts pity and confusion, as though wondering why she should care about one poor Iraqi kid. *Because this one knew John, or at least a part of him I didn't. Because in the midst of war they'd played ball together. Because I never gave my husband a son.*

Surrendering to a sudden fullness in her chest, Cate lurched to her feet and began to pace. Gulping cool air, she felt the panic that had gripped her begin to recede. In time, she turned back to Vincent. "All this talk of refugees makes me think — makes me want to tell someone." She held up the photograph. "This little Iraqi boy was probably seven or eight when this was taken, and that was two years ago. I don't know who he was. Is. But John took a bunch of pictures of him." The doctor's face was a study in compassion and sorrow. She moved to take her place beside him so that Vincent could study the photograph by the pool of a streetlamp's light. "I don't know why I'm telling you this, except that I think you'll understand," Cate continued. "Understand in a way others won't. You see, if I win the contest, I'll have money to care for my husband's grandmother. But if the book sells well, there might be enough to look for this boy. Although how I'll find him I can't imagine." Vincent's face registered only the barest flicker of surprise. "It's not that I think he might know something about John's death; I'm beginning to resign myself to never learning exactly what happened. But if this boy was injured, or in some way needs help —" The words she left unsaid swirled around them like a living thing. Maybe she could do for him what she hadn't for John. Maybe a contest sponsored by the VFW would end up helping an Iraqi child. And if it all came about because of her writing, because of the dream John had sacrificed so much for, there was closure in that — not the sort she had hoped for, but closure just the same.

Cate drew a steadying breath before opening her front door and flipping on the light. Her thoughts scattered at the sight of the journal entry awaiting her. Why? She'd been expecting it, had somehow known it was there. Turning back into the moment, she bent down to read.

When we learned Papa's house would be turned over to German-Poles, my brothers tried to map a path through the nightmare to come. I could not. Anger claimed me as never before.

I ran outside to stand amid my mother's roses. It was winter, and the plants that would soon explode with color and scent were only bare sticks stuck in the mud. How could we leave such a beautiful garden to the likes of collaborators? Grasping the base of a rosebush — the pale pink one that always bloomed in time for my birthday — I tugged hard. The roots went deep, and my hands slipped. Blood ran down my fingers where the thorns had fought back. Gritting my teeth, I grasped the plant farther down the root ball. Then I fell to the ground, weeping. Why should the roses die along with all our dreams? I looked up to see my brothers at the window, concern creasing their faces. As inept as all men in the face of raw emotion, they stood helpless. Getting up, I smoothed my skirt and took a breath to steady myself. Maybe the roses would survive the war and I would see them bloom again. Even as the thought flitted through my mind, I couldn't bring myself to believe it. The reserve of hope I'd once dipped into so easily was gone.

Weeks later, on that last morning, we talked in whispers as though in a sacred place. Then, one by one, we filed out the door. The last to leave, I stood for a moment in the silent house, hearing the clink of a teaspoon in Papa's glass of tea, smelling his pipe and straining for the sounds of my brothers wrestling upstairs. Echoes of who we were lived in the very walls of the house. For the last time, I touched the spot on the doorpost where the mezuzah had hung for a century. Without mezuzahs, it was no longer a Jewish home; it was no longer our home. Closing the front door, I locked it and stood staring at the key before slipping it into my pocket.

The day was warm for February, and

mud clogged the streets. Some families piled belongings on top of overturned tables that they dragged through the melting snow; others pushed wheelbarrows or wagons. All appeared crippled, bent forward to balance loads on their backs — carpets, pots, clothing, violins, paintings, and blankets bobbed up and down as far as the eye could see. Babies were crying, and the elderly shuffling; pregnant women clasped swollen bellies as young boys darted in and out of the crowd.

We joined the river of Jews that would soon overflow the Ghetto, moving only as fast as the slowest in the crowd. My knapsack held the last of our food, and I dragged two suitcases behind me. Joseph pushed a cart loaded with a few chairs, iron pans, dishes and tools. As he maneuvered around the puddles in the road, he recited prayers under his breath, periodically shifting the sack of books on his back. Samuel carried a suitcase in each hand and a mattress on his back. Benny's pack was tied around his waist, and the bed frame hoisted over his shoulder was soon dragging behind as he stretched out a hand to help me.

It happened so quickly. A flash of blue from the corner of my eye before Benny turned, grabbing for a little boy who had fallen in the road. A single gunshot rang out. As a scream rose in my throat, the crowd panicked and surged forward.

Benny lay crumpled on the ground, his face in the mud and a dark stain spreading across his best coat. I lunged for him, dodging plodding feet and wagon wheels. Joseph got there first. As he lifted his brother's body, a rifle butt struck him across the face. Then Samuel was beside them, shouting in German at the soldiers who shrugged indifferently before boredom drew them to another victim. Joseph and Samuel carried Benny, staggering under the weight. More shots rang out. I stumbled along with the surging crowd, clinging to the frail hope that my sweet, funny, kindhearted brother was still alive.

Turning the paper over, Cate found nothing more. Had Benny died that day? Or had he survived and been with his brothers when they were rounded up later on in the ghetto? She had to know, had to — then she caught herself. This had all happened seventy years ago! *But not for me. For me, this story is still unfolding.*

Reverently, she placed Miriam's words in a desk drawer she'd set apart for just that purpose. Then she brewed a pot of tea and reached for a bottle of aspirin. That afternoon she'd talked to Vincent about Miriam's last days before moving to the ghetto. Hours later, the journal entry had been waiting. Vincent hadn't left it; she was certain of that. For one thing, he didn't strike her as a liar. For another, she'd walked straight home from their meeting. So how had that particular journal entry found its way to her? How had any of them? She had no explanation, of course. And perhaps it was time she stopped looking for one. Perhaps it was time to focus less on how Miriam's story was being given to her and more on why it was. What was she supposed to do with what she learned? She thought of Gaby's gift, if one could call it that. Although unsure how she knew the things she did, still Gaby accepted the duty such knowledge imposed. Cate had to find a way to do the same.

CHAPTER 24

The morning of the county fair dawned warm and dry. Cate lay in bed watching creamy light creep over the horizon. Within moments, the skyline beyond her window was suffused with honey-yellow, and the lace curtains of her room began to glow. Soon the air resounded with the chirp of birds swooping down to visit the feeders that dotted Sheila's vegetable garden.

Cate slipped from bed and made her way to the living-room windows. Glancing down at Main Street, she noted storefronts festooned with flags and balloons. A banner hung across the road wishing Amberley a "Fun-Filled Fair," and people were already gathering beneath a cloudless sky. She was eager to join them, but the coffee pot beckoned.

As the first bubble of brown gold escaped the percolator on the stove, she closed her eyes in appreciation of the aroma filling the air. How anyone faced the day without caffeine was beyond her. Especially that morning, for she'd stayed up late the night before chatting on the phone with Jenny. The easy friendship of years ago was still beyond their reach, but since they'd reconnected each had made an effort to keep in touch. Cate was glad, but she was paying the price now for those hours of shared confidences. Still, it was worth it.

Since the day had a different color to it, she pulled on a navy-blue linen shell, red baseball cap, and white shorts that showed off the bit of tan she'd gotten. Fortunately, her hair had grown to the point a ponytail looked less stumpy than a month before, so she tied it back with a red band. Slicking on sunscreen, she stepped into a pair of white leather flats bought on impulse with her last paycheck. Wine-colored toenails peeked out the front for she'd indulged in a pedicure at the Clip & Curl salon the day before.

Standing in front of the small bathroom mirror, she strained to see her full reflection before stepping back with a frown. Such vanity! Really, what did it matter? Only it did. Not because of what men would think, but because she wanted to look — what? The part, perhaps. Yes, she wanted to look the part today. To fit in. This was her home, after all. And her friends would all be at the festivities.

After giving a final glance around the apartment that she had made her own, she tucked her notebook and wallet in her pocket and headed out. As expected, the grocery was closed, but abuzz with activity. Cate stuck her head in the back door to ask Sheila if she needed any help. One look at the neat trays of vegetables set out in the kitchen and the three-tiered trolley waiting to ferry them all into the delivery truck and down the street told her Sheila was as organized as ever.

Sure enough, she assured Cate, "I'm all set here. Go! Have fun!" Turning back to her assistant, she barked out some last-minute instructions. "No, no. You have to load the skewers just so. Grilled eggplant, then sliced mozzarella, then beefsteak tomato, then grilled zucchini. It looks best that way. Come on, get a move on!"

Cate threw the beleaguered girl a smile of sympathy before heading outside. The sky was dotted with wispy clouds, and a soft breeze unfurled the flags overhead. Spotting a familiar figure slouched against the closed door of the diner, she walked across Main Street with a wave of greeting.

Dressed in a red and white-striped halter

and form-fitting jeans that left little to the imagination, MaryLou was scowling. "How am I supposed to get through the morning without Gaby's coffee?" she complained. "I snagged this before she packed up, but it's inhumane to deny someone coffee!" In her hand was a sticky bun that she proceeded to devour in four bites.

Cate shook her head. "First of all, how can you eat like that without smearing your lipstick, and second, where do you put it all?" She gestured disbelievingly toward MaryLou's figure.

"No woman would respond to either of those questions," MaryLou shot back, but she was obviously pleased with the implied compliment because she smiled before licking her fingers each in turn. Draping an arm over Cate's shoulder, she lowered her voice conspiratorially. "Look, I'm only saying this because I like you. How about getting to know some of the kids in town? They're the future you know — those little rays of sunshine that are the next generation."

Cate slipped out of MaryLou's grasp. "I'm not running the carousel. They asked you to do it and you agreed."

"I must have been drunk!"

"You agreed," Cate recalled, "because it's a century-old piece of machinery that needs to be seen to properly or the kids riding it will get hurt. Sheila appealed to your sense of decency, and it worked. Can't back out now."

A fuming MaryLou trailed after Cate toward the antique carousel in question. It dominated the main entrance to the common and was a glorious sight. "Sheila sure plays the mayor card when it suits her! Drafts me into spending the day with a bunch of screaming kids and a creaky old contraption that will probably collapse after ten minutes. And you know the worst part?" MaryLou demanded, a dull crimson staining her cheeks.

Cate stopped, curiosity getting the better of her. "No, Lulu, what's the worst part?"

"I have to stay out of the beer tent all day! All day, I tell you. Can't risk getting a little tipsy when I'm the one keeping the youth of Amberley safe. It's not fair!"

As they continued walking, Cate suggested, "Why not ask Peter Flynn to help you?"

The words whipped through the air to crack the hard shell MaryLou wore like a second skin. "Oh, well, I could do that, I suppose," she mumbled, pulling a pair of sunglasses from atop her head and slipping them on.

"You like him!" Cate cried triumphantly. "I knew it!"

"Don't be ridiculous. He's seventy if he's a day. Probably needs to pop those horrid little pills before getting down to business with a woman. Really. Peter Flynn. Are you kidding? Why in the world would I be interested in him?" The disbelief meant to curl the edge of her speech instead gave the impression that she had asked the question before and hadn't found an answer.

"I think he's manly. Virile. And very nice," Cate countered, calling to mind her brief time in the hardware store. "Yes, he's older, but what of it? He still works a six-day week, and he can match you drink for drink — or so I saw the other night. He'd be good for you. Plus, you've got a lot in common. You're both always fixing things. And eating. He seems to be blessed with the same metabolism as you!"

"Peter's always been slim," MaryLou said, pressing her lips together as if a taste lingered. Then she sighed. "Muscular, but slim."

"And, most important, he's smitten with you."

"Smit— what century do you live in, Saunders? Besides, it's not as though I'm waiting around for him to be smitten or not."

Reaching for her phone, Cate teased, "Sounds like maybe you're afraid to find out. Like maybe you're scared you're losing your touch."

"Please! If I wanted Flynn, he'd be on his knees to me!" She tossed her head of curls and flounced off with a swing of her hips that sent a skateboarding youth crashing into the curb. Before Cate could ask if the boy was all right, he was back on his feet, eyes locked on MaryLou, who had proceeded to inspect the carousel motor. All business now, she muttered things like, "Drive belt's all but shot," "Damn thing won't last the day," and "I better be getting paid for this!"

Tuning out the rising tide of complaints, Cate studied the mechanical wonder that had graced every county fair in Amberley since Beatrice McLean was a toddler. It really was magnificent! Beneath the green canvas top, mirrors set in plaster panels of gingerbread work caught and reflected the light. She hopped onto the varnished wooden platform to admire the carved horses. Each a unique work of art, they were brightly painted and ornately decorated. Some had flying manes, others jeweled saddles inlaid with rhinestones or gold-leaf tassels.

"You're looking at the romance side, you know," a low voice pointed out.

Cate spun around to see Peter Flynn standing behind her. "You came."

He held up his phone. "You asked me to." He seemed about to speak again when MaryLou's one-sided conversation rose in volume. "Now I see why. Well, I'd best go and help. If she'll let me." He peeled off the denim shirt he wore jacket style over a white T-shirt and gave a nod of farewell.

Cate reached out a hand to stop him. "Hang on. You said I was looking for romance. That's not true!"

An amused expression played across Peter's face, one she now noticed was shadowed as if he hadn't had time — or hadn't bothered — to shave. Hooking an arm around the neck of the nearest horse, he said, "No. I said this is the romance side." He pointed to the row of horses nearest the edge of the platform. "The side facing out is always the most brightly colored, the most intricately carved. The decorations are meant to entice you in. To romance you." At the sound of a metal tool being flung amid a string of curses, he shrugged and gave a lopsided grin. Tipping down his sunglasses, he threw a glance toward where MaryLou worked and said, " 'Course, sometimes you find romance in the least likely places."

Cate smiled at his retreating form; he *was* a good match for Lulu. But had she been right to push them together? While she pondered the question, the cursing stopped and organ music rang out. When the carousel began to move, the children who had queued up for a ride squealed with delight. Cate hopped off and gave the scene a final, satisfied look before making her way to a corner of the common where animals were drawing a crowd. Leah Mitchell had set up a large outdoor cage in which a dozen cats dozed, kneaded the grass, or batted at flies. Children knelt around the cage to admire the white, gray, black, and calico fur, frustrated that they couldn't cuddle the cats and kittens. They turned pleading eyes on parents who grumbled that a holiday celebration was no place for the serious business of adoption, but more than a few left the common with one hand gripping that of an excited child and the other a cat carrier.

From time to time, Leah's gaze scanned the crowd to track a group of schoolchildren who'd volunteered as dog walkers. One was a pig-tailed girl wearing wire-rimmed glasses who was attempting to control a German shorthaired pointer. Her oversized T-shirt bore the dog's likeness and the words *2-year-old, neutered male, good with children, answers to Max.* Cate knelt down to pet the dog's velvet-smooth, brown ears. Looking into his soulful eyes, she felt confident he'd find a new home before the day was out. When she said as much, the freckle-faced girl threw her thin shoulders back confidently before continuing her walk with the prancing dog.

Ahead hung a sign that read USED-BOOK SALE TO BENEFIT THE LIBRARY'S NEW ROOF FUND. Marion Puttner, the librarian, stood before four carts of hardcover books and paperbacks. Cate gave her a wave of greeting, but didn't stop for she'd spotted Gaby. Apron-clad and smiling, she stood in the center of four tables. Each was covered in a checked tablecloth atop which were dozens of pies. A huge banner strung between bamboo poles read: AS AMERICAN AS APPLE PIE . . . OR CHERRY, RHUBARB, AND BLUEBERRY. Gaby called out a greeting and picked up a paper plate. "So, which will it be?"

Cate debated before announcing that she'd start with the apple. Gaby cut her a wedge, and Cate handed over two paper tokens, giving a mental thumbs-up to Sheila for planning so well. "Vendors lose so much time making change," she'd told Cate the day before. "And little kids never have enough money for what they want. So we sell paper tokens. Each costs a dollar, so some things cost one token, some two tokens, and so on. Plus, money is so dirty, and a lot of our vendors are handling food. This works much better all around." And that, Cate concluded, was why it paid to have a mayor who understood business.

As if on cue, Sheila stepped into view and strode toward a raised platform in the center of the common. A microphone had been set up, and Cate glanced around to see that loudspeakers hung from the surrounding trees. "Good morning!" Sheila called out in a commanding voice. The hum of conversation lessened gradually. Only when silence descended did she glance at her watch. "We've a special surprise this year," she said, her eyes raking the sky above them.

The distant roar of jet aircraft could be heard, and then a murmur ran through the crowd. A palpable excitement communicated itself to Cate. Tossing her empty plate in the nearest recycling bin, she asked a neighbor, "What is it? What's happening?" In response, he inclined his head toward the eastern sky. Following his gaze, she saw three jet fighters arrow past, leaving trails of red, white, and blue smoke as a patriotic signature. A roar of applause followed, and Cate got caught up in the moment. Americans might not favor parades of tanks and robot-like soldiers as the Soviets had, but they certainly enjoyed a Hollywood-style flyby.

"Now isn't that something?" her neighbor asked, a light flaring behind his hooded eyes. He'd removed his worn cap as a mark of respect, and when Cate turned to him she noted the flag pin on his lapel.

"Are you a veteran?" she guessed.

The man straightened slightly. "Korea. '51 — '53. Got the Bronze Star for bravery under fire. Chinese fire, that is." Then he seemed to shrink a bit, his spine surrendering to the pull of time. When his eyes flew skyward again, seeking the imprint of smoke that was now only a memory, Cate wondered how the peaceful twilight of his life compared with those tension-filled years. She couldn't — wouldn't — ask, but before turning away she patted the man's arm in farewell.

CHAPTER 25

Weaving her way through stalls of produce, handicrafts, and food, Cate heard vendors hawk their wares in boasting voices that rang though the air. "Get your hot dogs and hamburgers here;" "onion rings and French fries;" "doughnuts;" "pizza by the slice;" "caramel popcorn." There were baskets of fresh bread, mounds of crisp apples, and fat triangles of seedless watermelon. An herb farmer was selling great bunches of just-flowering basil, wispy fennel, flat-leaf parsley, and gray-hued lavender. She breathed deeply for the air was heavy with the scents of late summer.

A white-haired man in shirt-sleeves, walking shorts, and a baseball cap brushed past her with a mumbled, "Excuse me."

She recognized the voice. "Father Sullivan!" The priest stopped.

"Oh, hello, Cate."

She blinked. "You're out of uniform!"

"So are you," he teased.

"But —"

"I'll be judging the Main Street hundred-yard dash in a bit. There'll be lots of hurrying about, or as much of it as I can manage," he explained, gesturing toward the brace on his knee. As pliable as an ace bandage, it allowed for freedom of movement, but certainly not running. "Plus, it will be a scorcher today. Can't work in a suit and collar."

"Father! We're ready to start!" a child's voice called out.

"Got to go!" He gave a quick wave of farewell before moving off with a hobbling gait.

Cate spied Helen beside a flower seller up ahead. She was speaking with a little girl Cate recognized as the one she'd suggested plant a memory garden. "That one's pwetty," the child said, pointing to a bubblegum-pink petunia in a ceramic pot. "Mommy loves pink."

"Does she?" Helen asked, slipping off the five-dollar price tag. "Well, it's only a dollar. Do you have a token?" The girl eagerly surrendered the bit of paper she gripped. "Great," Helen said, adding four more tokens and passing them to the cashier. Picking up the pot, Helen handed it to the child. "Here you go. Now, you'll need to keep it watered." The girl nodded quickly before running off, a huge smile on her face.

"That was nicely done," Cate said.

Helen started. "Oh, well, she's a good kid." Her tone was brisk, and she took a sudden interest in the grass at her feet.

"You're as uncomfortable with compliments as MaryLou!" Cate observed.

Helen's laugh was quick. "I saw her as I came in. Well, heard is more like it. Quite colorful speech for someone who works with children."

"Yeah, I mentioned that to her. She said she'd modify her cursing today. Say bloody instead of f— well, you know. Hopefully, the kids won't understand."

Helen tapped her forehead. "Smart woman." Then she caught sight of the little notebook in Cate's hand. "So how's the book coming?"

"All right." It was her stock answer, but less than a friend deserved. "Slowly, actually. I used to write so easily. Well, not easily, but I didn't stare at a blank screen for an hour. And half of what I write is such fluffy garbage, I wind up deleting it."

Helen considered. "It's just that your writing muscles are out of shape. Flabby. So it's hard to get going."

"I hadn't thought of it like that," Cate admitted, although the description fit. "So all I have to do —"

"Is keep trying," Helen finished the thought. "You'll get back in shape soon enough." Her gaze lit on a row of flags lining the walkway. "This is a good day to finish our talk about Mama. Have you got time now?"

"Sure."

Iced coffees in hand, Cate and Helen settled themselves in a corner of the common where they could watch the comings and goings. Opening her notebook, Cate pulled out the latest journal entry she'd received. She passed it to Helen, who bent to read the familiar writing.

When Charlotte spoke of those lost years, she said it was like walking through a thick fog that obscured her feet. She wasn't sure if she was coming or going, moving toward the future or the past. Until that haze shifted, she couldn't reconnect the woman she'd been with the one she'd become. Or wanted to be. I knew part of her was desperate to join the Charlotte that had been Robert's wife with the one who was mother to Helen. She just didn't know how to bridge the years, how to thread the past through the void of lost time without fraying it irreparably. But she found a way.

"What did Miriam mean?" Cate asked when Helen finished reading.

Helen downed her coffee before answering. "I think I should start with the blouse. When I saw it, I knew Mama had found her way to the light." Leaning back on the bench, Helen half closed her eyes and began a story that had Cate scribbling in her notebook.

When Charlotte Connolly made her way into town for the first time in decades, no great burst of wind announced the future with all its changes. What Charlotte felt instead was the suggestion of movement at her back, a soft breath on her neck and an eddy of air about her ankles. It was enough to propel her forward. She went to McLean's for the store had a familiar, safe feel. Beatrice was there, in some ways older than the memories Charlotte kept in the eaves of her mind, but in some ways just the same. Beatrice helped her old friend pick out a shocking-pink peasant blouse. Wrapping it in a pretty box with violet tissue paper and grosgrain ribbon, she remarked that the right packaging could transform the ordinary into something magical. Charlotte hoped that was true.

"The box was on the dining room table when I got home that night," Helen said. "I remember standing there just staring at the card. The handwriting was shaky. Smudged. But as familiar as my own. It said: *TO HELEN, FROM MAMA.* Needless to say, I poured myself three fingers of whiskey."

Cate continued writing.

That long-ago morning, when dawn cracked the sky to spill a ray of yolk-yellow sunlight across the table, Helen sat hugging the peasant blouse to her chest. Jeans dusty and feet filthy from a frantic search of the attic undertaken the minute she'd seen her mother's gift, she'd found what she was looking for in a dented box buried under a pile of Christmas decorations. The doll's skin had aged to a patchy yellow and one arm was broken, but otherwise Barbie was as she remembered: sky-blue eyes, lemon-yellow hair, and pert red lips.

"I can't tell you how many times I dragged

that doll onto Mama's bed and played games while she stared off into space," Helen said. "I used to hold Barbie up to her face, desperate for a blink or a flinch — any sign of life. Then I'd get mad, and the games would change. Instead of mommy-to-be, Barbie would be the independent career woman who needed no one. She'd be who I was determined to be, you see. I'd make her march up Mama's arm, a tiny plastic briefcase clasped in her hand as she pounded the fleshy sidewalk. But Mama never reacted. Or so I thought. As you've probably guessed, my 1970s Barbie wore a shocking-pink peasant blouse." Helen wiped a tear from her face. "The enormity of what Mama did blew me away. She found the courage to leave the house and go into town. All because she remembered how I loved that Barbie doll. Oh, Cate, I can't tell you how much I cried that morning. I cried for a little girl who'd played with a piece of painted plastic in the shadow of her mother's sorrow. And I cried for all those years I'd put on a brave face so everyone would see how confident I was that Mama would get better. But I never *really* believed it would happen," Helen confessed.

They sat companionably, Cate replaying bits and pieces of what she'd heard in her mind until something Helen had said had her sitting forward with a start. "Pink. Of course." She gestured toward Helen's pink sunglasses, called to mind the mauve and pink scarf she'd seen Helen wearing the first day they'd met. "You always wear something pink. When we went to Vitelli's and talked, it was a belt."

Helen gave a quick smile before their voices crossed. "It's my —"

"Favorite color!" Cate guessed.

"That's right."

"But what changed that morning for your mother? How did she find the courage to go into town after so many years shut off from the world?"

Getting to her feet, Helen said, "Well, that's the last piece of the puzzle. Come on." They crossed the common together and walked around St. Joseph's to a graveyard at the back. Helen stopped before two small graves, and Cate glanced down to read the names: Sean Michael Connolly and Conor Patrick Connolly. "My brothers," Helen supplied. "Father Sullivan moved them to consecrated ground."

"But how? They weren't baptized. Didn't he get in trouble?"

"No," Helen explained. "Church policy had changed by then so that unbaptized infants could be buried in hallowed ground so long as they *would* have been baptized had they lived. Seeing my brothers safe was what finally brought Mama around. Miriam suspected it would. She knew the importance of graves." Helen's eyes sought a larger headstone across the way. "My father's stone has no body beneath; still, there was a grave for Mama to visit. A place where he was remembered."

Cate nodded, thinking that for all the horror of burying John, at least he'd been returned to her. Charlotte hadn't had even that minimal comfort.

Helen sighed. "So now you know Mama's story and the part Miriam played in her recovery. Father Sullivan, too."

"And you," Cate pointed out.

"And me," Helen conceded. Drawing a deep breath, she let it out with a whoosh. "So when is this book of yours going to be done?" The question seemed to hang in the air. "Like you've been saying, it's important for women to share their stories. And writing about war and how it shapes women may help you understand how it's shaped your life. Plus, using the skills you say your husband cherished is a way of honoring him. So," she asked again, "when is this book going to be done?"

"I don't know," Cate admitted. "I don't know if I can finish it. I don't know what voice to use. Or voices. How to tell the stories — one by one, or intertwined? I just don't know yet."

"You will," Helen assured her. "When the time's right."

"How can you say that?" Cate asked in surprise. "You've never seen my writing."

"Maybe I inherited Mama's instinct for reading between the lines. You've made a lot of headway — on the book and in town. People have shared their stories with you, and patients have come to trust you. Hell, you got me to open up about the past, and I don't do that often. Now, you've talked to me, and you know about Miriam. And I'm sure Beatrice has shared a bit about the war here at home. Whose story is next?"

"I — I don't know."

"What about Sheila and Leah? You've spoken with them about their father?"

"No. Well, I've spoken to Sheila about Vincent. And with Leah about her animals. Why? Is there something else — ?"

"Oh," Helen said quickly. "Sorry. It's not for me to tell." With a glance at her watch, she said she was due at the hospital and took her leave.

Cate stared after her, wondering about

Sheila and Leah's father. Should she — no, not today. Starting back across the common, she was assailed by the gleeful screams of children and the aroma of frying meat. She stopped and turned back toward town. She wanted — needed — to be quiet. Doubting such a thing was possible given the fireworks planned for sunset, she was still determined to carve a few minutes of peace from the day. With that thought foremost in her mind, she picked up the pace for home.

The sidewalk was crowded, and she stood aside for a woman pushing a baby stroller. The toddler within grasped an American flag in one hand and a dripping ice cream cone in the other. Cate smiled at the little boy, who beamed back. After he passed, she turned to wave good-bye, and sunlight glinted off her wedding ring. That she still wore it was a subject of conversation in town. She knew that. More than once, she had considered taking it off, but the truth was she still felt married. And seeing the gold band gave her a sense of continuity. It was a link not only to John, but to the Cate she'd been when the world was filled with possibility and promise. Then her mind circled back to Charlotte's story, and she wondered if, in her own way, she was hiding in the past. Losing today in missing yesterday. She slipped the ring to her knuckle and stared at her hand. The spot where the gold band had been was a lighter color, like new skin over a wound — healed but still vulnerable. She slid the ring back into place and tried to imagine the day it would rest in her jewelry box.

Chapter 26

"I learned how to make gravy from Rosa," Sheila explained, nodding toward a pot of spaghetti sauce bubbling on the stove. The smell of basil, garlic, and onions hung in the air, and Bon Jovi sang on the radio. Cate's stomach growled loudly, and Sheila smiled, pointing toward an oak table nearby. "Sit," she commanded, moving to slice a piece of what looked like rolled-up egg. When Cate licked her lips in anticipation, Sheila said, "It's frittata arrotolata — eggs, spinach, and onions." She plated a serving, adding a heel of bread and a thick wedge of white cheese before passing it to Cate.

"Is there coffee? Please tell me there's coffee!" Leah groaned from the open doorway. Shifting a box to her hip, she shut the door behind her, and the distant drift of voices died away. When Sheila reached for a stainless steel percolator that sat on the stove, Leah let out a low whistle before flopping down on the seat next to Cate. "Wow. Look at that old thing. I keep telling my big sister to get rid of it."

"She won't," Cate supplied, glancing up from her meal. "Modern coffee makers have plastic parts and doodads. Sheila thinks they leach toxins."

"I think that because they do," Sheila pointed out, pouring two cups of coffee. She crossed the room to place one before Cate and hand the other to Leah. Then she shook her head in disapproval at Leah's fur-coated clothing. "Oh, look at you!"

"What?" Leah asked, reaching for a crust of bread that lay on the prep counter.

Slapping her hand away, Sheila scolded, "If you're hungry, I'll make you something. You don't have to eat scraps like one of your puppies." Then her gaze lit on the flaming russet mane she knew so well. "What the —" She flicked a hand toward Leah's hair for it was tied back with what looked to be a bit of black leather. "That's a leash! You're wearing a dog leash!"

Leah's hands flew to her head. A guilty look sketched its way across the perfect symmetry of her features only to be replaced by one of defiance. "It's a cat collar, actually. What of it?" A soft meow sounded from the box Leah now held on her lap.

Sheila threw up her hands. "What's that? You know I can't have animals in the store! The health inspector could have my butt for this." She peered into the box. "For goodness' sake, can't you leave those cats for even an hour?"

Unruffled, Leah proceeded to bottle-feed a squirming kitten. With its eyes screwed shut, the white ball of fluff was no larger than a baseball. "They need to be fed every two hours. I couldn't leave them behind. Besides, Cate doesn't mind. And nobody else is here to." Her eyes swept the room before coming to rest on her sister's flushed face.

Watching the give-and-take, Cate felt a pang of longing. *I wish I had a sister. Or cousins. But then, if I had the real thing, I wouldn't have learned to write characters to say the words I never heard. Yet, I would trade it all for that comfortable familiarity Sheila and Leah share.*

Muttering that her sister was a lost cause, Sheila filled a plate with food and handed it to Leah. Then she returned to the stove and gave the gravy a stir. Thrusting out a hip as if in inquiry, she turned to ask, "So why are we here, Cate? What did you want to talk about?"

"You tell me," Cate replied, pushing her

empty plate away and choosing her words carefully. "I've heard mention of your father and something that happened to him during WWII. If you don't want to discuss it, I understand completely. But if you do —"

"We don't," Sheila said sharply.

"Speak for yourself," Leah cut in. She held a kitten in one hand and her fork in the other. "I can talk, eat, and feed at the same time." She turned to Cate, "What do you want to know?"

"Leah! That's family business, not something to be — I don't know, written about. Spread around."

"Everybody in town already knows about Jack," her sister pointed out. "Who else matters? Cate can change those details we want her to or not use our real names even. Right?"

"Absolutely," Cate answered quickly. "The agreement I've made with everyone so far is that I'll show them what I write, and anything they don't want revealed won't be. Most people have actually found the experience of talking through the past sort of liberating."

"Life is in the telling," Sheila said, repeating the phrase that was making its way around town. "Your grandmother had that right. And it's a good tagline for the book.

You may be right that when women on the home front begin to share their stories, the way men see war will change. At least I hope you're right. But our story's our own."

"Again, speak for yourself," Leah repeated. "I'm going to talk about him. You don't have to, but I want to." Addressing herself to Cate, she explained, "By the time I was born, my father was gone. I only met him after I'd grown up. Sheila and my mother never spoke about him. They wanted to shield me from what he'd done. I understand why they did that — well, now I do. But years ago I was really angry about it. Sheila has always thought it was her job to protect me. The big-sister mentality. I love that about her. And it pisses me off." She fixed her sister with a loaded look, and their eyes held.

Sheila's chin jutted up. Then contrition laid a hand on her, and she conceded, "I didn't tell you anything about the bastard because I didn't want to see you hurt. I see now that keeping the truth from you was wrong, even if I did it for the right reasons."

Pressing the advantage, Leah said, "Cate will hear the story eventually, Sheila. It's best she does from us. But you know, it would be easier to talk over dessert." Returning the last kitten to the box, she tucked a blanket around the now-silent litter.

Sheila pursed her lips as if considering. Reaching up to a shelf over the stove, she pulled down a small box and brought it to the table. When she lifted the lid, the scent of chocolate filled the air. "Try these. I've been experimenting with praline truffles. Seventy percent cocoa. Let me know what you think." Before she'd finished the description, Leah was reaching out a hand. After sampling a piece, she moaned in appreciation.

Cate popped a truffle in her mouth, savoring the tart, dark chocolate paired with a dusting of sea salt. Then she bit down, and there was a sweet explosion as the creamy center hit her taste buds. "Divine," she pronounced. "Just heaven."

"As usual," Leah added, licking her fingers in turn.

Nodding as though she'd regained command of the room, if not control of the conversation, Sheila returned to the stove as Leah began to speak of their father. Cate learned that Jack Mitchell grew up in Amberley and was as eager as his friends to enlist during WWII. When he boarded a bus and headed off to Georgia for basic training, a brass band played in front of McLean's. "Like so many in Amberley, my grandmother stood on the sidewalk waving good-bye. She was crying — tears of pride for the nation he would defend, tears of fear for what the future held, and tears of sorrow that her son would soon be schooled in the art of death and sent to kill some other mother's boy," Leah explained. "Grandma wasn't alone; my mother was with her. She was younger than my father, but they'd grown up across the street from each other. Nobody was surprised when they fell in love and got engaged."

Sheila picked up the narrative by explaining that she could never conjure the image of her father as the sweet boy her mother used to speak of. Although Sheila accepted that people could change, she didn't see how life could change them beyond recognition. Shaking her black bangs as if to clear her thoughts, she said, "Curiously enough, given the man he became, my father apparently served his country with distinction. After he was discharged, he married Mama. With the help of a GI mortgage, they bought a house, and my father built an auto body shop on River Road — the one that Lulu owns now. There was a lot of work in town after the war, and he had a reputation for honesty — well, then he did. Seems he used to joke that if he could keep Patton's tanks rolling, there wasn't anything on Amberley's streets he couldn't handle. The life my parents built began to fall apart the day my father learned who Miriam Rosen was."

"Miriam?" Cate asked, surprised.

Sheila nodded, methodically stirring the pot of gravy. "Mama was working at McLean's then and got to know Miriam. They spoke of her life in Europe. When Mama repeated the stories to my father, he stormed out of the house and rushed over to McLean's where he made quite a scene, yelling at Miriam in front of Beatrice. My father was stationed in Germany after the war. He picked up enough of the language to get by, so nobody knew what he and Miriam said because it was in German. When he came home from McLean's that day, he packed up his clothes. Mama was beside herself. She begged him to explain, but he wouldn't. He shook her off when she grabbed at him as he tried to leave, throwing her to the floor." The hand that held the wooden spoon whitened. "It was as if, in an instant, my father became a different person — angry and hurtful. Scary. I was standing upstairs watching them, peeking between the banisters. I was young — so very young — but I remember my father's red face, or at least I think I do. Maybe I just remember

Mama telling me what happened afterward. Anyway, he stormed out of the house, leaving her in tears. Oh, he came back the next morning, all apologies, but he was only biding his time. A week later, he sold the auto body shop. Mama suspected something because he was at home in the mornings, watching at the window for the mailman. I guess he was waiting for a check from the sale of the business. Well, it must have come, because one morning we heard the car roar to life and he was gone. He cleaned out the bank accounts, leaving Mama with nothing."

Cate was silent for some time before asking, "So what was your father's connection to Miriam?"

"Mama never asked her," Sheila said. "Talking about the war years was hard for Miriam. Mama understood that, or came to with Beatrice and Rosa's help. Plus — plus I think part of her didn't really want to know. She couldn't let go of this image of my father as the boy he'd been before he went to war."

"It wasn't just an image," Leah cut in, the exchange so sharp Cate suspected the issue was something the sisters had long debated. "Daddy loved her when they married. We were conceived in love; she always said that!"

A shiver of forewarning ran down Cate's spine when she saw Sheila take a steadying breath. "Leah's always believed that the man my father was when the war ended wasn't his doing. Believing that is easier than accepting that war only brought to the surface something that had always been there." Sheila inclined her head toward the boiling marinara, and Cate rose to her feet as though bidden. Making her way to the stove, she glanced over the rim of the pot to see islands of orange foam floating in the sputtering liquid. Sheila explained that to make good gravy, she cooked tomatoes until all their impurities floated to the surface. The trick was to skim off that bit of bitterness as soon as you saw it, before it disappeared. "If you wait long enough, even perfect-looking tomatoes surrender something impure." Sparing a glance at her sister's averted head, Sheila said. "Some people are like that — proper looking on the outside, but hiding something bitter within. Sooner or later, that badness shows itself. As it did with my father when he went to war." Turning her attention back to the pot, she carefully skimmed the bubbles off with a metal spoon before flinging them into a nearby sink.

Sheila's words hit home, and Cate began to wonder if war was a crucible or transformative, for the distinction was significant. She had always believed as Leah apparently did — that war affected change in people. But was it possible that it merely burned away what was extraneous and façade? If Sheila was right, then war was a paring knife — a disturbing concept since the logical extension of such thinking was that war refines the individual by exposing his true self. No, Cate decided with grim certainty, that wasn't true. Couldn't be true.

Silence filled the room, and her gaze moved from Sheila's flushed face to Leah's pale oval. She felt a lump rise in her throat, for her questions had forced two women she respected to dredge up old memories and past pain. "I'm sorry to have reminded you of your father," she apologized. "Please forgive me."

"No, it's my fault," Leah said, rising to her feet and walking toward her sister. "I insisted on talking about him. I thought it would help, but it never does." Sheila turned to give her a quick hug. When they separated, Leah explained, "Sheila and I disagree, as you can see. I've always believed that war changed Daddy. If that's not the case, then his life before was a lie. Or at least partly a lie. And to live a lie means he was — I don't know, twisted in some way. I worry that maybe that part of him, that evil seed, could be part of who I am, too."

Sheila's voice rose. "How many times do I have to tell you that there's nothing of that bastard in us?"

"I have his green eyes," Leah countered.

"But you don't see the world like Jack did! You're kind, gentle, and loving! Nothing like him. Nothing!" Sheila spat the word out, her face hard.

Leah merely shrugged. "Maybe. Maybe not."

In that moment of indecision and doubt, Cate understood the unique burden each sister carried. The shadow and stigma of whatever sins their father had committed shaped their lives. Sheila, in characteristic maternal fashion, tried to shield Leah from painful truths. For her part, Leah championed their mother's judgment by arguing that Jack Mitchell had once been a decent, loving man. And both sisters had chosen careers that reinforced the roles in which they'd been cast. Sheila's protective nature led her to nurture friends and strangers alike with food, the most basic of comforts. Leah believed firmly that horrific experiences could be overcome — by animals as well as people — so as a vet she advocated rehabilitation over euthanasia. And she undertook to retrain war-zone animals. Still, although the dark aftermath of war had shaped the women they became, they'd managed to fashion lives defined by love and kindness. That might have been due to their mother's influence, but it was also their choice and testament to their strength.

After a time, Sheila concluded, "We should tell her the rest of the story, Leah. We've come this far." She turned off the stove and moved to join them at the table. Sitting down wearily, she rested her feet on a chair and rolled her shoulders. Then she described the day she told her family she was marrying Vincent. After hearing the news, her mother had gone to her jewelry box to withdraw a small velvet box. Nestled in its white satin lining was a magnificent gold ring. "It was her engagement ring — a marble-sized purple stone ringed with diamonds. She'd only worn it on special occasions and never to work or just around the house. And once my father left, Mama took it off for good. When she offered it to me, well, I was stunned that she would give it up because she had really never stopped loving him. And I was surprised to find I wanted it."

"You always called it the grape-jelly ring," Leah reminded her.

Sheila's laugh rang out like that of the young girl she'd been. "When I was little, I thought Mama's ring was filled with grape jelly, like the kind that used to come in glass jars with cartoon characters on them — the Flintstones or Casper the Friendly Ghost. You're both too young to remember those." Her gaze fixed on the past, she described holding the ring toward the light and seeing a star shape flicker within. "It was a star ruby, you see. Surrounded by eighteen flawless, brilliant-cut diamonds. I stared at it for the longest time, imagining it on my finger — the finger of a grown-up, married woman. I asked Mama where my father had gotten the ring, and she said a jeweler in New York. I believed her — why wouldn't I?"

In slipping the ring on her finger, Sheila had set in motion a chain of events that would change so many lives. As she relayed what had happened, Cate made notes. That night, she put the story to paper.

CHAPTER 27

EXCERPT FROM *THE TAPESTRY OF WAR*

In November of 1990, Sheila Morazzo was elected mayor of Amberley. The local paper ran a story entitled "Half a Century of Female Rule" that profiled Sheila and former mayor Beatrice McLean. After it was picked up by the national press, Sheila went to great lengths to avoid the appearance of impropriety, so business from anyone even remotely connected with government was politely refused. The grocery's bottom line suffered accordingly. Resolved to turn a healthy profit despite the challenges she faced, she accepted a catering job in late December. A blizzard prevented her staff from getting to work the morning before the order was to be ready, but it didn't stop Sheila. After bundling herself against the cold, she headed into town, grateful to get out of the house. All morning she had been battling indigestion, and the cold air was invigorating. Vincent had been called to the hospital, and it was just as well; she knew her husband wouldn't approve of her working so late in her pregnancy.

A biting wind snatched at her hair, and, although snowplows had been working all morning, not a single car passed as she shuffled along. When she turned onto Main Street, the storm began to gather strength. Stamping her feet on the ice-slicked sidewalk outside Vitelli's, she pulled off her gloves and blew on her hands. A gust of snow numbed her face as she fumbled with the front door alarm, and she slipped into the warm interior with a sigh of relief.

The first labor pains struck while Sheila was pulling a tray of pignoli cookies from the oven. Letting out a cry, she doubled over and clutched the stove, white-knuckled. Fear pounded through her like the heartbeat of her unborn child. Why had she gone out in a snowstorm? Idiot! She was an idiot! As the pain crested, her eyes sought the phone. She stumbled toward it, lifted the receiver, and heard — nothing. The line was dead. Drawing a ragged breath, she gripped the wall and made her way slowly around the room. By the time she reached the front of the store, another contraction hit her like a wave.

When she heard the sound of muffled laughter, the sharp prick of reality burst her panicked thoughts. Sheila peered outside. Two boys stood across the street. Jerking the door open, she shouted, but the rising wind tore the cry from her. Drawing a breath, she tried again. Had they heard her? The snow was falling faster, obscuring her vision until the two boys were just a few feet away. They were brothers by the look of it, for the same red hair framed faces sprinkled with freckles. "Help me," she called, one hand grasping the doorframe while the other reached out.

"It's the lady Mommy knows," the taller boy said, handing the cookie he held to the younger boy. "She's sick. Let's get her inside." He half dragged Sheila onto a chair before looking around the empty store.

"Help," Sheila cried. "I need help." The boys shifted their feet uncertainly as the panic Sheila felt sharpened into hysteria. "Don't leave me," she begged. "Please!" She recognized the boys, but from where? Then she remembered: Her friend, Helen Doyle, had adopted two brothers from an Irish orphanage. "You're Helen's boys, aren't you?" Both nodded, and she saw that the younger held two cookies in his gloved hands. "The cookies. Where — did — you

416

— get — them?" She struggled to get the words out as another pain hit.

The older boy spoke. "The nice lady who works at the diner."

"Gaby!" Sheila sat up straighter. "Gaby's at the diner?" They nodded. "Go, go and get her." Sheila was shouting now. "Bring her here. Go now!" The boys tore from the store, leaving the door open behind them. Snow drifted in, and Sheila could hear the wind rising. She slumped in the chair. What was taking so long? Had Gaby gone home? And then the question uppermost in her thoughts: Was her baby all right? She hadn't felt her move since the pains began — was that normal? Surely, if there was something wrong, she'd know it; she'd know if her child was in danger. Then she remembered that Miriam hadn't known her son was dead, and Rosa hadn't known hers was alive. A wave of terror washed over Sheila, numbing her mind and sapping her strength. Her eyes closed.

"Sheila! Sheila! Wake up!"

Sheila heard the voice from a distance. It was wrapped in cotton batting, like the quilt her mother had made when Leah was born. "Sheila!" Now the voice scraped like chalk on a blackboard. *Have to stop the voice. It will wake the baby. Baby.* Sheila struggled to open her eyes, swimming to consciousness with an effort that exhausted her. "Gaby?" she asked weakly.

"I came in to check on the generator," her friend explained, peeling off the mittens she wore and blowing on her reddened hands. "Thank God I did. I saw Helen's boys and gave them some cookies. Then the storm got so bad, I decided to head out and look for them. I was just locking up." Bending over Sheila, she pitched her voice low. "Is there anyone else here? Is Miriam upstairs?"

"No. She's away. And the phones are out. I didn't bring my car phone with me. Why didn't I bring it?" Sheila's voice rose and she began to shiver.

"Boys," Gaby instructed in a no-nonsense voice, "pick up Mrs. Morazzo's feet."

Sheila drifted off before awaking to find herself lying on the kitchen table beneath a pile of towels. Water was boiling on the stove, and she was alone. She tried to sit up, but the pain was worse, and she managed to move only a few inches.

"I'm here, honey," a voice said from behind her before a hand stroked her arm. "I was just getting some more towels. I sent the boys out to wait in the store. We're alone. Sheila, you need to try and relax."

The front door banged open, and Gaby started. "I told them to stay put!" A moment later, she moved to stand between the table and the kitchen door. What she saw sent a shiver down her spine. The man who stood before her was bathed in an inky film of corruption and regret. *Oh, of all the times for this to happen,* Gaby thought. Blinking rapidly to clear the image from her mind, she shifted her gaze away from his face. "I'm sorry, but we're closed."

"I'm looking for Sheila Mitchell," he said.

Sheila started at the voice. Straining her neck, she inched her way up to a seated position and gasped. "Jack!" The name was torn from her as a contraction lashed her body.

Gaby took in the decrepit figure before her, finding little of the Jack Mitchell she remembered from her youth. For a moment, the dark waters that covered his soul parted, and Gaby saw with startling clarity that he cared for Sheila.

"What's wrong?" Jack demanded, moving toward the table and taking his daughter's hand in his before she jerked it away.

Gaby's mind was racing. Jack Mitchell was at an emotional crossroads; even now, the surge of concern she had seen was warring with his darker nature. Most important, the

419

reunion was upsetting Sheila, and that anxiety would be felt by the child. Grabbing the sleeve of Jack's cashmere coat, she shifted her gaze between Sheila's pale face and the man she knew her friend despised. "How did you get through the storm? Do you have a car?" Gaby asked in a rush. "Sheila's having a baby; she needs to get to the hospital. The phones are out and —"

He was already moving toward the door. "I parked down the street. Had a hell of a time getting here, but I made it. I'll pull around front."

"No!" Sheila's scream cut the air. "Gaby, don't let him near me. Please."

Gaby nodded briskly. "I won't, honey." Turning toward Jack, she demanded, "Get to the hospital and bring back Sheila's husband."

"Husband?"

"Dr. Morazzo," Gaby added impatiently. "Hurry up!" She shoved him out the door into the store, her eyes scanning the room. "Where are the boys?"

Jack looked confused.

"Two little boys, dressed in matching snowsuits. Weren't they here when you came in?"

"No. There was no one in the store."

Gaby swore under her breath. "They've

gone out in the storm! I told them to stay put, that it wasn't safe." Her eyes strayed toward the front door, but she couldn't leave Sheila alone. Her dilemma was obvious even to a stranger.

"I'll keep an eye out for them," he assured her. "After I come back with the doctor, I'll keep looking."

Gaby stared at him. "Why? You don't exactly have the reputation for —"

"Kindness?"

"Or decency. What are you doing back here anyway?"

He threw her a calculating look before the mask that had slipped for a moment settled back in place. "That's none of your business." Pulling his coat closed, Jack Mitchell opened the front door, letting in a blast of cold just as Sheila's cries split the air.

The lady from the diner had told Brian and Jimmy to stay in Vitelli's, and for a few minutes they had, warming their hands before the brick oven that blazed in the corner. That's when Brian got to thinking. The sick lady was Sheila Morazzo, an old friend of his mother's. When he was sick, his mother put him to bed with hot chocolate and a pile of comic books. But the time he'd been bitten by a dog, she'd taken him to a doctor. There had been lots of blood, and he'd gotten stitches. Although it hurt something awful, now he had a cool scar on his hand and a story to tell. After studying the scar for a moment, Brian knew what to do. If he helped his mother's friend get better, his mother wouldn't mind so much that he'd broken her fancy china cup that morning.

Reaching for his coat and mittens, Brian announced, "We have to find a doctor for that lady." Pulling his brother out the door, he tried to shield the younger boy from the snowy wind whipping through town. He knew he should have left Jimmy in the warm store, but his little brother had begun to cry, and Brian hadn't the heart to leave him behind.

Slowly, they made their way down the street, grabbing onto parking meters and streetlights to keep their balance. "Just follow me," Brian shouted, his breath white vapor. Jimmy nodded, eyes tearing from the cold. Brian saw the woman first, silhouetted against a wall of packed snow piled behind the hotel. A pair of cross-country skis was propped against a Dumpster, and she was bent over a drainpipe that snaked its way up the side of the building. "She's still here," he shouted to his brother, running faster now, his feet slipping out from under him. "Doctor Mitchell!"

Leah turned at the sound of her name, eyes scanning the street before settling on the two figures bundled beyond recognition. Dragging a box from behind her, she deposited the squirming kitten she had rescued inside. "What are you boys doing out in this weather?" she cried, pulling on her gloves. "Brian? Is that you?" She peered behind the nodding boy. "And little Jimmy? Does your mother know where you are?" It took only a minute for the story to tumble out of their chapped lips.

Leah took off at a run, clutching the box under her coat and dragging the boys behind her. She rounded the corner of Main Street and hurried toward Vitelli's, her heart pounding even as she registered the image of a silver sedan fishtailing its way down the street. A drift of snow blocked the front door of the grocery, and she threw her weight against it before tumbling inside. The boys were right behind her, slipping on the wet floor as they hurried toward the back of the store. Leah shut the door and checked on the frightened, trembling kitten. She punched holes in the box and set it on the floor beside the stove before running for the kitchen.

■ ■ ■ ■

"We g-got the doctor," Brian stuttered, falling into the room with Jimmy a step behind.

"Thank God," Gaby breathed, wiping Sheila's forehead before shooing the boys away from the table. "Sit down and take off those wet things." When the door swung open again, she looked up expecting to see Vincent. "Leah!"

"She was outside. We saw her before, feeding the cats up the street." Brian rushed on, teeth chattering but eager to tell his story.

Gaby put a restraining hand on his arm. "Yes, Brian, you two did well. Now sit quietly while Dr. Mitchell helps her sister. Can you do that for me?"

Two carrot-topped heads nodded solemnly.

Leah flexed blood back into her numb fingers before rushing to the table. Her sister's pulse was strong. "Sheila? Can you hear me?"

"Leah?" Sheila's eyelids fluttered open. "Am I dreaming?"

"No, sweetheart," Leah laughed nervously. Throwing her coat and hat aside, she plunged her hands into a basin of water and began to scrub up. Drying them on the cloth Gaby held out, she lifted her sister's skirt and examined her. "Sheila, I need you to rest until I tell you to push. Can you do that for me?" Leah's voice was calm and soothing, the voice she used with frightened animals and anxious owners. Sheila nodded, her eyes saucers, before tensing and letting loose a cry of pain. She went limp, her eyes rolling back in her head.

"Sheila! Stay with me." Leah turned to Gaby. "We have to keep her awake. Bathe her face with ice or —" Leah turned toward the boys who now stood behind her, swallowing hard and looking as if they'd like to both flee the room and edge closer. "Brian! Take that copper pot and go get me some snow from outside. Move!" He jumped, grabbing the pot and making for the door just as it swung inward.

Jack stepped aside for the running boy. "Can't get through." He coughed before his eyes locked on Leah's — the same green as his own. "Who are you?"

"Get out of here!" Leah ordered with all the authority of her medical training. Addressing her patient, she cooed, "It's all right, Sheila, you're doing fine. Just stay with me."

Brian shuffled in, dragging the now heavy pot. Leah packed a handful of snow into a ball and held it to her sister's forehead. Sheila started at the touch, and her eyes fluttered open. Gaby stepped toward Leah and whispered, "This is your father."

Leah turned, taking in the aged form before her. "You're Jack Mitchell?"

"Do I know you?" The voice was accusatory and suspicious.

"No," Leah stated flatly. "Why would you know your own daughter?"

"Daughter?" He scrutinized her face with narrowed eyes. "Fay was pregnant? Why didn't she tell me?" he asked angrily.

"From what I heard, you didn't give her the chance to say much before you left," Gaby hissed.

"Who the hell are you, anyway?" Jack demanded.

Gaby saw the Doyle brothers watching with rounded eyes and ordered, "Go out and sit in the store." She pointed a warning finger in their direction. "And don't even think about leaving again. Your mother must be worried sick about you two. Until I can get in touch with her, stay put! Do you understand?" Only when they had nodded and scurried out the door did Gaby glare at Jack. "I'm a friend of Sheila and Leah's, and if you do anything to upset them, you won't walk out of here. Is that understood?"

His face broke into something between a grimace and a smile. "Loyalty. I admire that." Addressing himself to Sheila, he said evenly, "I saw your picture in the paper. After the election, the national press picked up the story — small town run for decades by women."

"And you wanted to offer congratulations?" Eyes fixed on her sister's pale face, Leah threw the challenge over her shoulder. "Get out! Can't you see what's happening here?"

"I saw the ring in that picture," Jack hissed, his voice low and menacing. "It's mine by rights. And I need the money."

"What ring?" Leah asked. Then her gaze settled on the star ruby her sister always wore. "Mama gave that to Sheila!"

Sheila gasped as a contraction took hold. "Leah," she panted, twisting the ruby ring off her swollen finger. "I don't care. Give it to him. Make him go."

Leah accepted the ring, turning it over in her hand before holding it out to Jack. As he reached out for it, she pulled her hand back, frowning. "Sheila, the markings inside are Hebrew. I spent some time in Israel, remember? Working with that animal-rights group? I — I recognize the alphabet."

Gaby grabbed Leah's arm. A memory was

struggling to the surface of her thoughts. "Miriam! That's the connection. It was after your father spoke to her that he left town." She turned toward Jack. "Miriam is somehow connected to the ring, isn't she?"

Jack's eyes narrowed to jet-black slits in an ashen face. "That bitch ruined my life. Where is she? Tell me!"

"She died." Gaby had the presence of mind to lie before Leah or Sheila could respond. "Years ago. She didn't have an easy life."

Jack rocked back on his heels, relieved. "So she won't be making trouble." Then he stepped closer to his daughters, pulling all the air in the room toward him. "What did she tell you?"

"She told us everything, as it turns out," Gaby punted with a knowing look at her friends. "We just didn't put it together until now."

"Well, I didn't take the ring from her; a German officer did that years before. I just bought it after the war. For a pittance. There was so much money to be made then, I'd have been a fool not to take my share." He gave a brittle laugh shot through with disbelief. "Somehow Miriam found out I had the ring and tracked me down. I warned her to keep her mouth shut. What's done is done, I told her. No use digging up the past. But she wouldn't let it go." And then, as if to himself, "I should have made her see sense instead of running. But I panicked." His hands fisted slowly before his gaze found the ring again.

Gaby moved to stand between her friends and their father. Pitching her voice for his ears only, she said, "Get out."

Jack smirked. "Why should I?"

For a moment, Gaby's courage faltered. Jack Mitchell had done horrible things in his life. Like wine splattered across a linen cloth, the sins he'd committed dotted his soul. Here and there, she glimpsed a clear patch where the power of love had diluted the stain of evil, but was it enough to save him? She didn't know. Nor did she care. Throwing her shoulders back, she drew a steadying breath. While Leah and Sheila prepared for the coming birth, Gaby told Jack Mitchell what she'd seen of his past. When he blanched, she hinted at what his life would become.

In response, he turned hunter's eyes on the ruby ring for a moment that stretched to breaking. His gaze flicked to Sheila's sweat-stained face, and Gaby glimpsed a hint of humanity. Maybe even remorse. "Okay. Sheila can keep it. Damn thing's brought me nothing but trouble. Besides, it's probably too distinctive a piece to unload."

Only after she'd locked the front door behind Jack Mitchell did Gaby let out the breath she was holding. She'd never used her gift to intimidate before, and she was unnerved by how good it had felt. Moving to stand beside Leah, she soothed, "Forget him; he's gone. Sheila needs you now."

"Yes, yes," Leah mumbled, with a silent prayer that she would be up to the task before her.

Sheila's daughter, Sara, was born an hour later. At Sheila's insistence, Gaby weighed the baby on the scale in the kitchen of Vitelli's and pronounced her six pounds, three ounces. Then Gaby relegated Brian and Jimmy to a corner of the kitchen and poured them hot chocolate. They reached eagerly for the blue crockery mugs, grateful for the simple comfort of warm hands. As the two boys began to rehash the day's adventures, the frightening moments wore smoother with each retelling.

When the storm eased, Vincent arrived, breathless and frantic. As pallid winter sunlight filled Vitelli's kitchen, he took in the scene — Sheila lying still on the table, Leah bent over her, Gaby boiling water.

Then a bundle on the table stirred, and a baby's wail filled the air. With a grin of joy, Vincent rushed to embrace his family.

CHAPTER 28

After reading the manuscript, Sheila looked up with shining eyes, and Cate knew that all the effort she had put into the story had been worth it. They sat together in the kitchen of Vitelli's, the room where Sheila had learned so much from Rosa; confronted her father; and, given birth to her daughter. Cate had yet to meet Sara, but calculated she must be about twenty and Helen's sons a few years older. She asked what had become of the boys.

Sheila hesitated, wrinkling her brow. "Brian does something with investments. He was on Wall Street, but moved back here a few months ago. From what Helen said, he's saved a pile of money."

"And Jimmy?"

"He's a priest, actually. Helen hopes he'll replace Father Sullivan when he retires." Sheila shook her head. "We were all surprised when Jimmy chose the priesthood,

Sara most of all. She used to trail around after him when they were kids. Puppy love and nothing more, but Helen and I couldn't resist matchmaking. Still, Sara's found a different kind of love: being a chef. She's away at culinary school, you know. Not that Vincent didn't try to push her into medicine from day one. He gave her a little nurse's uniform when she was a child. She took one look at it and announced that if she decided to work in medicine, she would be a doctor like her father, not a nurse. I howled at that one. Anyway, she wants to open a pizzeria here in town. Maybe take over a section of Peter Flynn's place, and knock down the wall so that customers can enter from the street or through Vitelli's."

"Sounds like a good idea."

"I agree, not that I'll let on to her. She needs financing, but I can't just hand my daughter a business; she'll have to earn it like I did."

"I can understand that. It took you years to work your way up to owning this place."

Sheila eyed Cate sharply. "That's right; you know the story now. Before long, you'll know all our stories. Well, at least the parts we're willing to share." Then a broad grin spread across her face. "Speaking of the pizzeria, I have to give Sara credit for emotional blackmail. She wants to name the place Rosa's. Ha! She thinks that will sway me."

"Will it?"

Sheila's eyes lit at the thought. "Probably. But I'll make her sweat a bit first." Her voice dropped a note. "Miriam was her godmother, you know. She was shocked when I asked her, but so long as one godparent is Catholic, it's okay. That picture of her outside the church so proudly holding my baby is one I carry close to my heart. Oh, Cate, you should have seen Miriam's face the day I returned the ring to her. She was overcome. Speechless. You see, it was the last thing her father made. When she first slipped it on her finger, she made a vow that no one would take it from her. She tried to keep that vow and safeguard it through the war, but as the ghetto was being emptied out and the last survivors were sent to Auschwitz, Miriam was betrayed by someone who thought to curry favor with the Germans. She told me how an officer yanked the ring from her finger and held it to the light to appraise it. Miriam wanted to scream at the sight of him touching something her father had poured so much love into. She saw the ruby flash one final time before it was thrown into a box like so much junk. After the war, Miriam tracked down the officer who had stolen it. He was living back in Germany, having picked up the threads of his former life as if nothing had changed."

"How in the world did she find him?" Cate wondered aloud.

"Through some of her brothers' friends who were tracking down German officers and, well, dealing with them. They helped Miriam find the one who'd taken her ring, but when Miriam confronted him, he didn't remember anything. I think that made her angrier than anything. Her brothers' friends endeavored to refresh this guy's memory with their fists, and finally he revealed that after the war he had sold a truckload of stolen valuables. They tracked down the buyer. He'd sold the ring to someone else — you can imagine how it was. All those years Miriam was in Europe searching for her brothers, she was also looking for the ring. The promise she'd made when she slipped it on her finger weighed heavily on her; she had to find it. When she learned that one of the black-market operators was an American soldier, Miriam was elated. She thought that if she spoke to this man — to my father — and explained everything, he would return the ring to her. Once she learned Jack had been sent home, she made plans to follow him. Then she found out about the resettlement program here."

"Wow." Cate exhaled. "What a story. If Father Sullivan hadn't set that up —"

"Miriam might not have made it to Amberley. Traveling was expensive in those days, and she had so little." Sheila paused. "I can't imagine Amberley without her. My life without her. She was such a good friend to Rosa and Beatrice. To so many. Strange to think about how interconnected we are — how a good deed or an evil one ripples outward." Sheila sighed. "As soon as she got to town, Miriam started looking for Jack. In the service his name was Jonathan, and there are quite a few Mitchell families in the area. By the time Miriam was sure she'd found my father, she already knew Mama for they both worked at McLean's. Miriam had no idea — not then — that Jack had given Mama the ring, because Mama only wore it on special occasions. Never at work. Mama must have mentioned something to my father about Miriam that aroused his suspicions, because before Miriam could confront him, Jack stormed into McLean's looking for her. Well, you know the rest. Jack must have told Miriam that Mama had the ring, but Miriam never asked her for it."

Cate leaned forward. "Why not? After everything that had happened, after searching for so many years —"

"Something Gaby said." She held up a hand to forestall Cate's question. "I don't know exactly. Gaby never told me. And I wouldn't bother asking her, because she never breaks a confidence." Sheila frowned. "I appreciate that when it's my secrets she's keeping, but not when I'm trying to find out something. She did say that the truth would come out one day — whatever that means."

"And you never asked Miriam why she kept silent all those years?"

"No, I just couldn't. Talking about the past was too painful for her."

Summer was over, taking with it the last of Cate's hopes that Eddie Fallon would succeed in locating the two corporals who'd been with John the day he died. Every time Eddie phoned, her heart began a measured pounding before a heavy feeling took hold when she heard the undercurrent of regret in his voice. He would explain that he'd made little progress, his efforts hampered by the fact that perhaps the two men didn't want to be found. Cate's own attempts to pressure the army for information — with letters, phone calls, pleas to her congressmen, and e-mails to the press — had amounted to nothing. Reminding herself that she was doing all she could, she channeled her frustration into finishing the book. The submission deadline was November 11th, a date creeping ever closer.

Cate spent every free minute before her laptop. There was nothing more frustrating than staring at a blank screen as the stories she'd heard circled her mind, and bits of description and dialogue scrambled to find their place. When that happened, a trickle of panic made her question whether she was up to the task. Then she would draw a calming breath, settle her hands over the keyboard, and try to breathe life into the words that filled her heart.

Late one afternoon, after struggling to write a difficult passage, she felt antsy and decided to walk to the common. Settling herself on a bench, she reached in her pocket to withdraw a journal entry she'd found slipped under her front door earlier that week. Ten more had followed. Some were gut-wrenching, and others poignant. But how should they be fused together, if at all? She felt a shiver run up her spine and wondered if it was a reaction to the sudden gust of wind brushing past or a foretelling of challenges to come.

Part of her longed for an evening away from writing when she could sink into a bubble bath and let her thoughts drift. Perhaps she'd finish unpacking the last boxes she'd had shipped from Boston — boxes filled with memories she'd consigned to storage rather than let loose on her new life. Or maybe she'd just crawl into bed and wait for the sun to tiptoe its way in the window of her bedroom. Her bedroom. Miriam's bedroom.

Dropping her gaze to Miriam's handwriting, she tilted the paper to catch the fading light.

One chilly spring morning, I decided to tell my good friend Fay Mitchell about her husband and how he'd been a war profiteer. A black-market dealer in goods stolen from those slaughtered during the Holocaust. I kept silent for months because I knew the truth would hurt her, but lies help no one. I was sitting in a park trying to work up my courage. Fay was a sweet woman raising children alone. But she deserved to know the truth, and I wanted so desperately to see Papa's ring again. To feel it on my finger where it belonged.

A young girl, cute as a button, walked up

and sat down next to me. I'd seen her in town and tried to place where when I remembered that her parents owned the diner. The girl was carrying a cookie I recognized as one of Rosa's. She broke it in two and held half out to me. I smiled and accepted it. She introduced herself as Gabrielle, the name too formal for one so young.

"My name is Miriam," I replied. "You know, your namesake, the angel Gabriel, is very powerful."

"I don't have any power," the child said matter-of-factly, "but I can see broken things that my mommy can't."

"What do you mean?" I asked, only half minding her chatter for I knew how fanciful children could be.

"I can see you're broken and want to get back the part that's missing," she continued in a voice more grown-up than she. "Only" — she hesitated — "taking it back will break someone else."

I felt an odd sensation on my skin, like the edge of fear mingled with something I hadn't known for many years. How could this child I'd never met see what I planned to do? How could she know it would hurt Fay?

"Why would you say that?" I asked, my

440

voice barely a whisper. "Why?"

She shrugged and got up. I couldn't let her go, yet I didn't want to hear more. Know more. After taking only a step, she looked back and gave me a dazzling smile. What she said next both terrified and comforted me, for the words weren't those of a child. She said, "You can repair the world, Miriam. We all can, one break at a time."

As she walked away, tears stung my eyes. My mind replayed everything Papa had taught me about *tikkun ha-olam* and all I'd learned watching my brothers live up to those teachings. Pious Joseph risked his life to safeguard G-d's written word; sweet Benny died saving the life of a stranger; and, idealistic Samuel put his dreams of Palestine aside to stay with us in Poland. Then I knew, with a crushing certainty, that I could never hurt a good woman like Fay Mitchell even to recover Papa's masterpiece. I couldn't add to the brokenness of this world.

While the last rays of sunlight fled the onslaught of evening, and the day moved into memory, Cate refolded the journal entry and slipped it back in her pocket. Her mind replayed the conversation she'd had with Gaby after receiving it. "When I met Miriam in the common all those years ago and said what I did, I didn't know about the ring," Gaby had said. "All I saw — sensed — was that she'd lost something precious. That she wanted to get it back, but was conflicted. Since that day, I've seen many people confront the same question she did: whether it's okay to build their happiness on another's pain. But few of them have been as unselfish as Miriam. Or as courageous."

"So she never told anyone what Jack Mitchell did," Cate had marveled.

"Well, not then. But she did get the ring back eventually," Gaby had reminded her. "And wore it until her death. Then it was entrusted to Sheila. She keeps it in a safety-deposit box; I'm sure she'll show it to you one day. It's beautiful: a fiery ruby surrounded by cool diamonds. Miriam used to say that it represented the light of Torah learning burning like a beacon in a cold, hard sea of doubt and ignorance."

Cate glanced around her. Downtown was quiet save for the soft breath of a rising wind rustling the trees and the occasional sound of a car driving by. The stillness was in marked contrast to the questions swirling in her mind. In sifting through the stories she'd been told, she returned time and again to Miriam's. Although she couldn't secure a consent to tell details of the dead woman's life, she had decided to include Miriam's story in the book. But she was still ambivalent about the decision.

As she made her way home along a silver pathway laid by a full moon, her shadow trailed beside her. She imagined surrendering the self-doubt that filled her heart to that darkened part of herself. In the cleansing light of day, the two Cates might merge, but when the noise of the world died away and her mind quieted, perhaps shadow Cate could carry the burden alone. But no, that was cowardice. People had trusted her with their stories, and someone had given her the journal entries, because the book she was writing had merit. Because it had to be written. And she was the only one who could do it. With that thought uppermost, she and shadow Cate ducked into the grocery's side door as moonlight bathed the sleeping town.

CHAPTER 29

Cate opened her bedroom window to a gentle breeze that carried the astringent scent of basil. Glancing down at the garden, she smiled in anticipation of the pesto Sheila would make from the bush-like plants. In the cutting garden, dahlias bloomed, the cosmos were a six-foot-high wall of pink and fuchsia, and the peony foliage had faded to a rich russet. In the vegetable garden, fat tomatoes hung heavy on plants that had outgrown their stakes, and the last of the zucchini buds glowed orange against the chocolate-brown soil. September winds had begun to rob the maple tree of a few brilliant yellow leaves that now lay strewn on a stone wall. Along the slate path ran a pair of chipmunks, their cheeks stuffed with sunflower seeds salvaged from beneath the bird feeder.

Deciding on a walk, after breakfast she made her way toward the common. Her thoughts turned to Father Sullivan, Peter Flynn, and Vincent Morazzo, for they'd each played a part in the stories that informed her book, but not the leading roles. "They're quite sensitive, really. For straight men." MaryLou had observed one day. "Still, it's the women of Amberley who've kept this town alive, the force of their will that's gotten us through. We survived the last century because of Beatrice's grit, Sheila's tenacity, Leah's passion, Miriam's humanity, Helen's selflessness, and Gaby's empathy."

"And your strength," Cate had reminded her.

MaryLou had shrugged. "Stubbornness is more like it."

Cate wondered if the incredible women she'd come to know would have become who they were without the unique community that was Amberley. Could Beatrice have saved McLean's without the town's women stepping forward to work during the war? Would Sheila have succeeded in business without Rosa as a role model? Where would Helen be without the help of neighbors and friends who raised her when her mother couldn't? And would Leah have become who she was if her big sister hadn't shielded her from the truth about their father?

When Cate had first moved to town, she'd dismissed so many of the women of Amberley as meddlesome busybodies, intent only on poking their noses into her life. Now the scales had fallen from her eyes, and she saw how amazing they were. The more she learned, the more she became convinced that the daisy chain that was Amberley had no beginning or end. The people of her town were linked, one to another, by tragedy, triumph, and trust. And she was part of that now, a fact that would have meant nothing to her months before, but now made her feel proud.

Lost in thought, she started at the sight of an ambulance speeding past, lights flashing. After it pulled to a stop somewhere near Vitelli's and shut off its siren, Main Street filled with an eerie quiet. Cate turned around and broke into a run, heart sinking when she saw the paramedics pushing a stretcher out of the diner. Was there someone on it? She couldn't make anyone out before the stretcher was secured inside the ambulance. As it took off down the street, siren blaring, she yanked open the diner's front door and scanned the interior. The room was full because Gaby had been holding a fundraiser for the hospital. Sick at the thought that one of her friends might be ill, a wave of guilty relief washed over Cate when she spotted Sheila, for she knew it couldn't be Leah or Vincent in the ambulance or Sheila would have gone, too. Her eyes took in Father Sullivan sitting in a booth, eyes closed in prayer. She spotted Beatrice, breathing heavily and holding Zelda's hand. Who was missing? Wetting her lips, she tried to call out, but no sound came. Helen saw her and came over. "It's Gaby," she said in a dead voice. "She just collapsed. It all happened so quickly. Mary-Lou went with her." When Cate's gaze shifted to the door, Helen anticipated her. "No, I wouldn't try and see her today. Tomorrow. We'll know more by then."

Cate stared at Helen, trying to process what she'd heard. In the months she'd worked as a home care aide she'd seen so much illness, helped so many people. But this — this was different. This was a friend. Brain cancer. Incurable. So that's why Gaby had seemed so weak at times, as though she'd been doling out her dwindling strength with a terrible frugality.

When Helen handed her the care plan, Cate's eyes blurred with tears. Then she grabbed her handbag and rushed across town to Gaby's huge Victorian. MaryLou answered the door, her face devoid of makeup but heavily lined with grief. She gingerly fingered a purple bruise above her eye. "Damn cancer's changed her personality. She's not herself, she — she threw a glass at me." MaryLou shook her head in disgust. "My reflexes are shit; I didn't duck in time." When Cate drew a breath to respond, MaryLou held up a hand and rushed on. "Don't say it. Please. I'm fine, more hurt inside than out. What's important now is that Gaby doesn't want to die in a hospital. She wants to be here. At home. The folks at hospice are stretched pretty thin. They can send someone at night, but during the day — look, Gaby won't let me near her. That's why I asked Helen to send you. But if this is too hard, if you'd rather not —"

"No, I want to help," Cate stated with conviction, eyes straying toward a hospital bed in a corner of the living room. "Because she's my friend and because I need to keep busy. Keep my mind off other things."

"You mean the contest?"

Cate waved a hand as though shooing a fly. "That's not important. Well, not compared to this. No, I mean Eddie Fallon. He phoned this morning to say he's following a new lead. I don't want to get my hopes up. In fact, I sort of wish he hadn't told me." She ran a hand through her hair. "Bottom line is that I need to work now. A lot." Her eyes moved to where Gaby lay on the white sheets, looking pale and frightened. Taking charge, Cate checked her patient's vital signs and emptied the nearly full catheter bag.

"I'm s-sorry," Gaby sobbed, gesturing toward the urine.

"It's nothing," Cate assured her, all business. "I'll have you all set in no time."

MaryLou hovered at the foot of the bed. When Gaby averted her face as if ashamed at her best friend's seeing her in such a state, Cate said, "MaryLou, you have to leave." The mechanic's eyes widened, and she shot back that nobody was going to give her the bum's rush. "Gaby needs rest," Cate insisted. "You can come and see her later, but now you have to go." After looking as though she would protest again, instead MaryLou threw Cate a look of grudging respect before quitting the room.

Gaby's strength ebbed and flowed. Some days she was strong enough to meet with her staff and take an active role in running the diner, and others she couldn't get out of bed. The cancer wrought changes in her personality and mood — changes that made her impatient and ill at ease with friends she had known all her life. Plagued by seizures that left her disoriented and angry, she often alternated between fits of sobbing and uncontrollable laughter.

One stormy morning, the lights flickered for a moment before the power went out. Milky sunlight filtered in through the windows, lending an unreal quality to the day. As she often did, Gaby clutched a well-thumbed copy of Augustine's *Confessions* that Cate knew bore the inscription:

To Gabrielle,
Like the Saint, we're all sinners.
Yours in Christ,
James Sullivan

Gaby had been thumbing her way through the book, but now pushed it aside and said in a clear, lucid voice, "You must have heard rumors about how my parents died."

Cate blanched. She hadn't, actually. "Why don't you rest now? We don't need to speak of it."

"It was my fault," Gaby whispered.

Cate felt a shudder run down her spine;

she didn't want to hear what sounded like a confession, but after her experience with Lourdes Garcia, Cate knew that dying patients needed to talk. She'd come to accept that it was part of her job to be there when that happened, to hold their hands and make sure that what they said was heard. And perhaps by doing so she could atone for not being there when John had needed her. So she sat on the edge of the bed and waited while Gaby gathered her thoughts.

"Every year, my parents came to Yale to pick me up for Christmas vacation," Gaby began. "My last year of graduate school, it was snowing something awful by the time we reached Amberley. A blizzard like we hadn't seen in years. My father was tired, so I drove. We were arguing. He wanted me to move back home, but I was finishing my doctorate and so full of other plans. I told him all I hoped to do in life even as dark thoughts — angry thoughts — flapped in the shadows of my mind. We were on River Road, harsh words flying like the snow pelting the windshield. I was so focused on my own needs and the rosy future I was sure was mine for the taking. I couldn't believe he expected me to live in Amberley. I didn't even ask why he did. I just shouted, 'What do you want me to do, be a waitress at the diner?' It was the last thing I said to my father. The car hit a patch of ice and swerved into the river right across from the old graveyard — you know the spot." Cate nodded wordlessly. "I wasn't wearing a seatbelt and was thrown clear before it submerged. But my parents were trapped." Tears ran down Gaby's face, but she kept talking. "The snow was blinding, the road so slippery. I fell to my knees and crawled toward the river. I — I dived in, gagging on the icy water. But the car was gone! I couldn't see anything!" Her eyes were desperate, pleading. "It was so dark, so black. Helen was at the hospital when they brought me in. She — she told me later that I was in shock. But that was nothing to the guilt. I was overcome with guilt." Gaby's brow pleated with the effort of remembering and confessing. "I still dream about the accident. Even now. Sometimes my dream self manages to swerve the car in time to avoid the river. Sometimes I fall in the freezing water with them. We sink together. Die together." She squeezed her eyes shut as if to keep the images that haunted her sleep from claiming her.

So we both lost our parents to a crash. And carry guilt because of it, although mine is nothing to hers, Cate thought. Yet how often had Gaby pulled friends and neighbors back from despair and pushed them toward hope? As horrible as those few moments on River Road had been, they weren't her friend's true legacy. Pathos. That was the word for Gaby's gift, for she had an ability to see people as they truly were. Or hoped to be. And she had made it her life's work to both feed people's bodies and sustain their spirits. In her mind's eye, Cate saw Gaby sitting in the common with Miriam; feeding friends and strangers the food that made them feel special; and, welcoming MaryLou to town. Welcoming Cate to town.

"I used to dream of my parents' death, but now I dream of John's," Cate confided. "I put myself in the scene, and we die together. Sometimes, I dream that I save him, but not usually. I don't know why that is. When it happens, I wake up terrified, my heart pounding." She put a hand to her throat in memory of all the tears she had cried. "Actually, I haven't had that dream in a while. I've had it less and less since coming to Amberley." Her voice trailed off.

Gaby reached out a shaky hand to grasp Cate's. "That's why I had such a connection to you when we first met. I knew how you felt about John's dying. I knew you'd understand." Some of the tension in her rail-thin body lessened. She spoke of her parents again, the words coming more quickly. "When the storm cleared, they searched the river. It took days. Their bodies were under the ice, trapped in that frozen, choppy water so long. Hitting rocks and —" She fought for control. "When their bodies were found, I was still in the hospital. In the psychiatric ward because I was overcome with guilt. You see, my mother was sick. Breast cancer. In those days, that was all but a death sentence. That's why my father wanted me home. Not to destroy my life, but to help save my mother's. To help him care for her. When I found out, I broke down. I was suicidal for a while. Helen helped me so much. She was a nurse-trainee then." Gaby drew a steadying breath. "After I pulled my mind back together, I didn't know what to do. Not at first. I couldn't stay in school. Oh, I finished my thesis years later, but then — then I didn't care. I had some half-formed wish to atone, so I took over running the diner. As a sort of penance, I think. And to honor my parents. Curious that I came to love the place. Still, it's been my prison, too."

As the morning wore on, Gaby sobbed quietly for those she had lost and the bittersweet life she had found. She marveled that she'd once sought her destiny in the ivy-covered halls of academia only to find it behind a diner counter. "But then, it's in the half-light of obscurity that I came to see myself most clearly."

"Obscurity?" Cate repeated. "That's hardly the word I'd use to describe your life. As you did with Miriam and so many others, you can see what's broken in people. And help them heal. Who knows how many lives you've changed, how many ripples can be traced to your kindness? I can only imagine how you've punished yourself over what happened during that horrible storm. Just as I have over John's death. And I see how becoming a waitress was an act of penance, even if in time you found a vocation as true as any priest's. Maybe," Cate whispered half to herself, "you need to find a way to forgive yourself. I'm doing that. Some days I succeed. If — if you want, I can help you." She chose her words carefully, feeling her way forward. She was rewarded when she saw a change in Gaby's expression, like the edging of light beneath a closed door. Cate knew from experience how quickly that light could fade. "You helped me so much when I came to town," she rushed on. "You all did — Beatrice,

Sheila, Lulu. And Leah. Let me help you now. Not just with this" — she waved a hand toward a table piled with medicine bottles and medical supplies — "let me help you with the rest, too. It's one of the few things I know something about. Guilt and remorse, I mean."

In the weeks that followed, Gaby did just that, and Cate noted the progress her patient made — physically and emotionally. It was very much a matter of two steps forward and one step back, for although on some days Gaby was peaceful, on others she was anxious and distracted. But through it all a curious thing happened: Gaby's strength returned. Her energy level improved, and she began to put on weight. Everything changed that late October morning when Gaby's oncologist called. After speaking to him in muted tones, she hung up the phone and stared at Cate.

"What? What is it?"

Gaby wet her lips, unable to form the words. Cate took her cold hands and rubbed them gently, unsure how to help. Finally, Gaby nodded that she'd found her voice. "Remission. I'm in remission."

CHAPTER 30

Halloween dawned dry and cloud-free, with temperatures cool but not chilly. The air had that burning-leaf quality one only finds in New England, and there was a lush, extravagant beauty to the day. The maple trees lining the common flamed like torches until a sudden breeze undressed their graceful limbs, sending scarlet leaves dancing in a cobalt sky.

Sunlight gilded downtown as it prepared for the onslaught of children and parents, for Amberley's Halloween parade drew trick-or-treaters from all the surrounding towns. Main Street was closed to traffic. Although the festivities didn't start until noon, people gathered early to admire the decorations. Skeletons hung from streetlights, spider webs fluttered from stop signs, and jack-o'-lanterns covered the parking meters. McLean's storefront paid homage to the Wicked Witch of the West's penchant for black dresses, while Vitelli's opted for a vampire theme, albeit one where the undead drank imported marinara instead of blood. The graveyard in the window of the garden center was planted with colorful mums labeled ON SALE, and the Corner Pharmacy featured a display of zombie attack first-aid kits.

Grateful to have the day off, Cate took a quick tour of downtown and paused outside A Spoonful of Sugar. The shop was painted in stripes of complementary colors — orange next to blue; yellow next to purple; and red next to green. Its awning was a cleverly designed, oversized umbrella from which hung polka-dotted balloons that swayed in the breeze. As expected, the Mary Poppins theme was reflected in the front window display, but in addition to merchandize that celebrated the über-nanny — children's tea sets, miniature carpetbags, themed coloring books — there were building blocks, Lego sets, and board games. Cate eyed them eagerly before her heart gave a lurch. She had no children to shop for, would never have — no, that wasn't true. She opened the carved oak door and stepped inside, leaving a few minutes later with a stuffed animal for Catherine tucked into the tissue paper of a gaily wrapped box.

Heading down Main Street, she passed MaryLou and Peter who waved in greeting before continuing a heated debate. "Peanut butter cups go better with coffee," MaryLou argued, twirling the tail of her Catwoman outfit. "They're creamy, too."

"No," Peter disagreed. "Hershey bars have been number one for a century. You can't improve on a classic."

Continuing on to the grocery, Cate found the place mobbed with locals and visitors. Layered over the familiar aromas of just-baked bread and ground coffee was the smell of spiced pumpkin. It drew her to the bakery counter like a bee to honey. The holiday treats on offer — cupcakes, muffins, cookies, and cakes — paid homage to bats, broomsticks, spiders, crows, and ghosts.

As Cate debated what to order, a voice urged, "Try this."

She turned to see Sheila holding out a black, cat-shaped cookie. Accepting it eagerly, Cate bit first an ear and then a whisker. "Chocolate. Yum."

Sheila nodded with satisfaction. "It's all right, then?"

"You haven't tried any?"

Sheila moved a hand to her abdomen. "Not feeling up to snuff today. My stomach's doing backflips. I haven't felt like this since —" She blanched. "No, that can't be."

"You're pregnant? Oh my gosh. You need to sit down. Put your feet up." Cate reached out a supporting hand that Sheila briskly slapped away.

"Don't be ridiculous! I'm just overtired, and I must have eaten something that didn't agree with me." She gave a shaky laugh. "You think I'm pregnant at my age!"

"How old — ?"

"Fifty-two. Old enough to be a grandmother," Sheila said in a tone that turned the lock on that topic.

At the sound of a drum beating, Cate glanced outside. "Band's warming up. Looks like you guys put on quite a show, but then I've been spoiled. John was from Salem, and we went there every year for Halloween."

"Oh. Salem." Sheila shook her head in defeat. "Nobody can top them I guess. But we do our best. And the parade is wonderful. Parents march with their kids. And dogs. Everybody dresses up. There's a contest for best costume at the end. It's all very small-town America."

"Who are the judges?"

"There are a bunch. Father Sullivan's one this year. I give out the award."

"Mayor Morazzo." Cate sketched a salute.

"You're such an overachiever. Just like Beatrice."

"Yeah, well, I'd just as soon put my feet up and let somebody else do it today." She blew out a sigh before squaring her shoulders in characteristic fashion. "I'd better get ready for the kids." She reached for a basket and proceeded to fill it with assorted Italian candies.

"That's quite a selection. Maybe somebody should taste — ?"

For the second time, Sheila slapped her hand away. "You're no better than Mary-Lou." Placing the candy at the far end of the counter, she began to fill a second basket with what appeared to be toothbrushes.

"Are those —"

"Yes. Vincent insists we give these away, too. He worries about kids eating so much candy this time of year. He always does." At the question in Cate's eyes, Sheila beamed. "He's getting back to normal. Back to himself. Bit by bit." She stared at the pile of toothbrushes before reaching out a hand to sort through them. "At least he chose colorful ones. The X-Men and Superman, Cinderella, and Sleeping Beauty." Her hands stilled. "I was like Sleeping Beauty. In a way. But meeting you woke me up."

"What do you mean?"

Sheila explained that she'd finally found the courage to tell Vincent how his leaving hurt her. "I didn't ask him not to go again, but he needed to know how hard it is when he does. I don't think, no, I *know* I wouldn't have done that without your example."

"Me? What did I do?"

"More than you know," Sheila said simply. "If you can take on the U.S. Army, how can I refuse to level with my own husband?" Not by nature demonstrative with her friends, Sheila took Cate aback when she gave her a quick hug. "It was a good day when you came to town, Cate Saunders. All those months ago, when I first saw you here looking so lost, I thought I could help."

"You did."

Sheila shrugged. "Maybe a bit. But you helped me, too. I didn't see that coming."

When Sheila stepped back to arrange the baskets just so, Cate felt a lump rise in her throat. A companionable silence settled over them. Snatches of band music drifted in the front door, and they could hear the day's soundtrack of laughter and chatter rising in volume. After a time, Sheila acknowledged what lay waiting on the outskirts of their conversation. "We've talked of cookies and Halloween, my queasy stomach, and Vin-

462

cent, but neither of us has touched on the big news."

"Gaby," Cate said simply. "Will she come today, do you think?"

"I don't know. I hope so, although she doesn't like using that new wheelchair. Still, it's only temporary. Once she gets all her strength back —" Her mouth set in a determined line, Sheila whispered the next words as fervently as a prayer. "The remission has to last, Cate. It just has to."

Gaby recalled a winter long ago when she'd cried for flowers she was convinced lay dead beneath a mountain of snow and ice. Only after her mother explained that what appeared dead was only sleeping did the grief that tore at Gaby's heart recede. *I'm like that. As the coming winter will freeze the garden, so remission has frozen my death. But there's always a thaw; it's nature's way. Spring may come in chilly garments, may tantalize with games of hide-and-seek, but it always comes.* Terror at the thought of her cancer's returning pounded through her like a heartbeat. Sometimes, it drowned out the voices of her friends and the call of the birds. Then Gaby would struggle to the surface of her fear and remind herself that every day was a

463

blessing and every moment not wasted a victory.

That she didn't know what the future held scared the hell out of her, but it also made life shimmer in a way she couldn't put into words. For so many years, she'd lived with only one foot in the here and now. If she was chatting with a friend, she was also planning the next day's menu; if she was taking a customer's order, she was also tallying up his check. Looking back, she likened such thinking to a highway where even as she drove in the center lane, part of her was hopping on and off exits, backtracking, or speeding ahead. Since her illness, she'd tried to imagine life as a winding country road where the promise of what lay around the next bend kept her living in the moment.

On Halloween morning, she was determined to embrace the day and all it held. Making her way downtown, she rounded the corner of Main Street and found herself in a crowd of children lining up for the parade. Hearing the future in their laughter, she watched sunlight stroke the faces of zombies, cowboys, witches, and clowns. A little boy in a Spider-Man costume played catch with a teenaged Batman, while a princess tipped her crown to a pint-sized

Darth Vader. Robots trailed behind a bumblebee, and a trio of bunnies hurried to catch up with a tall boy in a Superman cape. Once upon a time, she'd been one of those children, donning first a Raggedy Ann costume, then a Cinderella gown, and finally Wonder Woman tights. *I could use a bit of Wonder Woman's strength now,* she thought, massaging her sore biceps. Maneuvering a manual wheelchair was a challenge for muscles gone slack from weeks of bed rest.

"Let me help," a familiar voice suggested.

Gaby threw a grateful look behind her. "Helen, you don't have to. I'll manage."

"I'm sure you would, but we're going in the same direction, so it's no bother to push you."

"How do you know where I'm going?" Gaby asked.

Helen bent down to scrutinize her friend. "You've the look of someone in need of a bite to eat. And as the diner's closed, I'd say you're headed to Vitelli's."

Gaby smiled. "Yes, actually. I never get there on Halloween because we're always so busy. But this year, I decided not to open. I wanted to give my staff the day with their families; they've been run off their feet covering for me the past few weeks." Her eyes sought the darkened windows of the diner. "Still, it's strange to be closed."

Turning her friend's thoughts toward the light, Helen reminded her, "But, as you said, this will give you a chance to check out what Sheila's made. And spend some time with your friends. Plus, you'll see the parade from start to finish. When's the last time you've done that?"

"Can't remember," Gaby murmured.

Helen held up her hands as if to say, "See? It's all for the best."

As they waited their turn to cross the street, Gaby reached up to squeeze Helen's hand. "Thank you for acting so normally. People haven't been, you know. As weirded out as they were by the cancer, it seems remission is even harder to handle. It's like they don't know how to treat me. But you do."

"Just give them time," Helen advised. "They'll come around. It's a lot to take in."

Gaby soon saw that Helen was right. When she was first wheeled into Vitelli's, an uncomfortable silence gripped the crowded store. People looked at each other and then at Gaby, unsure how to greet someone they'd assumed was near death. Then Sheila announced that surely Gaby was on the mend because of the Italian food she'd been eating. Leah reminded the group that Gaby had two rescue cats and that being around animals speeds recovery, while Beatrice pointed out the psychological benefits of dressing smart. Fingering Gaby's jacket, she said proudly, "It's a McLean's Original. Part of our summer line of washable silk. Available in five colors and made right here in town, not in some Asian sweatshop."

"Bea!" Sheila cried. "Nobody sells in my store but me!"

Laughter rippled through the group, energizing people to break off into twos and threes. Some continued shopping; others lined up at the register or claimed tables near the front windows. As the hum of conversation increased, Gaby watched with concern as Cate scrolled through a text message on her phone and went quite pale. After Helen wheeled her over to where Cate leaned against the deli counter, Gaby asked, "What is it? What's happened?"

"It's Eddie Fallon. He's — he's found those two soldiers. He's coming to Amberley. Today." She glanced out the window as if expecting to find him standing on the sidewalk. "He apologized for the short notice, but he's in Boston and didn't want to put it off. Why would he say that unless — unless he has bad news." Her voice trailed off.

"Or he just wants to put your mind at ease," Gaby countered. "Stands to reason given what's at stake and how much this all means to you."

"I don't want to see him," Cate whispered, folding her arms across her chest.

All brisk assurance, Helen dismissed such trepidation. "You're not a coward! I should know; I've been watching you these seven months, haven't I? No, it's best to see this man and have done with it."

"Helen's right," Gaby said, taking up the standard. "Sometimes, what we dread hearing can change our lives for the better. When my doctor called to tell me about the remission, I didn't want to pick up the phone. I was convinced it was more bad news, you see. But it wasn't. So you can't be afraid, Cate." She spared a glance across the crowded room to where Sheila stood chatting with a customer. "Not with all your friends close by."

Revealing a smile she kept in reserve just for Gaby, Cate said, "You're right, of course." Relaxing her shoulders, she shook them gently as if discarding something.

Gaby blew out a breath. Leaning back against the seat of her chair, she said, "Good. Now, you should use the diner for your meeting. It may be the only quiet place in town today." Guessing correctly, she added, "You probably don't want to take him up to your apartment." Handing the keys to Helen, she asked her old friend, "You remember how to open up?"

"Oh, sure. And, as you say, it will be quiet there. Private." Then to Cate, "Unless you want one of us —"

"No, no," Cate said quickly. "And I know Father Sullivan's busy so — so I'll talk to Eddie alone." She nodded briskly. "Yes. I think that's best."

Helen shot a glance at Gaby. "All right. But we'll be close by should you need help."

Gaby could have picked Eddie Fallon out of the downtown crowd even if she hadn't seen him throw a wave in MaryLou's direction. That he was a soldier through and through was clear to see, for the residue of combat clung to him and had for so long it was like a second skin. There was a spare, chiseled quality to the man's angular face that was reflected in his lean frame. He moved with economy through the crowd, weaving in and out like — a cat. Why she thought that she couldn't say, for he wasn't graceful per se; rather, he gave the impression of both stalking and walking in that tightrope fashion felines manage with ease. Then she saw a shadow trailing behind him — one not his own. In that moment, Gaby knew that whatever Fallon had brought with him to Amberley, whatever negative energy had attached itself to him, had something to do with Cate. Fumbling with the wheelchair, she regretted not bringing her phone. She needed to get a message to Cate, to warn — but it was too late. Fallon had already moved past her. Telling herself that Cate was stronger than when she'd first come to town and could handle whatever truth lay ahead, Gaby wrung what comfort she could from the thought.

CHAPTER 31

The awful, slimy thing Eddie Fallon had unearthed was too difficult to grasp; every time Cate tried, it threatened to pull her beneath the dark waters from which it had come. As she struggled to find her mental footing, she felt his eyes on her. The intensity of his look was born of concern and something more she couldn't see. Not then. All she could manage was to gather the words that seemed to scatter whenever she reached for them. "What are you trying to tell me?"

Eddie repeated what he'd driven two hours to say. "Those two corporals believe they were betrayed by a kid named Samir Falah. Apparently, your husband used to play football with him. And give him food."

Cate's thoughts scrambled. Was this Samir the child in the photograph? No! It couldn't be! Surely that smiling boy with the open face could have nothing to do with murder!

She pulled back against the leather of the booth, recoiling from Eddie's words and what lay behind them even as her peripheral vision took in the diner's familiar surroundings. There was the counter where Gaby dispensed wisdom and sliced pies, the jukebox that played Sinatra and Santana, the specials board where someone had drawn a jack-o'-lantern. Surely in such a comforting place she wasn't hearing that a child she'd so long thought was a friend to John might have conspired to kill him! And how was it possible John had so misjudged the boy? She sat up straighter at the realization that for two years she'd assumed that the pictures meant they'd been friends. What if that wasn't the case? What if the photos had been taken for another reason? Oh, how was it possible she knew so little and had assumed so much?

She slit her eyes against the harsh truth of her ignorance, and for a fleeting moment wished she could shut down as Charlotte had all those years before. Tuning in and out, she heard distant parade sounds and remembered it was Halloween. Halloween — when children dress up and pretend to be something they're not. Ghosts and goblins, superheroes and — murderers? Traitors? No! She focused on the smiling faces marching by the diner. Strange that she'd never realized cries of joy could so easily be mistaken for cries of pain. Mirror images, like a coin flipped in the air that catches the light before falling into shadow. Then the scene outside the diner's window shifted, and the children weren't marching down Main Street, but being herded through an Arab village. No, they were being driven toward a train station in the Lodz ghetto. She gripped the table so hard the metal edging bit into her fingers. *Pain. Pain is real. What I'm hearing isn't real, but the pain is.*

Eddie jumped to his feet and moved away, returning a moment later with a bottle of water. "Drink," he urged, holding it out. Cate's hands shook too much for her to manage, and he sat next to her and folded his powerful fingers over hers. "It's all right. You're going to be all right."

She managed to sip, grateful that the mechanical action required no thought. No real decision. Some time passed before she noted that the noise outside had lessened. A shift in the light signaled the approach of dusk as Eddie slid out of the booth and took the seat across from her. Then he picked up the edge of their conversation, pulling it taut and tucking in the stray bits. As he detailed his meeting with the two corporals, in her mind's eye Cate saw Kapunski — short and stocky with the cocky air of a bully. Lance Bruno was described as gangly and younger, in years and experience. "Bruno told me most of what I learned. Kapunski was more closemouthed."

Of their own volition, her hands reached into her wallet and withdrew the picture. She held it for a moment before placing it on the table. "Is — is this him?"

Eddie studied the photograph. "I don't know. Could be. Seems to be about the same age. Samir was probably seven at the time. Where'd you get that?" She told him and he nodded. "Lots of kids hung around the soldiers. Trailed after the patrols. Soldiers gave them candy. Kapunski and Bruno did." Hearing this, Cate softened toward the corporals. As if reading her expression, Fallon tried to set her straight. "Don't get the wrong idea. Kids are valued as human shields. Insurgents might hesitate to shoot into a crowd of civilians. At least that's the thinking. Not true, as it turns out. So, you see, kids — civilians — are just fodder for both sides. Same as any war."

Same as any war, she repeated in her mind. Like the children of the Lodz ghetto, or those Father Sullivan met in Korea.

Those children had been caught in the crossfire or used to draw fire. "Nothing changes," she whispered. "War after war and nothing changes. Children pay for the sins of their parents."

"That's true," Eddie conceded. "But sometimes kids aren't so innocent. I wish that wasn't true, but I've learned otherwise. The bottom line," he summed up, "is that Kapunski and Bruno believe this Samir betrayed them." Eddie seemed to be considering what else to say — how much of the story was to be her portion. That realization broke the spell that bound her, and she asked herself why he was putting himself out to help her. That she was able to do so given how broken she felt would surprise her afterward. At the time, it was as if her thoughts ran forward on two tracks: one so cluttered with debris it was impassible, and the other an express that flew along at breakneck speed. So even though the news he'd shared had crippled her first train of thought, she was able to recall that Eddie was a dear friend of MaryLou's. But why had he gone to such lengths to help a stranger? In a corner of her thoughts the answer lay, but she turned her back on it, unwilling to name the hunger in his eyes. Men had been interested in her since John's death, but with Eddie it was more than lust, and that was something she couldn't get her mind around. Or didn't want to.

When she asked him to tell her what else he knew, he shrugged in a way that suggested he'd warned her of the minefield ahead and, if she chose to blunder into it, there was nothing he could do. "The kid's father was an informant. He used his son to pass on information about insurgents because one more kid hanging around the soldiers didn't arouse suspicion. Samir could go where his father couldn't, and in time the soldiers got to know him. According to Bruno and Kapunski, your husband knew him best of all."

"What makes you think these two corporals are trustworthy?" Cate demanded.

"I'm a good judge of character," Eddie shot back, before smoothing out his voice. "Look, they're pretty messed up after what happened. Not just with your husband, but everything over there." Jabbing a finger on the table, he continued, "There was only the flimsiest of missions in Iraq; the rules of engagement changed with the weather; the body armor was a joke, and the intelligence crap. Contractors — mercenaries, really — were swarming around like cockroaches, taking the plum jobs and the salaries to match. They scattered when a light was turned on, by Congress or the press, but only for a time. Common soldiers like Kapunski and Bruno are chewed up and spit out by war. They're not victims maybe, but they're not given what they need to be heroes, either."

"I accept all of that, but it doesn't mean they spoke the truth."

"I believe them. Which is to say I believe they believe what they told me."

She sat forward. "And what else *did* they tell you? How exactly did this Samir betray John?"

"Ah. That's where things get a little murky. First, let me ask you something. Is it true your husband spoke Arabic?"

"He was learning. Or at least he was trying to before he left. I don't think he knew much."

"Could he read?"

"I — don't know," she faltered.

"Try to think!"

"Well, probably not much. I mean he learned the letters and all, but —"

Eddie's exhale was that of a satisfied man.

Cate suppressed a shiver of foreboding. "Why is that significant?"

In answer, Eddie reached for a napkin and drew a figure:

"This is the fourth letter in the Arabic alphabet — *tha.*" He held up a hand to silence her question. "On that last morning, the kid was hanging around the base. He ran up to your husband's vehicle as it was leaving. Samir didn't say anything; well, there were other people around. Instead, he handed something to your husband. 'Slipped it to him,' is how Kapunski put it. A small piece of paper. Kapunski and Bruno saw what was written on it only for a second as your husband opened it quickly and then stuck it in his pocket. I think what they saw was this." He tapped the napkin where he'd written the letter *tha.* "Your husband would have recognized this Arabic letter, but not Bruno and Kapunski. To them, it looked like a smiley face. That's what they remember seeing." He reached for another napkin. The smiley face he drew seemed so bizarre under the circumstances that Cate glanced away. "No, look at it," Eddie urged. She did, seeing the familiar depiction through a curtain of tears she couldn't control. "Look, what Kapunski and Bruno said they saw makes no sense — a smiley face from an Iraqi kid? On the other hand, I don't think

478

they were lying to me. So I got to thinking about what they might have seen. And I think it was *tha*."

Cate blinked for the two drawings looked alike — but no. In the Arabic letter what looked like a nose was where the eyes should be. She pushed the napkins away. Smiley faces, Arabic letters — none of it explained why John had died. How he'd died. "I don't understand! Even if you're right, what difference does it make? How does it get us any closer to the truth?"

Eddie's voice was low, his tone patient and gentle. "*Tha* would never appear like this because Arabic is written in cursive — the letters connected. Unless" — he paused for emphasis — "it was an abbreviation of some sort. The one that comes to mind, given the situation, is the word *thaniyah*."

"What's *thaniyah*?"

"It means second. Sort of like saying, 'Go to plan B.' "

"So?"

"The village where your husband died could be entered one of four ways. The army alternated the route daily. The plan that morning was to enter from the north. If they had, they would have avoided the bomb. But instead, your husband took the second road. The eastern road."

"Road 'B,' " Cate offered in a whisper.

"Yeah." Eddie glanced down at the napkin. "Maybe because he trusted Samir. But not completely, of course."

"Meaning?"

Eddie paused, his mouth pressing into a hard line. "As I told you before, your husband ordered the vehicle stopped just inside the village. He got out and proceeded on foot, taking the lead."

"But why would he do that? And why — wait a minute! So they stopped by choice; they didn't break down!" When Eddie nodded, a wave of relief washed over her. She sat for a time. Thinking. Absorbing. Sifting. A flash of light behind the darkness of his words caught her eye, and she tracked it to its source. "I know you believe what they told you, but you can't be certain of any of this. You can't know if the message is as you say, or whether Samir wrote it or his father. Maybe Samir didn't even know what he was delivering. Besides, you can't even be sure Samir is this boy!" She shook the photograph for emphasis. "And — and your explanation of the Arabic and what it might mean makes even less sense," she suddenly realized, her voice rising. "If John saw that letter and understood it as you do, he'd have thought it was a warning or a trap. Either way, he would have told someone. Radioed in!" At Eddie's stony silence, she pressed, "Right? Isn't that right?"

"Yes, that would be procedure."

Her voice fell to a whisper. "But John didn't follow procedure. He drove farther away from the base. Got out of his vehicle to walk. In front of the others."

"Bruno and Kapunski said your husband always took the lead," Eddie offered quickly. "That's to be commended. And in this instance, it saved his comrades."

In the moments that followed, Eddie sat still and contained, but Cate got the impression his mind was ranging far and wide. At his grim expression, she felt a fresh prickle of dread. "What? What aren't you telling me? There's more, isn't there?"

Eddie shifted his weight and folded his hands purposefully. "There would have been no reason for your husband to risk his life if he thought there was something wrong. And he must have known something was wrong because he changed the route. None of this makes sense, so there's something else going on here." He shrugged slightly. "We may never know what the Falahs did. If anything. The family was moved soon after your husband was killed. Or they took off. I couldn't find out where."

Cate's heart leapt in her chest. "So it's possible they were relocated by the army. That they were helping us."

"It's possible, but that doesn't change the army's conclusions regarding your husband's death. He violated procedure and put himself and others at risk. There are only two explanations for that: he didn't understand or appreciate the danger or —"

"Or?"

Eddie frowned.

"Please. Finish what you came here to say. I — I have to know."

Eddie drew a deep breath and held it for a moment. "I told you before that the stress of combat can make people careless. Reckless. It's not in any official report, but your husband's commander thinks he might have been, well, self-destructive. Even suicidal."

"They think John was suicidal? He wasn't! I don't know if this boy in the photo was Samir, or if Samir was a friend to John. But I know my husband loved his life. He loved me." She stabbed a finger at her chest. "He was coming home to me. To our marriage. To the family we never had a chance to make together. He was coming home to me!" When self-control fell away, a wail like that of a wounded animal broke free. Then Eddie did what he told her afterward he'd wanted to do since the moment they'd met: He enfolded her in his arms and held tight.

CHAPTER 32

That meeting with Eddie Fallon was one of the most painful experiences of Cate's life. In the immediate aftermath of his revelations, she was in turns disbelieving, furious, and devastated. Rehashing, questioning, and analyzing what he'd said, and what lay in the hollows between his words, she lamented the time lost to ignorance even as she longed for its embrace. As the days slipped by, suspicion and self-doubt that the light of reason and the intensity of love had for years been consigned to the shadows of her mind stole their way to center stage, cast in starring roles. She gave herself over to sorrow, pushing friends away, ignoring Jenny's calls, and coming close to losing her job. Again.

Perhaps John had been careless. Perhaps the army was right and the stress of combat had been too much for him to bear. Perhaps, perhaps, perhaps. The word ricocheted through the corridors of her mind, nicking the treasured bounty of love. What saved her in the end was the very thing that plagued her uneven sleep: memories of John's funeral. For as his casket was lowered into a muddy hole and the teeth of a savage storm sharpened her grief, she'd glimpsed a path through the pain. She'd strayed from that path in the years since, had stumbled and chanced her way back upon it since coming to Amberley. But she hadn't strode it surefooted until Eddie's words ripped her world apart.

After the pain born of his visit dulled, she found her thoughts stretching back to that dark day when blinding rain curtained the Salem church where John had been baptized, married, and then buried. Lightning flashes had thrown the trees that ringed its graveyard into relief, smudging the world beyond. After the service, what seemed like a sea of mourners had flooded out the church door. They'd scattered briefly, like a string of beads suddenly undone, before reforming to square the gravesite. She'd stood with them beneath a sky of black umbrellas, watching reflected light drip off the metal spikes that encircled each of them like a halo. Then darkness had begun to lose ground to light, and instead of menacing the rain had seemed beautiful, like shining water dancing all around them. With the priest's final prayer, milky sunlight had broken through the bruise-colored clouds to soften the leaden day, and a clump of daffodils at her feet had swayed in the wind. Feeling a prick in the surface of her grief, she'd stared at those yellow flowers as golden memories flooded her mind — John's hair, the color of an August sun; corn on the cob from their first garden, dripping with butter and crusted with salt; sunshine twinkling on a Cape Cod beach during their honeymoon; and, the snap of a campfire on July 4th. Burnished by time, those images had pulled her back from despair. As much as their power seemed to fade when the world pressed in again to scatter her thoughts, in truth her memories of John kept her grounded. Centered. For it was precisely when the surface of her life resembled nothing more than bogland dotted with questions, doubts, and worries that his love shone brightest. That was her lodestar: the pure center of her being. Let the world fling at her what it might, let fate buffet her this way and that, so long as she held tight to the certainty of John's love, she would endure.

She thought of the lone birch she'd seen

months before. Although denied the protection of a wood, it had withstood nature's pounding without bending. Where bark had been ripped away raw gashes were visible, yet the trunk had not become twisted. She'd felt a kinship with that solitary tree and often wondered how it had fared in the time since. If he were here, John would say they should pack a lunch and bike out to look for it.

"You'd make a special day of it," she whispered in the predawn darkness one morning. "A magical time. We had such magic together, didn't we? Because you loved me and I loved you. I know you weren't reckless. You were coming back to me and the family we would have." Her voice hitched. "Oh, John, I loved you as I'll never love another. And for all I got wrong — for all I messed up, I was a good wife. I was the love of your life; I know that. I'll never doubt it again." The words became a mantra that gathered steam in the weeks to follow until they rolled through her mind unchecked and fell from her lips in a clear, strong voice.

Building on the foundation that John had loved her and she had not failed him, Cate began to put her insecurities to rest. In doing so, she came to believe as Sheila did:

war doesn't change a person's core. Chaos might breed flashes of aberrant behavior, but a good, kind, considerate man doesn't become reckless or suicidal no matter what the pressure. People became who they were by choice. Those choices might be informed by circumstance, but they were freely made — the product of a lifetime, not a split second. The soldier John became was the sum of all he'd been: the little boy delivering newspapers along Salem's sleeping streets; the high school quarterback; the philosophy major who'd brought his puppy to class; the craftsman who transformed wood into works of art; and, the lover who could heat her blood with a slow smile.

She would never know how war had shaped him, but she was certain it hadn't fundamentally altered the man he was. And it hadn't made him suicidal. As the truth of that knowledge settled over her churning thoughts, she came to appreciate the good turn Eddie Fallon had done her. If not for the news he'd shared, she might have continued living in the half-light of guilt, doubt, and recrimination for years. She might never have discovered that on some level — the most important level — it didn't matter if she ever pieced together exactly how John had died. His life wasn't defined by his death any more than her inability to learn the truth of that horrible day evinced failure. And if she meant to become the woman he'd believed she could be, she had to accept that even if she reconstructed the final chapter of his life, the last page might forever be missing. As haunting as an unanswered question, or an unfinished thought, ambiguity settled uneasily into the landscape of her thoughts. But she was learning to share her mind with its swirling darkness and still find her way to the light.

Cate thought of the boy in the photograph. Was he Samir Falah? She didn't know. Had he been a friend to John? She hoped so. Determined to find out, she was grateful for her first lead: a name. She was also grateful she wouldn't be searching alone, for before he'd left town Eddie had vowed to help despite her plea that she had no money to pay him. Perhaps they'd find the boy together, perhaps not. She was prepared for failure, but also for the daunting prospect of success.

And the larger issue of culpability? If she found the boy, she would confront him and learn the truth. If it turned out that Samir had been involved in John's death, what then? What would she do then?

While Cate moved through the day, that

question circled her thoughts, alighting for a moment or two only to take flight again. As evening descended, her gaze sought the desk John had made her. She kept Miriam's writing there, for it was a special place — the most special place. Crossing the room in quick strides, she reached out her hand only to draw it back. Surely she wouldn't find the answers she sought in the past of a woman she'd never met! *Yet I know her through her writing. Funny that we connected that way. Or perhaps not, for would I have been so open to Miriam's story if we hadn't met writer to writer?*

Pulling the top drawer open, she sorted through the journal entries before finding what she was looking for. Sinking down on the couch, she read.

A few weeks after Poland's surrender, we awoke to a fierce pounding on the front door. I jumped out of bed and slipped Papa's ring off my finger and into a special pocket I'd sewn into my underwear. As I moved into the upper hallway, my brothers scrambled downstairs. Samuel was the first to the door. He opened it to our neighbor, Jan Schultz, who pushed his way inside with a soldier who began throwing books to the floor and breaking furniture. I heard the crash of Mama's Passover china and a cry of triumph when they found the silver candlesticks used for the Sabbath.

"Where is it?" the soldier asked Samuel in stilted Polish.

"Where is what?" Samuel replied in flawless German.

"Your radio."

My heart hammered in time with my thoughts, for we'd sold the radio the week before.

"We haven't got a radio," Samuel responded coolly.

"Ask him about the diamonds," Schultz hissed. "Their father was a gem merchant."

Before Samuel could respond, Benny spoke. "If we had diamonds, don't you think we would have sold them and fled the country like so many others?"

Schultz started, as though plagued by a sinking feeling that the plunder he had promised his new friend might not exist after all. Then the smug certainty he had embraced since Poland's surrender broke through. "I don't believe you. You lie. You all lie."

With a flourish, Joseph reached down to the floor and retrieved a book that had been trampled upon. Its front cover was torn, and Hebrew writing was visible on the exposed page. "Herr Schultz, you know me to be a religious man."

The German-Pole shrugged.

"This is the *Tanakh* — the Hebrew Bible," Joseph said calmly, grasping the book to his chest. "I swear I know of no diamonds hidden in this house. If this be untrue, may G-d strike me dead."

No one spoke. I was wild with fear. Then I understood. My ring had never been hidden before! And when we divided up Papa's diamonds, Joseph hid his share in the garden! I wanted to sing, to recite a prayer of thanksgiving, for my wonderful brothers had fought violence with honesty!

As the door shut behind Schultz and the disgruntled soldier, I felt Papa's presence. I knew he was proud of how his sons had averted disaster, just as I knew Schultz wouldn't forget being embarrassed.

We were safe, but for how long?

Putting aside the journal entry, Cate sat quietly as moonlight inched across the floor. The bitter thoughts that her mind had been turning over since she saw Eddie had now fully shriveled under the light of reason. Even if Samir Falah was the boy in the photograph, he couldn't be compared with

Jan Schultz. Or any adult. The modern world might hold otherwise, but the court of conscience shouldn't. And she couldn't. A child manipulated by adults wasn't solely responsible for his actions. If a boy that young was used — by his father, insurgents, or someone else — he was a victim. Not as John or Miriam had been, but a victim nonetheless.

And yet if Samir had betrayed John, she couldn't forgive him. Never that. But he wasn't like Schultz.

CHAPTER 33

On November 11, Cate threw open her bedroom window and breathed in crisp air gilded with the glow of autumn. Her eyes skimmed the vivid tapestry of Sheila's small piece of paradise. The foliage ringing the yard flamed with jewel tones of scarlet and rust, and Cate caught her breath for a moment. Strange to think that such heart-wrenching beauty was born of death, but then dormancy was an intermission more than an ending. She imagined Father Sullivan reminding her that what appeared to be dying was only transforming, for spring would bring resurrection and renewal. And what of her life — what change would the next six months bring?

As the sun climbed over the horizon and the future beckoned, Cate tried to match her spirit to the promise of the day. Although there was satisfaction in finishing the book, it had been a challenge to weave the stories together. In the end she'd found a common thread: Miriam's tale.

The novel explored how war had fashioned Beatrice into a combination Land Girl and entrepreneur; the toll a volunteer physician's commitment took on his family; Sheila's and Leah's differing views on whether war is a crucible or transformative; Father Sullivan's experiences as an army chaplain; and, how Helen had filled the void born of her mother's emotional paralysis. Cate's tale of loss had found its way into the narrative as well.

Thumbing through the manuscript, she wondered if her writing would hold a reader's attention. Had she merely done an adequate job, or "hit one out of the park" as John would have said? With a glance at the clock, she brewed a pot of tea, opened a tin of biscuits, and settled herself in a comfortable chair. There was just enough time for a final read-through before the manuscript was due, provided she could quiet her mind enough to concentrate. Active stillness — that was what she sought. Ignoring the nervous fluttering around her heart, she tried to focus instead on the journey ahead, one for which all fiction lovers keep a bag packed. Just in case.

Cate would always recall her first Amberley Christmas as a series of black-and-white images. Snowballs flew as dark figures darted behind snowbanks; black gloves were left to dry on white radiators; and ice skates flashed on the murky surface of Skitter's Pond. And on Christmas Eve, she joined her friends to watch in wonder as a sleeping tree came to life in the common when Sheila threw a switch that sent a thousand bulbs twinkling against a velvet sky.

Over coffee and a bagel on a snowy morning before the new year, Cate switched on her laptop to check her e-mail. There in her in-box was a generic "Dear Author" message thanking her for taking part in the writing contest. Her eyes blurred as she called to mind all the rejection letters she'd received from publishers over the years. Those that began with a thank-you always ended with a rejection. She pushed her half-eaten breakfast away and reached out to punch the Delete button only to jump at the sound of the doorbell. It was barely seven o'clock. Who would be — Sheila, of course. As mayor, she doubtless knew the contest results and was coming to offer what comfort she could. Although Cate appreciated the gesture, talking about the hundreds of hours she'd wasted writing a book that would sit forever on her hard drive was the last thing she wanted to do. The bell rang again before a voice called out, "Open this blasted door!"

Cate hurried to let Beatrice in. The old woman's face was flushed, and she was sweating despite the cool temperature. "I need to sit," she announced simply, moving toward the couch. Cate recoiled inwardly, for the face she'd come to know as a roadmap of lines and wrinkles that spoke to a long and fulfilling life seemed to have lost its inner fire. For some time, she'd been noting changes in Beatrice who feared only two things: losing her mobility and what she called "my marbles." Arthritis, osteoporosis, and her recent surgery had the former under assault, and some days the mind that had seemed like a steel trap only months before was anything but. "The sliding fortunes of old age," Helen had remarked when Cate shared her concerns. Yet perhaps Beatrice's paper-thin skin was the result of nothing more than fatigue, Cate thought. Still, the aura of fragility that clung to the strong-willed matriarch brought tears to her eyes. She turned away, determined that

Beatrice not see her dismay. Cate was equally resolved not to don the blank, impassive face of so many home care aides, for she couldn't repay the old woman's trust with such false coin. "Beatrice, can I get you anything? Something to drink?"

"No, no." Beatrice waved her cane dismissively before pointing to the rocking chair opposite. Cate sat. "You've heard, then?"

"Heard?"

"About the contest! Sheila told me you're not a finalist. Bunch of old men making the call. They were never going to let a slip of a girl win. Still, no matter. You've got the thing written; that's what's important." She paused to take a deep breath. "So, what are your plans?"

"Plans?"

Beatrice cocked her head. "To sell the book. It's good — at least the parts I've read. So will you use a literary agent or approach publishers directly?"

Cate raised a hand to her forehead, wishing she'd thought to get her coffee before the grilling began. She sent a longing glance toward the kitchen. "Beatrice, I only just found out. And I don't know anything about literary agents and all that."

"Well, find out. And fast. Once life gives you a shove, it's best to kick back quick as you can. I know a thing or two about that."

Cate hesitated, for the truth was that suddenly the contest didn't seem that important. The book didn't seem that important, not after what she'd lived through the past few weeks. "I'll give it some thought; I promise."

"Fine." Getting to her feet, Beatrice nodded once. "Well, that's one chore off my list. Now to Sheila."

"Sheila?" Cate stood. "She's all right, isn't she?"

"Of course. Or she will be once the morning sickness passes." At Cate's stunned silence, Beatrice added with a chuckle. "It's twins, you know."

Cate joined Beatrice in congratulating Sheila, who seemed by turns ecstatic and frantic at the thought of being a mother again. Afterward, Cate traded texts with MaryLou, Leah, Gaby, and Helen about baby shower ideas. Then she settled herself in front of her laptop with a pot of tea, a glass of whiskey, and a pound of almond cookies. It took her hours to compose a synopsis of the book. E-mailing a handful of boutique literary agencies, she described the women of her town as having, "survived the ravages of war linked together in a daisy chain of love at once more powerful and more fragile than they realize." Over the course of the next few weeks, she received a few lukewarm responses, but no requests to read the manuscript. *This takes time,* she thought. *Months. Years even. I just have to be patient.* Then a confident voice — had it always been there? — whispered that Beatrice was right: The book was good. Most important, it was timely. So much so that Cate didn't want to wait a year for a literary agent to take notice, then another two years before a publisher released it. What she'd written might encourage sisters-in-arms to begin telling their stores. The sooner that happened, the sooner men would start listening. And maybe stop dying.

After so many years of struggle, during which she'd doubted she would ever succeed as a writer and cursed the dream that had so dominated her life, Cate did what she'd promised herself she never would: She considered self-publishing. It had certainly worked for that wonderful writer from Salem who'd penned *The Lace Reader.* Not that Cate was comparing her novel to that best-seller, but she did look to the book's author for inspiration. It guided her decision, one she was determined to act on sooner rather than later.

On her next day off, Cate set to work. Hours later, she glanced at her watch. With a start, she realized that she'd worked through the day, for what had begun in the clear light of morning was ending under a puddle of lamplight. Hoping the effort had been worth it, she sat back and considered the book cover she'd designed. It depicted women working in factories, tending children, and plowing fields against a backdrop of flames and barbed wire. The significance of a blue jay perched on the edge of an upturned spade she alone appreciated, for it had been that bird's plaintive cry that had pulled her to the mailbox that last day at the house she and John had made a home. If not for the bird, she wouldn't have seen the letter that brought her to Amberley.

Eyeing the book cover with approval, she uploaded the image to a do-it-yourself e-publishing Web site. Then she checked that the manuscript was properly formatted. For a moment, her hand hovered over the Return button. Once she pressed it, her novel would be out in the world. Where it would go, whom it would touch, she couldn't know. Perhaps no one, perhaps — no. The book was good. Better than good. She punched the Return button before she could second-guess her decision. Then she went in search of the Bushmills bottle.

As they sat together over the remains of Sheila's signature St. Patrick's Day dinner of corned beef and cabbage, Beatrice took in the smudges of fatigue beneath her friend's eyes and the rigidity in shoulders that bore so much. Yet Sheila was glowing, too, doubtless because her husband was thrilled with the pregnancy. "A positive, life-affirming start to the year," he'd said, before swinging his wife into the air and setting her back down reverently. When she'd seen that, Beatrice had stopped worrying about how Sheila would handle this latest challenge, for worry she had, despite her confident words to young Cate and others. Now over fifty, Sheila was a bit long in the tooth to carry a child, let alone twins. But, then, she wasn't like other women. *I know that,* Beatrice thought. *Vincent does, too. Just have to make sure Sheila comes to believe it.*

"You're a good mother to Sara, and you'll be to the next two," Beatrice observed, sipping the cordial Sheila had just set before her. "And before you tell me that you won't have time to keep the business running, remember who you're talking to. I've been watching you since the day you were born.

You've set a strong pace all your life, and you're an overachiever of the first order — someone I'd go into combat with. When I needed something done at the store, it was always my practice to ask a busy person. This is no different. You're like me: always running at full steam." For a moment, Beatrice was tempted to confide that where once the inner landscape of her mind had been well lit, now shadows crept ever closer. Instead, she checked the impulse. Comfortable in the roles of matriarch and mogul, she didn't embrace vulnerability. Well, not easily. "I bet," she teased, "even now you're multitasking, your mind skipping over all the things you have to do tomorrow. Am I right?" When Sheila blushed, Beatrice slapped the table. "I knew it! You're made of tougher stuff than even you know, my girl. Just as young Cate is. I told her that when she found out she didn't win that contest. Damn shame. So now she has to get the thing published herself and has a bit of a mountain to climb. Nothing to yours, of course, but one she didn't expect to be tackling. In my opinion, you'll both succeed. And as much as my body betrays me these days, some things haven't changed."

"Such as?" Sheila asked, unconsciously rubbing her belly.

"I'm *never* wrong."

By Easter, *The Tapestry of War* was an e-book sensation. Argument raged about whether it was a novel or narrative nonfiction, but all the talk only fueled sales. So many war widows reached out to Cate that she set up a companion blog where readers could post comments and share their stories of sacrifice, loss, and recovery. Every morning when she turned on her computer, she was stunned by how many had visited the site, for women from all over the globe and every walk of life were connecting with her characters. Marion Puttner, the puffed-up librarian who'd been so abrasive when they'd first met, now considered Cate her discovery and promoted *The Tapestry of War* with gusto. As a result of her efforts, libraries across New England hosted readings, and local book clubs encouraged members to keep journals.

Cate's hope that women affected by war would tell their stories snowballed in ways she could not have imagined. People stopped her on the street to talk about the book, and she spent hours each day responding to e-mails and letters. A number of publishing houses announced the release of war memoirs penned not by soldiers but by the sisters-in-arms who mother, marry, and mourn the warriors. Across the country, high schools were including an oral history component in their study of war and its aftermath. So many nursing-home residents had expressed a wish to record their experiences of World War II that a foundation stepped forward to cover the costs of preserving what it called, "the receding tide of our collective memory." Most important, military widows were banding together to demand full disclosure of the circumstances surrounding their husbands' deaths. Forced by circumstance, the Pentagon was responding, albeit at a snail's pace.

Given how impressively the e-book was selling, Cate was approached by an independent print publisher that championed the work of debut authors. With the help of an entertainment lawyer friend of Jenny's, Cate negotiated her first publishing contract. Although the print publication was more than a year away, Cate was brimming with ideas. She suggested to her editor that signings be held in diners. Those who attended would receive a LIFE IS IN THE TELLING pen and advice on keeping a journal. She envisioned a Web site that called to mind a diner's paper place mat. By clicking on different sections, visitors to the site could take a virtual tour of Amberley, and links were provided to the town's many businesses. When a follow-up book that would delve into the backstory of the novel's main characters was proposed, Cate set her mind to what she came to think of as book two in the Amberley series.

Once it became known that the book would be released in print form, Cate was kept busy with media requests for interviews, podcasts, and photo shoots. "If you're promoting the book, you need to look good. Separates are best," Beatrice argued. Repeatedly. Although she no longer ran McLean's, Cate's first and still favorite patient talked up its in-house label with the skill of one born to retail. "Our silk's top quality. It breathes, looks expensive, and doesn't wrinkle much. Don't forget that you're representing Amberley, so you should wear something produced locally that's both accessible and polished."

So Cate took to dressing more carefully, surprised to find that she enjoyed the caress of silk and the swirl of a wrap skirt. Wearing such clothes made her feel sexy, something she was still coming to terms with. Although her new friends told her, in ways both subtle and not, that John wouldn't expect her to remain celibate, Cate hadn't found her way back to the sexuality that had once been such a part of her personality. In time, she would, but until then she was content with baby steps: growing out her hair and dressing well.

For months, Cate hadn't worked as a home care aide. Still, she made an effort to keep in touch with certain patients. Every few days, she stopped by the rectory to check up on Father Sullivan. Most Saturdays she met Beatrice at the Clip & Curl, where they'd chat while having manicures. And like many in Amberley, she also tried to keep an eye on Zelda. Although at first visiting the newsstand seemed an obligation, in time those few minutes each day became as welcome a part of Cate's routine as a morning espresso at Vitelli's, or lunch with Helen at the diner.

CHAPTER 34

As a consequence of how run off her feet she was, when Cate received the e-mail from Israel, it lay in her in-box for days before she read it. The morning she finally did dawned with no indication that two things would occur to change her life. First, she learned from Eddie Fallon that Samir Falah was, indeed, the boy in the photographs she now kept in a small album. After months of searching and a bit of luck, Eddie had found the Falah family living in London. The father had apparently died, but Eddie had spoken with Samir's mother who'd recalled her son's befriending a soldier matching John's description.

That the family had been granted asylum in the UK suggested they hadn't been involved in John's death. Still, Cate was determined to speak with Samir in person. For just a moment, she questioned the wisdom of such a plan. Was it rash and a waste of her newfound income to fly to London? And what if her meeting with Samir went badly, what if — No. She wouldn't allow "what ifs" into her life again. Before she could question the decision, she booked a ticket and e-mailed her travel details to Eddie. It was then she noticed the message from Israel that her publisher had forwarded.

Dear Ms. Saunders:
Could you tell me please if the character named Miriam Rosen in your novel is based on a real person? My father's little sister had that same name, you see. She was lost to him in the Lodz ghetto, and it would bring him such peace to know she survived the war.
    I look forward to hearing from you.

Sincerely,
Rabbi David Ben Yehuda
39 Elazar HaModai
Moshiva Germanit
Jerusalem, Israel 93148

The calls had been hurried, just the sketchiest of details and an urgent plea to come to her apartment as soon as possible. They arrived as a pale moon rose in a sky dusted with stars. Some hurried up the steps, while others leaned on canes or the arm of a friend.

As the evening was chill, Cate lit a fire, and it snapped a cheerful greeting. After she handed around coffee, hot cider, and whiskey, her gaze traveled over the faces of Miriam's friends — her friends. Sheila and Vincent; Leah and Gaby; MaryLou and Peter; Father Sullivan and Helen; Zelda and Beatrice. When they'd all settled into seats or found pieces of wall to lounge against, Cate told them about the e-mail and the phone calls that followed. "After he was taken from the Lodz ghetto to fill a slave-labor quota, Miriam's brother Samuel was eventually sent to Auschwitz." Someone gasped, but Cate hurried on. "He survived and made it to Palestine — to Israel — after the war."

"Thank God," Father Sullivan murmured, crossing himself. "And her other brothers?"

"They died during the war," Cate said. "At least as far as I know."

"And this rabbi who wrote to you?" Leah asked. "Who is he?"

"David is Samuel Ben Yehuda's son."

"Ben Yehuda," Gaby repeated. "Not Berkson. So he changed his last name?"

Cate nodded. "Samuel took a Hebrew name, I suppose associating his old name with the horrors of those last years in Europe. Ben Yehuda means son of Judah — Judah was his father. The name change would have made it harder for Miriam to find him."

"And she tried to," Helen pointed out. "I know that for a fact. She looked in Europe and Israel."

"Did you speak with Samuel directly?" Sheila wanted to know.

Cate shook her head. "David wants to move slowly. His father is quite elderly, and David doesn't want to risk all of this — well, overwhelming him. He said he'll tell him soon, but not quite yet. Samuel's in the hospital, you see. An infection that's not life threatening, but David wants to be careful nonetheless."

"Smart man," Vincent observed. "Even treatable infections in someone Samuel's age are serious."

Beatrice agreed that hearing unexpected news — even if it was good — wasn't easy once the years pile on. "I never did like surprises, and now I positively hate them."

"And you're sure this Samuel is Miriam's brother?" Leah asked. "Not that it seems possible there could be two people with the same name and so much in common, but —"

"I'm certain," Cate said. "It was talk of the journal that clinched it. David told me he'd always heard how his aunt used to keep diaries when she was a girl. Miriam kept one right through those last days before moving into the ghetto. She hid it, actually; but then she had three older brothers."

"And feared they'd go through her things," Zelda offered with a knowing nod. "She was probably right."

"Samuel told his son stories of how Miriam used to tuck what she wrote into a hiding place beneath her windowsill. He said she'd sit at that window for hours, dreaming of the life she'd one day have. Dreaming of —" Cate stopped, the hand that had reached out to pour a cup of coffee loosening its grip. The crash that followed made her jump. She stared down at the brown stain on the carpet and then back at her hands. "Oh my God. Oh my God!" She was running from the room before anyone could react.

They were behind her in an instant, filling the bedroom and spilling out into the hall. "What? What is it?" Sheila asked, pushing her way to the front of the crowd. She found Cate clawing at the windowsill above the padded window seat.

"Damn it, he's good," Cate said to no one

in particular.

"Who?" Sheila asked.

"I think she means me," Peter Flynn answered.

Cate turned around, her eyes pleading. "You've nailed it into place too well!" And then to Sheila: "It was loose and sort of warped. Peter fixed it for me." She gave another tug. "I can't budge it now."

Peter pulled a screwdriver from his back pocket while MaryLou whispered that her man always had the right tool for the right job. Cate wrung her hands impatiently while Peter tried to undo his careful work and pry the windowsill apart. When the wood groaned in protest, he sent a questioning look in Sheila's direction.

"Oh, the hell with it!" She waved at the now-splintering wood. "Rip it off. We'll worry about fixing it later."

Peter nodded and gave the piece of mended wood one final tug. It came apart with a crack. Cate leaned forward to peer into the space between the wall studs. She saw — nothing. The sigh that escaped her was eloquent.

"Hang on," MaryLou said, holding out a tiny flashlight she kept clipped to her keychain. "Check again to make sure."

Cate flipped on the light and shone it into

the narrow space. Two spiders slithered out, and she jumped back reflexively, recalling the moment she'd found the first journal entry all those months before. A sudden prickling at the base of her neck, and she knew. Sure enough, a moment later the flashlight's beam hit a sheaf of paper. Her breath came more quickly now. She handed the flashlight back to MaryLou and reached a hand into the dark cavity. Wordlessly, everyone gathered around as Cate unfurled the first of over a dozen sheets. It was yellowed with age and dotted with water stains, yet the writing was unmistakable. At the sight of the familiar, cursive script, Cate's throat closed. "I didn't think I'd see her writing again. Didn't think there were any other journal entries." Reverently, she held the first page out to Sheila.

"No," Sheila said. "You read it, Cate."

"But —"

"It was to you Miriam reached out," Gaby reminded her. "And it's your book that brought her story to the attention of her family."

Wetting her dry lips, Cate blinked away a sudden film in her eyes and read aloud:

After Isaac and my sweet baby died, the little house in Krakow where we had known such happiness was filled with shadows. After the mourning period, I packed my things and returned to Lodz. Joseph had lost his young wife in childbirth and his infant son soon after. Awash with grief, he had moved back into our family home. So as the rumble of war grew louder, we four Berkson children were together again. I settled into my old room the day the conscription notices arrived. Benjamin and Joseph were charged with supervising the digging of ditches around the city. Fluent in German, Samuel was designated an interpreter with the mayor's office.

Cate turned the page.

After the invasion, I told my brothers we should dig up the diamonds we'd hidden. "People are being pulled from their homes with no notice. If that happens," I reasoned, "there won't be time to pull up floorboards or tear apart the garden. The stones have to be where we can get to them quickly. We won't carry them openly. We'll hide them in plain sight." Glancing up at the ceiling, I asked, "Would you be able to distinguish a diamond from the crystals of that chandelier? No, because if diamonds are disguised as something they resemble, they aren't noticed."

Benjamin patted my hand. "Good thinking, Miriam. You were always the best at hiding the Passover afikomen. You left it out in the open because no one expected it. When Papa asked why, you answered that the simplest way was usually the best because people like to overcomplicate their lives. He laughed so hard; you were only a little girl at the time."

I smiled with pride. "We'll keep this simple as well. I want each of you to choose an overcoat — one that won't attract attention. I'll sew the diamonds on like so." I pulled out a tattered wool coat, one I had meant to give to charity long ago. Pointing to a row of brown buttons, I asked, "Can you tell they're diamonds?"

Samuel grabbed the coat. "They look so ordinary. How —"

"I painted them," I said proudly. "Then glued them onto old buttons. I'll do the same with your coats."

Cate looked up, her eyes moist. "There are more pages, but I'm not going to read them. It seems wrong somehow. It didn't when I found that first one, for she was nameless then. Faceless. Without family. And when the others were given to me, it seemed right to include Miriam's story in the book because that was what she initially intended for her journal. This is different. Knowing Samuel is alive and waiting, well, I can't read more. Not before he does, at least. So, I'll just send these on to David along with all the others." She carefully rerolled the entries even as some in the group questioned whether it was wise to pass up the opportunity to learn more about a friend they sorely missed.

Beatrice settled the matter as only she could. "Cate's right about this," she announced, knees creaking as she shifted her cane from one hand to the other. "The journal entries should go back to Miriam's family." Like a ship with sails unfurling, she straightened her shoulders and lifted her chin in challenge as though daring anyone to disagree. No one did.

"Instead of sending them to David," Sheila suggested, "why not deliver them in person?"

"Go to Israel?" Cate's voice rose in surprise.

"Of course. We can't mail Judah Berkson's masterpiece." As realization dawned on the faces around her, Sheila added, "You need to bring Miriam's ring to her brother." She patted her belly protectively. Now eight months pregnant, she was in no position to travel. "I can't do it, but you can. Besides, you'll be going to England next week, won't you? Now that Eddie Fallon's tracked down that little boy?"

Cate nodded slowly and explained to her other friends that she'd decided to go to London. As Sheila's suggestion settled in her thoughts, Cate considered continuing on to Israel. "I don't know. I don't think it should be me going. You all knew Miriam. Knew her in life." She looked at Father Sullivan, who held up his hands.

"I'm far too old for such a trip."

Helen spoke up. "Me too. It's a fourteen-hour flight, I think. But I'll want to hear all about it when you get back."

"I may have gotten out of that wheelchair, but I can't go either," Gaby said before, one by one, they all demurred.

"You're the one to do it," Leah agreed. "Just like Sheila said. It was your book that got Miriam's story out there. And you'll be in London. That cuts the travel time in half, more or less."

"You can take letters from us. We could all write something," MaryLou suggested.

"He should see Miriam's sketchbook," Beatrice put in. "She was so talented."

"Maybe we can make a little video of Amberley," Zelda proposed, adding proudly, "It's such a lovely place."

"Great idea," Sheila agreed. "And I've got that photo album. There are lots of shots of Miriam through the years. He should see how happy she was here. You've got to tell him how much we all loved her. And miss her."

As they exchanged ideas, their voices rising in excitement, Cate was caught up in the moment. Learning that his sister had built a new life might give Samuel a measure of peace. And returning the ring to him would help right a historic wrong, for perhaps it was the only work of his father's to survive the war. And maybe she *should* be the one to go for she felt such a connection to Miriam.

"It's quite a responsibility, but I'd be honored to bring the journal entries to Samuel. And take the ring on its final journey," Cate said to the approving murmur of her cherished friends. In many ways, Miriam had entrusted a piece of her story to each of them, and the ending of that story had yet to be written.

CHAPTER 35

"The kid suffers from night terrors," Eddie explained, gesturing across the street toward the low brick building Cate had learned was Lambeth Hospital. "They get bad enough every few months that he needs treatment. Outpatient counseling, not drugs."

Cate pulled her jacket closed. The day was cool for May, or perhaps the chill she felt was due more to Eddie's words than the sudden gust of wind. "Night terrors. Are those just bad nightmares?"

"No. I thought the same until I spoke with a doc friend of mine. Seems that nightmares happen during REM sleep, but night terrors only in deep sleep. And you don't remember them when you wake up. Apparently, the Falah kid has them bad. He screams for an hour or so. Top of his lungs."

"Oh my God. How horrible."

"If this kid saw what I think he did in Iraq, well, he must be pretty messed up. I've known grown men who couldn't cope with what he probably had to, and they had training. How the hell is a kid supposed to handle what grown men can't? It's asking too much to expect that." Eddie's voice caught before he lashed down his emotions, as though the wind that now swirled dead leaves into the street might scatter them beyond his reach.

The next moments passed in silence until an elderly man in a wheelchair approached. Stepping back to give him room, Eddie moved closer to Cate. When he met her gaze, she saw that the muscles of his unshaven face were tight. Funny that she'd never noticed the gold flecks in his eyes. Or the scars. There was the ghost of one across his forehead and another one on his chin. How had he — ?

Taking a step back, she folded her arms across her chest. "So I can't see Samir today?" Eddie shrugged, and she exhaled a breath.

This latest disappointment came on the heels of a day filled with setbacks. She'd had a horrible headache on the plane, and her flight from Boston had taken longer than usual because of a security scare. At the sight of Eddie waiting at the Heathrow arrivals gate, she'd thought that finally the long months of wondering what she'd learn from Samir Falah would end. Eddie had told her the boy was in the hospital, and she'd been sympathetic but no less determined to see him. Yet when they'd arrived at Lambeth, Eddie hadn't led her inside as expected. Instead, he'd suggested they grab a cup of coffee from a vendor across the street. Then he'd described Samir's mental state.

Cate felt her temper rise. She'd waited so long for the final piece of that beautiful mosaic that was John's life. As much as she'd accepted that she might never find Samir, now that she had she wouldn't be put off. Crumbling her empty cup, she tossed it in the trash and asked, "What about his mother? His brothers?"

Eddie pulled out a pair of sunglasses and slipped them on despite the cloudy weather. "I only spoke briefly with Mrs. Falah. Jameela's her name. I don't think she knows anything about the bombing. What Samir knows is another matter. And he'd be the one who would know something, because his father's dead and his brothers are too young. So your only chance of finding out what you want to know is to talk to the kid. I can help you do that. Translate for you.

Problem is, his mother never leaves his side. So —"

"So she'll know what I'm asking," Cate finished the thought. "She'll know that her husband, her son, or both, might have been involved in killing John."

"Yeah." Eddie shifted his weight. "I thought you should know that before you go in."

"Which means you think I shouldn't?" Cate guessed, pacing back and forth on the sidewalk in an effort to warm her body and cool her head. "I can't believe that after all this time — after waiting so long —" Her mind was racing. "That boy knew John, may or may not know what happened that last day." She read judgment in Eddie's silence. "Hey, it's not my fault he's sick!" Her voice rose. "Maybe it's just guilt over what he's done. Did you think of that? Maybe that boy feels guilty!"

Eddie shrugged. "Maybe he does."

"You don't expect me to walk away from all this, do you?" She spread her arms wide. "For how long? A day? A month? Forever? I don't even get to ask the questions that I've lived with for years because they might upset Samir? Might upset his mother?" When Eddie didn't respond, she snapped, "I need time to think. Take me to the hotel."

And then, in a calmer voice, "Please."

It was while sitting alone at the hotel's small bar that Cate's thoughts began to settle. Funny how alcohol can both clear the mind and muddle it, she thought, before deciding that, as with all things in life, drinking was a matter of balance. Pushing an empty wine-glass away, she got stiffly to her feet. Balance. She took a step, then another, feeling the impact of little food, no sleep, and a slight buzz. All she needed was some fresh air; that would clear the cobwebs.

When she stepped through the hotel's front door, she felt the cool breeze like a slap. As she buttoned her cardigan, her thoughts returned to the concept of balance — so akin to perfection. Miriam's father had believed that prayer and good deeds repaired the world. Sheila mended it one meal at a time, while Peter made the discarded useful again. Leah healed animals, Helen people, MaryLou machines, and Gaby the broken-hearted. *And me? I write stories. Give life to words. Surely, I can do more.*

Patting her pockets, she pulled out the slip of paper Eddie had given her when he'd dropped her off earlier. In block letters was written an address in the London neighborhood of Hackney, which he'd described as "poor and crime-ridden." Should she — ? A moment later, her hand shot out to hail a passing cab, and the alcohol's final grip on her dissolved. She read the address to the driver, asking, "I may not find a cab back, so can you wait for me while I — while I visit a friend?" He hesitated until she produced a fifty Euro note and held it out.

They moved quickly through the city, the well-lit order of downtown gradually giving way to more littered, treeless streets until they were in what could only be described as slums. The cab pulled to a stop across from a row of boarded-up storefronts. When the driver gestured toward a low-rise apart-ment building covered with graffiti, Cate's stomach lurched. She got out and took a few steps along a broken concrete walkway littered with beer bottles before glancing back at the cab. The driver had pulled out a newspaper, but was, blessedly, waiting as arranged. Drawing a deep breath, she quickly exhaled the scent of rotting garbage and urine before pulling her sweater over her nose. She moved toward the building's entrance only to find that the door's upper panel of glass had been replaced with a piece of plywood duct-taped into place. Bits of paper had been slipped next to each of the eight call buttons, and she felt her heart hammer when she read the neat handwriting beside apartment number five: FALAH.

Cate stepped back, her breath coming quickly as she scanned the building's small windows. Four sets on the first floor, four on the second. Apartment 5 must be on the second floor, but was it the apartment on the far right or the left? Lights were on in both. In one, an old man stood silhouetted before he drew the shade. She shifted her gaze to the other apartment and waited. Surely that one was number five! *Why don't I ring the bell and settle this once and for all? What am I waiting for?* As the argument raged in her mind, she stood rooted in place, unable to move forward or back.

Then the window was flung open. A hand drew the gingham curtains aside, and she heard a woman singing. The language was foreign, but the soothing tone unmistakable. A moment later, a figure came into view. Clad in a flowing dress, she was dark-haired and graceful in her movements. The child at her hip was fretful, and the woman was bouncing him up and down in an effort to comfort. Then another figure appeared. He was turned toward the woman, but Cate could still make out the boy's features. She knew them well, although the face before her had aged from the photographs she'd seen. Samir Falah rested his head against his mother just as her hand reached out to tousle his black hair.

That unconscious gesture — so natural and maternal — fueled a flash of rage that burned through Cate. She would never bear John's children or see the father he might have been. Never hold their grandchildren or face old age with the love of her life. Not wanting to see more — know more — she turned away, and her heel slid out from under her. She fell to the pavement, crying out. Tears of pain became those of anger. She was such a coward! Why hadn't she charged right into the building and pounded on the Falahs' door? After years of wondering and months of searching, how could she have wanted to run away, even for an instant? She'd flown to London to confront Samir, and she'd damn well do it!

Before she could rethink the decision, Cate scrambled to her feet and ran the few steps to the building. Through a veil of tears, she reached out to ring apartment 5. In a moment that lasted forever, her thoughts circling round and round as her finger hovered over the buzzer. A bundled figure shuffled out of the building, and Cate caught the door before it closed. She pulled it open and stepped inside to the stench of urine and fried food. A fluorescent light sputtered overhead, throwing gruesome shadows across the foyer's peeling walls. Spotting a staircase, she moved toward it, her mind dully registering the fact that her knees were bleeding.

When she rounded the top of the stairs and turned toward the apartment where she'd seen the Falah family, she stopped dead, for the door was open. What now? She took a faltering step forward only to inhale sharply when a green plastic ball came bouncing out the doorway. One, two, three bounces before it rolled toward her. The child Jameela had been holding waddled into the hallway, hands outstretched and eyes fixed on the toy. Instinctively, Cate bent down to grab the ball before it disappeared down the stairs. Holding it up for the boy to see, she was rewarded with a gurgling smile of gratitude. She'd taken only a step toward him when a shadow fell across the doorway, and Samir emerged in pursuit of his brother. He grabbed the little boy's hand and said something before tensing at the realization they weren't alone. His gaze swept over Cate, and he relaxed visibly, concluding she wasn't a threat. She wondered if John had done the same, trusting that a child couldn't be a murderer.

Suddenly, the words she'd crafted for months deserted her. As if from a great distance, she watched her arms lift the neon green ball. When Samir released his brother's hand to take it, Cate's scrambled thoughts snapped taut. She pulled back, and Samir's brown eyes narrowed in confusion. But something more than surprise stirred in those muddy depths, and Cate sensed it was just breaking the surface of his emotions when the door squeaked open further.

Jameela Falah appeared and said something to Samir in a scolding voice. She scooped up the younger boy before catching sight of Cate. Smiling, she shifted the child in her arms to reach out a free hand for the ball. Then her gaze traveled to Cate's bleeding knees. After guiding her two children inside, she hurried back to the hallway and spoke rapidly in Arabic, pointing to the blood.

"I don't understand you," Cate said, shaking her head. "But I'm fine. Really." She turned to leave, but Jameela took her arm and inclined her head toward the apartment. "No. Please. I'm fine." Jameela's touch was gentle but insistent, and Cate allowed herself to be led. When they reached the doorway, Cate's gaze traveled inside. A single naked light bulb hung from the water-stained ceiling, lending a sulfur glow to the small room. A sink and mini refrigerator stood in a corner of the apartment, and through an open doorway she glimpsed a tiny bathroom. She had long imagined the moment she'd come face-to-face with Samir — anticipating and dreading it in equal measure. Yet when she stepped inside the Falah home, Cate felt only an unexpected pang of conscience, for she was there under false pretenses.

After shutting the door, Jameela moved toward a cannibalized armoire in the corner. Two drawers lay on the floor. In one, an infant lay. Face screwed up and legs flailing, it sent forth a fussy cry. Another drawer appeared to hold layers of newspaper, and Cate guessed it did duty as a changing table. The third drawer remained inside the armoire frame. It was piled with pillows and probably served as a bed for the toddler.

Looking up from her baby, Jameela indicated that Cate should sit on the room's worn couch. She did, and when Jameela raised and lowered her hands as if to say, "Stay," Cate's mind emptied of whatever anger had gripped her earlier. The Iraqi woman tucked a blanket around the infant before speaking briskly to Samir, who

530

blinked as though awaking from a dream. He rummaged in a kitchen cabinet for a blue and white first-aid kit as his mother moved to kneel down in front of Cate.

When the boy's gaze met hers again, Cate saw that he was trying to puzzle something out. Reaching a hand up to touch his thatch of black hair, he lifted his chin slightly toward Cate. The light in his eyes seemed like recognition. But surely she was imagining things. This boy didn't — couldn't — know who she was. Unless — unless John had shown him a photograph, one taken when her hair was longer.

Cate's heart thudded in her chest. She jumped at the burn of alcohol on her cuts and looked down to see Jameela dabbing at the wounds with a cotton ball. Murmuring something soothing, the Iraqi woman worked quickly. The infant had stopped crying, and the toddler was curled up in his makeshift bed, green ball clutched to his chest. Cate glanced at Samir, and in the thick silence that followed, they continued their *conversation.* He inclined his head toward a leather-framed photograph on the far wall. From a distance, Cate could see little but a bearded face. Surely it was Samir's father! Preparing to jump up for a better look, she tensed, and Jameela looked up. The Iraqi woman smiled encouragingly and held up a bandage as if to say, "Almost done." Nodding mutely, Cate tried to relax, but she felt Samir's gaze like a question. The naked fear on his face was a jolt that shredded the last of her nerves. *He's afraid of his dead father. No, that can't be. Of me then. Of what I know or might find out. What I could reveal to his mother.*

A cry from the baby brought Jameela abruptly to her feet. She placed a hand briefly on Samir's shoulder as if to keep him from following her and then hurried to her infant's side. Cate glanced down at her neatly bandaged knees, and, before she could question her actions, pulled out her wallet. Her hands were shaking as she slid the snapshot out from behind its plastic protector. Samir's eyes locked with hers, and a question passed between them. Slowly, so slowly, his gaze dropped to the photo of a smiling man with sea-green eyes and wavy blond hair. The boy reached out a hand to John's image before pulling it back. The anguish on his face told Cate all she needed to know.

Lurching to her feet, she felt the room spin for a moment. Jameela was beside her then, speaking quickly. Cate shook her head, hugging John's photograph to her chest.

Eyes locked on the door, she mumbled, "I have to go. Thank you. Thank you for helping me."

If she could have run, she would have. Instead, she managed only a shuffling walk. After fumbling the door open, she turned back for the briefest moment. Jameela's hands were draped protectively around her eldest son, and there was a smile on her face. Samir stood waiting, head bowed and shoulders stiff. Something had to be said to close the wound between them, and Cate tried to recall any of the Arabic John had studied before his deployment. She remembered nothing except one word that sounded like shalom. It emerged from her memory slowly, and she tested the pronunciation in her mind before saying, "Salaam." *Peace.*

Samir's head shot up, surprise and relief transforming his features such that she glimpsed an echo of the child John might have known. Jameela was nodding and speaking rapidly, but the roar in Cate's ears drowned out everything but the sob rising in her throat. She turned toward the stairs, retracing her steps as quickly as she could. Once in the lobby, she threw herself against the front door, pushing it open to a chill night.

She gulped air, the cold piercing her lungs like ice crystals. The first sob escaped her as she reached the cab. Alarmed, the driver jumped out and yanked open the back door, asking if she was hurt. "No, no, I'm fine," she managed, climbing into the warm interior. "Just take me back. Please!" The cab sped past a burned-out car, and Cate twisted around in her seat to see a gang of hooded youths cross the road toward the Falahs apartment building. A store alarm sounded, and police sirens could be heard in the distance. As the cab moved through the darkened streets, she closed her eyes to the poverty and decay of a city as divided between privileged and poor as any war zone.

Sinking back against the seat, Cate imagined the past half hour of her life as pieces of memory to be saved or discarded. She might choose to remember seeing the Falah boys in the hallway and meeting Jameela, but she didn't want to recall the pain in Samir's eyes when he'd looked at John's photograph. Or how his body tensed at the sight of his father's face and relaxed when he heard his mother's voice.

After a hot shower, Cate ordered room service and fell on the platter of grilled cheese and French fries with an appetite she hadn't felt in months. Only then did she find the courage to acknowledge what she'd known to be true the moment she'd seen what was left of the Falah family. She couldn't do to Jameela Falah what Miriam had refused to do to Sheila and Leah's mother. Even if Jameela's husband had been a terrorist, even if her son had been complicit in John's death, Cate couldn't shatter Jameela's world. Not even to mend her own.

How strange that life's biggest decisions could be made so quickly, but it had always been so with her. It might have taken her mind months to realize that she would love John forever, but her heart had known it from the moment she'd seen him. It had been the same with the house they'd made a home. Even before the realtor had opened the front door, Cate had felt the pull of the place. She'd felt that same certainty at the sight of Jameela comforting her sons. That reason, fear, and self-interest had sought to weaken her resolve in the hours since hadn't changed what she knew to be true — what her conscience told her was the only truth that mattered. With that knowledge came peace of mind, or the beginnings of it.

But before she patted herself on the back, she had to ask the question: Was she simply taking the easy way out? Was she walking away because part of her still didn't want to know what had happened to John? His death might have been more horrible than she imagined, yet she'd already imagined the worst and lived with one horrific scenario after the other for years. Bringing those final moments of his life into focus would only free her spirit. Yet she couldn't — wouldn't — buy that freedom with another's pain.

Her thoughts turned to the miserable neighborhood where the Falah family lived. It had to be better than Iraq, but how could a boy as damaged as she suspected Samir was recover his smile in such a place? Perhaps she should do what she could to improve his future. She rejected the half-formed thought as soon as it surfaced in her mind, for even if Samir wasn't solely responsible for John's death, she suspected he'd been a part of it. She couldn't bring herself to harm him for that, but she couldn't help him either.

Unmindful of the hour, Cate picked up the phone to tell Eddie what had happened.

"Hullo?" a sleepy voice answered on the second ring.

"Oh. I'm sorry." She glanced at the clock and saw it was three a.m. "I didn't notice

536

the time. Go back to sleep."

"No, wait." His voice was clearer now. "What's wrong?"

"Nothing. I just — I just wanted to tell you something. But it can wait until tomorrow." She heard the sound of a bed creaking and was struck by the intimacy of their speaking in bed, albeit separate beds.

"So you went to see them?" he guessed.

"How did you — ?"

"Instinct. I figured you'd have to. That's why I gave you the address. It's a tough neighborhood, but then you know that." He exhaled into the receiver. "So what happened?"

She told him, but not about her *conversation* with Samir. That was private. Or perhaps she simply didn't know how to frame with words what she'd experienced. "When I saw Jameela in the window, when I realized who she was, it was so unreal. Partly because I'd waited so long for that moment and partly because the poignant scene was so out of place in that horrible neighborhood where they live. Jameela was cradling one of her younger sons and trying to calm him, all the while patting Samir's head and holding him close. Her movements were so soothing, so intended to convey that she could protect them, would protect them.

But of course she can't, any more than she could in Iraq. Then I went inside and she helped me. A stranger. And all the while, she was taking care of the three children. In that depressing place, she was trying to make them feel safe. And it was working; I think they wanted to believe it was possible to be safe again."

"And that's why you don't want her to know what happened to your husband?"

Cate drew a breath and held it before letting go. "I lost my parents when I was quite young. And now I've lost John. I know what it is to be shattered. I can't do it to someone else."

"You'll speak with Samir someday, you know," Eddie assured her. "He'll probably be better in a year or so. And he'll learn English. In the meantime, I'll keep an eye on him. On them. And I'll keep in touch."

Cate opened her mouth to tell him not to bother, that she'd made her decision and it was final. Then she realized that she wanted Eddie in her life — even in such a minor way. "All right." Before she could second-guess herself, she added quickly, "And next time you're in Amberley visiting MaryLou, let me know. We can — maybe — umm —"

"I will. We will." His voice was soft. "Do you need a ride to the airport?"

"No. No thanks." Twirling the phone cord around her fingers, she said, "Well, good night then."

"Good night, Cate. Take care of yourself. I'll see you soon."

When he hung up, she sat staring at the phone. How was it possible that the day had ended like this? Or that she could think of another man at such a time? Besides, Eddie wasn't her type, was nothing like John. And yet —

CHAPTER 36

When her flight touched down at Tel Aviv's Ben Gurion Airport, Cate marveled at the twists and turns her life had taken in little more than a year. What if she hadn't checked the mailbox that last time and found the letter from Amberley, hadn't entered the writing contest or found Miriam's journal entries? What if — ? Giving herself a mental shake, she jumped up in time to join the last passengers moving toward the exit.

She stood among Israelis returning from vacations abroad, wide-eyed tourists gripping guidebooks, and a mix of secular and religious Jews visiting relatives. Shouldering her carry-on, she followed signs to the taxi stand and climbed into a communal cab headed to Jerusalem. The other passengers nodded in greeting, and Cate gave the driver Samuel Ben Yehuda's address before settling back against the seat. As they pulled away from the curb, she slipped on sunglasses, her gaze sweeping the area outside the terminal. There were small knots of soldiers, tourists with backpacks, and Israelis speaking a harsh-sounding language she knew to be Hebrew.

An hour later, the taxi maneuvered its way up the steep hills that encircled Jerusalem. She tensed at the sight of a burned-out tank before the elderly woman next to her leaned in to say in accented English, "It's from the War of Independence. We leave it there so we don't forget how the capitol was cut off and under siege."

Cate opened her mouth to say that all that had happened back in 1948, but was sixty-odd years really such a long time? She sometimes felt that Beatrice and Zelda saw the past as clearly as the present, and what was such a time span in a land as ancient as Israel? Surprised by the built-up suburbs and shopping malls they passed, she whispered, "It's all so modern."

Her neighbor chuckled. "You expected camels, maybe? We've all that, but in the Old City."

A few minutes later they entered Jerusalem, and the driver pulled to a stop in a quiet, residential neighborhood. "This is the German Colony," he said, directing himself to Cate.

"Oh. Right." She climbed out with a wave to her fellow passengers. Standing on the sidewalk as the taxi sped off and the street settled into quiet, she recalled her surprise when David had given her the address. "Why would your father live in a German settlement?" she'd asked. David had laughed then. "It's a very nice place. Close to downtown, and with lots of parks. But yes, it was settled by Germans."

Slinging her bag over her shoulder, Cate crossed the street toward a two-story apartment building. Four mailboxes bore residents' names. Of the four, only one name had two words. Reasoning that Ben Yehuda was two words in Hebrew just as it was in English, she pushed the bell of that apartment.

"Ken?" a female voice answered.

"No, it's not Ken. It's Cate. I'm Cate."

The woman's laugh rang out. "Yes, okay. Come in." The entrance door buzzed, and Cate pushed it open, shifting her bag from shoulder to shoulder. There were two apartments on the ground floor, and the nearest door swung open to reveal a young woman dressed in a long-sleeved cotton shirt and ankle-length denim skirt. She smiled broadly. "Welcome."

Cate relaxed. "Oh. Hi. So you were expecting me — but then, who's Ken?"

The woman laughed again. "Ken, it means 'yes' in Hebrew."

"Oh. Oh!" Cate joined in the laughter. "I meant to pick up a phrase book, but everything's been so hectic. Well, I never got around to it."

"There's no need. English is fine. For all of us. My father studied in England, and Grandpa Samuel taught there." She inclined her head a bit. "I am Rachel Ben Yehuda. Come in, please." She held the door open, and Cate's gaze moved over the brightly furnished living room floored in cool marble. Bookshelves lined the walls, and glass doors opened onto a garden. Rachel lowered her voice. "My grandfather is resting. He has been sick. I don't know how he will react to seeing you."

"I don't want to upset him," Cate said quickly. "That's not why I've come."

"Oh, I know," Rachel rushed on, taking Cate's hands in hers. "Thank you for coming all this way. My father was so pleased to get your e-mail. He's out now, but will be back soon. I'll make coffee while we wait."

"Coffee would be wonderful," Cate said, her stomach growling on cue.

"And something to eat, perhaps," Rachel

added. "Come."

Cate stepped inside, peeling off her coat and following Rachel into the kitchen. The scent of just-baked bread filled the air. Taking a seat at the tile-topped table, Cate felt the nervousness that had gripped her in the cab fall away. She chatted easily with the Israeli, avoiding mention of Miriam, for doing so seemed improper before she'd spoken with Samuel. They'd just finished coffee and cake when a middle-aged man she guessed was David strode into the room.

"You've come," he said with a broad smile, stating the obvious with such relief that it brought a lump to Cate's throat.

"Of course. I told you I would." She got up to extend her hand before remembering Father Sullivan's saying that religious men don't shake hands with women.

Seeing her discomfort, David smiled again. "My father's not observant, by the way. And he's having a good day, as it happens. He knows about Miriam, about you, but I haven't told him you were coming today because —" He paused, a flush staining his bearded face.

"You weren't sure I'd show up, and you didn't want to disappoint him," Cate guessed.

"Just so. Come," David said. Cate and Rachel followed him toward a closed door.

David knocked once, opened it, and peered inside. "He's awake," he said softly, pushing the door open. An old man sat hunched in a chair across the room, an open newspaper on his lap. David made the introductions. "Cate Saunders, this is Samuel Ben Yehuda." Samuel struggled to his feet and took Cate's hands in his. His hair had perhaps once been the same blond as Miriam's, but was now thinning and gray. Yet his piercing eyes were undimmed and the same blue as his sister's had been. From her conversations with David, Cate knew that the ninety-five-year-old Samuel was a legend in the family. He had survived the Lodz ghetto and the death camps, run a British blockade to get to Palestine, fought the Arabs in three wars, fathered six children, and built a life in Israel as a respected professor of history.

"Cate has come a long way to tell us about Aunt Miriam," David said, guiding his father back to his chair.

"So it's true. She survived. I wouldn't allow myself to believe it when David told me," Samuel said in heavily accented English. "What — what happened to Miriam?"

Cate drew a deep breath. "I don't know where to start; I've so much to tell you. To show you."

When she faltered, David asked softly, "When did Aunt Miriam die? You didn't say on the phone."

"About three years ago." At Samuel's sharp intake of breath, she rushed on. "She was very happy, or as happy as one who'd known so much sorrow could be. She lived in Massachusetts. In a small town there. I never had the pleasure of knowing her, but many of my friends loved her dearly. Miriam kept a journal." Reaching into her bag, Cate drew out the journal entries. "We think much of the journal was lost, but these pages survived." She handed them to Samuel. "When they learned I was coming here, Miriam's friends gave me pictures to share with you." She held out Sheila's photo album. Setting the journal entries aside, Samuel reached in the pocket of his sweater. His hands shook as he slipped on his reading glasses. Cate surrendered the album reverently. At the sight of his sister's face, Samuel's eyes streamed.

Cate stood. "This is a private moment — a family moment. I'll come back another day. I've a reservation at a hotel downtown. Maybe —"

"You will stay here," Rachel said firmly. "You can share my room. Then Grandpa can visit with you when he's able. When he's strong." At Cate's hesitation, she added, "Please stay."

In truth, Cate longed for the anonymity of a hotel where she could rest undisturbed and recover from the trip. But one look at the eager young woman's face decided it. "Of course I'll stay," she said. With a nod toward David, she turned to follow Rachel from the room.

"America," Samuel said in a low voice. "After the war, I tried the agencies there. Tried to look for her."

His words tugged at Cate who looked helplessly from David to Rachel. Finally, she said, "It took a long time for Miriam to get to America. She stayed in Europe long after the war. She was looking for you and your brother Joseph."

"He died in the ghetto," Samuel stated simply, his face guarded. "And Benny — Benny was shot dead before we even reached it." At Cate's nod, he said, "I see you know that. So Miriam was looking for me and Joseph. She wouldn't have known he was dead. And because I changed my name, she wouldn't have found me here." His voice was flat. "I never considered that. And as much as I looked for her, part of me didn't believe she could have survived. Not alone. Not without us."

Troubled that her coming had only added to the old man's anguish, Cate searched for something to say that would bring comfort. Unconsciously, she fingered the chain around her neck. "Oh God, I almost forgot." She pulled the chain until the ring was visible; it caught the light and seemed to glow.

Samuel blinked. "That's not —"

"Yes." She drew the chain over her head and passed it to Samuel. "It's your father's ring." She hesitated, searching for a way to tell the truth and still offer comfort. "Miriam did her best to safeguard it. She was wearing it when she died."

As Samuel's hand closed over his father's masterpiece, he trembled with emotion. Concerned, David drew up a chair and draped an arm around his father. After a time, Samuel fixed his son with a nostalgic look. Holding up the ring, he said, "Your grandfather made this. Made so many beautiful things. He died before the war; I thank God he never saw Poland crushed. When he knew his time was coming, that he'd be gone before the wheel turned for a new year, he kept to his workroom. He was desperate to finish the ring for Miriam. One day, he called me in. He was so sick — coughing blood and unable to stand. He made me promise to save Miriam and my brothers, trusted me to get them to Palestine. So many of my friends were Zionists, and there were still ways to get out of Europe. But I failed to get them out. I failed!" He squeezed his eyes shut for a moment as David murmured that it was all right. Samuel seemed not to hear. "They wouldn't leave!" he rushed on. "They couldn't see the Germans for what they were! And because they wouldn't emigrate with me, I stayed. But the promise I made my father weighed heavily. I was not religious, but I'd been taught how broken the world is. It can be repaired through hard work, prayer, and charity. I thought of that when Poland surrendered, thought that if I found a way to guide my family through the madness to follow, I could repair the broken promise I made my father. But I didn't find a way."

Samuel fell silent for so long that Rachel knelt down beside him and took his hands in hers. "Aunt Miriam survived," she reminded him.

Samuel gave a weak smile. "Yes. Yes, Miriam and I survived. Two out of four children. We were luckier than most. And perhaps one day we'll be together again. My father believed in an afterlife." He stared at the ring, then into his granddaughter's eyes. "Perhaps he was right, and I will feel their love surround me again as it did in that little house in Lodz that so haunts my dreams."

In the weeks to follow, Cate explored Jerusalem. She shopped in the New City and walked atop the walls that encircled the Old City's four neighborhoods. As she wandered along streets paved with honey-colored stone, climbed the Mount of Olives, and made her way through cobblestoned alleys, she had a curious feeling that she was doing so in Miriam's stead. In coming to Israel she'd kept faith with the dead woman, and Cate would come to describe her journey in those terms. Yet as serious as her visit was, she often reduced Rachel to giggles by her attempts to eat a falafel with anything approaching a clean face. When Cate made the mistake of stirring her Turkish coffee, the young Israeli took her in hand and explained the finer points of Middle Eastern cuisine. For his part, David made an effort to drive Cate around the country — up to Galilee, over to Haifa, and down to Masada. She saw the caves where the Dead Sea Scrolls had been found, hiked the hills of Judaea, and swam in the Mediterranean.

Over glasses of sweet tea, she sat with

Samuel in his rose garden, speaking of the present and the past. They forged a unique friendship despite differences in age and background, connecting through Samuel's love for his sister and Cate's identification with her. In time, Cate spoke of John's death and Samuel of the loss of his beloved wife many years before. But it was in talk of Miriam that they found common ground. As Cate shared pieces of Miriam's American life, Samuel listened intently. He studied her sketchbook with interest, the pride on his face evident when he heard all his sister had accomplished. Many of Miriam's friends had sent letters, and Samuel read them before pouring over her journal entries. He asked questions about Amberley and McLean's, devouring every scrap of information Cate could recall or phone home to uncover.

One day, Samuel reminisced about his early life in Lodz. Through his eyes, Cate came to see Miriam as a girl. She learned that after Judah Berkson lost his wife in birthing their only daughter, he found with his three sons a friendship he had never expected. Each boy made his father proud — Joseph was studious, Benjamin sensitive, and Samuel the iconoclast. So different in temperament and inclination, the brothers disagreed about most everything except how much they adored their little sister. Denied the love of a mother, Miriam was spoiled by her father from the day she drew breath. When the demands of his profession called Judah from their home, the little girl turned to her brothers for love and security. Joseph taught her Hebrew; Benny made her laugh; and Samuel encouraged her to question authority. "My brother Joseph was the scholar, and Benny the peacemaker. I was rebellious. Irreligious." Samuel gave her a sorrowful look. "I don't speak of my brothers enough, for sometimes all I see is their deaths. But now, having the ring back, I'm reminded of a time before war. Before the horror." He reached out to lay a hand over Cate's. "Thank you for that."

They spoke at length about the ring. When she learned how Samuel's father had labored eighty years before to make it, Cate tried to imagine a teenaged Miriam slipping the star ruby on her finger. Through the darkness that followed, that ring had doubtless been her touchstone, reminding her of love and family, beauty and art. After the war, the ring had lain dormant as though waiting to be found. Sheila and her mother had each treasured it, but as custodians only, for the ring was destined to find its way home. And now it had.

That she'd been given the privilege of taking Miriam's ring on its final journey humbled Cate. It also made her feel connected to the women of Amberley. She thought back to those first days in town when she'd been so broken and scarred by grief. Bit by bit, she'd rebuilt herself in that healing place. The path she'd traveled had been uneven, and she'd stumbled more than sprinted, but each day she'd found a reason to keep going. The journal entries had helped, and for that she would always feel a deep connection to Miriam.

From Miriam and Samuel Cate had learned about the Jewish concept of *tikkun ha-olam:* repair of the world. Gaby used her gift of empathy to fix what was broken, as did each of Cate's friends in some way. Yet when Cate imagined repairing the world one break at a time, it was through the strength of community, for she'd come to value how women's stories were intertwined. Interdependent. Standing alone, she and her friends were as vulnerable as that lone birch tree struggling to survive. But together they were shielded and protected, supported and nurtured. Together they could weather any storm. Bend, but not break. Just like Miriam.

■ ■ ■ ■

One sunny morning Cate found the courage to ask Samuel how a survivor of the Holocaust could come to celebrate and embrace life after witnessing such horror. "The light beckons," Samuel said simply. Fixing his faded eyes on the sky, he lifted his shoulders briefly. "You wake up one day to find that the darkness has receded just enough for life to warm you again. And you move toward it, for the instinct to survive is too strong to do otherwise. We're animals, after all. Bred for survival. But you always see the past from the corner of your eye. Or superimposed on the present." He stared down at his hands, wrinkled by time and swollen by arthritis. "Even as these hands built a homeland, I saw them coated with my brothers' blood. I still see the blood, still feel the weight of their broken bodies." He clenched his fists.

When he paused, Cate whispered, "You don't have to talk about it. Don't have to relive it. I — I know how Benny died."

Samuel nodded. "A little boy fell in the street. He was crying. Benny tried to help him and was shot. I remember staring at the blood staining my brother's coat, not believing it could be real. Benny was the best of us — the kindest and most gentle. How could such a beautiful life end so quickly? There was no warning. No time to say good-bye or tell him we loved him. I heard Miriam scream and saw her move toward Benny. But the shooting had frightened people. They were pushing and shoving. I thought she'd be crushed. We were being carried forward with the crowd, hauling our belongings and our dead. Miriam was hysterical. Screaming." He shook his head in disbelief. "I don't know how Joseph and I got them both inside the ghetto, but we did."

Snatches of the stories she'd heard and read replayed in Cate's mind. "I know that eventually you and Joseph were separated from her. Taken away."

Samuel nodded slowly. "We feared it might happen as roundups were common. Thankfully, Miriam was out when we were grabbed. So she didn't see. Didn't know. I thought we'd be sent to a labor camp. But we were only moved to another part of the ghetto. We couldn't get word to her, though. Couldn't get back to her." Samuel fixed his gaze on Cate's taut face. "We were assigned to pull the excrement wagons, you see. My brilliant scholar of a brother, the one with the finest mind, was tied to a wagon like a workhorse. Like a beast. Yet even as we pulled those putrid barrels through the ghetto, Joseph's mouth was moving. Praying." Samuel blinked and wiped at his eyes. "No one could last more than a few months at such work, and every day we grew weaker. Joseph had never been strong, not in body. He died in my arms."

The silence that followed was broken first by the distant laughter of a child. Then birdsong cut the air, and a breeze rustled the trees above them. Finally, Cate asked, "And — and after?"

"Eventually, I was sent to Auschwitz. I couldn't get word to Miriam. I told you how I looked for her after the war, but I didn't really believe she could have survived the ghetto on her own. I took some comfort in that, convinced that she hadn't been sent —" The words he left unsaid swirled around them like the shadows Cate feared would always fill that corner of his mind.

CHAPTER 37

On the morning she left Israel, Cate felt tears sting her eyes. She'd said good-bye to Samuel in the rose garden he loved so much, promising to come back and see him again as soon as she could. David insisted on driving her to the airport, and, while he carried her luggage to the car, Cate sought out Rachel. She found the younger woman in the kitchen packing some cookies.

"For the plane," Rachel explained, handing them to Cate. After Cate hugged her in thanks, Rachel held up her right hand, smiling when Cate saw Miriam's ring. "Grandpa wants me to wear it, wants to see it being used. Being loved." The star ruby glinted in the morning sunlight, and Rachel gazed at her inheritance with something approaching awe. "This ring has been through so much. And because you shared Aunt Miriam's story in your wonderful book, it's back with our family." Her gaze swept the tidy kitchen.

"It's home."

Eighteen hours after leaving Jerusalem, Cate pulled her rental car into a parking space in front of Vitelli's. It was six o'clock in the evening and the sun was low in the sky. She saw Sheila in the grocery's front window, bagging an order with one hand and massaging her belly with the other. Her due date was fast approaching, and Cate was grateful she'd gotten back before the babies' birth. Across the street, Zelda was standing beside the newsstand chatting with Peter, who was walking the puppy Leah had convinced him to adopt.

As she got out of the car to stretch her legs, Cate's cell phone beeped with a text from her editor. Her heartbeat quickened when she learned that a Congressional oversight committee had been established to review whether the Pentagon was misleading the families of fallen soldiers as to the details of their deaths. Her thoughts turned to *The Tapestry of War*'s companion blog. It was now getting thousands of hits a day. Some readers wrote to ask Cate when she would publish the follow-up book that would delve into the background of characters so many fans had come to love. She'd been giving the project a lot of thought and wondered if she should share the story of Sheila's saving Leah's life when they were children. Or Beatrice's risking prison so her sister could have cancer treatment. Perhaps Cate would include the story of how Miriam and her friends banded together when Charlotte's in-laws had her committed to the hospital's psychiatric ward. *Amberley Sisters* would be a good title, for whether bound by blood, friendship, or circumstance, the women she would profile were truly sisters.

Slipping her phone in her pocket, Cate glanced up and down Main Street before hurrying toward the diner. She wondered if Gaby would be there. Maybe she was too sick to — but no, her friend was behind the front counter slicing a pie. Cate saw so many friends around the room that she paused a moment to take the picture into her heart. Then she stepped into the diner's warm interior to shouts of greeting.

MaryLou strode across the floor to give her a bone-crushing hug. "Well, it's about time! What the hell took you so long?"

"Cate! What happened in Israel?" Beatrice demanded, rising from her booth and fumbling for her cane.

"If anyone's going to ask Cate questions, it's me," Sheila announced from the open door before moving awkwardly across the floor. "I saw you out the window and tried to catch up, but my feet are killing me. These babies are anxious to be born, but wouldn't before you got back."

Cate smiled. "You're glowing."

"I'm perspiring," Sheila corrected, making her way to a chair.

"You shouldn't be working so much!" MaryLou chided Sheila. "I told you that."

"Oh, be quiet, Lulu, I want to hear what Cate has to say!"

As the two old friends sparred, Cate walked over to kiss Beatrice. Father Sullivan called out a greeting, and Leah raised a glass of lemonade in salute. At the front counter, Gaby held a piece of cherry pie up in the air and pitched her voice above the din. "Everybody stop badgering Cate! Let her eat a little something."

With a wave to Helen who'd just come in the door, Cate made her way to the counter. Giving Gaby's hand a squeeze, she slid onto a stool and dug into the wedge of pie. The room echoed with questions.

"So what happened with Miriam's brother?"

"Did you give him the ring?"

"What about that boy in London, did you see him?"

Cate swiveled in her seat, her gaze moving around the diner. How could she explain that she might never know what happened to John any more than she would learn who had left her Miriam's journal entries? But then they were all living with uncertainty. She thought of Sheila's anxiety over her pregnancy, the ebb and flow of Gaby's cancer, and MaryLou's fear that the love she'd found with Peter Flynn would wither and die. Every day seemed a battle for Beatrice who described aging as an un-mapped minefield where moving backwards in her thoughts was as tricky as forward with her body. And for all his bravado that he'd win this battle as he had all the others, Father Sullivan's announcement that the diocese had decided to close St. Joseph's had shaken them all.

There's so much uncertainty, but at least we're together. We suffer loss alone, but we heal in a community. I did. And as much as my new friends helped me heal, I've done my part, too. Sheila credits me with her newfound honesty about Vincent's war work, Gaby keeps saying I've given her a measure of peace about her parents' deaths, and Mary-Lou calls me the matchmaker of Amberley. The words Cate spoke in her mind were directed to John but also at that part of herself she'd held back since the day she came to Amberley. *These people accept me. Love me. I belong here.*

Gaby's voice cut across her thoughts. "So what have you got to tell us, Cate?"

"Quite a bit." Cate smiled at the familiar faces, the golden glow of late afternoon sunlight framing the front windows, and the lingering sweetness of homemade pie. At Amberley. "But mostly that it's good to be home. So good to be home."

ACKNOWLEDGMENTS

Without the vision of literary midwife Alicia Condon, this novel would not have been published. No writer could ask for a more patient, sage, and committed editor. I am indebted to Kensington's "tourism" mavens: Publicist Lulu Martinez, who guides readers to Amberley, and Rights Director Jackie Dinas, who insures its residents have passports. My thanks to Production Editor Paula Reedy, and the art and production teams for giving my characters a beautiful home with a stunning front door, and for insuring that all in Amberley speak the Queen's English.

We are all products of the love we've shared with others. I am privileged to have a mother whose strength of character inspires me every day. Over countless cups of tea, she shared the revision journey, never doubting I'd find a way to tell this story. I owe a special debt to Kit, my sister and best friend, who always believed I'd be a novelist. My brightest memories are lit by her smile. My brother, Matt, sees opportunity in every challenge. His contagious optimism and unshakable faith that all things are possible help me find the promise in every dawn. I thank him for reading an early draft and for all the baked goods that fueled the writing process! I am ever grateful to my reader/brother, Mark, for teaching his baby sister the power of logic, and for bringing his soul mate, Vicki, into our family. Eternal gratitude to my muses: L, MJ, I, and Mr. B.

Although the women of Amberley were born of my imagination, they were inspired by strong, compassionate friends: Margaret Villanova, Tova Glass, Jennifer Paton Smith, Suzanne Erez, Roxanne Epstein Rosenthal, Wendy Recore, and Noreen Nash.

During the writing of this novel, I turned to Benjamin Yosef for support many times. His friendship is a precious gift.

An acknowledgment of Shmuel Huss's good advice all those years ago is long overdue; he set me free, although I couldn't see it then.

My deepest gratitude to the Tilden Library's Ann Kurt — gentle reader and cheerleader — and to Professor Zdzislaw Pietrzyk, Director of the Jagiellonian University Library in Krakow.

David Llewellyn saw promise in this novel years before it grew into itself. He encouraged me to persevere, and I owe him my thanks.

I am indebted to two amazing poets. The novel's title, *Sweet Breath of Memory,* is taken from a line in the poem "Memory" by Anne Brontë, and the poem "Be My Friend" that Vincent recites to Sheila was written by my mother.

This story would have lived forever in my imagination but for my characters' persistence. When self-doubt gripped my heart, they coaxed and prodded until I found my way again. I set them free to roam the world beyond my laptop with faith they'll find their way into the hearts of readers . . . and back home again should a sequel be their destiny.

AUTHOR'S NOTE

Writing about the Lodz ghetto is a daunting task, for by definition the horror of that time is beyond description. Readers interested in learning more about the ghetto have a plethora of research materials at their disposal. The basic facts are as follows. A few months after conquering Lodz, the Germans sealed off the poorest section of the city. 245,000 people — a figure that included refugees from other conquered lands — were imprisoned in an area that measured 1.5 square miles. As the ghetto was a slave-labor camp, one hundred factories were established. Food and fuel were rationed, and many died of disease and starvation. Some Jews were sent from the ghetto to work as slave laborers in other towns, but the majority were eventually deported to the death camps. It is impossible to know how many Jews survived the Lodz ghetto; the highest estimate I have seen is 4 percent.

Haunting images depicting everyday life in Lodz were captured at great personal risk by ghetto photographer Mendel Grossman. Tasked by the authorities with photographing "official" subjects, Grossman took more than 10,000 secret photographs before dying on a forced march. After liberation, his sister returned to the ghetto and dug up tin cans in which Grossman had hidden the negatives. As per her brother's instructions, she sent them to Israel. This unique visual record of the ghetto was destroyed by the Egyptian Army during Israel's War of Independence. Thankfully, prints and negatives that Grossman entrusted to a friend have survived.

I ask the reader's indulgence on a point of historical fact. In the novel, Miriam's husband is a medical student at Krakow's Jagiellonian University in 1938. In reality, the 1937 class was the last that accepted Jews (11.5 percent of the student body). As a result of the *numerus clausus* (anti-Jewish quotas) in the years leading up to WWII, Jewish enrollment in Polish medical schools dropped by 60 percent. By 1938, Jews were banned from both the study and practice of medicine.

The scene set in the ghetto's Marysin

graveyard is based on fact, although eyewitness reports differ as to whether the Red Army liberated Lodz the following day or thereafter. Similarly, reports differ as to whether eight or nine mass graves were dug at Marysin. What is undisputed is that the Gestapo spared from immediate execution the Jews who dug those graves. Although undoubtedly motivated by sadism, this decision saved their lives. Unlike Lodz's oldest Jewish cemetery, Marysin wasn't destroyed by Poland after the war. With 230,000 graves, it is the largest Jewish cemetery in Europe. The mass graves dug by ghetto prisoners have not been filled in, and serve as a reminder of that horrible chapter in Polish history.

The account of Miriam's husband's telling her of their son's death is adapted from a story told of Bruriah, the Talmudic scholar who was wife to Rabbi Meir.

The U.S. Army did authorize a printing of the Talmud in Germany in 1946. Unfortunately, due to a shortage of supplies and the need to secure a full set of Talmud from the U.S., what came to be called the Survivors' Talmud was not produced until 1948. A preface containing the work's only English began with the words "This edition of the

Talmud is dedicated to the United States Army."

The release Cate is urged to sign is not based on fact. To my knowledge, military families are *not* required by the government to waive their common law or statutory rights. That said, whether contractors serving in war zones are entitled to immunity is less a matter of settled law than has previously been the case. As this fascinates me as an attorney, and intrigues me as a writer, I decided that Cate should confront the issue.

■ ■ ■ ■

A Reading Group Guide: Sweet Breath of Memory

ARIELLA COHEN

■ ■ ■ ■

The suggested questions are included to enhance your group's reading of Ariella Cohen's *Sweet Breath of Memory.*

DISCUSSION QUESTIONS

1. Cate's memories of John are fluid, shifting in and out of focus and becoming abraded by time. She questions if this means her love was somehow flawed. Why do you think some memories remain crisp, while others blur and seem to dim with each dawn?

2. Cate speaks of memories as a shield against loneliness and despair. Like armor, they're "initially so shiny they dazzle and in time acquire the patina of use." Do you agree? Are there particular memories that have been your armor in life?

3. How does the life path of Cate mirror that of Miriam Rosen? Can the guilt Cate feels over John's death be compared with a Holocaust survivor's guilt?

4. Gaby does not initially tell her closest

friends that she is dying. Knowing how her parents' deaths shadow her life, do you think denying herself the comfort of friendship is a form of self-punishment?

5. Working as a home care aide, Cate wears the uniform of one valued more for what her hands can do than what her mind can imagine. Compare her initial attitude toward caregiving with Gaby's toward waitressing. Both women come to view such manual labor as a form of atonement. Is this healthy?

6. When Helen describes growing up with her mother, the anger and resentment she felt toward Charlotte is obvious even though it was tempered by great love. How can we help friends and colleagues face the unique challenges of caregiving?

7. Rosa Vitelli, whom we meet only through the memories of other characters, often said that, "Life's challenges are best confronted on a full stomach." Compare this with Vincent's outburst in the grocery when the sight of so much food disgusts and angers him. Could you relate to that scene? Have you had similar feelings after

traveling or living overseas?

8. Cate's book celebrates those who mother, marry, and mourn America's warriors. For Cate, such women are the silent casualties of war. Do you agree that these sisters-in-arms need to tell their stories?

9. Sheila and Leah differ in their views of how war changes people. Sheila believes that the experience will bring to the surface what was always there, while Leah feels that what is life-altering can also change a person's character. What is your view? Is war merely a crucible or fundamentally transformative?

10. After she understands Zelda's medical needs, Cate asks why the woman isn't in a place where she can be cared for. Helen points out that Amberley is such a place because Zelda's friends keep an eye on her. Do you think a community coming together like that is a good thing, or should people like Zelda be in care facilities?

11. In comforting Cate after her first patient dies, Helen points out that the choices Lourdes Garcia made can't be understood

by those living in comfort. One implication of Helen's words is that Lourdes was justified in compromising her ethics in order to survive. Can Lourdes be compared with Jan Schultz, the German-Polish collaborator Miriam wrote about?

12. Who do you think gave Cate Miriam's journal entries? Why were they given to her?

13. The novel examines the Jewish concept of *tikkun ha-olam* — repair of the broken world — from many perspectives. How do the main characters affect repair of their community and themselves? Discuss, for example, Cate, Sheila, Gaby, Helen, and Father Sullivan.

14. The ring Judah Berkson made for Miriam was the gift of a dying father to the daughter he would never see become a woman. Consider the ring's meaning to those who controlled its destiny: Miriam, the German officer who stole it, Jack Mitchell, Leah and Sheila's mother, Sheila, Cate, Samuel, and, finally, Rachel.

15. Cate realizes that she may never learn the truth about John's death. Ambiguity

settles uneasily in her mind but she comes to accept it as the "new normal." Could you live with such uncertainty?

16. After meeting Samir Falah, Cate cannot bring herself to expose his possible complicity in John's death. In mirroring Miriam's actions, did Cate do the right thing?

17. The town of Amberley is a central character in the novel. How does living in such an iconic small town contribute to Cate's emotional journey?

18. At the end of the novel, Cate comes home to Amberley. Compare that scene with her arrival by bus in chapter one. Think about how the women of Amberley changed in the interim. Is Cate a catalyst for change much as Miriam was decades before?

ABOUT THE AUTHOR

Ariella Cohen is a graduate of Barnard College, the Hebrew University and the University of Michigan Law School. Her short fiction appears in *A Cup of Comfort for Couples, Heartscapes,* and *Flashshot.* Although she makes her home in New England, her dream self resides in County Mayo, Ireland. Visit the author's website at: www.ariellacohenauthor.wordpress.com.